FALL IN LOVE WITH AMALIE HOWARD!

"Amalie Howard's books sit at the crossroads of history and herstory—Victorian romance, but with a dollop of strong women who take charge of their destinies...and as a result, who rescue the men in their orbit. Refreshing, steamy, and stocked with characters you don't normally get to see in the genre—her books are a must-read for me."

—Jodi Picoult, #1 *New York Times* bestselling author

"Amalie Howard tells a story with self-assured style, wit, and energy...her writing sparkles!"

—Lisa Kleypas, #1 *New York Times* bestselling author

"The fresh voice historical romance needs right now....I will read every word she writes."

—Kerrigan Byrne, *USA Today* bestselling author

ALWAYS BE MY DUCHESS

"Fabulous writing...such a delicious escape. Utterly delightful!"

—Eloisa James, *New York Times* bestselling author

Always Be My Duchess

AMALIE HOWARD

A Taming of the Dukes Novel

FOREVER

NEW YORK   BOSTON

Forever
Hachette Book Group
1290 Avenue of the Americas, New York, NY 10104
read-forever.com
twitter.com/readforeverpub

First Edition: July 2022

Forever is an imprint of Grand Central Publishing. The Forever name and logo are trademarks of Hachette Book Group, Inc.

The publisher is not responsible for websites (or their content) that are not owned by the publisher.

Library of Congress Cataloging-in-Publication Data
Names: Howard, Amalie, author.
Title: Always be my duchess / Amalie Howard.
Description: First edition. | New York : Forever, 2022. | Series: Taming of the dukes
Identifiers: LCCN 2022004293 | ISBN 9781538737712 (trade paperback) | ISBN 9781538737705 (ebook)
Subjects: LCGFT: Romance fiction. | Historical fiction. | Novels.
Classification: LCC PS3608.O89695 A79 2022 | DDC 813/.6—dc23/eng/20220203
LC record available at https://lccn.loc.gov/2022004293

ISBN: 9781538737712 (trade paperback), 9781538737705 (ebook)

Printed in the United States of America

LSC-C

Printing 2, 2022

CONTENT GUIDANCE

This book makes reference to sex work and sex workers in the Victorian era, which ranged from prostitution in the streets to highly paid companions. In keeping with the conventions of this period, words such as *courtesan* and *light-skirt* are used as descriptors, and I have tried my best to keep these both authentic and sex-positive within context. Some derogatory inference and language are used in conversation. The duke has a mental and behavioral disorder, which might not have been diagnosed at the time but was certainly in existence, and there is also some ableist bias in the way he views himself as well as some ill-treatment by his father. There are also scenes that may be violent to some readers, in which the heroine defends herself against potential assault as well as reference to her sister's injury at the hands of a theater patron.

For Thao Le,
who has my infinite gratitude

CHAPTER ONE

1865
London, England

Lord Lysander Blackstone, the very pragmatic and always sensible Duke of Montcroix, was well and truly lost. On the outskirts of St. Giles. Well past the hour most sensible people would be abed. One could argue that was neither pragmatic nor sensible.

It could be worse…he could be passed out in a dark alley somewhere, fleeced of his clothing, buttons, handkerchiefs, boots, hat, and coin. Perhaps worse, if any flash-men were out for blood. Thus far, he'd been fortunate, though he could feel eyes upon him from windows and shadowy passages.

A duke in the rookeries! Sound the bullhorn!

He upped his pace, peering at the nearest grubby street name etched into the building stone—Great White Lion Street. He couldn't be completely certain, but that was not the correct direction. Mayfair was west, was it not?

Why the hell are there no hackneys?

Stumbling slightly, he shook his head to clear it of the terrible fog brought on by equally terrible liquor and cursed his friend who had dragged him from a perfectly acceptable night in, tracking his investments and poring over local railway ledgers, to the opening of a new ballet at the Lyceum. He'd nearly pummeled the persistent Earl of Lushing, aptly named, before giving in. A foolish idea, clearly.

"Come on, mate," Lushing had cajoled. "All you do is work. What kind of duke worth his salt *works*? Don't you have people to add the sums for you?"

"I like numbers," he'd replied. "It keeps my mind calm. I also like money. The estate is profitable, and yes, I have enough stewards, but I want my own eyes on it."

Lushing had scoffed, "I have the perfect solution for calmness, and it involves a pair of long legs, a perfect arabesque, and a face to die for."

"Are women all you think about?"

"You wound me, Stone. It's the theater with the usual stiff-lipped crowd." A melodramatic hand had found his chest. "I'll have you back at the stroke of midnight, pet, I promise."

Lysander had wavered, despite his passion for the theater. The last time he attended the opera, he'd been positively swarmed by every matchmaking mother with an available daughter seeking an introduction...and a coronet.

These days, even his business acquaintances had expectations.

Do you intend to settle down? Family is important to the peerage. When will you do your duty and wed?

The Earl of Bolden, a man Lysander was soliciting for a piece of property imperative to his new railway venture, had been especially vocal at White's last week.

"This bachelor lifestyle of yours must be exhausting," Bolden had remarked, and Lysander's collar had felt hot at the unspoken judgment. "Perhaps you should pick one."

The notion had left him cold. He'd proposed to one woman… and she'd jilted him for greener pastures that were much too close for comfort. As such, he hadn't thought much past his reply, articulated if only to placate the earl. "Indeed, Lord Bolden."

Lysander stumbled on an uneven patch in the street and caught himself from crashing headfirst into the dirt and losing a few front teeth in the bargain. Hobbling, he recalculated his bearings. Right, there was the opera house. He frowned. Didn't he just come from the opera? No, that was the Lyceum. Then Lushing's public house slash social club, Lethe.

Yes, *yes*, his current misfortune was all Lushing's fault. The rotter.

The earl was a profligate who could not be trusted, since the very excellent ballet he'd convinced Lysander to attend had been followed by a debauched demimonde party at Lethe that would make a sybarite blush. Bored and in no mood for empty flirtation, he'd left on foot…and now found himself on the wrong end of yet another poor decision.

Lost, sir, you are lost.

Christ, even his bloody conscience was caustic.

Squinting at the street name again, he hunched down into his coat and turned back the way he'd come. He'd lost his hat at some point as well. Hearing raucous laughter from a nearby tavern, he debated venturing inside to ask for directions, though he might as well be asking to be robbed at this hour. He shifted course, recognizing the Royal Opera House—*huzzah!*—when his attention was caught by a slight figure pacing back and forth with angry, mincing steps.

A woman, if his eyes could be trusted. He squinted. His gaze fell upon the shapely bosom visible beneath the rise of the cape as she stalked toward him and then whirled in the other direction. Definitely female. Why was a woman alone outside a closed theater? Unless she was a light-skirt. Prostitution, like crime, was rife in these parts. Then again, it would be much safer asking *her* for directions than entering a public house full of drunks and ne'er-do-wells.

He hesitated, his notice caught by a delicately boned hand lifting to swipe furiously at her cheeks. The movement was so elegant and graceful that Lysander froze midstep, and then he blinked as his brain registered what she was doing.

Good God, was she *crying*?

Scowling, he turned on his bootheel when a whimper reached him, followed by a shriek of agony or rage. Or perhaps both.

Nothing to do with you. Mind your business. Don't do it, you fool.

But of course he did. The well-bred gentleman in him could not ignore a woman in distress, even if it were a ruse to rob him blind or seduce him with erotic offerings. Not that he was interested in the latter at the moment. Or at all—women were much too unpredictable, and he liked his life the precise, organized way it was.

On cautious feet, Lysander approached the woman, attempting not to fall face-first into the street covered in God knew what filth. No need to advertise his sotted wits and give the chit, should she be one without scruples, any advantage.

As he neared, she was back to pacing, hands curled in her skirts, her mouth muttering what sounded like filthy obscenities in both English and French that made his own foxed brain stutter. Did such words actually exist? Perhaps she was simply repeating things she'd heard. But when she spewed out a particularly colorful oath involving men's organs and dark spaces, his brows slammed into his hairline. Now *that* was creative.

His mouth twitched with reluctant amusement.

"Miss? Are you well?" He almost didn't recognize the harsh croak that emerged as his own voice.

She came to an abrupt halt and stared at him before snatching a flintlock pistol from her pockets. "Stop! That's far enough."

Lysander's eyes widened as he lifted his hands in view of the lethal weapon pointed at him. Did she even know how to wield the thing? His dubious expression must have been evident because a cocking noise filled the street, and his ballocks tightened. Why yes, of course she did. This was the seedy west end, after all, and here he was approaching a potential cutpurse like a naive imbecile. Bloody hell, he was going to get shot, murdered, *and* robbed.

By a chit half his size.

All because he couldn't have minded his own damned business.

"Please don't shoot, I won't come any closer," he said, his woolly brain clearing somewhat at the sight of the pistol. Good to see his self-preservation instincts hadn't hightailed it with the rest of his common sense.

He felt the press of her eyes as she scanned him from head to toe, no doubt taking his measure to determine whether he was a threat or not, and the marginal dissipation of his whiskey-fueled fog allowed him to take in the details of the small but fierce female in front of him as well. Her clothing appeared to be well-made and sturdy. She was of average height and slender build. He couldn't get an idea of her coloring, her hair hidden under a plain bonnet and her eyes in shadow beneath the brim, but her confident, fluid movements fascinated him. There was veiled poetry in them. Could she be an actress or a dancer then?

As a longstanding patron of the arts in London, he was familiar with most of the popular leading faces. Lysander narrowed his gaze on her bow-shaped pink lips—the only feature he could see clearly—and felt his own mouth tingle at the plump fullness of it. He suddenly wanted to kiss those lips. Run his tongue over them.

By God, he truly *was* drunk.

Reining in the sharp eerie jolt of whatever the hell that nonsense had been, he cleared his throat. "You're not safe here."

"I'm safer than you, I'd wager, monsieur," she shot back, a hint of a musical French accent dancing over her words. She spoke English as though she were well educated, but then again, if she was an actress, they were professionally trained to mimic their roles. "Considering you're at the business end of my faithful friend here."

The business end that was currently trained on him with faultless aim. Should she pull that trigger, he would not be able to escape it. He should go. A smart man would leave. And yet, he remained where he was.

"You seemed upset before," he said instead. "It's why I stopped. You were crying."

Those plush lips went tight. "I wasn't *crying*. I was angry. Those were *angry* tears. Completely different thing."

"Why?"

She glared, fire sparking from shadowed eyes, her lips slamming together at first and then parting as if they could not help themselves. "Because I cannot get a job in this cursed town."

"You're an actress."

"Ballerina, if you must know." She blew out a frustrated hiss through her teeth. "At least until recently."

Lysander's eyes skimmed down her form again, noting the precise stance and the turned-out soles, her weight evenly distributed on the balls of her feet even as she wielded a pistol at him with unflinching aplomb. So beautiful and so fierce! What would she look like onstage in full costume in the glow of gaslights, passion imbued in every line of her body? He felt that strange otherworldly jolt again.

"An out-of-work dancer," she added with a feminine growl, "with no chance of being hired anywhere, thanks to that rotting, rodent-souled roué…" She trailed off in a vicious slew of muttered French insults. Her chin lifted toward him after her diatribe as if daring him to remark upon it, and then she sighed. "Apologies, sir, I am…not myself. May I assist you with something? Are you lost?"

He gave a sheepish nod. "I was at the Lyceum—"

She grimaced. "I know it. They turned me away there, too."

"I seem to have veered in the wrong direction."

The lady slowly lowered the pocket pistol to her side, but not before glowering at him. "I'm as excellent a shot as I am a dancer, so don't make me ruin that pretty face of yours. What is your name?"

Lysander's mouth curled. He wasn't a man whom any would call pretty...and hope to get away with it. He had the harsh kind of face that made people feel wary rather than swoon.

He inclined his head with a slight frown. "Call me Montcroix, or Stone, if you prefer."

"Stone? What kind of a name is that? A nickname?"

"Just so."

Her full lips pursed. "Suits you. Cold and menacing like a gargoyle."

The blunt assessment stung, for no reason at all. That had to be the effect of the whiskey again. He was not a man who cared what anyone thought of him, particularly foulmouthed, feisty, and impertinent out-of-work ballerinas. Then why was he so bloody insulted?

Because gargoyles are hideous.

At least she hadn't called him pretty again. Once was quite enough.

"You've deduced that from a few minutes of idle conversation?" he asked in a patronizing tone. "How original."

She pointed between her own brows and then the sides of her mouth, which drew his attention there again. Lysander scowled. "Yes. Exactly. You have deep grooves here and here, which suggests you rarely smile but glower much like you are doing right now." She grinned when he instantly tried to relax his tight expression and failed. "You hold yourself upright as though your skin and bones are made of marble and steel instead of flesh and blood. And your tongue is as thick as any mallet, as though you mean to cut, crush, and pound with your words."

"I do not pound," he muttered.

One eyebrow lifted in an amused quirk, and heat shot through him. "I mean, I pound. I can absolutely, categorically pound." He blinked at her mirthful expression and shook his head hard. *Oh the idiocy.* "No, that's not what I meant. *Never mind.*"

Stifled giggles burst through the air. God above, the irreverent chit was *laughing* at him and not even sorry about it!

Lysander sputtered, his mouth opening and closing in irritation, more at her current reaction instead of her unflattering, cool assessment of him. He was not a man led by his emotions or his temper. Or his stirring nether regions. Wait, why *were* they stirring? He needed to take the situation in hand.

"Look here, Miss—"

"Valery," she supplied, a residual smirk tugging at that full pout.

Lysander stared at that sinfully curved mouth, and suddenly, his vexation shifted into something else, something deeper and a thousand times more dangerous because it *wanted*. It craved. It yearned. A wave of lust engulfed him so violently that his knees nearly buckled.

What the ever-loving *hell* had been in that whiskey?

Alarmed at the tide of desire dragging him under, Lysander stumbled back but was halted by the sound of footsteps. Many footsteps and drunken singing as men lurched out of a nearby alley across the square from the tavern he'd seen earlier. The slovenly group's attention flocked to the two of them like moths to light.

"Oy, what 'ave we 'ere, lads?" one yelled out. "A sweet little dolly-mop for the takin' and a fine nob with a purse full o' coin."

His companion's entire body went rigid, the pistol in her palm lifting. "Merde. If you want to survive tonight, you'll follow me. I won't have your death on my conscience, even if you are as arrogant as you are senseless for being here on your own."

Lysander blinked. "You're alone in the streets as well."

"I live here," she shot back, her gaze spearing his expensive coat and shiny boots. "You, monsieur, I am assuming, do not. Now come! Or stay, if you choose, I don't care."

He didn't have much choice. It was either follow her or face the five rough-looking men currently strutting across the square with greed on their faces. He was capable in a fight, but not five against one, and certainly not in his inebriated state. Catching sight of the flare of the ballerina's dark cape rounding the corner, he took a deep breath and chased after her.

Curses followed and footsteps mimicked his pace. "Oy! Come 'ere, little rabbits!"

He'd barely caught up to her when she whirled down a filthy alley, nearly disappearing around another tight corner. He'd been lost before, but now, he hardly knew which end was up. All the narrow streets looked the same and not even the light of a lamppost or a sliver of moon showing the way. Lysander came to a panting halt, his eyes searching the darkness, his heart threatening to burst out of his chest. Devil take it, he'd lost her!

He heard the thudding sounds of the men behind him, their laughs and catcalls echoing between the buildings. There were healthier-than-good odds that they knew this area much better than he did. He had to keep moving or risk getting trapped like a hare in a snare. Perhaps he would come to a street he knew...or keep going in circles. Either way, standing still was a sure way to get caught or killed.

Suddenly, a hand curled into his lapel and yanked him into a narrow lane. It couldn't even be called an alley—more like a dank drainage passage between two buildings—and he was smashed up against a slender and very warm female shape. His physical reaction was instant and unavoidable. Lysander shifted away as best he could in the confined space.

"Miss Valery—"

"Shush," she told him in a whisper, gloved fingers reaching up to cover his parted lips. "Quiet, or so help me Dieu, I shall shove you out there."

Nève Valery had been in close quarters with men before, even intimately so with the male dancers who partnered her. It was to be expected, and part and parcel of being a ballerina, especially at the Théâtre Impérial de l'Opéra in Paris. But none of those men—not a single one—had ever made her disciplined body react as it did now. Here in this dark alleyway with *this* man.

This complete *stranger*.

Gracious, she was a woman of the world—a ballerina who had danced on the most celebrated stage in Europe. She could seduce with a glance, lure with a subtle sweep of an arm or a gracefully pointed leg. Wealthy and handsome gentlemen toppled at her feet for a smile from her, all vying for a blown kiss from the rise of the stage beyond the gaslights.

Plying the audience was just one tool in a dancer's arsenal, but through it all, Nève had remained resistant to the men who viewed her only as a lovely object. As much as charm was a weapon, cynicism was her armor. Those men had coveted her as a thing of beauty, not as a person of individual worth. She'd learned *that* lesson firsthand.

The tiniest exhale left her compacted lungs. Nève felt his hot breath shudder against the fingers that were still foolishly clasped over his mouth, and prudently, she withdrew her palm, pressing as hard as she could to the wall behind her to put a sliver of space between them. It was no use. The more she shifted and squirmed, the more she felt every impressive inch of him.

And he *was* impressive.

Nève could feel his wickedly rigid arousal prodding into her stomach, and though she knew it couldn't be helped given their cramped situation, her own body couldn't help its primal reply. Her lower half was flooded with liquid heat, and her nipples were attempting to cut their way out of her bodice to profess their fidelity.

Why was he so hard? Not just at his hips, but everywhere! Weren't gentlemen supposed to love padding in their clothing? This man had none. Even his face was hewn from marble. He gave the smallest groan, the only sign of his discomfort, and Nève licked dry lips, not daring to look up. Once more, she blessed the bonnet that kept her face hidden from his.

He was a gentleman of means, she guessed, if only by the

exquisite cut of his clothing. Even in the dim light of the square, she'd been struck by his uncommon looks. He was not pretty as she'd mocked earlier, because nothing about the man was *pretty*, except perhaps his golden hair, and even that had been groomed to within an inch of its life as if not even the wind would dare dally with it. This man was attractive in a way that came from confidence and power.

He was tall and hatless, those dark blond waves touching his collar, but the length had softened the brutal cut of his cheekbones, that heavy brow and strongly drawn nose, and the severe, unforgiving mouth that for some inexplicable reason had made her blood thicken in her veins. Everything about him was too austere, too controlled, and too *hard* to be appealing, and yet, her throat had dried in explicit, instant want.

He wasn't pretty, no, but he made her heart kick all the same.

Tiens but she was a romantic dolt. The man was no one to her. A sotted brick of a gentleman who was lost, being chased by cutpurses, and she had stupidly decided to rescue him. Her sorry condition over a few nonpadded muscles was her own fault.

Nève licked her dry lips and took in another small sip of air. He twitched again, an infinitesimal movement that she felt nonetheless...because *that* part of him was jammed up against her abdomen and currently the cause of the indecently damp condition of her drawers wedged over his stone-hard thigh. Stifling a moan, she inched her legs apart to provide some much-needed relief from the unrelenting pressure, and heard a pained indrawn hiss from above.

"Do. Not. Move." The command was raw, his voice pure gravel.

She exhaled raggedly. "I can't help it, Stone, my muscles are burning."

"Miss Valery," he bit out, "unless you wish to have your lady-like sensibilities thoroughly and wickedly debauched in this filthy hole of an alley, you will not move."

His words turned her core to liquid.

Oh, la vache, this would not do!

Think of the movement from the first act of the last ballet, she ordered herself.

Pirouette, glissade, pas de deux. A split in midair, twirl, rond de jambe. Run and a grand jeté on the other side of the stage, followed by a leap and fall into her partner's waiting arms. Her breathing stuttered but settled as the sequence took precedence in her brain.

Again.

And once more for good measure before she felt marginally composed.

Which wasn't much considering she was scandalously squeezed into an alley in Covent Garden with a strange man, her body no longer under her own command. The minutes bled by while the flames between them built into an inferno. Her blood was running so hot, Nève was sure she'd have blistered, reddened skin. Her reaction to the man was as absurd as it was unwelcome.

Every breath in that restricted, bricked-in space began and ended with Stone. She'd never been so in tune with a man in her life...not even the talented and handsome dancer from the corps de ballet whom she'd danced with for an entire production. She'd kissed him at a party once, and though he'd wanted more, she hadn't.

What would it be like to kiss Stone?

To feel that stern slash of a mouth molded to hers.

Would it be as hard as it looked or soft to the touch? Overheating once more, Nève forced herself to run through her ballet sequence again, but the scintillating fantasy of Stone's lips on hers refused to be erased. Piroutte, lick. Jeté, suck. Plié, bite.

Dieu, have mercy.

CHAPTER TWO

Lysander was acutely aware of the entirety of the supple female form currently plastered to him—from the chin pressed to his chest, to the firm breasts mashed against his torso, to their intertwined limbs wedged in between each other's in the most intimate of positions. It was certainly never a circumstance in which he'd ever found himself before. Not that he was complaining, considering survival was at stake, but he was still a duke.

"This is highly impro—" he muttered.

"Hush, espèce d'idiot!" Her hand went up to his mouth again in a panic.

"Did you just call me an idiot?" he muttered against her quelling fingers, resisting the wicked urge to clamp them between his teeth.

"I can't help it if you're a babbling blockhead."

He blinked. No one had ever accused him of being such a ridiculous thing. "I am not. I assure you—"

Her fingers pressed down, one settling between his lips and grazing his teeth. "Dieu, you prattle on like a chatterbox. Don't make me regret saving you. Now, *hush*."

Saving *him*?

Well, she wasn't wrong.

His rescuer wriggled against him, inching them farther back into the shadows, her pliant body doing intolerable things to his. They stilled as they heard the violent oaths of hunters who'd lost their prey from only a few feet away. Neither of them dared to breathe.

An inconvenient erection was vastly preferable over a slit throat.

Lysander hadn't responded to a woman like this in, well... forever. Not that he'd searched out female company—his interests and work had kept him busy, and his annoyingly adventurous friends like Lushing kept him entertained. He was simply not willing to offer what the women in his circles craved—declarations of undying devotion, proposals of marriage—all for the grand title of duchess. Even during intermission at the theater earlier this evening, they had watched his every move, ambushed him for introductions outside his private box, and one young lady had even pretended to confuse him for someone else in a not-so-veiled attempt at an introduction.

Though now, Lysander's extraordinary reaction to *this* woman made the wheels turn in his head, and he saw a chance meeting become opportunity. Even while on the brink of discovery by footpads and still half-sotted, his brain was in constant motion.

He'd been too often accused by his dead father of being slow and too methodical, but the precise skill that had earned him a caning many a time had served him well in adulthood. A familiar instinct wound down his spine. He hadn't gotten to where he was in life without taking careful but highly lucrative risks. Lysander did not ignore his gut in matters of business, and right now, his instincts were screaming for him to make her an offer she could not refuse.

She was an actress looking for a job. He was a duke who did not want to be swarmed by debutantes or grasping widows. If his intuition was right, they could help each other. She was in need of a role...and he required a deterrent on his arm.

Fate had handed him the perfect solution.

The building blocks were there—he could see them clearly— they just needed to be put into position for what he was about to propose. The idea was unconventional, but it could work. The more he thought about it, the more it made practical sense that they were a good fit. He could tell from her diction, despite the lilting and charming French inflection, that she was educated, even raised as gentry, if he had to guess. She carried herself with poise and pride. She could easily be a lady.

Except for that savage wit of hers.

His lip kicked up in the shadows. She wasn't afraid of him. In truth, she didn't seem to have a lick of respect toward him at all, and for a man who was accustomed to people groveling at every turn, it was refreshing. Not that he *liked* it, of course. She was simply not the kind of female he was used to.

Notwithstanding her pirate-worthy oaths and dauntless spirit, he couldn't deny that he was intrigued. She had a delicate, elfin beauty that was captivating in its elegance—pointed chin, sweeping cheekbones, long swanlike neck—but that outer fragility was fortified by a spine of pure steel. The contrast fascinated him to no end. Much like the plush lips that housed her razor-sharp tongue.

He envisioned those full pink arches and nearly groaned. His groin, jammed up against her svelte curves as it was, twitched its vigorous approval. Lysander froze, all his muscles locking. Bloody hell, he hoped she hadn't felt that.

"It won't be too much longer," she whispered with a tilt of her head, the husky tones feathering over the skin of his neck above his cravat.

"Fine," he gritted out.

He could *do* this. He could be a statue—an appallingly erect statue—for a few more minutes. Sweat dampened his hairline, the maddening scent of lemon cakes torturing his nostrils.

Think about railroads and shipping. Expenses and dividends. The House of Lords.

But all that was for naught when Miss Valery's hips shifted infinitesimally against his, and his unruly cock reacted as if it had been shown a white flag of surrender, rearing up like a conquering hero on a battlefield of pure lust. Her smothered squeak made Lysander cringe. There was no way in hell she hadn't felt *that*. The bloody thing was like a branding iron against his waistband. His neck burned.

For a moment, Lysander was grateful for the cover of darkness and the merciful fact that he stood a head and shoulders over her. He didn't know if he could live down the fact that he, the seventh Duke of Montcroix, a man known for his complete lack of emotion in Parliament and his infamous inscrutability, was *blushing* like a lad caught with his short pants around his ankles.

"I think they've gone," Nève whispered.

Their pursuers' voices had faded, and enough time had passed that she was fairly certain they would not be coming back this way. Slowly, she and Stone shifted from their cramped hiding spot. He rolled his neck to each side and rotated his shoulders before his hands descended to his hips. Nève didn't dare follow them, knowing where her eyes would undoubtedly land. *That* part of his body didn't need any more attention than it had already received.

"Thank you," Stone said, his voice a gravelly rasp that did untoward things to her fragmented senses. "That was close."

"You're welcome. Can I direct you somewhere?"

He nodded, a movement that she could barely discern in the shadows. "A hackney, if by chance you know where we are."

Nève peered down at the lane and canted her head. Her own shoebox lodgings were a stone's throw away. "This way."

Keeping a careful eye out for the ruffians who'd chased them, she made her way through the warren of streets before coming to another, better-lit square. Relief ran through her, but it was short-lived as a triumphant and loud bellow reached her ears.

"There they are! Get 'em, lads!"

"Fuck me," Stone muttered.

Nève bit back her laughter at the sound of the unexpected oath. He didn't look or seem like a man who swore often or at all. He was much too put together. Too *stoic*. Too lordly for something as pedestrian as swearing. But the unexpected vulgarity humanized him somehow.

"Now?" she teased with a grin, taking off into a sprint. "Might I remind you we're on the run for our lives here? Those two things are mutually exclusive."

He caught up to her easily with those long legs of his, eyes glinting. "You'd be amazed at what I can manage when put to the test."

"Arrogance is not a virtue, sir."

"I have supreme confidence in my ability to juggle multiple tasks." If any one of those men caught them, they'd be done for, but she had the unspeakable urge to halt, grab Stone's lapels, climb him like a tree, and demand he prove his boast.

"I suppose I'll have to take your word for it," she said instead. The voices behind them grew closer, and her lungs and legs burned with strained effort, but mercy was in sight. "Look, there's a hack! Move those limbs of yours and run!"

Hitching up her skirts, she grabbed his sleeve and half dragged him to the street corner. She put two fingers to her mouth and made a loud whistle. The coach barely slowed to a stop before she grabbed hold of the door.

"Tell him to go! Those louts are nearly upon us and they won't stop without their pound of flesh, and I'd rather that not be from either of us."

A panting Stone gave the man garbled directions and reached into his pocket to toss up a crown to the coachman. Nève's eyes widened—it would pay for a few dozen hackney rides, but she was grateful as they tumbled inside.

Luckily, the carriage sped forward at Stone's command, and Nève crashed back against the worn squabs, her heart nearly climbing out of her throat. She put a hand to her chest to calm her racing pulse as her blood thundered in her ears. From the looks of him, Stone was doing the same, hauling great gulps of air into his lungs.

He tugged at his cravat, loosening the immaculately tied folds. "Now that was truly *too* close for comfort."

She smiled at the echo of his earlier words and then peered through the grimy window to make sure they weren't being followed. "Where are we going?"

"Grosvenor Square. My residence."

Nève's eyes went wide. That was a fancy address for usually very fancy occupants. Her curious gaze fastened to him. "Who are you?"

Stone or Montcroix or whoever he was stared at her in silence, the crunch of the wheels against the road the only sound between them. Long, gloved fingers tapped on one knee—the only sign that he had heard her question. He did not reply for a handful of heartbeats as if the answer were a complex one that required thorough analysis.

Was his identity truly that complicated? Nève's interest swelled. "Well?"

"Someone who wants to make you an offer of employment for one evening of your time." He cleared his throat. "For a role."

Suspicion rose on the heels of curiosity. She narrowed her eyes on him. Yes, he was well-heeled and didn't seem like a villain at first glance, but Nève was well familiar with how a pretty face could hide a foul core.

She might believe in fairy tales, at least enough to embody them confidently on a stage, but she'd seen many a handsome gentleman come to the foyer de la danse with sweet promises to get what they wanted before exposing their true nature. They didn't want romance; they wanted a popular gem to own. Lord Durand was a perfect example of such nauseating privilege.

And she hadn't been his only victim.

The knave had pursued her sister, Vivienne, who had been badly injured when he'd ended her career overnight in a jealous rage. Nève's jaw tightened. Confined to bed for weeks with two splinted, bandaged feet, Vivi was told she might never dance again by the surgeon. Care for the terrible injury had consumed what was left of their inheritance, the remnants only enough to pay for a lady's maid and nurse for her sister in Paris while Nève was in London looking for work.

Work that couldn't be had... except for this decidedly scandalous proposition.

"Are you a theater owner or director?" she asked Stone carefully.

"No," he said. "But I am a devoted patron of the arts with many connections."

Nève stared at him, searching those hard, austere features and the eyes glimmering in the shadows. They gave away nothing. She should be more fearful, but for some reason she wasn't. Any other man might have taken liberties in that alley, and he hadn't. Besides, if he meant her physical harm, she still had her pistol in her skirt pockets. Very deliberately, she placed one palm over the weapon, scowling when his eyes tracked the movement and the corner of his lip curled.

In amusement? Nève bristled, her temper sparking.

"And what is this role?" Her flat tone made it clear what she was expecting. "A night spent in your bed perhaps? Despite what you might assume, whoever you are, I'm no courtesan."

"I know you're not," he replied. "I wish you to play a performance. I will, of course, reward you handsomely for your time."

She frowned. "What kind of performance?"

"You will play the role of my companion at a ball tomorrow evening."

Companion. There were other words for that. Mistress. Paramour. Paid consort.

Dieu, could she be more gullible? Vivi always laughed at Nève seeing the world through rose-colored spectacles, despite its obvious and many pitfalls. Nève had argued that a few bad apples didn't mean *everyone* was bad, but maybe her sister was right. They were all rotten, just like Durand. Nève shook her head, swallowing down the bitter taste of despair. Couldn't she meet one man who didn't want to creep under her skirts?

"Stop the coach."

"You misunderstand my intent."

She glared. "Monsieur, I assure you I know how to recognize a scoundrel's proposal when I hear one. I was not born yesterday."

He lifted both palms in a gesture of conciliation. "Hear me out, please. If you still wish to leave after I'm finished, I will not stop you. We will part ways and I will wish you well. But you said to me yourself that no one will hire you. I am offering you a temporary position."

"A scandalous one!" she hissed. "What if someone found out?"

"You are an actress, Miss Valery. A dancer. If anything, you will gain instant notoriety for being seen on the arm of a duke for one evening."

Nève gulped down her shock. He was a *duke*? She should have known. Even as foxed as he'd been when she first saw him weaving and stumbling across the square, the man had worn hauteur and power like a second skin.

"Moreover, the logistics of our arrangement will be your secret to tell," he went on. "It is one evening of your time and your company. I'm certain your reputation will not suffer and I know for a fact that Edmund Falconer, the manager of the Lyceum Theatre will be in attendance. He will not turn you away, I assure you."

That gave her some hope, but Nève wasn't completely reckless. Though the fact that she was contemplating the completely asinine proposition suggested otherwise.

"Why would someone like you"—she lifted a palm, gesturing from his shiny cropped hair to his polished boots—"even need to pay someone to pretend to be their companion? You're titled, you clearly have money, and you're fit. Any society lady would be happy to be on your arm at a fancy ball. Why do you need *me*?"

"Because you won't want more than this." His lip quirked. "We work well together, don't you think?"

That stern mouth cracked into the semblance of a smile, baring the shine of teeth for a marginal second, did things to her. A cynical twist, tugging at her insides and warming her. Idiotically, she wanted to see it again. It was ludicrous how desperately she suddenly wanted to make the glacier surrounding him melt.

Furious with her absurd thoughts, Nève bit her lip hard. She could melt his ice for one night, and then what? She'd be completely ruined and still in the same state as when he'd found her...out of work and days away from the poorhouse.

The lofty principles she'd clung to when she'd fled Paris would be for naught. Those same principles that left her short on another month's rent for the tiny one-room flat on Queen Street.

"Tell me the truth," she demanded. "What do you get out of it?"

"I don't want a wife."

"So can you just not say so, or is that tongue of yours just as uncooperative and hard as the rest of you?"

Oh, mon Dieu, her *own* tongue required a muzzle.

Cheeks on fire, Nève hoped he'd overlook her tart reply. She would be adored for her face and feet, never her mouth, as the theater director at the Théâtre Impérial de l'Opéra had told her on countless occasions when she'd spoken without thinking.

To his credit, the duke did not respond in kind. "The matchmaking mothers of the season will not care whether I am bucktoothed, gout-ridden, poor, or uninterested in matrimony. They will still foist their daughters upon me at every turn. It is ceaseless."

Nève blinked in disbelief. "Oh, you poor, *poor* sought-after, venerated duke, I feel so dreadfully sorry for you." Her mouth twisted as she rolled her eyes. "Imagine a ballerina's world where men treat women like their own personal playthings, and when we have the gall to say no, we're forced to pay a dreadful price. At least you have a choice."

A piercing gaze fastened to hers, his lips thinning. "Has someone...forced you to do something you did not want?"

"No," she said, surprised by the odd reaction on her behalf. He seemed furious *for* her. "But they have tried. When a ballerina takes the stage, some of the more ardent sponsors hope to keep some of that magic for themselves *off* stage. I have said no more times than I can count to unsavory men, but it doesn't make them any less persistent."

"That is reprehensible," he said, and Nève shrugged but didn't reply.

She blew out a breath. "C'est la vie. Now tell me why you require a lady knight-errant."

Mouth twitching at her description, Stone scraped a hand

through his hair, disturbing the deep gold strands. She liked him disheveled thus…more man, less duke. She itched to muss his locks even more, but curbed the idle inclination.

He frowned, and cleared his throat. "Very well. The simplest answer is that I need to convince someone I am not an eternal bachelor in order to conclude a matter of business. With you at my side, I will convey the necessary image."

Skeptical brows shot skyward. "The *image?* With a ballerina?"

"With a potential duchess," he clarified. "Your performance as such will also help to dissuade the matchmaking mothers."

D'accord. Very well, she could understand that. He desired a shield.

"I'm to be your bodyguard then?" Nève laughed, the sound loud in the confined coach. "Fending off the virginal hordes. Can't have you yelling, 'Fuck me,' to the aristocratic misses without repercussions, can we?"

At her words, strong fingers flexed on the seat bench, and Stone angled his body forward as if to close the small gap between them. His mouth parted, and for an interminable second, Nève was sure he was about to chase the vulgar oath from her lips with his kiss. She sucked in a breath, heart pounding wildly beneath her bodice while his face hovered inches from hers. Banked fires burst in those fathomless eyes, nostrils flaring like a hound on the hunt.

But with a ragged sound, Stone thrust himself back and pinched the bridge of his nose. Was that a throb of disappointment she felt? Or relief? She was not in the habit of kissing strange men in coaches, nor was she in the habit of considering outrageous propositions, either, but here she was. Desperate to lessen the brewing tension, she gave a dismissive sniff.

"What is this matter of business you hope to conclude?"

"The purchase of a very valuable piece of property." His lips flattened in displeasure as if he resented the question, but Nève didn't care. If he wanted her help, she had to know what was in it for him.

"Buying up land? Isn't that below the attention of a duke?"

"I like making money."

"Don't we all," she muttered and then eyed his expensive clothes. "You don't seem to be suffering from a lack of it, however."

He let out a low exhale. "One evening of your time, Miss Valery, for me to convince the current landowner that I am not a rake and have plans to settle down with a wonderful young lady. In addition to compensation, I will, of course, provide everything you need for the ball including a gown and other accoutrements, which you are free to keep. You will incur no expense."

His proposal, laid out so pragmatically, did not sound seedy or untoward in the least. No, it sounded quite rational and logical. She was to play the part of a thorny hedge, keeping the marriage-hungry riffraff away, while he hoped to convince a seller of his suitability with a possible bride on his arm.

She felt a giddy sort of laughter build in her chest. Once upon a distant time, she might have been a peer's bride. She and Vivienne had been born and bred for such, despite having fallen on desperate times and being forced to pursue more desperate measures to survive.

Much like this one.

Tapping her chin, Nève considered playing the part. She'd performed harder roles onstage, convinced thousands she was a snow maiden, a dryad queen, and a sylph. A potential duchess would be easy. Tiens, was she actually considering this?

"What kind of payment do you have in mind?"

"One hundred pounds."

Nève could hardly contain her gasp. A fortune! She could never make that in one night, not even if she were a prima ballerina in the most sought-after ballet on the Continent. A sum like that would help her settle her overdue rent and pay for her sister's medical expenses. And if things did not work out with a theater in London, Nève could go back to Paris with enough breathing room to figure out a new plan. She was resourceful enough.

Though...was she *resourceful* enough to be a duke's pretty decoration?

An image of a fairy-tale duke who would sweep her off her feet from the back of a white stallion and ride off into the sunset filled her brain, and she nearly laughed. There would be no dashing heroes, no sunsets, and no wishful fantasies, only a curtain call.

But *that*, she was trained to do.

This would be a different kind of stage, one that toed the line of integrity she'd drawn in the sand. Pride warred with the dragging weight of poverty. A hundred pounds was a *hundred* pounds. She'd be a fool to walk away when her situation was so dire. If it was safe—if *she* would be safe—then what was the harm?

"If I were to agree, what happens next?" she asked softly.

"You will accompany me home to Blackstone Manor." She frowned and he met her instantly wary stare. "You will be given your own private guest room. Don't worry, my aunt is in residence and she will act as a chaperone so that propriety is met."

"Propriety?" Nève snorted even as relief filled her at the fact that he wasn't expecting her to share his bedchamber. "You're paying me a fortune to be your private escort. One would think we're overstepping modesty as it is, Your Grace."

The change of the road beneath the wheels was obvious as they drove into the area where the upper crust of British society lived. Nève had moments to decide whether she would take the duke up on his offer. These funds he was offering meant she would not be homeless…or so *hopeless*. And the fact that she could potentially meet the owner of the Lyceum Theatre was a golden opportunity she could not ignore.

The pros far outweighed the cons.

This was a logical, *smart* decision.

The coach drew to a smooth stop, and the duke peered at her, his gaze unreadable once more. "What say you? Do you accept my offer or shall I have the coachman return you to Covent Garden? The choice is yours, Miss Valery."

Nève felt as though she were standing at the edge of a precipice, about to leap off the edge into open space. Her heart thrashed like a captive bird in her chest, but she bit her lip. "One hundred pounds for my attendance at one ball, that's it?"

"Correct."

"Nothing more?" she pressed.

Stone slanted a brow, his lips twisting in that sardonic lift that barely passed for a smile. "I'm not certain I know what you mean, Miss Valery."

He was mocking her. Nève glared at him. "You won't expect me to lift my skirts and climb into your bed?"

The answering heat in his gaze nearly singed her where she sat. The man's blood might be coated in hoarfrost, but ice could burn, too. She would do well to remember that. "Only if that is your desire."

"It won't be." A lie had never tasted so bitter on her tongue, but she swallowed it down like the medicine it was. "Very well then. I accept your offer." She paused. "But on one condition."

"Which is?" The low rumble of his voice made the hairs on her nape rise.

Nève swallowed. "Instruct the coachman to return me to Covent Garden this evening. I prefer to stay in my own lodgings, but will agree to return at a reasonable hour to be fitted on the morrow."

"It's already the morrow," he said, opening the door and pointing to the predawn sky.

"Then I will return in a few hours." She peered out the window. "To Number Eight Grosvenor Square." The window of time gave her some control over a situation that felt much too much *out* of her control, and she needed to be out of his orbit to see whether she was inclined to change her mind.

His face was inscrutable. "Anything else?"

"Half the payment upon my arrival, and the rest after the ball."

"Agreed." He hesitated. "Allow me to send a coach for you."

"No need. I can find my own way."

The duke descended the carriage and bowed. "Good night, Miss Valery. Thank you. This has been an unforgettable evening. I look forward to our . . . next act."

She smiled with as much grace as she could muster, but as the hansom rolled away, Nève could only hope she hadn't made a huge, *huge* mistake.

Chapter Three

It was unconscionable what he'd done.

No, it is not, Lysander's ever practical brain argued. She was a ballerina. An *actress*. She already worked for money, and he was offering her a paid performance, no more, no less. Then why did he feel so blasted guilty? Miss Valery could hardly be considered an ingenue—he suspected there was a clever, incisive mind behind those svelte dancer's curves. But still, indecision roiled within him. Christ, why was he suddenly going soft?

He'd made an offer and she'd agreed. The end.

It was a business transaction, nothing more.

A transaction that could close a negotiation that had been ongoing for months. The Earl of Bolden required convincing that Lysander was suitable. On top of that, Viscount Treadway, whose family-owned Clareville Railway, which Lysander intended to buy, needed careful managing. The fop had no interest in railways, but he had inherited the small station that was to be the cornerstone of Lysander's plans. Treadway was a problem for the future, however. Getting Bolden to sell was the priority.

Scrubbing a hand over his chin, Lysander paced the study, his footfalls making no sound on the thick carpet. He let out a curse. None of it would matter if the ace up his sleeve didn't come! He pulled the timepiece from his pocket. He hadn't specified when she should return to Blackstone Manor, though it was well after breakfasting hours. He'd also called on his longtime friend the Marquess of Marsden, who'd recently made an unconventional match himself with a modiste. Not that he was a connoisseur of fashion, but Lysander had seen Lady Marsden's creations, and the woman had a gift with fabric. It was the single reason he'd coerced the marquess into loaning him his wife.

Lysander glanced at the tiny dark-haired lady who sat on the settee in the morning salon, surrounded by a small army of helpers. Piles of fabric and unfinished gowns lay beside them. Marsden's marchioness nursed her third cup of tea and was being poured a fourth. Tightening his jaw, he strode to the window and peered out onto the busy street.

There was no sign of anyone matching the description of the woman he'd left in his coach a handful of hours before, not that he'd seen much of her in full light. He could identify her by her lips, a pair of burning eyes, her keen whip of a tongue, and the graceful, economical movements of her body. Not much to go on at all.

He turned with a frustrated sound. "Apologies, Lady Marsden, she will be here."

The marchioness inclined her head. "It's no trouble, Your Grace. I wanted to escape anyway. It's a madhouse getting ready for the ball tonight. I swear Marsden gets more agitated than I do about making sure everything is *just right*." She placed a hand to her mouth to hide her amusement. "Don't tell him I said that, please. He does so enjoy a good ball."

"I wouldn't dream of it, my lady."

"Miss Valery has arrived, Your Grace," the butler intoned. At the announcement, the tension in Lysander's frame loosened as though every muscle in his body had been wound tight. He found the reaction strange. If she had decided not to come, his evening would have been more challenging but not insurmountable. Something inside of him, however, had been desperate to see her again.

And now, there she stood in the doorway.

His memory had barely done her justice.

"Thank you, Finley," he murmured, dismissing the butler.

His midnight ballerina was lovelier than his fevered dreams had conjured. Divested of her cloak and bonnet, a mop of burnished mahogany curls was looped into a haphazard knot that he longed to bury his fingers in, but it was her face that struck him dumb—small, heart shaped, and dominated by a pair of luminous sea-green eyes that sizzled with intelligence and internal fire.

Now that spirit he hadn't misremembered.

Those eyes . . . they *blazed* with passion.

He'd thought her elfin in stature before, but this wasn't some dainty fey creature . . . she was a warrior queen ready for war. Her mouth would be ready to do battle as well, he'd wager. The thought made him look at her lips—they were just as pink and full as they had been hours earlier in the carriage.

"You came," he murmured, and then cleared his throat, remembering himself as well as present company. "Miss Valery, may I present Lady Marsden, who will be assisting with your gown for this evening." He pointed to the woman who was half-asleep in the corner, a forgotten embroidery hoop dangling from her fingers. "And my aunt, Lady Millicent."

The latter let out a small snore, but the marchioness rose with a smile. "A pleasure, Miss Valery."

"Please, call me Nève."

Lysander noticed that she didn't seem overawed by the grandeur of the room, another sign perhaps that she might have been accustomed to luxury herself. Was she French gentry then, as he'd suspected? Or a lady fallen on hard times? Both were possibilities. It wasn't unheard of for ladies of unfortunate circumstances to seek out work, though it was more along the lines of governesses than ballerinas. Dance required years of training and skill.

Idly, Lysander wondered if she had any real talent or had been cast for her beauty alone. A face like hers would lure a mob. He blinked, reconsidering his earlier assessment that she might be a lady. On second thought, perhaps she was simply an outstanding actress, able to mask her feelings and adapt to her surroundings. The guise of high society could be studied and imitated. *Faked.*

"Your Grace?"

Lysander started, turning toward the marchioness. "Yes?"

Lady Marsden bit back a smile, and Lysander cursed himself. Had he been woolgathering in front of them? "Shall we continue here, or is there another room we can use?" she asked, her amused tone making it clear that she'd asked the question before.

"Oh yes of course." He strode over to his napping aunt and

gently nudged her awake. "Aunt Millicent, dear, will you accompany them to the upstairs guest room?"

"Oh, good Lord and troubles, Lyssie-lad, is it time for tea?"

Lysander did not acknowledge the strangled giggle behind him at the nauseating nickname. "You've already had tea, Aunt. Our guest is here, the one I mentioned at breakfast, if you recall."

Watery gray eyes the exact color of his brightened. "Oh yes! Our dear...distant cousin by marriage. Miss Valery from Paris!"

"Indeed."

He rotated, and the little minx's face was as blank as an artist's canvas at the lie, though Lady Marsden's eyes danced with devilry. Lysander frowned. Apart from her considerable talents with a needle, Marsden always grumbled about his wife's cleverness and outspoken nature, though he claimed they were both a small price to pay for being in love.

Lysander disagreed. There was no price he'd ever pay when it came to something as fickle as love. Certainly, he could *love* his aunt in that he appreciated her role in his life. He esteemed and respected his friends. But the idea of falling in love—of giving up all self-governance, especially after his last foray into a courtship—was alarming. He needed order and structure, not chaos. His eyes slid to the ballerina, whose demure gaze remained hooded and hidden from him, a Mona Lisa smile full of secrets gracing her lips.

She was chaos incarnate.

For the barest moment, Lysander wondered if he'd made a mistake...if his impeccable instincts in business had finally failed him. He frowned, hesitancy cutting through him, and then he firmed his jaw. It was one night. Surely he could survive one evening with a beautiful woman on his arm?

At the end of the ball, she would go back to her rooms in Covent Garden a hundred quid richer, and he would finally close the deal with the Earl of Bolden.

He cleared his throat. "I will be in my study if I am needed. Luncheon will be served at your leisure. Please excuse me."

Devil take it, he wanted *her* at his leisure.

A pair of shuttered sea-glass eyes met his as he strode for the exit, and never had he been more tempted to stay in a woman's presence just so he could take the time to sift through each stunning color, to catalog them for future study in private. Had he ever seen their like? Emerald, jade, and gold striations flecked her irises, mesmerizing in hue like the sun hitting the surface of a tropical ocean. A man could get willingly lost in such eyes.

Flinching at his overly mawkish thoughts, Lysander picked up his pace. A sharp wit combined with a dancer's body that he yearned to see on a stage, and now a face that could launch ships, would be his willing ruin. If he had taken the measure of her true appearance, he might never have made the offer. Never would have put himself in this position.

Because, without a doubt, he felt it...the buzzing over his skin that came from facing an unseen change, from knowing that some intense storm brewed on the horizon.

As though she were rain...and he, a vast, barren desert.

This most definitely had been a mistake.

The gentleman before Nève screamed nobility. The noblest

of the nobles. The bluest of the blue bloods. The man from last night was well and firmly buried beneath an unshakable mask of Mayfair. Even as he swept past her, draped in full ducal hauteur, he barely spared her a glance. All the logical arguments she'd presented to herself in her tiny attic room, of how helpful the sum of a hundred pounds could be, vanished at his arctic demeanor.

She swallowed her bubbling uncertainty, resisting the frantic urge to turn on her heel and scurry back the way she'd come. What in botheration had she anticipated? Rose petals on the floor? Sonnets? Perhaps not, but maybe a smile of welcome or some indication of their shared misadventures hours before. She had not expected to be made to feel like a beggar at the scullery door. She was doing him a favor!

No, he's your employer, a calm voice reminded her. How they'd met, accidental misadventures or otherwise, had no consequence on where they went from here, and she had a role to perform. Nève squared her shoulders and turned to where the pretty brunette with deep umber skin was directing the other women with the ease of a seasoned general. They gathered armfuls of colorful, expensive fabrics and marched from the room.

Lady Marsden smiled, gesturing for her to follow the seamstresses. "Come along then, we have lots to finish and not much time in which to do it."

Nève moved obediently, her eyes devouring the space—the wide foyer with its impressive staircase, the rich mahogany paneling, and the marble floors. She was no stranger to wealth, though perhaps not quite as excessive as this. Before her father had lost his fortune to awful investments and hovering vultures, they had lived in a fashionable part of Paris in a home that boasted sixteenth-century French architecture.

Despite being disowned, he'd had a sizable inheritance of his own, which had bled from his fingers like water through a sieve during her childhood. As kind as he was, her father had always been a target for unscrupulous rogues seeking to relieve him of his fortune. By the time Nève was twelve, they'd sold off their fancy apartments on the Boulevard des Capucines along with most of their possessions and had been reduced to renting a small flat in a decidedly unfashionable arrondissement on the Left Bank.

Private tutoring in music and dance had stopped, with the exception of ballet that her mother had staunchly continued to teach her daughters. Both girls had shown an uncommon aptitude for it, but back then, dance had been a lovely diversion for two aristocratic young ladies, not a means of income. A few years later, when sickness had taken both her parents, ballet had become both respite and necessity.

Nève swallowed hard. Need was a complex thing—bellies needed to be filled and expenses needed to be paid—and sometimes, survival demanded compromise. She refused to be under the control of any man like Durand, but barring that, her body and her time were hers to command. Once more, she would do what was required of her . . . within reason.

"Are you thirsty or hungry?" Lady Marsden asked, once they were settled in another luxurious set of rooms with blue-and-gold trim.

"No, thank you, my lady."

"Goodness, I insist you call me Laila," she said, wrinkling her nose adorably as if the formal address offended her. Nève liked her already. "Disrobe behind that screen down to your undergarments and step up on this box, if you please."

Nève did as she was bid and then dropped her jaw in shock as Lady Marsden approached armed with a tape measure, a dress draped over one arm, and a full pincushion. "Wait a moment, what are you doing?"

"Taking your measurements and fitting you," she replied.

"But you're a *lady*."

One dark brow arched high. "Also a modiste. Is it so incredible to you that a woman of my station can be both wellborn and clever with a needle?"

Nève closed her mouth, reminded of her own situation. "Well, no, but one would expect needlepoint rather than dressmaking."

"Needlepoint." Lady Marsden gave an eloquent sniff as she proceeded to efficiently measure Nève's chemise-clad shape from head to toe. "It's a rather exceptional kind of torture, I assure you. I much prefer design. These dresses, for example"—she paused and pointed to the arrangement of heavily embroidered silks that the other women held—"are my own creations. Inspiration from India, where my parents are from."

Oh, how wonderful! The gowns were exquisite in their color and construction, with a gorgeous Eastern flair, and Nève couldn't help but be impressed. "You design gowns for yourself?" she asked, curious as to whether her efforts were a hobby, or heaven forbid, work.

"And a few other ladies," she replied. "My marquess encourages my passion."

Nève blinked. Dieu, she was a marchioness! One step down from a duchess. She frowned at the unassuming lady who was currently happily on her knees, hair askew and dark eyes alight, squinting thoughtfully at a parchment in her hands with numbers scribbled upon it. "The duke mentioned a partiality for blue, but I think green or maybe even a bold red. What colors do you like? Do any of the fabrics the girls are holding take your fancy?"

Nève let out a breath of surprise. Montcroix had requested blue? He hadn't seemed to care beyond the fact that she had arrived at his home as agreed.

"Blue is fine," she blurted and then fought a blush as the marchioness's glittering gaze met hers. "And red or green, or anything really. I'm not particular."

The assistants held out four dresses—one was an emerald-green satin with blond lace, another was the color of flame, the third was an ice blue that made her lungs squeeze for no good reason at all, and the last was a rich topaz satin with richly detailed embroidery on the bosom and hem. She should choose the blue. The duke was paying for her time after all, and she should dress to please him.

"Actually, the brownish gold," Nève said firmly. She was a dancer, not a court jester. She'd dress to please herself. If the duke didn't like it, he could go hire someone else.

Laila's lips curved. "Excellent choice. That's my favorite. The metallic threads are Zardozi embroidery of Mughal origin."

The girls fetched her stays and petticoats, fastened them efficiently, and then slid the gown over her head. Cool satin rushed over her body in a shimmering waterfall, clinging to her modest décolletage and rustling over her hips. Where the fabric gaped, Laila pinned with deft movements, pursing her lips and squinting. It was a tad long, but with a few more pins and five women working in unison, the right length was achieved in no time at all.

Laila let out a pleased sound, walking back a few steps. "There, that's lovely. Heavens, you do this gown more justice than it deserves, Nève. Come look."

Nève stepped down, careful not to dislodge the handful of pins or get accidently jabbed, and joined Laila in front of a standing mirror. She blinked in surprise, mouth agape at the image that greeted her. The dress hugged her sparse ballerina's curves to perfection, the tawny color making her porcelain skin seem richer. She did not have much of a bosom, but the little she did have was emphasized to blush-worthy extremes by the fancy brocade. Fitted through the waist and flaring out over a bustle in lush buttery folds to the floor, it was by far the prettiest ball gown she'd ever worn. Not that she owned many—after the decline in her papa's fortunes, invitations had dwindled, and all their fancy dresses had been sold.

In this creation, she looked like a duchess.

A frown marred her brow in the reflection. *No*, she looked like a paid thespian.

"It's a beautiful gown," she said to the marchioness. "You're very talented."

"Thank you. It might have been designed with you in mind. A match made in heaven. I shall be thankful for the free advertising."

Nève turned. "Your marquess does not mind that others know of your interests?"

"The ton already considers me an eccentric, mostly because I am not fully English." That was no surprise—but Nève was a firm believer in judging on character rather than bloodline. Considering she and Vivienne had been shunned for the choices they had made, she was hardly one to cast stones from her glass house.

Laila led Nève back to the small dais in the middle of the room and gestured for the seamstresses to carefully remove the dress, leaving the pins tucked for the adjustments. "I'm certain you'll hear all the gossip tonight, arriving on Montcroix's arm and entering his circles."

"Circles?" she muttered. "I'm surprised people actually want to be around him."

"He's a powerful man."

"With the personality of a whetstone." She clamped her lips shut in horror, but Laila only laughed.

"Oh, you are lovely! I always wondered what sort of woman would catch Stone's eye. Clearly one who isn't made mute by him."

"I haven't caught his eye," she said quickly. "I'm his distant cousin by marriage, that's all."

The marchioness canted her head. "As you say."

"You call him Stone as well?" Nève asked.

"He and Marsden went to Eton together. They've been sworn best enemies since boyhood." She rolled her eyes. "Believe me, my dear, anything one of them can do, the other can do better.

Marsden has been goading him about a bride for months now. It's not unheard of for distant cousins to marry. Perhaps that will be you."

"I doubt it," Nève replied. "Our association is not of that nature."

Laila shot her a shrewd glance, and for a moment, Nève felt as though she were being pinned to a wall and dissected. "Oh? Pray tell, I do love a good story."

Nève opened her mouth and closed it. Their arrangement was Montcroix's business, and while she had a deep sense of camaraderie with Laila and felt in her bones that the marchioness could be trusted, it wasn't her place to say. She was saved from replying by a sleepy voice in the corner.

"The duke said she's visiting from France and only here for a short while," Lady Millicent interjected from where she sat, and Nève was grateful for the interruption. Her savior's face fell as she propped herself up in the chair, watching the seamstresses pack away all the bolts of fabrics. "Oh, bother, did I miss the entire fitting after all?"

Laila smiled. "It will be the grandest surprise, Millicent dear! But now that we've finished and can sit for a moment, shall we all enjoy a spot of brandy?"

Millicent brightened and rose, waddling over to where Nève stood, once more clad in her plain, serviceable walking dress. Without the topaz gown, she felt much too frumpy and plain to be in such a lovely chamber, but this was her best dress and it would have to do. Millicent smiled and produced a small wrapped parcel. "My nephew told me that I should give this to you once the fitting has been concluded." Her rheumy eyes lightened gleefully. "Perhaps it is a gift. A pair of earbobs for this evening or a bracelet."

Nève knew exactly what it was—half the money for her services as she'd requested in the hansom. Something in her chest seized when she took the parcel as though some idiotic part of her romantic heart were hoping for a tender gesture instead. She bit the inside of her cheek.

This wasn't an amorous gift from a dashing suitor to his lady.

It was payment.

Blinking, Nève forced away the spark of shame that arose. She had nothing to feel awful about. This was a role, a *lucrative* role, and she had arranged the terms of compensation. She should be pleased that he was a man of his word. She lifted her chin—there was no room for regret. Not for this. She'd made the choice with her eyes wide open and of her own free will.

And now she had a part to play.

Lysander paced in his study, wearing a tread in his carpet as his ears strained for any sound...any sign that Miss Valery was still in residence, even though everyone else had departed hours before. His guest was, of course, ensconced in the guest wing, but he couldn't hear a thing. The floors were thick hardwood and soundproof. But just the knowledge of the fact that she was above stairs, undressing and bathing, having a gown molded to that lithe body, while she was a stone's throw away from his own bedchamber, had done unthinkable things to him.

Objectionable things.

What exactly was it about her that got under his skin so?

She was lovely, but it wasn't as though beautiful ladies did not surround him on any given evening at the theater or the opera. Was it the tactile memory of the pliant and firm feel of her flesh pressed up against his frame in that narrow alley? Or the edible lemon-cake scent of her that had made his mouth water and his groin tighten in tandem?

One would think he'd never been with a woman before, though admittedly, it had been a while. His estate and investments kept him busy—kept him focused. Knowing Miss Valery was *here*, he'd been on tenterhooks, unable to function. After he'd left the salon, he'd barely been able to concentrate, not for lack of trying, and he'd given up when he'd penned the same notes on his forthcoming meeting in an illegible scrawl that even he could not decipher.

It was unlike him.

Hell, he needed to pull himself together. The ball this evening was critical to secure Bolden's approval, and Lysander could not lose the opportunity to change the man's mind. Which brought him back to his "companion" for the evening.

It was a gamble. *She* was a gamble.

Hiring a woman he'd met on the streets had been imprudent. He'd only been thinking of winning Bolden over, and at the time, his strategy to use her as a foil had seemed sound. Likely because the bloody earl himself had goaded him: *Perhaps you should pick one.* And so he had.

Picked one.

Off the streets in Covent Garden, no less.

Tension gathered in his skull, and he pinched the bridge of his nose, willing it to dissipate. Everything about this felt different. She wasn't Charlotte, the woman who had played him like a fiddle and left him for his own father, though he felt dread tightening inside all the same. Betrayal never went away; it bled into everything. But that was why this was good. It was business.

Cut and dried. Clear. Sensible.

He would not be affected.

Even since he'd been a boy, Lysander had never put one foot out of line. He went to the expected schools, studied the required subjects, walked the path extrapolated by the former duke, and tried to meet his father's every expectation. If he hadn't or if he failed in any way, the consequences had been dire. The lash had been the least of it. He'd been beaten, humiliated, punished—all in the name of grooming for the dukedom.

But it'd been more than that. His father had been ashamed of him.

His brain simply did not work the way the duke expected it to.

At times, hot embers of rage had flared inside of him, but they had been doused so many times, he wasn't sure they would ever burn again. But those embers had never died. He'd wanted to prove his father wrong and to inure himself from the duke's cruelty. He didn't need the rest of the ducal fortune held over his head as though it were a golden ax. He'd been determined to take his inheritance and make his own fortune.

You're a dunce, boy, you'll never amount to anything.

And so, a younger, less wiser Lysander had used the first portion of his birthright to invest in his first railway company. But naivete had been his downfall. That and his father's cunning. Of course the old man had found out. The railway had been sunk and buried beneath a mountain of paperwork in the House of Lords, at the perverse whim of his father, the too-powerful Duke of Montcroix. Lysander had lost every penny.

It had all been a twisted display of power, of course. Mont-croix would never disown or shun his only heir. A man's son, even shamed and scorned behind closed doors, only made the duke stronger in the eyes of the rest of the aristocracy. A son was proof of his virility, that his line was strong and would continue. Mont-croix was king of his domain...and Lysander had been nothing but a powerless pawn.

A knock on the study door made him whirl. "What is it?"

"Your Grace?" a feminine voice inquired. "The butler, er, Mr. Finley, said you would be in here."

"Enter."

The door opened and everything stopped—his breath, the air, the very world—at the woman standing there. If those singular sea-glass eyes and the sardonic twist of her mouth didn't proclaim who she was, he wouldn't have recognized her.

Lysander's mouth dried of speech as he took her in, savoring every stunning inch. He surveyed the rich tawny gown that made her complexion glow like opals, the knot of curls tamed into lush submission and framing her face, the graceful creamy column of her neck and the tantalizing display of flesh at its base. He'd desired blue, but he'd been wrong...so very wrong.

In burnished bronze, she outshone the sun.

At his prolonged scrutiny, she let out an exhale, looking uncertain. "Is this too much? The marchioness insisted it wasn't, but it's so extravagant."

"She's right. It is perfect." Lysander frowned at the unfamiliar dry rasp of his voice. He cleared his tight throat. "Would you like a glass of sherry before we leave?"

Nodding her thanks, she entered the study in a swish of

golden-bronze skirts, perusing the spare masculine space before her gaze came back to rest on him. Her eyes swept him from head to toe. "You've come up to snuff."

"As opposed to what?"

Her mouth twitched as she trailed one gloved finger over the surface of his desk. "Well, you were rather a mess when we met. You'd lost your hat as well as a few buttons. Your cravat was askew, you had dirt on your boots, and you reeked of spilled ale and everlasting regret."

"And yet you weren't afraid of me," he said, hiding his humor at the last.

Those eyes lit, and his breath sputtered. "What romantic heroine worth her salt would abandon a nob in need of assistance? That would be in poor form for the starving poets, sir."

Amusement filled him. God, she was like a breath of fresh spring air in a closed-up, boarded room. "The poets?"

"Lord knows those poor, uninspired souls need some new source material other than men rescuing women all the time. Women are capable of such heroic actions, as well you know."

"Indeed." He arched a brow as he prepared the drinks. "Though my heroine seemed determined to have a brawl with the walls of an empty theater in the middle of a square with no thought to her own well-being."

She smirked. "I had a pistol for protection. I seem to recall your being on the business end of it, Your Grace."

Lysander walked over with the glass of sherry and a refreshed glass for himself. "What weapon do you have on you tonight? Surely a pistol won't fit into your reticule or go with that ensemble."

"You'd be surprised at how spacious ladies' reticules are," she replied. "But no, there's no need to worry on my behalf. I won't be spilling blood on any fancy carpets tonight. I'm armed with something much more dangerous than a gun."

"Which is?" He was almost afraid to ask.

A wicked smile curled her lips, something like delight flashing in those green eyes as she tapped her temple with an impish wink. "Woman's intelligence. The dread of the patriarchy and the scourge of the aristocracy. Provocative at best, deadly at worst."

Chapter Four

Drat and botheration, Nève couldn't breathe. Every inhale in the confines of the carriage made smaller by the duke's large body brought his scent with it—that wintry mix of pine, sage, and sin—a combination that wrought war upon her senses.

She'd nearly swallowed her own tongue when she'd seen him standing like a brooding Ares in his study, attired in raven black from head to toe, the only relief to the unrelenting darkness a snow-white shirt and cravat. With that uncompromising jawline, bold features, and primal magnetism, he'd had the air of some fallen king from some fallen kingdom. A dark, sulky god among unsuspecting mortals.

Nève hadn't been able to catch a proper lungful of air since.

He'd liked her dress. The sudden flare of admiration in his eyes had been unguarded, not that he'd hidden any of his response from her. He'd let his appreciation show, and she'd basked in it like a feline preening in the sun on a warm day. She'd chosen the gown for herself, but his thunderstruck expression hadn't gone amiss.

Now, ensconced in his fancy ducal coach with its rich velvet interior on the way to the ball, Nève felt the first frissons of apprehension. Montcroix hadn't offered up a word as to his expectations for the evening, other than what he'd explained hours before: she was to deter any distractions of the female persuasion.

"Perhaps now is a good time to go over what you expect of me for this evening," she ventured, choosing her words as carefully as she could, given Millicent's presence.

Glittering eyes met hers. "As opposed to wielding your female wits, you mean?"

"Better than thinking with parts of my body that have no sense."

He blinked as her quick parry struck home, and Nève hid her grin.

Lady Millicent made a strangled noise from where she sat on her side of the bench. If Nève didn't know better, she'd think the older woman was stifling a snicker, but her pensive face gave away nothing. That useful skill must run in the family.

Nève wondered how much he had told his aunt of their arrangement. Not much, she'd wager. Everything about this stone-cold duke was padlocked and impenetrable, every emotion on the shortest of leashes. He was a vise, even with his own family.

For a moment, Nève pondered what had made him that way . . . or *who* rather.

"I expect you to be my honored guest, Miss Valery," the duke replied, capturing her attention. "People will speculate on who you are to me, of course. I expect you to be gracious and equally enigmatic. Let them sweat on ferreting out who you are and whether you're the future Duchess of Montcroix."

His words, even as disingenuous as they were, sent a hollow thrill through her. "Are we courting then, *Cousin?*"

The last was for his aunt's benefit, though Nève was certain the woman was not as bird-witted or oblivious as she seemed. The sudden arrival of a long-lost relative from France who had to be fitted for a ball gown in the space of a few hours was a stretch at best, even if the all-powerful, lord-of-all-things Duke of Montcroix declared it to be so.

"Let it be a mystery, Cousin *by Marriage*."

It was Nève's turn to blink at the emphasis. She could read all sorts of things into that. His tongue flicked out to wet his lip, and a sudden pulse of damp heat ricocheted between her thighs. Nève pressed her knees together, only to catch him watching her with a sharp, hooded stare...as if he, too, had felt the answering press of desire.

"Not too much of one," Lady Millicent chimed in. "Or the gossip won't be pleasant. You know how cruel the ton can be with outsiders."

Breaking her stare-off with the duke, Nève bristled. Given she was half-English and the daughter of a viscount, she would have no trouble handling herself in polite circles. But despite her self-righteous prickle, Lady Millicent was right, because the gossip would be unstoppable if the ton ferreted out the truth that she was nothing more than a duke's *paid* companion. Her ties to the aristocracy would not make much of a difference. They would rip her to ribbons without a qualm, no matter who her father was. No, tonight's performance had to be flawless.

"Naturally," Montcroix murmured.

"I will be the perfect amount of mystery and charm, and besides, beyond this evening, I don't intend to stay in London long enough to make a lasting impression, my lady," she said to Millicent with an effusive sweetness that made the duke's brow arch.

Lady Millicent patted her arm. "Oh, I do wish you were staying awhile, darling girl. The place is so dreary without female companionship. And my nephew can be such a dreadful bore, he's practically a marble bust himself. It's honestly a wonder he's even out socializing tonight."

"I socialize," he said.

Millicent scowled. "You go to your club. To the Lords. Once or twice to the theater. In that order. It's no life for a gentleman in his prime. Ever since that conniving—"

"Aunt."

She looked put out at the interruption, but did not heed the soft reprimand. "Don't Aunt me. You have not been the same since, and you know it. You're not getting any younger, and just because one devious, title-hunting tart made you hide with your tail—"

"Enough," the duke said softly, but the warning in that single word was enough to make the older lady clamp mutinous lips together.

Nève blinked. *Title-hunting tart?*

She couldn't imagine this man skulking away from anyone with his tail between his legs, much less a woman. And yet... given his aunt's passionate outburst, there was clearly more to *that* story. One Nève would give anything to hear. Something whimsical deep in her heart hummed...did this stoic, impassive duke have a beating heart, after all?

Oh, arrête, c'est la folie!

Nève's curiosity spiked, but she squashed it down. Romanticizing him in any scenario was nonsensical. It wasn't any of her concern who had broken his heart or leached the warmth from him.

Because after tonight, the Duke of Montcroix would be firmly in her past.

"His Grace, the Duke of Montcroix, Lady Millicent Templeton, and Miss Geneviève Valery," the majordomo intoned upon their arrival.

Lysander stilled at the sound of her given name. He hadn't heard her offer her name to the efficient butler upon entry, but she must have. Geneviève slid through Lysander's senses like silk over bared skin, but he buried the sudden interest. He had no business thinking of her by any name but her last.

Aunt Millicent promptly disappeared to find the punch, so he turned himself and Nève toward the receiving line for their hosts.

"Well, hell has truly frozen over now that the devil has left his domain," the Marquess of Marsden crowed. "Good God, when my dear wife informed me you would be in attendance to *our* humble ball, I had to see it with my own eyes to believe it."

Lysander canted his head with a dry look at his friend. "One would think I was an undisputed hermit the way you're carrying on."

"If the shoe fits, Stone. You *loathe* balls."

"Stop teasing him, Husband," Lady Marsden chided the marquess with an unaffected smile. "Your Grace, it's lovely to see you again."

She looked elegant in a shimmering emerald gown that instantly made Lysander want to see Nève in the same color. He squashed *that* errant thought as quickly as it came.

"And you, my lady." He bowed, turning back to the marquess.

"Marsden, allow me to present Miss Valery, a distant cousin visiting from France."

"Ah, yes, the reason you required my lady's talents." He took Nève's hand and fawned over it, making every muscle in Lysander's body wind tight. "Good to meet you, Miss Valery."

"And you, Lord Marsden." She curtsied. "Lady Marsden."

The marchioness inclined her head with a grin. "My word, Miss Valery, but do you look stunning in that remarkable gown. Might I inquire which extraordinarily gifted modiste crafted that magnificence?"

Nève smirked. "Would you believe that a wondrously talented marchioness appeared like a fairy godmother and, poof, waved her magic needle, and here I am at the ball wearing a gown any woman with a pulse would die for."

They shared a chuckle, and Lysander's gut clenched at the rich, throaty sound of Nève's laughter. He could feel Marsden's curious stare settling on him. He deliberately did not look at his friend, schooling his features into his usual unreadable mask. "Is Bolden here yet?"

"He arrived some time ago," the marquess replied, though his probing gaze promised that Lysander would be held to the fire later about the mysterious Miss Valery.

Leaving the receiving line, they moved past the foyer and into the ballroom to ridiculous amounts of staring and whispering. Lysander let out a grunt of distaste. One would think people had nothing to do but gossip about his social habits. It wasn't that unheard of for him to be in attendance. Or with a woman. Then again, he couldn't think of the last time he'd been to a ball on the arm of a lovely lady, or *any* lady for that matter.

Not since...

No, he would not think of her. She was only at the forefront of his mind because of Millicent's well-intentioned fury on his behalf in the carriage. But Charlotte Blackstone, his former betrothed, and rather uncoincidentally, his late father's duchess, did not deserve a single speck of his time. Not after her betrayal.

"May I interest you in a waltz, Miss Valery?" Lysander asked, shocking himself and his companion as well, by the looks of it. Dancing was *not* part of the plan.

He should seek out Lord Bolden, do what he'd come here to do and leave, but he couldn't. *Not yet*. Not without one dance. Suddenly, the notion was as imperative as breathing. He wanted one memory of the evening for himself; he'd paid a small fortune for her company, after all.

"If it pleases Your Grace," his companion said with a demure smile that nearly made him lift his brows in surprise. His gaze narrowed on her. Spine straight and shoulders back, she had the definitive air of a lady of quality, but everything about her suggested shyness and sweetness. Lysander blinked. She wasn't in the least bit shy. Or sweet.

Who *was* this woman?

She was playing a part, he reminded himself, and doing it well.

His palm on her elbow, Lysander led her to the ballroom floor, feeling dozens of probing eyes following their path. A waltz would give the tongues more incentive to wag, but Lysander didn't care. He had to satisfy the urgency to touch her...to have her in his arms once more, even if the reasons were hollow and much too indulgent.

Much too *dangerous*.

But Lysander's skin buzzed with excitement as her gloved hand gripped his and his palm slid about her waist. They were a foot apart, nowhere near as close as they'd been in that alley-way, and yet even at this distance the hunger in him settled from a roar to a satisfying hum when they drifted into the first turn. She moved with an effortless, supple grace—her steps flowing into the next as though she were treading upon a cloud. Pure joy filled her eyes, lighting the green from the inside until it was a blaze.

God above, what would she be like onstage?

Lysander tore his gaze away, only to fasten on the long, elegant line of her throat leading to her collarbones, the satiny cords beneath her skin prominent, as if they, too, were caught up in the emotion of the dance. He wanted to lick them . . . nip into the hollow of her neck where her pulse was beating. Gorge himself on the lemon and vanilla scent of her.

His mouth watered. Would her skin taste as good as it smelled?

"You waltz well, Your Grace," she murmured, that sea-glass-green gaze catching his, and he couldn't help noticing how the color of her dress brought out a hint of gold flecks in her irises.

"I am rusty." So was his voice, emerging from his throat like pure gravel.

"One wouldn't know it," she said, her own reply husky.

Was she thinking about the alley as well? About how her body had felt flush against his? Was she thinking of narrowing the gap between them now? His fingers flexed on her trim waist, as if to yank her closer, and a small, clipped exhalation left her lips.

"You're acquitting yourself quite well, too," he gritted out, restraining himself. Barely.

"I am a dancer, Your Grace. It would be embarrassing if I could not perform a few steps of a simple waltz."

"Indeed." For a moment, he *had* forgotten...what she was. Who they both were. He cleared his throat, willing his rioting emotions under control. "What was your last ballet?"

"*Giselle* was the last production I performed, but I was supposed to dance the sylph in *La Sylphide*."

"Supposed to?"

Green eyes flashed. "I was regrettably replaced."

There was a story behind that, but for the life of him, Lysander could hardly concentrate, the sinuous shape of her in his arms too distracting. His fingers contracted above the curve of her hip. A sharp exhale left his lips as her skirts swept against his trousers on the next turn, leaving embers in their wake. Her small waist became his anchor, her gloved fingers his only tether.

Twelve inches of charged air did not seem like nearly enough of a gap to be platonic. One tug and her breasts would graze his chest. One pull and she'd be in his arms. One step and his mouth could be on hers.

If they weren't in a public venue!

Hissing out a breath, he tore his gaze from her, taking in the other couples dancing around them as well as the many raised fans of spectators hiding the frenzied whispers behind them. The foot of space between them had shrunk to half that, her body distractingly close.

On the next turn, Lysander set her back into place.

The requisite distance of forced clarity.

A chasm and yet not far enough...not for all the ice inside of him to stop melting into steam. He wished he'd never asked her to dance in the first place. He wouldn't have, if he had known. He cleared his throat, striving for control. "Why were you replaced in the ballet?"

"I refused to entertain an indelicate offer." She paused. "From a gentleman."

"Indelicate?"

Her mouth twisted before resuming its pretense of a demure half smile. "Surely I do not have to explain what that means to you. He wanted the use of my body in exchange for my place on the stage. It's quite a normal contract for most ballerinas."

The coldness he'd fought for flooded his veins. "But not you."

"No, not me," she said quietly. "But nothing is ever free. Choices come at a price. It just depends on what one is willing to barter or give up. One's body...or one's soul. One could argue that the latter is a far greater cost."

Lysander nearly balked at her piercing look, wondering if she was referring to his offer. He opened his mouth and shut it. There was no argument he could make. The *job* he'd offered her flirted with indecency, and once more he felt an uncomfortable swell of complicity. Had his practical offer backed her into a corner? Forced her to make a hard choice?

He blinked, seeing the situation—and her—in a different light. "I regret to have put you in a similar position."

"At least you were honest about what you wanted."

"Nonetheless, I am sorry."

Her eyes searched his, as if trying to see the truth of his words, but then her lashes dropped, a false serenity coming over her features. "We do many things in the name of love, Your Grace. Mine is the love of a sister, for whom I'd pay a steep price. Even take money from a duke to be paraded through the ton as his prize."

Lysander swallowed as an odd discomfort filled him. "I prefer partner," he murmured. "Not prize."

"Do you care what I think?" she asked.

Strangely, he did. "Yes."

A soft laugh left her lips. "There are many layers to you, Your Grace, if one took the time to look, despite how insultingly blunt you can be." But then her eyes narrowed as if she could see right through the many protective battlements surrounding him. "I think you're running from something. Not footpads, this time. Something in your past, perhaps."

"And how do you know that?"

She shrugged. "We all have our demons, Your Grace."

"You seek to rescue me again, petite ballerine?" he asked with a dark look.

She lifted a brow. "Do you wish me to?"

"No."

"Are you always this morose?"

"Are you always so sanguine?" he countered.

She rolled her eyes. "It is an act, Your Grace, don't forget. A smiling prima ballerina gets more applause."

Lysander grunted. How could he forget? He twirled her again, once more enjoying the effortless grace of her body. She made a simple waltz seem like something ethereal.

"Why are so many people staring at us?" she asked as though

only just noticing their rapt audience. "Including Lord Marsden. One would think they'd never seen a duke waltz before."

"Because I don't."

A pleat formed between her brows. "You don't waltz?"

"No."

"Then why put yourself through the torture? You hardly strike me as a gentleman who does what he dislikes under any circumstance." She stared at him with a curiosity that was edged by a disturbing sliver of compassion. "Shall we stop?"

"No."

The frown deepened. "No, *what*? Sometimes, you are impossible to speak to, do you know that? It's a wonder that anyone understands you when you are fluent in monosyllables."

She shook her head, her teeth rolling her bottom lip in a habitual reaction he was beginning to associate with annoyance on her part. The reappearance of it made him want to snatch it between his own teeth right there in the middle of the ballroom floor.

Get in control, Stone.

He did it the only way he knew how . . . with practiced antagonism. "No, I don't typically do what I dislike, but here we are, waltzing. Maybe I wanted to get my money's worth and test out the merchandise."

"I am not a toy to be sampled, Your Grace," she shot back, a shimmer of something that looked like injury in her eyes before they shuttered, hiding any emotion from him.

"Then perhaps I wanted to see whether you were full of hot air about being a ballerina and had cleverly fleeced me out of a hundred pounds."

Those green eyes flashed with fire.

"A waltz is hardly a measure of a professional dancer." Her mouth flattened, and slender fingers dug into his shoulder as though she couldn't help her reaction. She sought to injure him as he was injuring her. "I did not lie or exaggerate my position. Nor did I propose this asinine scheme on a whim because I have money to spare and needed a woman to protect my ducal virtue." She scowled, scorn dripping from her words. "Pardon me, I meant ducal purse. Without a doubt, the only one full of hot air here, Your Grace, is you."

"Is that so?" His reply was silky. Quiet. Delivered in a tone meant to unsettle the most stalwart of men. He was a duke, for God's sake. How dare she speak to him thus? He'd ruined others for less.

The vixen in his arms only glared. "If the shoe fits, *Stone*."

Marsden's words, now delivered by a tongue ten times sharper in a meaning much more cutting than its predecessor's. She found him lacking, did she? As the waltz drew to its close, he did not release her, relishing the dark pupils that swallowed up the sea green. Was it fury or was it desire? Both emotions twined through him, determined to leave destruction in their wake.

Without another word, he shepherded her out to the terrace and down the stairs leading to the lamplit garden, leaving a storm of feverish whispers behind them in the ballroom. Something he'd regret later, he was certain.

"Do I need to remind you of your place?" he growled, once they were in the cooler air of the arbor and out of view behind a hedgerow and an enormous marble statue.

"My place?" she echoed viciously. Fierce eyes flayed him as she yanked her arm out of his grip. "Considering the role to which you've elevated my lowly, humble self, Your Grace, I can hardly forget, can I?"

"Then do your job. Perform."

The chit actually stamped her foot. "Gracious, you are maddening! I wasn't the one deviating from my course with a completely unnecessary dance whereupon you decided to judge me with your vulgar comments about my person. You will apologize, sir."

"For what?" he asked incredulously.

"Dieu, you really are thick, aren't you? I've never met anyone so arrogant in all my life. I am not a thing to be bloody tested for your pleasure, you odious, blockheaded man!" She took a furious step toward him. "You might have paid for my time, but you do not own me!"

The last five words were punctuated with sharp jabs against his chest. She was magnificent in her anger, like a hissing beast, all claws and teeth and voracious spite. Lysander couldn't help it. With one step, he met her chest to chest, tension exploding like fireworks between them, rushing like a thundering drumbeat in his ears. Blazing green eyes dropped to his lips, passion warring with her wrath.

God, he was desperate to kiss her. Desperate for *her* to kiss him. Frozen, he stood and stared, imagining how she would taste—like salt and burning sunshine—and felt his body tremble with need. He should go. Leave. But he couldn't tear his eyes away from her.

"Stop looking at me like that," she whispered.

A shudder rocked him at the huskiness in her voice. "I want to kiss you."

Those eyes dilated, lips parting as if the thought had been consuming her as well, right before her lashes dipped. "Then kiss me."

With one swift move, Lysander drew her to him, bracketing her with his body up against that very stone statue that hid them from prying eyes, and crashed his mouth to hers.

Chapter Five

At first, Nève couldn't decide whether she preferred to kiss him or kick him. For now, she'd enjoy the former. Maybe afterward she'd give him the kick he deserved. Everyone in attendance had witnessed him practically drag her out here, and though they were concealed by a flowering hedge and a marble sculpture, it wouldn't take much to imagine what the Duke of Montcroix might be doing. Or perhaps it would be beyond imagining, if said duke wasn't known for frequenting balls, or dancing, or seducing young ladies in secluded arbors.

Nève's fingers reached up to his lapels, with the full intention of ending the kiss, only to curl into them and yank him closer when his tongue flicked hard across the seam of her lips.

Oh, sweet baby angels...

Her fingers wound tighter as remaining upright won out over kicking. At least, that was what she told herself. The kissing was secondary. A distant second. Another indelicate lick to the inside of her upper lip, and lust twined up her spine to blanket her brain. Who was she fooling?

Kissing him was *everything*.

Because she was weak when it came to this duke. Weak to the stern but so deliciously soft lips currently possessing hers. Weak to the breaking tide of desire currently storming through her veins like a hurricane flood. And the taste of him—rich wine and dark, potent lust—well, that was her sodding demise.

The silken lash of his tongue touched the roof of her mouth, and Nève felt the sinuous stroke echo between her legs. She could already imagine the havoc it could do to the rest of her. Her nipples, already tight shameless points, tautened to the cusp of pain. She let out a breathless whimper, and he took full advantage, flicking deeper.

When Nève gave in with a moan and parted her lips wide, that sleek tongue found hers, teasing and torturing, sipping and delving. They dueled for dominance, much like their earlier verbal exchange, neither willing to give any quarter. This wasn't a kiss. It was a war. Pleasure was edged in pain, hardness tempered only marginally by softness. As one palm curled into the hard planes of his chest, the other crept up to his jaw, pinning his head in place as he explored every inch of her with a raw hunger that made her see stars.

Forget stars . . . she was seeing whole actual planets.

Bloody cosmic galaxies.

Pleasure spiked and crested along Nève's nerve endings like wildfire. Stone seemed to be equally lost, the needy growls ripping from his chest so primal and raw that it made her burn. This man could consume her and leave her in a smoldering heap, if she let him.

She *couldn't*.

Shouldn't, if she had a lick of sense left in her.

Hitching her arms up around his neck, she threaded her fingers through his thick locks and yanked hard on his hair, making him groan into her mouth. With one final decadent nip of his lip, she ducked beneath his arm.

"Kissing was not part of the agreement," she said huskily, touching two gloved fingertips to her tingling lips, her heart pounding like a galloping horde behind her rib cage.

Montcroix looked as stunned as she felt, those gray eyes like pools of shifting mercury as he visibly composed himself. "Fuck."

"Definitely also not part of the agreement."

The joke fell flat, despite the unseemly thrill it gave her.

"Please forgive me," he said in a tight-lipped whisper. "You're right, of course. My apologies."

For a heartbeat, Nève felt a dark sense of power that she'd been able to bring such a controlled man to such an ungoverned state, to unravel him so completely. Loss of control frustrated him, too, if the frown currently smashing his brows together was any indication. He was not someone accustomed to losing the upper hand or being led to action by base, physical emotions. And yet, he'd done so…because of her. Because of one, albeit shattering, kiss.

"I'm sorry, too," she said.

The duke raked a hand through his hair and then smoothed it back into place as if it gave him ease to have every piece of his armor intact. "You have nothing to apologize for."

"I was angry."

His brows rose. "Do you believe standing up for yourself was wrong?"

"Well, no," she replied after a beat of hesitation. "But I do tend to be forward with my opinions. It's the Frenchwoman in me, I suppose. I could have been more tactful considering you are paying me to provide a service not a setdown." Her lips quirked with mischief. "That will cost you extra."

Stepping away, he put some more space between them, the soft murmur of voices filtering in from the other side of the hedge. Nève narrowed her eyes, watching him. He'd already donned his ducal mask, but now the shutters drew up over his cool eyes, dampening the heat of his stare and altering his face. It was remarkable to observe the shift from flesh-and-blood man to stone duke. Within a handful of seconds, he was as chilling as the ferocious gargoyles who guarded the Cathédrale Notre-Dame de Paris.

Nève didn't know whether to be impressed or alarmed.

It was hard to believe this cold effigy was the same fiery man who had been kissing her minutes before as though he would die if he didn't. As though she were the air in his lungs and the blood pumping through his veins. Her eyes traced over the hard, swollen curve of his lips, and she felt a ripple down to her toes. She ducked her head to hide her blush.

"Shall we go back in, Miss Valery?" he asked, extending his arm, the veneer of frost in his icy stare a cautionary tale...a warning should she or anyone dare to trespass.

With a breath, Nève took his arm and smiled as though she were onstage for an encore. It was his show after all. "Lead on, Your Grace."

Lysander was obsessed with her mouth—the taste of it, the texture of it, the soft heat of it—so much so that he hadn't heard a single word the Earl of Bolden had spouted in the last quarter of an hour. How could something so soft and inviting harbor the sting of a wasp? In the garden, she'd been in the midst of giving him the crushing setdown he deserved, and all he'd wanted to do was to sample those lips to see if they were as tart as the words coming from between them. When she'd consented, it had been all he could do not to fumble like a novice.

Contrary to her biting words, they'd been sweet.

Venomously sweet.

He wasn't even sure if the wild handful of heartbeats they'd spent in that impassioned tangle could be called kissing. Regardless, it had been impulsive. Stupid. *Reckless.*

He closed his eyes.

"Am I boring you, Montcroix?" Bolden demanded, watery brown eyes piercing him. "You seem distracted."

Lysander frowned, giving himself a mental shake. Nothing was more important than getting this man on his side and convincing him to sell, not even a vixen with sugared belladonna for lips. "I beg your pardon. No, of course not. You were explaining how long that acreage has been in your family. Please continue."

The earl gave him a dubious look. "As I was saying, it's unentailed, but very dear to me. It belonged to my countess and came with her as part of her dowry, God rest her soul."

"I was not aware." Of course he knew. Lysander made it his business to know everything in great detail about his investments.

"It was exceedingly important to her, and this is why I had second thoughts about your suitability, Montcroix, and what your plans are for the estate."

Lysander was all ears now. He frowned—his plans should not matter. It was a piece of property. A *thing*. His offer had been far beyond the market value for the estate. Suitability had nothing to do with it, and yet here he was, hopping to this man's absurd tune.

"It would honor my late wife's memory to have the new owners maintain the castle and raise a family there, put down roots in the childhood home that was near and dear to her heart." He pursed his lips. "And, well, that is not you, Your Grace."

"And what do you think I am?"

"Ruthless. Callous. Materialistic. Rootless."

Lysander fought the urge to cringe.

Those were all true, though the fourth stung slightly. The sentimental foolishness of the notion scraped Lysander raw, but he kept his thoughts to himself. The man's wife was gone. Who cared who bought the property? Or what they did with it? Yes, the castle was beautiful and had a long history, but it was in the way of progress...and his railway.

Before Lysander could reply that he *was* indeed a man who intended to put down roots, thanks to the timely Miss Valery, the earl's face shifted as another gentleman joined them. Christ, could Treadway's timing be any worse? The man was a brainless dandy, and he was about as subtle as a bull in a china shop.

"Montcroix, Bolden, good to see you both," Treadway said with a jaunty grin. "I'm sure no introduction is needed for Her Grace."

Time stopped and resumed at a pace too fast for Lysander's narrowing mind to follow. His gut tightened at the woman trailing in Treadway's wake. The evening had just gone from bad to worse in a matter of thundering heartbeats.

What the *bloody hell* was Charlotte doing on Treadway's arm? It could be coincidence, but Lysander did not put much stock in that, especially where the dowager Duchess of Montcroix was concerned.

Distaste filled him. How had he ever been so blind? Lysander had proposed to Charlotte, not out of love but of duty, and he'd thought them at the very least well matched. Yet when his mother had died, delaying their nuptials until the requisite year of mourning had passed, the beautiful and ambitious Charlotte had turned around and married his father. Lysander hadn't seen it coming. No one had.

The duke had clapped him on the back after the wedding. "Never turn your back on anyone, son. They'll stab you in it, the first chance they get. Even me."

"So this was another lesson?" Lysander had asked.

"Never cross me."

From that day, the ashes of anger in his soul had reignited into an inferno. He'd slowly and methodically begun to dismantle and destroy everything his father held dear. That first investment failure hadn't deterred Lysander—it had only made him more determined. To win. To have more money than his father ever possessed. To grind the memory of the previous duke to nothing but dust.

Swallowing the urge to turn on his heel, Lysander scowled, his eyes falling on Charlotte, whose eyes glittered with their usual cunning. It was unfortunate he had taken too long to see her true nature. He detested games, but for the moment, he was caught between the devil and the deep sea...between his desires to win Bolden over and his deep mistrust of the woman standing before him.

"Your Grace," he greeted her coolly.

"So formal, Lysander," his former betrothed cooed.

"Do you prefer I call you *stepmother*?"

"Don't be cruel, darling," she said, sidling closer. "You know I cherished your father."

Yes, she cherished the fact that he'd made her a very wealthy duchess, only to keel over from apoplexy five years later. Lysander wanted to walk away, but he couldn't risk giving Bolden any more ammunition against him, not when he needed to salvage the situation.

Ruthless. Callous. Materialistic. Rootless.

Charlotte drifted a finger down his arm, making him cringe. "When Treadway said you would be here, I had to come, now that I'm finally out of mourning."

Of course she was—the ivory-and-gold gown she was wearing instead of somber half-mourning colors declared it to all and sundry like a bull's rag. "On the prowl for a new husband already?"

"Should I be?" She preened, fluttering her eyelashes in a way she probably thought was seductive. "Come now, surely you've missed me."

Christ, did she mean *him*? Lysander was trying to think of a delicate way to extricate himself, when he felt a gentle touch on his sleeve. "Stone, my dearest, I've been looking for you."

The duchess glowered at the intimate address, her painted lips pursed as though she'd swallowed something sour when she caught sight of his rescuer. "Who is this?"

Lysander ignored her, clutching the lifeline his ballerina had unknowingly handed to him. He gripped Miss Valery's elbow and pulled her close. She was his out…his saving grace. The very thing he needed to convince the earl that he was a changed man.

His gaze dipped to Nève, and he pushed away the pulse of guilt. She'd understand what he was about to do.

Maybe.

"We've not yet made the announcement public, but, Bolden, may I be the first to introduce you to my fiancée, Miss Geneviève Valery." He felt Nève stiffen at his side, felt her surprise, though, to her credit, nothing of it showed on her face. He forced a laugh that sounded hollow. "Well, soon to be, anyway. We are in the middle of negotiations. I am attempting to convince her as we speak of the sincerity of my suit."

The earl bowed, a look of delight filling his eyes. "A pleasure, Miss Valery. A pleasure, indeed."

"The pleasure is mine, my lord," she replied sweetly.

Treadway cleared his throat, an appreciative gaze casting down Nève's form in a casual way that made Lysander tense. "I didn't know you were in the market for a wife, Montcroix."

"It was unexpected like the sparks and fireworks all the poets write sonnets about," Lysander replied, and turned to Nève, meeting her eyes for the first time since his outrageous falsehood. Those sea-green orbs sparked with the promise of retribution, and something wild in him rose up to meet it. God, she fired his blood. Even while going along with his latest charade, she clearly intended to eviscerate him once they were alone. Was it foolish that a part of him was looking forward to it?

"Chérie," he said to Nève. "May I present Viscount Treadway and my late father's widow, Her Grace, the dowager Duchess of Montcroix."

Treadway made a smacking sound with his lips, and Lysander could feel Nève recoil. "A pleasure, Miss Valery."

Nève curtsied, and Charlotte's cold eyes swept her form with disdain. "Miss Valery, how is it we have not been introduced? Are you new to town?"

"Why, yes. From France, actually."

Her voice was honey sweet, her expression open and full of wonder as though nothing the other woman could say or do would steal her joy. Lysander wanted to blink, to see if this was the same smart-mouthed vixen who had given him a brutal set-down and kissed him with the fire of a seasoned lover, but no, his ballerina was wearing the face of a wide-eyed, guileless angel.

"Good Lord, Montcroix, you'll eat this one alive," Charlotte drawled with venom.

Nève smiled and clutched his arm before he could answer. "My sweet, charming Stone?" She let out a musical giggle that was so syrupy it nearly gave him a toothache. "Goodness, Your Grace, he wouldn't hurt a fly. Or *eat* anyone."

Stone couldn't stop the smirk that appeared on his face.

With an unflattering huff, Charlotte swept away with the viscount, leaving them with an uncomfortable-looking Bolden, who quickly made his own excuses to leave. But not before Lysander asked the earl to reconsider his position on the sale, and much to his relief the earl promised to think about it.

"Well, that went well," Lysander murmured when they stood alone. "I almost didn't recognize this version of you."

"We are not engaged, Your Grace," she hissed, all pretense of the angel gone as she attempted to drag him behind a potted fern. "What are you doing? What will happen when your supposed fiancée goes missing after tonight?"

"No one will know."

Her mouth dropped open. "No one will *know*? You are a duke. By the end of this ball, *everyone* will know of your change in bachelorhood, trust me. If not Bolden or the duchess, someone else will have overheard. Nothing in the ton stays secret for long, I know that more than anyone." She clamped her lips shut as though she said something she shouldn't have.

Lysander wondered if she was thinking of the same gentleman in France she'd spoken of who had taken undue liberties, or whether it was more. This sounded deeper, and more personal.

"What do you mean?"

"Not that it's any of your business, but my father was an English viscount, Viscount Reeves. When he got his lover, an opera dancer, with child, they tried to keep it a secret, but it got out anyway. He was cut off."

"You're illegitimate?"

She shot him a withering look. "As opposed to half the bastards in the aristocracy? No, not that it matters, my parents married before I was born. My sister and I took my mother's name. We did not need his family's name or their charity, not that being the Honorable Geneviève Reeves would do me any favors." Nève broke off abruptly, as if realizing the same thing he did. She would not be bartering her presence for a hundred pounds if she *weren't* in need of charity.

"Your father was a viscount."

She slanted a sidelong glare. "That's what you heard out of all of that?"

"You have connections to the peerage."

Nève huffed, her voice low. "Ciel, you English and your obsession with aristocratic lineage! Where were those peers when my sister and I were penniless? Where was my father's family? They shunned us. I wrote letters that they ignored." She clenched her fists, eyes glancing over the crowd. "I would not be surprised if they are here somewhere, enjoying their pretty lives while my sister withers in bed."

"Then do something about it."

She let out a snort. "By pretending to be a future duchess?"

"Yes."

"It's that easy for you, is it?" she bit out. "Everything in stark black and white with no middle ground?"

Lysander frowned. From her tight expression, he was missing the nuance of the conversation, but to him, it *was* easy. Middle ground only muddled things. "Precisely. Life is a series of equations, and the answers are there. You apply one to the other. It's simple."

Yet again, it seemed to be the entirely wrong thing to say as low, hard laughter left her. "Life is not an *equation*, Stone. Neither is it simple. By default, you are assuming that *I* am simple." Lysander opened his mouth to disagree, but she let out a ragged exhale and lifted hurt eyes to his. "Please excuse me, Your Grace, I require a moment."

At a complete loss as to what he'd done wrong, he stared at her as she left the ballroom. He couldn't have fouled that up more if he'd tried. She wasn't simple, she was *remarkable*, and he'd wounded her. Frowning, Lysander rubbed at his chest, wondering why it ached for a woman he'd just met.

Ironically, he had no ready answer to that.

Chapter Six

Nève's heart was pounding a raucous tempo in her ears as she pushed through the crowd, searching for the retiring room. She could go back outside, but she did not want to be followed, not by him and not after she'd confessed something that should have remained hidden away. She was already hampered by the lies of Lord Durand; she did not need the fact that she was the daughter of an English viscount being public knowledge. No one would hire her then.

She sighed through her teeth. No one was hiring her now.

The retiring room, unfortunately, was crowded, so she headed toward a pair of armchairs tucked into a nearby alcove. Pressing her fingers to her temples, she circled them against the knotted tension there. She only had to get through the rest of the evening and then she would put this evening behind her. One hundred pounds was more than enough to get back to Vivienne and cobble together what their next steps could be.

"There you are, little frog."

Nève's jaw clenched at the unoriginal slur and the approach of the Duchess of Montcroix and her slimy viscount. If she was a frog, this woman was a viper. Nève had run into many of her ilk in Paris, draped in jewels and furs and looking down their noses at the dancers who more often than not warmed their husbands' beds. They primped and simpered when the curtains were up, and when they fell, the talons came out.

Falling into character, she pasted an innocent smile to her lips. "Your Grace. Viscount Treadway. How wonderful to see you again so soon."

The lady's eyes narrowed, but Nève kept her smile firmly in place, her gaze wide with sincerity. As a dancer, one had to be prepared to adapt to any role, even one that went against the grain as much as this one did.

The viscount leaned in with a wink that made her flesh feel as if it were covered in spiders. "If you ever get tired of him, let me know. He's a bit on the nose and rather slow on the uptake, if you know what I mean."

Nève ignored that disparaging opinion, keeping her focus on the duchess, who was the much greater threat. "Do you miss His Grace, the late duke?" she asked. "I am sorry for your loss."

Her red mouth curled. "Not as much as I miss the current duke."

"The *current* duke?"

"Oh yes," she said, the smile turning vicious. "We were engaged years ago. I was the love of his life."

Something rushed up into Nève's chest then—a tearing need to vanquish this woman with her painted face and her petty remarks—not that Nève held any claim over Stone, but her sense of outrage spiked all the same.

"And you decided to break his heart and marry his father?" The question was delivered in all sweetness, but the duchess reared back as though Nève had slapped her. "That doesn't say much about your character, I'm afraid, Your Grace."

"You silly chit, how dare—"

"Heavens, Charlotte," a tall blonde drawled, approaching with Lady Marsden, who had a fierce expression on her pretty face. "Put your claws away before you poke someone's eye out. Didn't your mama ever teach you your manners?"

"This is none of your business, Vesper."

"But it is *my* business," Laila said, coming to a stop. "And I will kindly ask you to refrain from harassing my guests, or I shall ask you to leave."

The duchess whirled in a huff. "Well, I never."

The woman called Vesper snickered and hooked a cheerful thumb over one shoulder. "The exit is that way in case you're lost."

Nève instantly decided she liked her.

"That was rather unpleasant," Laila said, gesturing for a hovering footman to fetch a third chair so they could all sit. "My husband said she arrived with Viscount Treadway." Her nose wrinkled as she watched them disappear into the throng. "That man is hardly any better, though those two are probably suited to each other. Are you all right?"

"Nothing I couldn't handle," Nève said, though she was grateful for the rescue. She was a hairsbreadth from shoving the odious woman right onto her sanctimonious arse if she'd come one step closer. Pretend angel or not, Nève was no pushover. She learned early in the corps to hold her ground or risk being trampled by those who felt they deserved more.

Laila pointed at the blonde beside her and grinned. "This is my dear friend, Lady Vesper Lyndhurst. Fair warning, she's rich and unmarried, and fancies herself a matchmaker, so don't let her get her paws on you or you'll be betrothed before you can say, 'Dreadful to meet you.'"

"Don't listen to her!" the lady huffed. "I'm perfectly harmless, I assure you. And besides, I thought I heard a few little birds chirping that *you* were already engaged to a duke."

"Not yet," Nève said, unable to deny or confirm it. The rumor mill was faster than she expected, but juicy news was like that—it didn't require much to spread.

Laila tossed her dark curls. "Vesper, meet Nève, Stone's distant cousin from France, if you can believe it."

"Stone has relatives?" she quipped. "I thought he was raised by wolves."

Nève surprised herself by replying, "More like stone gargoyles in a crumbling abbey somewhere."

Both women stared at her before dissolving with mirth, their giggles echoing loudly in the alcove. Nève was sure she heard a snort or two. "Oh, goodness, I adore you already. Oh, well put!" Vesper gasped, holding her sides. "I do look forward to getting to know you better over the season."

At that, Nève felt an instant pulse of regret. Under different circumstances, she could see herself liking these two charming women. But Vivienne was counting on her, and as much as she'd enjoyed the fairy tale for one night, it would soon be over. She would take off the beautiful dress and go back to being Nève with rent to pay and an injured sister to care for.

Even if the manager of the Lyceum was indeed here as Montcroix had said, there was no guarantee that she'd be offered a job in London. She was an unknown, and she had to focus on what was achievable. "Lamentably, I must return to Paris at the end of next week." She cursed inwardly, remembering she was now supposed to be engaged. "For previous commitments."

There, she'd made her decision. Her flat was rented through the end of the month, which meant one more week for a few last-ditch auditions in London, and if nothing came of it, she would leave.

Vesper looked dejected but brightened. "Then you shall come to Harwick House for tea before you depart. I insist. Please say you will."

"I'd just give in," Laila advised with a resigned grin. "She's like a hound with a bone once she's got her mind set on something. Just be grateful it's not a man she intends to match you with."

"I'm not *that* bad," Vesper grumbled. "But yes, please come."

What would it hurt, Nève reasoned. Her time with Montcroix would be done and her hours would be her own. If she was still "engaged" by then, she would play the part, but that was his mess to navigate, not hers. "Very well, I'd love to."

Vesper clapped her hands, her blue eyes bright. "Wonderful! It's settled. Next Saturday, Harwick House at four o'clock. Now, tell us everything on how a stick-in-the-stone like Montcroix managed to get his hands on someone as refreshingly lovely as you."

In the study at Blackstone Manor, Lysander fetched the rest of the money he'd put aside for Nève. His fingers traced the edge of the packet as though he were averse to picking it up, giving it to her, or letting her go. Perhaps all three. He turned slowly to where she stood, garbed in the plain dress and cloak she'd arrived in. She was no less lovely for it. Nève had made the golden gown shine, not the reverse. He noticed she did not carry it with her, and frowned.

"The gown is yours to keep, Miss Valery."

She shook her head. "I couldn't accept it, Your Grace."

"It was part of the agreement," he said. "And besides, no one else will wear it. Do what you must with it. Sell it or give it away. It's yours to do with as you wish."

"Thank you."

In the next breath, Lysander found himself involuntarily committing each of her features to memory, from that high brow to the elegant rise of her cheekbones and the point of her chin, those fire-bright eyes and pouty lips, the elegant shells of her ears and the luster of her deep brown hair. He would not see her again.

The thought was oddly gutting.

He was not a man given to mawkishness, but this was different. This felt…huge, his instincts screaming for him to take her arm and never let go. It was foolish, of course. With a reluctance that he didn't want to dwell on, he handed over the parcel to her, watching her eyes settle on it before she graciously accepted it.

For a moment, their fingers brushed, making him catch his breath, and then their eyes met. Hers were an unfathomable green in the low-lit gloom of his study.

Nève cleared her throat, the slight tug on the packet forcing him to release it. "Thank you, Your Grace. I had a wonderful evening."

"All of it?" he couldn't help asking, remembering the ferocity of their kiss in the garden.

"Yes." Though crimson bloomed in her cheeks, she pocketed the money beneath her cloak and waved an arm. "Notwithstanding being accosted by your monstrous stepmother, I was also cornered by Lady Laila and Lady Vesper, who asked me to tell them everything of how we met." He laughed at her cheek, and she shot him a devilish look from beneath her lashes. "I hope you don't mind that I got creative."

His amusement dissolved. "How creative?"

"Oh, *chéri*, it was the stuff of dreams," she said with a theatrical sigh that made him want to kiss the saucy smirk from her lips. "When we caught sight of each other across a square in front of a deserted theater, it was love at first glance. Struck in the heart by Cupid's arrow, you tumbled like a duke-sized star falling from the heavens." A grin trembled over that lush mouth as she continued in wicked overly quixotic glee, warming to her story. "Unable to depart without a name or a touch, you fought your way through that square, braving a treacherous throng full of cutpurses and pickpockets, until I was at last in your arms."

Lysander fought back a choking noise. "You did not tell them that."

"It's the truth, isn't it?"

"Embellished. Very, *very* embellished." He let out a strangled breath. "No one in all of England would believe such hogwash of me."

Eyes sparkling, Nève gave in to her laughter. "Oh, but Your Grace, all the women were swooning all over themselves with delight."

He froze. "*All* the women?"

"I had quite the audience," she replied. "They all wanted to hear the tale of how the unromantic, obdurate, and utterly stone-hearted Duke of Montcroix fell to his knees for love."

"I did no such thing."

That teasing smirk grew, one hand going to her breast. "Upon my poor idealistic heart, you did, Your Grace. I could not refuse your impassioned words as you spouted Byron to the starry heavens and sank on bended—"

"You are devious, Miss Valery." He crossed the short distance between them and placed two fingers against her laughing lips. The heat of her skin seeped into his as uncontrolled laughter bled through the bracket of his fingers. "Now thanks to your inventive account, I will be the target of countless fops seeking courting advice."

"Consider it retaliation," she said and pretended to bite his finger.

"I'll have you know that I'm hardly the sort of man to drop to my knees, Miss Valery, not even for a beautiful woman."

"That seems to be rather extreme. A future without masculine swooning is no future at all."

Her smile wavered. As if suddenly realizing how close they stood and becoming aware of his bare fingers brushing her lips, she sucked in a lungful of air. But before she could move away, he slid his palm down to cup her jaw, his thumb coasting over the fullness of her lower lip. It was the only caress she allowed him before stepping out of reach.

"I was teasing. Don't make this any harder than it needs to be, Your Grace."

His hand drifted forlornly back to his side. "I'm sorry Edmund Falconer wasn't in attendance tonight. I was informed there was a mishap at the Lyceum."

"Was it serious?"

"No."

Nève lifted one shoulder. "Perhaps it wasn't meant to be, though I am grateful to you, nonetheless." She smiled brightly and gave a small curtsy. "This is goodbye then."

Lysander frowned, the finality of that word hitting him right in the gut. He wasn't ready for this—whatever *this* was—to be over. "What if it wasn't?"

She stalled. "What do you mean?"

"Stay for the rest of the season. Act as my fiancée. I'll compensate you for your time, for all of it. Name it and it's yours." He was aware of the slight note of desperation in his voice, but he couldn't help it. The thought of her walking out that door and out of his life was something he did not want to contemplate. Nor did he want to consider the whys of it. "Stay. Please."

He could see the confused emotion brimming in her eyes, the denial rising to her lips. One evening of pretense could be reasoned, but several weeks made it a different kind of agreement. One of deception and duplicity. One of questionable integrity.

"This was supposed to be just the once," she said softly.

"Don't give me your answer right away," he told her. "Please think about it. I will send a messenger for your answer tomorrow. The offer is on the table. You set the terms and the remuneration. A hundred pounds a day for eight weeks. More, if you prefer."

Her mouth parted at the astronomical sum. "I'm not for hire, Your Grace."

"Then don't think of it that way," he said.

"There are many courtesans in London who would be better suited to your needs."

He shook his head. "No, I don't require a courtesan. Consider it more of a dowager's companion. Think of me as an old widow with missing teeth, gout, and a bad spine. You wouldn't hesitate to accept the position then, would you?"

"You have excellent teeth, Your Grace, no hint of gout, and a strong back."

"I'm weak and corrupted on the inside. In danger of expiring this very moment."

A huff of mirth left her lips, but she shook her head, hand reaching for the doorknob. "There's a reason Laozi said there is no greater misfortune than wanting more. Sometimes, it's best to enjoy something for what it is and leave a good memory intact."

"If I heeded the words of every ancient philosopher, I would be in the poorhouse."

Her smile was bittersweet. "Farewell, Your Grace. Thank you for keeping your end of the bargain."

CHAPTER SEVEN

You cod-headed, bird-witted goose.

It wasn't the first, nor even the dozenth inventive curse she'd leveled against herself in the last week. In English *and* in French! Who said no to nearly six thousand pounds? An idiot, that was who. Six thousand pounds was a bloody fortune. A king's ransom. A dragon's hoard.

A ... second chance.

She and Vivienne could open their own dancing studio with that kind of money, one that they could run and manage together for the rest of their lives. Nève wished her sister were here. She would know what to do.

Stretching her legs and pointing her toes, she warmed up her stiff muscles in the cramped space of her single room. Concentrating on her ankles, knees, hips, and then her spine, shoulders, and wrists, she repeated the routine with meticulous focus before falling into several grand pliés, relevés, and extensions. There wasn't much room to move beside the small woodstove and the narrow cot, but there was enough for her to do what she needed to keep her body healthy and limber. She had to be in good shape if she intended to land a role, *any* role.

But so far, luck had not been on her side.

To her dismay, she had now auditioned at almost every theater in London, and all the meaty roles that might bring a decent income were filled. The two in the last few days had been especially gutting. One manager asked her to audition in his rooms above the theater. She had left without a word, and the second had offered her a pittance for a minor role that would barely cover her flat payment, much less leave anything to send to Vivienne.

She'd told the duke that she wasn't for hire, but right now, Nève would take a job scrubbing pots in his kitchens if he'd allow it. But there was no going back. Montcroix had sent a messenger the day after the ball for a final answer, and she'd replied with her regrets, integrity intact. Nève sighed.

Unfortunately, her pride didn't pay her debts or fill her stomach.

It didn't help that of late her dreams had been crammed full of the duke. Some had been tame while others were scandalous in the extreme, involving kissing, lovemaking, and other explicit acts that had nothing to do with love whatsoever. Nève bit her lip, trembling en pointe as her thighs clenched at the recollection of the past night's vivid dream of the duke dropping to his knees behind the stage curtains after a performance.

The girls in the corps in Paris used to discuss their liaisons as frankly as one would discuss one's preference for petits fours. Positions, body parts, orgasms, and pelvic acrobatics in bald, cheek-scorching detail. Unfortunately, at night, those lewd stories and her current fantasies about Montcroix collided into imaginings that left her body coiled tight, drenched, and deeply unsatisfied.

Stop obsessing over him! The duke's a cold fish. He probably doesn't know any of those positions. He'll climb on top of you and lie there like a slab of cold mutton.

But even as her brain valiantly attempted to convince her of his lack of prowess in the bedroom, a sly voice countered that any man who could kiss as ardently as he had would undoubtedly have other skills. Didn't she admit herself that ice could burn?

Oh, la vache! Assez, Nève.

With renewed focus, she finished up the last of her exercises, holding her arms aloft and extending her leg in a straight line behind her in an elegant arabesque. The pose would have been perfect if not for the small table that crashed onto its side and knocked over a cup of cold tea. Nève grimaced and released the position. She needed better lodgings, but she was loath to touch the money from Montcroix—that was earmarked for Vivienne's medical expenses.

After cleaning up the mess, she peered out the small, grimy window onto the narrow street. Costermongers with their carts of fish and fruit lumbered down the lane. Several washerwomen were already outside. It was late in the rookeries, but early for most of the ton. She didn't have much time before her tea with Lady Vesper at Harwick House. Nève sighed. She'd much rather devote her afternoon to looking for a job than taking tea in Mayfair, but she'd given her word, and when one had nothing, one's word had to mean something.

After a quick sponge from the cold basin of water in the corner, Nève pawed through her meager possessions, choosing a clean, dove-gray dress that had seen better days. Between that and the navy gown she'd worn a week before, it was her only other option. Despite being woefully out of fashion, it did have some beautiful vine-patterned embroidery around the neckline and hem that Vivienne had sewn herself, and the fabric was well made.

Donning her plain bonnet and cloak, she left the lodging house. It didn't take long for Nève to reach the square where she had met the lost and foxed Duke of Montcroix, though it looked rather different in the brighter light of day, noisy and lively with stalls, peddlers, and performers. A strange longing unfurled in her belly at the thought of him—how closed off and remote he'd been at first, and yet how different he'd been here and during their dance.

It was almost as though he'd forgotten he was a duke.

How strange that a mere handful of days should seem an eternity ago.

By the time she located a hackney and arrived at the very fancy address at Harwick House, all she wanted to do was turn around and leave. Her nerves were a chaotic, jumbled mess. Being back in this area of London reminded her of him. It wasn't as though she would see Montcroix, even if her stomach clenched at the glimpse of every tall, fair-haired man in a top hat visible from the carriage windows.

After paying the driver, she descended and dragged her feet up the steps, but it did not put off eventually reaching the door. With a resigned sigh, she knocked. A polite, efficient butler took her cloak but left her bonnet, and ushered her through the opulent house to the gardens, where a cluster of four women stood near a trellised arch covered in roses.

"Nève, you came!" Vesper squealed when the butler announced her arrival.

She didn't have to feign a smile at the woman's effusive greeting. "I wouldn't have missed it for the world."

Tiens, she was good at lying.

"Come, meet my friends," she said excitedly. "Let's dispense with all the honorifics, shall we? You know Laila, of course. This is Briar," she said pointing out a petite, dimpled brunette with tight corkscrew spirals surrounding a kind, freckled brown face.

"A pleasure" was all Nève could manage before she was dragged to the next lady—a tall, ethereal-looking woman with white-blond hair and a porcelain complexion. "This is Effie. She rescues lost animals, runs her own shelter, and is determined to remain a spinster for all her days."

"I am not," Effie protested. "I simply haven't found a gentleman whom I can put up with. Don't listen to her. She's just sour that I won't let her compulsive matchmaking hands get a hold of me."

"If you allowed me to pair your picky self with any eligible gentlemen," Vesper said with an exaggerated eye roll, "perhaps you would be able to find a man who will allow you to pet and groom him like you do all those beasts you collect."

"Newborn kittens are so much better than any gentleman," Effie said.

They burst into laughter. At the unabashed sound of it, all of the fears and worries that had plagued Nève suddenly fell away. These women felt like kindred spirits, and she'd welcome the reprieve from her life for a few hours. A nearby linen-covered table was set for five and dotted in tea cakes, fresh fruit, and tea. She took the last empty chair.

"So Nève, tell us about you," Vesper said, pouring each of the teacups to the brim with a grand flourish. "What do you do for fun?"

Nève busied herself with taking a sip of her tea. She was treading a narrow line here, between keeping her business with Montcroix private, and satisfying the curiosity of four very observant and clearly intelligent ladies. "What do you mean?"

"Well, *I* like bringing people together..."

Briar snorted and stuffed an entire tea cake into her mouth with no care for decorum. "What she means is that she's a meddling busybody who thinks she's Cupidella," she mumbled through a mouthful of crumbs.

"Briar here loves her pamphlets and her down-with-the-patriarchy protests," Vesper went on with a sly grin at her friend. "I've the perfect gentleman for you, by the way. He's old, can't hear very well, and is in need of a young wife with childbearing hips. In fact, I shall coyly suggest the match to your father when next I am at Foxton Hall."

"Don't you dare, you wretch!"

Vesper blew her a kiss. "As you know, Laila loves designing her fabulous gowns, and her handsome unconventional husband lets her do anything she wants. I shall take the credit for that excellent match, by the way!"

Seeing Vesper's inquisitive eyes settle on her, Nève grasped at the chance to redirect any conversation away from her. "How did you meet the marquess?" she asked Laila. "Did Lady Vesper truly arrange the match?"

The three ladies burst into laughter, and Laila rolled her eyes. "*Arrange* is rather mild for what actually happened. While we were admiring the swans on the Serpentine in Hyde Park, my best friend shoved me into the lake, and Marsden was forced to come to my rescue. He's never forgiven me for ruining his favorite pair of boots."

"You tripped, Laila. Admit it, you know how clumsy you can be." Vesper pinned her lips to stifle another round of giggles before glancing at Nève, her eyes glassy with mirth. "And please, it's just Vesper. We're all friends here."

"What's living in Paris like?" Effie asked. "I visited once as a child and found it so fascinating."

Nève hesitated, her fingers toying with the edges of the tablecloth. "It is a lovely place, though it has its advantages and disadvantages like any other. I live with my sister, Vivienne. We both love to dance. The ballet, mostly. We get that from our mother, I suppose."

"Was she a ballerina?" Vesper asked.

The question made Nève flinch, though she didn't detect any malice behind it, but she'd been wrong about people before. How well did she truly know these women? Aristocrats in the ton didn't change from country to country. They scorned anyone who wasn't born into their world, and the only reason she'd been invited here to tea was that she was supposedly engaged to the Duke of Montcroix. But that association was over—in a few days, she would leave English shores for good.

What did she have to lose?

"She was, though she danced as an opera burlesque dancer." Silence fell at her words, and Nève braced for the onslaught of disdain. To her surprise, there was nothing but genuine interest on the faces of her companions.

"Were you classically trained, then?" Laila asked. "When I was pinning your dress for the ball, I couldn't help remarking on the grace of your movements. In truth, you reminded me very much of a ballerina."

Nève nodded. "Vivienne and I both were as children, though my sister was recently injured."

"How?" Vesper asked. "Was it a fall? Did her partner drop her? I saw that happen once mid-performance at the theater, and it was awful."

Once more, Nève debated how much to share, but then decided to throw caution to the wind. She was leaving anyway, and these women did not mean her harm. "She refused the attentions of one of the wealthy male patrons, and not even a day later, she discovered glass shards in her slippers."

Effie gasped. "That's barbaric."

Nève nodded. Especially for a ballerina. It was the reason she and Vivienne had always been taught by their mother to check their footwear. Ballet, so beautiful to anyone from the outside looking in, could be vicious.

"Thankfully, she saw them before putting her slippers on." She took a breath. "When she tried to leave to search out another pair, she was waylaid in the wings by the man she'd refused. He shoved a nearby crate that held heavy pulley equipment for the stage right onto her bare toes." The women gasped. "The gentleman claimed it to be an accident, though we both know it for what it was. Punishment for her refusal."

Their gasps were loud and outraged. "That's sodding dreadful!" Briar said, bronze cheeks flushed with anger.

Nève nodded. "That is the world of ballet. Dancers exist solely for the pleasure of their patrons' entertainment. Much like everywhere else, men hold the purse strings and the power."

Briar cursed. "Isn't that the unjust truth."

"So, do you dance professionally in Paris?" Effie asked, the question soft as if she were worried about overstepping.

By that point, Nève was so relieved to unburden herself of some of what had been weighing on her for months that she didn't care if these women might think ill of her for it. "I used to. I was the understudy in *Le Papillon* for Emma Livry in Paris. She's a lovely ballerina. The same gentleman whom my sister spurned decided to pursue me, and I had the audacity to threaten to expose him for what he did to Vivienne, so he had me barred from the opera. I was removed as understudy and lost the part I'd been hired for—the leading role in *La Sylphide*."

"He could do that?" Vesper asked.

Nève lifted her shoulder in a shrug. "He's a longtime benefactor, worth much more than a burgeoning prima ballerina."

"Men are bastards," Briar said, angrily biting into a slice of orange.

"Not all men," Laila said quietly.

"That's true," Vesper agreed. "Marsden is a keeper, even if he is as vain as a rutting peacock."

"He is not!" Laila said, but then she snorted with laughter when Vesper lifted her brows and muttered something about a blindingly bright, saffron-colored waistcoat and matching trousers.

"It's deeply ironic that he's fallen in love with a modiste who has no sway over his awful fashion choices," Vesper said dryly. "Your husband has execrable taste and you know it."

Laila dissolved into giggles. "Oh, God, he truly does, doesn't he?"

Vanity aside, if marriage was ever in her future, Nève hoped for a man like the marquess—one who wouldn't seek to change her, one who would accept and love her for who she was. The image of a stern, uncompromising face filled her brain, and she shoved the vision of the duke away, focusing instead on the animated, sparkling grins of her companions.

Merde, she couldn't do it. She couldn't lie to these women any longer.

Lifting her teacup to her lips, she took a bracing gulp and made up her mind before her courage failed her. She didn't want to hide the truth from them, even if it would cost her their esteem and budding friendship. "I have a confession to make," she blurted out. "I'm not who you think I am."

Four pairs of curious eyes swung to her.

"You're not?" Effie blurted, pale gaze wide.

"I'm not engaged to the duke," Nève explained. "And I'm not really his cousin by marriage. I'm no one at all but an out-of-work ballerina, and the only connection I can claim to have with Mont-croix is one of brief, dubious acquaintance." At her confession, there was dead silence. She drew a shaky breath, daring a peek through her lashes at her hostess and her friends. Laila's face was flushed and her gaze was fastened to the table. "I understand if you wish me to leave."

"Why on earth would we wish you to leave?" Vesper asked.

"So what if you're a dancer? Laila stitches for a living, Briar is in constant danger of being arrested by the police, and Effie surrounds herself with mange-ridden, feral animals. I'm often accused of being a vapid, vain half-wit with a predilection for hat plumes. We're all misfits, in our own way." She waved a dismissive arm. "Besides, Montcroix has obviously vouched for you, and if there is one thing Lushing says about the Gargoyle King, it's that he's an excellent judge of character. Clever description, by the way, Nève. I think that one will stick."

"Thank you. Who's Lushing?" Nève mumbled, dazed by the unexpected acceptance.

"My charming brother, the Earl of Lushing, scoundrel, miscreant, and my father's greatest ducal disappointment."

Nève had almost forgotten that Vesper was the daughter of a duke. She hardly behaved like one. None of the women had any airs whatsoever. Once more, Nève found herself wishing that she had met these ladies under different circumstances. A marchioness, a duke's daughter, and two earls' daughters. In truth, they were the opposite of everything she'd grown to expect from the standoffish ton.

"Telling tales about my splendid self again, Sister?" an amused voice drawled from the terrace.

They all whirled in unison, and Nève's heart tumbled and crashed to her feet. Because there, beside a tall red-haired gentleman whom she assumed was the roguish Earl of Lushing, stood the man who had invaded her thoughts and dreams for the better part of a week. Her heart kicked hard against her ribs. Montcroix's brooding silver eyes met hers instantly, and a flash of raw awareness sizzled down her spine.

Dieu, the effect the man had on her was positively frightful.

"And be nice to Stone," Lushing went on, bounding down the steps to the grass where they were seated and snatching up a tea cake. "It's not his fault he was born with gravel in his veins."

"Go away!" Vesper screeched as her brother made quick work of a tray of cakes and sandwiches. "This is a *ladies'* tea, which means you have to be a lady! Don't you have somewhere else to be that isn't here?"

"We did, but Marsden let slip that his wife was at your little soiree with Sweetbriar, Lady Effie, and the delightful Miss Valery, whom I've heard so much about," he said. Laila frowned, but it was clear that *her* husband had been smart enough to stay away. "Besides, you know how I do love a good tea party."

Briar glowered. "Sweetbriar is *not* my name."

Nève nearly giggled as the unrepentant Lushing waggled his eyebrows at the scowling Briar. "Miss me, Prickles?"

"Like an in-growing toenail," she shot back.

The earl made a tragic moaning sound, his hands flying to his chest. "Such cruelty. You wound me mortally, my lady."

"Then why don't you do everyone a favor and expire?" she replied sweetly.

Nève choked on a bite of strawberry, but clearly, the others were already familiar with such squabbling between the two because no one else batted an eye. She forgot the offending piece of fruit lodged in her throat when Montcroix moved to stand slightly behind her chair. She didn't turn, but Nève was acutely aware of him, every nerve in her body coming to attention from his proximity. The distinctive winter and pine scent of him teased her nostrils. She swallowed hard.

"Apologies for the interruption, Lady Vesper," he said, his deep voice humming through to her bones as their hostess gave a gracious if annoyed nod. "Lady Briar, Lady Evangeline."

"Stone," both women chimed, and Nève belatedly understood that Effie must be a nickname. She also realized that they had to be on friendly terms with him if they were calling him Stone. No wonder they'd accepted her so readily on his approval.

When at last the duke set his attention to her, she tilted her chin up, though she couldn't bear to focus on those penetrating eyes. She let her eyes hover on the cleft in his chin instead…and the firm lips above it. A mistake, as a wild flush wound through her insides at the full sight of that ruthless, unbending, *talented* mouth…and the sinful memories it invoked.

"Miss Valery, what an unexpected pleasure."

"Your Grace." Her voice was hoarse…from swallowing the strawberry, she decided, not at all from the dark, intimate way he said *pleasure*. That word could not live up to what he intended it to mean, or what her rioting senses were imagining it to mean.

Cheeks hot, she glanced around to see if anyone else had taken note of the ribbons of desire unspooling between them like ink distilling into water, but Lushing and Briar were still insulting each other, and Vesper and Laila had their heads together, whispering about something.

"I received your message," Montcroix said in a low voice. "To my eternal disappointment."

"I am sorry," she said.

"As am I."

Silence grew between them, and Nève fidgeted in her seat, her body completely on edge by his nearness. Her skin heated and her pulse pounded beneath her skin. She usually felt like this before going onstage in front of an audience, not because of a man. Then again, the Duke of Montcroix was no ordinary man—he was an elemental force, a thunderstorm trapped in a bespoke suit.

Then why weren't the other unattached ladies at the table reacting to him as she was? Vesper was still whispering with Laila, Briar was glaring daggers at the Earl of Lushing, and Effie was preoccupied with feeding treats to the enormous hound under the table that had appeared on the heels of the earl. None of them seemed remotely interested in him.

"Reconsider." The whispered command was low and husky, drizzled in the warmed timbre of his voice, and Nève felt goose bumps lift on her skin. She dug her fingers into the sides of her chair, knuckles white, and bit her lip hard. The shocking effect of that graveled velvet command would have been the same if he'd ordered her to strip down to her undergarments there and then. She felt dizzy.

Goodness, had Vesper laced the tea? Everything inside her longed to give in to him, to scream *yes* to whatever he demanded. If she opened her mouth to reply, she couldn't trust what would emerge.

"I beg your pardon," she managed eventually.

His throat worked. "What would it take for you to reconsider?" He did not whisper this time, and curious stares flocked toward them.

"Reconsider what?" Vesper asked from across the table, snapping Nève out of the fugue of desperate desire.

A flash of irritation passed over the duke's face at the interruption. "Our negotiations have stalled."

"Negotiations?" Vesper asked with narrowed eyes.

"Betrothal."

Effie frowned at Nève, looking up from her furry friend with a confused expression. "I thought you said you weren't engaged."

"She turned me down," Montcroix replied smoothly. "My attempts to assure her of my suit have been rejected."

To Nève's surprise, the ladies didn't even try to smother their amusement, giggles and even a snort or two filling the air.

"Bully for you!" Briar crowed. "Not every woman drops her drawers at interest from a duke." She glared at Lushing. "Or any peer with a swollen head."

The earl made a choking noise, and Briar flushed.

"That is truly outrageous, Sweetbriar," Lushing chastised, though the wicked look on his face said he was relishing Briar's mortification at her unintended innuendo. He stuck his hands in his pockets. "But I thank you for noticing my...assets."

Not to be undone, she glared at him. "That would require a magnifying lens." She waved him away as she would a vexing gnat and turned back to Nève. "Out of curiosity, why did you refuse him?"

Nève frowned, not wanting her new friends to get the wrong idea of what she'd confessed earlier and Montcroix's intentions. This wasn't a normal courting. Nothing about what had happened between the duke and her was *normal*. He wanted her as a hired worker, not as an actual fiancée. There was a phrase for such a thing, and it wasn't *future bride*. She opened her mouth, but words failed her.

"I was unconvincing," the duke said.

"And how did you attempt to convince her, Stone?" Vesper asked, eyes glinting in a calculating way that had Nève shaking her head in instant dread.

His mouth tightened, adding more severity to his expression, though Vesper was not cowed in the least. "The usual ways via an ironclad, mutually acceptable betrothal contract. My title, my fortune, the fact that she will lack for nothing."

Lushing let out a snort, reaching for a silver flask from his pocket as he propped his hip against the table. "If your attempts at seduction come down to a lackluster, written betrothal agreement, Stone, then I'm afraid we can no longer be friends." He winked at Nève. "The Earl of Lushing at your service, by the way. Brother, friend, and speaker of hard truths."

"Nève," she murmured dazedly as the duke cleared his throat.

"Marriage is a business transaction."

Multiple gasps of outrage flew to the heavens. "Not everyone marries because of a few archaic, quantifiable requirements," Laila said hotly. "It's not a ledger column in your estate books, Stone."

Montcroix was unmoved. "Ladies don't seek a title? Impoverished peers don't seek a fortune to shore up declining estates? You are disillusioned if you don't see that the majority of aristocratic marriages are basic transactions in nature."

"Mine isn't," Laila said.

"Not anymore, but Marsden married because he had to inherit. The fact that fondness grew out of that bears no consequence on how or why either of you entered into wedlock." The duke's intonation did not change. He could be presenting a case in front of the Lords for the lack of emotion on his face. "I'm not trying to be cruel. I am, at heart, a realist."

Or perhaps you have no heart at all, Nève thought, and then realized she'd said it out loud when eyes the color of fallen sleet jerked to hers.

She flinched at the arctic sheen to them. Suddenly, she wished she'd kept her silly mouth shut. Everyone else had gone strangely silent, but after a fraught beat, the fractious duke simply inclined his head. "There's that, too. If you will excuse me, Lushing, ladies, I must take my leave. Miss Valery, safe travels back to France."

The mood did not improve after Montcroix's abrupt departure, despite Vesper's best efforts to do so. Even Lushing made an effort to be extra charming. But Nève couldn't help feeling the dour turn was her fault, calling the duke out as unkindly as she had, and she wondered if her flippant words had somehow hurt him. She could not have such power, could she?

It wasn't long before she decided she needed to leave as well, bidding a sad farewell to her new friends and promising to write. Thanking Vesper for the lovely afternoon, she left her address in Paris with Laila at the lady's insistence.

Upon her return to Covent Garden, Nève felt oddly bereft as she climbed the rickety stairs to her room, only to see that her door was ajar. She frowned. She was positive she'd locked it when she'd left. That meant only one thing—thieves. She didn't have much in the way of possessions, so whoever had broken in was in for certain disappointment. It was only when she crossed the threshold that she remembered Montcroix's money that she'd slipped into a hole cut into her thin, lumpy mattress.

Heart racing, she hustled to the bed, dropped to her knees, and lifted the threadbare sheets, her fingers digging into the narrow slit she'd made. With a despairing cry, she dug through the loose stuffing again, but it was no use.

The money—and all hope for her future—was gone.

CHAPTER EIGHT

Lysander paced in the spacious library—the only room in his house that had been completely overtaken by plans unrolled on every available surface. Shipping plans. Mining plans. Railway plans. Normally they offered him hours of distraction, but he could barely concentrate on any of them. He could not stop hearing the quiet sound of the words over and over in his head: *Or perhaps you have no heart at all.*

He wasn't a man of emotion. He never had been. Not when his mother had died of a wasting illness. Not when his former fiancée left him to marry his father. Not when his exacting, ruthless father had keeled over from apoplexy. But Nève's words had made him feel like he was flawed, as though some fundamental thing in him was missing. Lysander wasn't even sure why it bothered him as much as it did. She was no one to him.

But he *did* have a heart, damn her!

He just didn't trust it to make logical decisions.

As though offering to pay a woman six thousand pounds to be at his side for the season was by *any* stretch logical...

Swearing beneath his breath, he stalked to the mantel and poured himself a liberal glass of whiskey. He swirled the amber liquid and took a bracing sip, feeling its hot sting glide down his throat. Even the liquor reminded him of her—beauty with bite—smooth at first but layered with fascinating complexity. A ballerina who'd been born and raised a lady, a woman who straddled two disparate worlds out of obligation.

He shook his head free of thoughts that had no bearing on his present crisis. He had greater things to worry about. This land he intended to buy in Yorkshire from Bolden was critical for the route of the supplemental railroad line going to the river Hull. He was also in the process of petitioning Parliament to move forward with the act to approve the line as well as countless other shareholder responsibilities.

Connecting his mining investments to railroad and shipping was a natural next step. A new railway line meant jobs, convenience, and more opportunity, and the revenue it would generate would be exponential. That wasn't counting his private investment in an iron ore mining company in northern England and the benefits in transport the line would provide to his shipping port. Pouring his expanding fortunes back into his own ducal estates gave him enormous satisfaction. The Montcroix dukedom was on its way to being the richest in England, a far cry from what his father had expected him to do with it.

Use your brain, boy. Why are you so slow? These tutors are useless, coddling you. You need some direction... a strict boarding school that won't allow for failures. You'll grind this dukedom into the ground, mark my words.

Lysander flinched at the memories.

The thought of closing the deal with Bolden should have made him salivate. Then why was all he could think about a gamine ballerina with flames in her eyes?

He'd asked her to stay for the season for no other reason than he didn't want her to leave. It was the same motivation behind his purchase of companies or investment in businesses—when he saw something he wanted, he went after it. And Geneviève Valery made him want...and that was a dangerous path. One he did not wish to repeat.

She's not Charlotte.

No, she wasn't. But it was still better for him that she went back to Paris. He would simply put her out of his head, categorize their meeting as an unexpected distraction, and move on.

Exhaling, he stared at the engineering plans for the railway line...and at the castle that would be demolished. Aldenborough was a beautiful estate, but he wondered at the wisdom of the earl who would walk away from a fortune to honor the sentimental wishes of his late wife. That kind of devotion—or rather stupidity—was inconceivable to him.

"Your Grace?"

Pulled from his thoughts—*mercifully*—Lysander looked up to where the butler stood. "Yes, Finley?"

"A Miss Valery is here to see you. I told her you weren't at home to callers per your instructions, but she insists on an audience." Her name sent a wild jolt through him. Shouldn't the chit be on her way to Paris by now? "Since she was the guest you were expecting last week, Your Grace, I thought I would check with you first."

"Send her away," he bit out, though a part of him was screaming for the butler to contradict him and do the opposite. The servant wouldn't, of course. A duke's word was law, and the butler couldn't be expected to read his mind.

Lysander clenched his jaw so hard his teeth ached when the older man bowed his head and walked back the way he'd come. His brain roared that it was a mistake to let her leave. Should he have at least tried to find out what had brought her here? To him?

Feeling as if his cravat were choking him, he flung his coat to the floor and ripped the offending thing loose. He wasn't aware he'd pounded his fist onto the table until the pain ricocheted up his arm and into his numbed senses. Damn. *Damn!*

"I hate to imagine what that poor piece of furniture did to deserve such wrath, Your Grace."

The soft, slightly mocking voice spread through him like butter on a piping hot scone. Relief…he felt relief. He wanted to savor it, wallow in it for a few precious seconds before sanity intruded.

Pushing off the table, he turned, equanimity intact. "Clearly my butler needs some direction on following orders."

Lysander wasn't prepared for the blow the sight of her did to him, though he battled valiantly to ignore the tension of his muscles and the obnoxious hammering of his heart. She wore the same plain cape and bonnet she'd been dressed in when they'd first met, wide eyes peering up at him from beneath the unadorned brim. She did not need plumes or ribbons or anything to detract from that face—they would pale in comparison.

The hapless Finley hovered at her side, and though he looked put out to be thwarted, there was a distinct gleam of *something* in his eye. Lysander frowned, but dismissed him with a wave of his hand. Bowing, the butler retreated, but wisely left the door open in view of the nearest footman. It wasn't ideal, but it would do for propriety even though he and the lady in question were probably both beyond that designation at this point.

Lysander leaned his hips against the table, and his eyes fell to the discarded coat he'd thrown to the floor. His brows dipped. He wasn't a man given to such fulminating fits of temper either. Reaching for the coat and shrugging into it, he lifted his fingers to his loosened cravat and growled, unable to retie the deuced thing.

She was upon him before he could utter an apology for his uncouth appearance or summon his valet. "Allow me."

His eyes went wide when he realized her intent. "This isn't proper, Miss Valery."

"Have we ever been proper, Your Grace? And besides, there's no one here. That poor footman outside your door looks like he will expire from fear any moment, so your reputation is quite safe from ruination."

"I wasn't thinking about *me*!"

Lysander's breath thickened in his throat when the scent of her assaulted him even before gloved fingers reached up for the cloth around his neck. She wasn't touching any part of his flesh, but Christ, the sensation of each tug on the silk around his throat made his body seize. They'd been in a much cozier position than this in that alley, and yet he felt as if this was somehow worse. His lungs struggled to function, and his blood turned to mead in his veins.

It was too *much*.

There was that sensation, jabbing at him like a freshly forged blade, but Lysander couldn't form a single sound. She was too near. Too *close* for any kind of comfort.

"Don't blame poor Finley either," she said quietly. "I sped past him. I can be quite nimble on my feet, you see, and I've a good memory. I remembered the library when Laila pointed it out on my tour last week, though we did not enter."

He narrowed his eyes. "How did you know I was in here?"

"When Finley said you weren't at home to callers, then went to confirm that you were indeed not at home, I followed him."

Lysander blinked. "You followed him?"

"Don't get your drawers in a twist, Your Grace. Your silver is quite safe, never fear." She broke off and pinned her lips, a blush covering her cheeks. He didn't smile at her teasing tone, but God, he wanted to. *Badly.*

The pressure in his chest held him immobile as her fingers finished their task and she gave the fabric a final pat. "There, as good as any valet."

"Thank you."

"My pleasure." Whatever spell was holding him in place lifted as she stepped away. Her eyes flitted over the space, noting the floor-to-ceiling shelves crammed with books, and an awed smile touched her lips. "My sister would be in hog heaven right now."

"She likes books?" he asked. Christ, he was beginning to sound like a repetitive idiot, echoing her statements as if he didn't have a working brain cell in his head.

"More than life itself." She paused, something somber passing over her gaze. "She always has, but more recently, they've become her comfort. She enjoys novels, but her true passion is learning about medicine. In another life, she might have been a surgeon, I believe."

"That's ambitious."

Her eyes narrowed. "Why? Because she's a woman?"

He shook his head. "It's a demanding course of study. Whether she's a woman has no bearing on aptitude. I know of several women who are successful doctors or studying medicine. Elizabeth Blackwell and Elizabeth Garrett Anderson to name two, though the first was across the Atlantic, and many others here in England who practice without official status, much as some of the men do."

She looked surprised. He found he enjoyed tilting her off balance. After a beat, she cleared her throat. "Most gentlemen of my acquaintance expect their women to be docile and useless, to not have a brain in their heads or any passions and dreams of their own. Our sex is there to provide for the heir and the spare, nothing more." Her stare drilled into his. "A business transaction, as you've said."

"Then I pity you those poor acquaintances," he said, propping a hip on his desk. "Yes, aristocratic courtship is a transaction, but I would never expect a lady to be useless or without her own ambitions."

She stared at him as though trying to determine his angle. "So your wife won't be required to bear your heir?"

"Alas, primogeniture is a sacred duty." He nodded with a slight shrug. "I will do my part to secure the ducal line and my dukedom, and my duchess will be expected to do hers."

"Ergo broodmare."

If he didn't see her press her lips together, a dismayed expression crossing her face as if chiding herself for the caustic reply, he wouldn't have cared. But she was here for a reason and he was done playing games.

He schooled his expression to something blank. "Why have you come, Miss Valery?"

Nève licked dry lips, her nerves spiking again. His face was in its usual unreadable resting duke state. It had been impulsive of her to come here, but she'd had little choice. No one had seen anything, heard anything, or wanted to say anything about the theft of her belongings. Then again, the lodging house had a constant stream of unsavory guests, including the occasional flash-man. The landlord had outright laughed at her when she'd demanded the police be summoned. In the end, she'd had nothing left but her pride and the sting of the violation.

She was, in a word, desperate.

More desperate.

In her peripheral vision, Stone crossed one long leg over the other, folding his hands over that broad chest. Seeing him again, so disheveled and reminiscent of their time in Covent Garden, had given her a boost of courage. Nève could hardly believe she'd had the audacity to retie his cravat, or touch him so casually, but she hadn't been able to stop herself. Her wicked fingers had wanted to lay waste to the rest of his pristine clothing, but instead she'd put him to rights.

She needed to put *herself* to rights while she was at it.

The Duke of Montcroix was a complex puzzle box. On the surface, he was cold. Careful. Methodical. Underneath all that stony control, he was much less restrained. But the passionate man who had kissed her in the arbor, who had run with her into that alley, was not the man here now. *This* man was all business. Short of seducing him, which was *not* an option, she had to depend on the intelligence she'd boasted about. Appeal to his pragmatic sense. Convince him of the practical benefits of a working relationship.

"I'd like to reconsider." Nève gnawed the inside of her cheek, ignoring her pounding heart and the feeling of a complete lack of air in her lungs. "Your offer."

"You would?" he asked, his eyes fastening to her.

"Yes, I would. If it's still on the table."

Nève gulped past the growing knot in her throat, knowing that she'd put her own foot in her mouth when she'd insulted him in front of his peers at the tea party *and* just now called his future wife a broodmare. She did not know him well by any means, but he did not seem to be the forgiving sort. Or the second chance sort. But desperation gave one a bellicose kind of courage.

"Which offer is that, may I ask? I'm a very busy man and can't be expected to keep track of all of my various proposals. Be more specific."

Her jaw went slack. Was he in earnest? Nève had to work to keep her temper from rising at his banal tone. She peered up at him through her lashes and nearly growled at the blank look on his face, but then she saw the distinct twinkle of amusement in his eye. Was he being obtuse on purpose at her expense?

"The one to buy a pretend fiancée for the season, is that specific enough for you?" she snapped, only too late remembering that she'd come here to plead and bit her tongue.

Stupid, unruly temper.

"What if my needs have changed?"

The question jolted her into looking up, catching that piercing stare of his and feeling a deep-rooted instinct to back slowly out of the room. Even relaxed as he was against the desk, his body seemed coiled and ready for action. Nève directed another glance to his face—inscrutable as expected—his mouth an unyielding slash bracketed by an angular jaw. He was an intimidating man, but neither was she a wilting wallflower.

She straightened her spine and released the ties to her bonnet and cloak. "Then we negotiate."

"Is that so?" The press of that cold gaze slammed into her, and she lifted her chin, meeting it with a firm one of her own. Was that a beat of respect she saw there? Or was she imagining things? That was always a possibility.

"Isn't that your preferred form of entertainment, Your Grace?" She placed the folded cloak and bonnet on the seat of a nearby armchair and walked forward to the nearest chair at the end of the massive table. He was so close she could touch him, but she restrained her hands in her lap. She was being bold enough as it was by sitting without invitation, but boldness was all she had.

"You seem like a man who is exceedingly specific about what he wants, so let's get to it unless you've changed your mind and don't require my help."

Montcroix pushed off the table, and for a heart-stopping moment, Nève thought he was going to throw her out. But he walked past her and closed the door to a crack. Propriety was long gone, though she still felt a stroke of melancholy. She'd been joking about his reputation before, but in another world, another *life*, a lady being alone with a gentleman without a chaperone would have resulted in scandal.

But Nève was no longer a lady. Her *ruination* had come at the hands of fate, not the fault of some unscrupulous gentleman who'd compromised her reputation. The minute she'd been forced to seek work as a ballerina in the world of the demimonde, the fastidious rules of the aristocracy had ceased to apply. She'd fallen from grace, but her virtue and her future had become hers to command.

The former was no one's business, and now, she had to secure the latter.

Hopefully without surrendering the first.

Montcroix moved to the other side of the crowded table, but not before placing a glass of sherry in front of her. She sipped it gratefully to bolster her flagging confidence while he busied himself with rolling up some of the plans and maps that littered his desk and setting them aside. He hadn't kicked her out, so that was a good sign.

When he was done, he sat and lifted his glass. The duke peered at her over the crystal rim in what had to be some kind of intimidation tactic. Neither of them spoke for what seemed like an eternity, and though her fingers went clammy, she would not be the first to give in.

She could not capitulate so early.

Instead, Nève pretended she was onstage, staring out at a packed theater, her opponent's face fading to a blurry mirage. Glissade, pas de bourrée, pirouette. She tapped her fingers to inaudible music and took in a measured breath, running through the sequence and adding a few more complicated steps, ending in a grand jeté at the end that made her entire body lift in suspended motion. Her nerves settled. She released the air in her lungs, and reality came crashing back to her when she saw the duke staring intently at her. Nève felt her cheeks warm.

"What were you doing just then?" the duke asked, curiosity evident.

"Sitting."

His lips quirked. "No, you went away for a bit, in your head, and you were drumming your fingers. What was that?"

"It was nothing," she replied. "A simple measure to seat my nerves."

"Describe it."

She clenched her teeth at the blunt command, both resenting it and wanting him to get on with the negotiation. "It's a dancing routine."

His eyes lit with interest. "I think I should like to see you onstage one day."

"Perhaps you'll get your chance."

He lifted a brow. "Are you any good?"

"I suppose you'll have to see to decide for yourself." Nève drained her glass and set it down between them. *Think like a man*, she told herself. A man would not hesitate to lay out the terms, no matter how irregular or embarrassing they were, no matter how unconventional. "But in the meantime, shall we get to the business at hand? If I recall, your offer was six thousand pounds' allowance for two months in a position as a dowager's companion."

To his credit, he did not even react to the insult to his masculinity. "Four."

Nève's eyes narrowed. "Four months?"

"Four thousand pounds."

"What? No, you said six." That was a third less than what he'd proposed a week ago. Even as Nève scowled at the ruthless maneuver, she quailed that he would go even lower. Four thousand pounds was still a fortune.

"The terms have changed. It's the law of supply and demand," he replied with cool composure. "This is what happens with re-negotiation. Amounts change. Needs change."

Her nails curled into her palms. God, he was a ruthless bastard. They were negotiating the terms of a highly unprincipled position, and he couldn't help taking advantage of the fact that she had come back with her head bowed to beg for a second chance. She shouldn't be surprised—men with power did that... toyed with their prey.

Well, she wasn't prey! His, or anyone's.

Nève let out a frustrated breath and swallowed the fulminating reply on her tongue. Telling him to go to hell would not help her cause. Though he held all the cards, she wasn't quite powerless. He obviously needed her or she would not be sitting here... *negotiating.* "Five thousand. And the terms remain the same as the first evening."

He leaned back in his chair. "Before we advance, will you enlighten me on those, Miss Valery? I seem to have difficulty remembering what we discussed."

The cad. He knew very well what the bloody terms were! She gritted her teeth, her confidence feeling flimsier than the threadbare gloves she wore. She barely had a leg to stand on, but by God, she would not crumble to this man. Leaning back in her own seat to mock his nonchalant posture, Nève made her voice as dispassionate as possible.

"In return for the monies and accommodation as agreed, you

will introduce me to the manager of the Lyceum, and in return, I will perform the role you require. As your companion, I will provide company and conversation, and entertain your guests as instructed. I will accompany you to social events and protect you from the hungry jaws of the ever-hopeful debutantes, as well as assist with any domestic responsibilities beyond your capabilities." She couldn't quite curb her mutinous tone. "If needed, I will also sew, crochet, and perform needlepoint, though I cannot vouch for my skill with a needle beyond stitching the ribbons of ballet slippers. I will pour His Grace's tea, play the pianoforte, and read bedtime stories while His Grace takes his afternoon nap. How does that sound?"

His mouth twitched. "You don't mince words, do you?"

"I admit, mincing is not my forte." Ears hot, she exhaled. "Are we agreed then?"

He stared at her, those mercurial eyes swirling with wolfish intrigue. Well, she'd wanted to catch his interest, and now she had. She could hardly complain about the result…but the way he was looking at her climbed under her skin and sank into her bones. Every hair on her body stood at attention, as though understanding the implicit peril she was in, even if her brain was slow to comprehend the danger.

Nève blinked and licked dry lips. A breath hissed out when his silver stare dropped there, and her sense of agitation heightened. She opened her mouth—self-preservation taking over— but before she could speak or do something drastic like change her mind, the duke smiled, the predatory intensity fading from his eyes. Somewhat.

"Yes," he said softly. "I believe we are."

"Half now and half at the end," she said.

"Agreed."

Nève rose, the sense of relief mixed with residual fear almost making her light-headed. "Then I shall take my leave and collect my belongings."

"Please feel free to avail yourself of my coach to do so."

"Thank you." With a small frown, she paused at the door. "May I ask why you changed the offer? It's no hardship to you."

"Because this is business. Your perceived value decreased because of your pressing need to sell. Whatever your change in circumstance, Miss Valery, you should not have accepted less."

"Was I so obvious?"

"To me, yes. I've learned to read people—understand their motivations and how far they're willing to go to get what they want. Our first agreement was motivated by a combination of curiosity and necessity. This time, it's more of the latter in your case." He lifted his glass and scrutinized the amber liquid. "It's important to recognize your worth. Overestimate, if you must, because it's always higher than you think." His cool gaze fastened to hers as he downed the remainder of his drink. "Especially if you are female. Your sex does not determine your value."

Dieu, he confused her. Nève felt as though she were a mouse being toyed with by a bored feral cat—a diversion one moment and dinner the next.

"That's an unconventional way of thinking," she said. "After all, a lady's value is determined by her ability to choose a husband in exchange for the prize of her unblemished virtue."

"Is that what you think?"

"Hardly. A woman determines her own worth."

"Precisely." His mouth curled at the corner. "Don't underestimate yours."

Letting out a breath, Nève nodded in an attempt to turn the tables on her discomfort. "Thank you for the advice, Your Grace, but I would have stayed for much less."

The duke canted his head, and the sudden appearance of the smallest and rarest of smiles made heated sparks erupt like tiny fireworks in the pit of her belly. "And I, Miss Valery, would have paid whatever sum you asked."

Chapter Nine

Her suite of rooms was different from the one she'd stayed in the last time. No, this one was sumptuous in the extreme, done in shades of pale green and luscious cream. The heavy furniture was rich and dark, offsetting the lighter tones of the elegant wainscoting, patterned wallpaper, and plush carpeting. Like everything else in the house, the decor was opulent, a degree of luxury she hadn't seen since her childhood home a lifetime ago.

Nève wandered to the window, which looked out onto the pristine gardens where not one blossom seemed out of place. Everything was picturesquely perfect, from the graveled walks to the painstakingly groomed shrubs. She had the urge to run down and muss up the flower beds, but such a subversive act might not go over well with the garden's fastidious owner. Nève had a feeling that the duke did not like disorder.

She grinned. Too bad she was the epitome of messy.

Passion, much like pandemonium, did not like being boxed in.

Nève supposed that was what made her the dancer she was. In terms of technique, she was nowhere near as accomplished as ballerinas who had studied under Russian greats, but what she might lack in precision she made up for in enthusiasm and love of the dance. The duke himself seemed to have an interest in the theater. He'd said he wanted to see her onstage, and the idea of his watching her made her stomach dip.

She let out a breath, misting the windowpane. His interest was professional, of course. She was here to play a part, not to solicit or bask in his admiration. She walked to a nearby door to the adjoining bath chamber.

After the dismal facilities of her lodging house and rental flat, this was a slice of heaven. Brushed metal fixtures with copper piping framed a porcelain tub large enough to fit more than one person. She wouldn't have to bathe out of a basin or heat water from the kitchens. Her knees went weak. It was indulgent and extravagant, and she planned to make use of it as soon as humanly possible.

Though Montcroix was wealthy, he didn't seem to be the indolent kind of duke, the ones who sat around on their laurels, spending their inherited wealth, gossiping at their clubs, and passing their time doing absolutely nothing, besides lauding their own importance. From the look of his desk earlier, covered in obsessively neat piles of papers, parchment, and rolled maps, he didn't seem to be cut from that idle kind of cloth.

When they'd first discussed his need for a companion, he'd mentioned obtaining a piece of property from the Earl of Bolden, whom she'd met. After seeing all the estate plans on the table, it made her curious about his intentions. More than merely curious, if she were being honest. Montcroix—*no, Stone*—was driven to a fault. She sensed that whatever his objectives may be, he would make them a reality.

The more she got to know him, the more she saw they were opposites in every way.

He might have seemed different when they first met, but in actuality, he was the moon: cold, hard, distant. She was the sun: fiery, passionate, hot-tempered. He saw things in absolutes, in black or white, while she viewed life in every hue imaginable. He was winter; she was summer. Nève let out a sigh; despite their differences, she *was* attracted to him. Perhaps there was some correlation between opposites and attraction. Or perhaps she was inventing a hero where one did not exist.

Stone was a man of business, not a storybook prince. And she was not a girl who'd lost a glass slipper; her slippers were threadbare, bloody, and tattered. Best to get any of *those* ideas out of her head.

Nève returned to the bedchamber to eye her meager trunk of belongings. She was lucky that the landlord on Queen Street hadn't thrown them out on the street before she'd returned. He hadn't taken her threats about going to the police very well and had glared at her when Stone's burly coachman had accompanied her to fetch her belongings. She knew the driver's presence had been at the duke's instruction, but she'd been glad for it when she saw the landlord's surly expression. She had a sneaking suspicion that *he* had been the one to rob her room . . . and that she might have been in dire straits if she'd come back alone.

Men with the slightest bit of power were unpredictable.

Stone has plenty of it.

Frowning, Nève rubbed her arms, wondering what kind of situation she'd gotten herself into this time. Was the fat now in the fire? Feeling suddenly nervous, she marched over to the bedside table and reviewed the parchment outlining their contract in detail.

Exactly half of the amount they'd discussed sat in a thick package in neatly stacked notes. Apprehension filled her as she stared at the money. She'd already counted—it was all there. The agreement itself was straightforward and honest, but that didn't mean deception wouldn't be lurking in the wings. She would just have to be vigilant.

"Are you settling in, dear?" a voice said from the doorway, and Nève jumped, looking over her shoulder to see Lady Millicent standing there. She shoved the packet under a pillow and turned.

"Yes, thank you."

The older woman shuffled in. "This used to be my sister's room, though the palette is quite different now. She preferred bolder colors. Reds and blues and whatnots. It's been through so many changes."

Nève swallowed. "This was the duchess's room."

"Yes." She let out a puff of air. "Both of them."

For a second, Nève frowned, but then remembered the obnoxious woman who had confronted her during the Marsdens' ball a week ago—Stone's former fiancée and his father's duchess. Millicent must have noticed the look on her face because she gave a small laugh.

"Don't worry, Charlotte was hardly here. She coaxed my brother-in-law to buy her a much grander residence a few streets over. It had a bigger ballroom, you see, in a house she insisted was properly deserving of a duke's wife."

Grander than this?

Nève hadn't seen the ballroom or the residence in its entirety, but she had a hard time imagining anything more lavish.

"Do you need anything?"

"Not for the moment, no, my lady."

The older woman gave her a guileless smile and raised a hand. "Please, call me Millicent, now that we are to be a little more than distant cousins."

Nève felt a flicker of guilt. She had an inkling that the lady already suspected she wasn't a relative. "I'm not really a cousin, Millicent."

"I know that, dear." She gave a conspiratorial twitch of her paper-thin lips. "You think I don't know my own family tree? Least of all a cousin by marriage in France?"

"Why didn't you say anything?" Nève asked, discomfort heating her neck.

"And miss all the fun?"

Nève frowned. "Fun?"

"My dear nephew trying to scheme his way into something. I might have my faults and be a spinster with a head full of wool at the best of times, but I have known Lysander a very long time, and there is nothing that boy would not do to get what he wants." She paused for breath, fingering the lace embroidery at the edge of her cuffs. "Including finding a woman to play the part of his fiancée."

Her heart sank. "He told you."

Millicent shook her head. "No, dear. You just did." At Nève's crestfallen expression, she continued. "Don't worry. Your secret— and my nephew's—is safe with me. Lord knows that boy needs some distraction in his life." Nève blushed at her dry tone. Surely Millicent didn't mean *that* sort of distraction, but the older woman grinned. "I may be unmarried and quite in my dotage most days, but I still have a working pair of eyes."

"It's not like that, I assure you."

Millicent arranged herself in an armchair near the window. "Then what is it like?"

Nève worried her lip, bursting at the seams to talk to someone—anyone—about the situation she found herself in. It was an hourly flip and flop about her motivations and whether she was doing the right thing.

Finally, she let out a breath. "It's a mutual agreement. He helps me, and I help him." She swallowed, her fingers tracing over the edges of the fine carvings on the post at the end of the bed. "I need to get back to Paris or find work here in a theater."

Millicent nodded. "Oh yes, my nephew is a fond supporter of the arts. But why *him*, dear?"

Nève blinked at the blunt question. Something in the older woman's piercing stare drilled through her to the bone. Picturing Montcroix's starkly compelling face, Nève's heart skipped in her chest. Why him, indeed. Would she have done something like this for any other man?

The answer was a resounding no. She tried to imagine Lord Durand in the duke's position instead, and a sick feeling coiled through her.

"I suppose…I trust him," she replied eventually.

"Your instincts are sound, though I am biased." She gave a fond if sad smile. "I will warn you, though you must already know, that my nephew is a fractious man. He might be cold and callous, but he is honest. Lysander does not trust easily, and I find it impossibly intriguing that he has chosen to go this path."

"Which path?" Nève asked, curious.

"A bride. I'd thought he'd put all thought of marriage aside after his last experience."

"A *pretend* bride," Nève clarified, and then took the seat opposite. "I met the Duchess of Montcroix last week at the ball. She accosted me in the retiring room."

Millicent did nothing to hide the distasteful expression that came over her face. "That woman is foul. Her husband, my brother-in-law and Lysander's father, God rest his soul, was not any better. What they did to that poor boy was—"

She broke off just as Nève felt every nerve in her body stand at instant attention at the arrival of the tall, handsomely dressed man crowding the doorway. Her heart lurched against her ribs. Dieu, would she ever get used to the presence of him?

There was no expression on his austere face. Nève spared Millicent a glance and saw that the older woman had gone red, her thin lips pursed as though she'd sucked a lemon.

Remembering her manners, Nève rose swiftly from her seat, aware of his piercing gaze tracking her every movement. "Your Grace."

"Are you well, Miss Valery?" he asked, his deep voice humming through her. "I see my aunt is making sure you are settled."

Nève nodded. "I am, thank you. And she is."

There must have been an underlying reprimand in his words because Millicent's blush deepened and she stuck her chin mutinously high. "Someone has to see to it," she muttered.

Nève hid her smile behind her palm. Even Stone looked surprised at the waspish outburst. He blinked and then cleared his throat. He could only stand there as his aunt gave a last aggrieved huff and departed from the room, but not before throwing a surreptitious wink at Nève.

Her breath stuttered on an exhale as her eyes met and held the duke's. Those silken ribbons of awareness unraveled anew between them, making her skin tingle. Could she stand months of this? Warm air hissed out through her lips as she forced her normally agreeable body to obey her commands. At long last, her hands lifted from her sides to clasp at her front. It was a small, simple movement, but enough to break the spell between them.

The duke cleared his throat again, a faint flush spreading over those aristocratic cheekbones as though he'd been trapped in the same trance. "You are free of appointments for the rest of today, however, I will require your presence at dinner tomorrow evening. Nine o'clock on the dot. Lady Marsden will be here for a final fitting tomorrow morning."

Nève frowned. "Final fitting?"

"I took the liberty to commission a full wardrobe in the hopes that you would agree to my proposal."

Shock filled her. Had she been *that* predictable? "That sounds like a little more than hope, Your Grace," she said, keeping her expression cool.

He eyed her. "It was a calculated decision, yes."

"One that paid off," she said. "What if it hadn't? What if I hadn't changed my mind and you ended up with a mountain of women's clothing?"

"I would have sent the items to a women's shelter."

The items. Nève wondered if she was disposable, too. When he was finished with her, would he discard her as well? She blinked away her unhelpful thoughts. What did it matter what he did when their arrangement ended? They would go their separate ways. It was up to her to keep her emotions in check and to keep her heart guarded.

She arched a brow, reaching for her stage poise. "Tell me, Your Grace, does it ever get easy?"

"What?"

"Carrying that enormous ego around? It must weigh you down. Honestly, I can't imagine how you manage to hold your head up most days."

He narrowed his eyes at the jab. "It's no burden when I'm right."

"Let me guess," she drawled, stepping away. "You're never wrong?"

Stone mimicked her stride and closed the distance, the movement cornering her against the mantel. "Rarely."

She bit her lip hard and heard his sharp, indrawn hiss. The duke's silver stare was pinned to the hold she had on her bottom lip, something hot darkening his eyes. His nostrils flared, and for a fraught moment, Nève wondered if he might ask to kiss her again. Dieu, she did not know if she could handle another of his kisses without wanting more. Exhaling, she released her lip, licking it unconsciously.

What sounded like a growl rumbled from his chest, but without another word, he whirled and left the room. Her entire frame slumped. Thank the heavens for the piece of furniture that propped her up and kept her from sliding to the ground in a sad, sad heap of pent-up, unsatisfied despair. A self-deprecating laugh broke from her. She was a mess. It took every ounce of strength left in her to direct her leaden legs toward the bathing chamber.

Clearly both her body and her brain needed a good cooling.

Chapter Ten

This is never going to work.

Lysander had been a hairsbreadth from giving in to his base instincts and begging like a fool for her favors. White-knuckled, his fingers dug into the wood of his desk instead as he fought anew for control. His entire body felt as though his skin were about to fly apart and come back together in a patchwork mess. Who knew that lust could be such a catalyst for his downfall? He was a man who valued order, not chaos. He exalted discipline and restraint.

And yet...he *lusted* for chaos. Lusted for *her*.

He thumped the desk hard. Blast, he needed to get out of this house. Where was Lushing when he needed him? The man was supposedly in the country seeing to one of his father's estates. He considered going to his club, but he did not want to socialize or be civil. His fingers flexed, tapping against his sides. Music?

No, he needed *more*.

Like a round or ten in the boxing ring.

The devil Lysander kept buried under layers of civility reared its head with interest. Though bare-knuckle boxing was illegal, it remained popular, and he enjoyed it.

Used to enjoy it.

While the gloved Queensberry rules made it seem more of a gentlemanly sport, Lysander preferred the feeling of flesh on flesh. He could head over to the London Athletic Club for a few sedate rounds in the ring or to the public house and underground boxing club that Lushing owned in secret and go a few gloveless, less restricted rounds. He'd made up his mind to do just that, when Finley announced a visitor.

He did not have time to respond that he wasn't at home to callers before Viscount Treadway marched into his study.

"We need to talk," the viscount said. "Is Bolden going to sell? Word is our competitors have his ear for the same tract of land."

Lysander's frown deepened. "I'm working on the earl."

"Work harder."

The man's tone loosened something in him, reminding him too much of the late duke perhaps. "Careful, Treadway. One would think you were trying to command a duke."

A pair of narrowed eyes met his. "Apologies, Your Grace."

"No need." Though Treadway was trying at the best of times, it wasn't his fault that Lysander was on edge. Still, the man's presence was a welcome disruption. "Who is the competition?"

"North Eastern Railway," Treadway said.

That was not surprising. The growing company, led by George Leeman, had a near monopoly on the territory it covered from Yorkshire to Cumberland and had been amalgamating smaller companies for the last several years. It was a good thing Lysander had shares in that railway as well and considered George a colleague. He had diversified investments in many railway companies all over Britain, but his interest in Treadway's Clareville

Railway was quiet. Lord knew if Leeman got wind of it, the price would go through the roof.

Which was why he needed to close this bit of business with Bolden as soon as possible.

"I'll handle the earl. You make sure things are square on your end." Lysander cleared his throat. "Is there anything else you wished to discuss? I was on my way to a prior engagement."

"Ah, yes, apologies for bursting in unannounced, Your Grace. Speaking of engagements, yours was quite a surprise. How have I not heard of Miss Valery before?"

Because you and I are nothing remotely close to friends.

Lysander let out a patient breath. "She lives in France. Our engagement was recent."

"Strange that you never mentioned her."

A muscle flexed in his cheek. "I prefer to keep my private life separate from my professional interests. Whether I am engaged to be married bears no consequence on anything else."

A wily smile settled over the viscount's mouth. "Who knew you had it in you, Montcroix? The ever-hardened bachelor succumbing to the temptations of the marriage mart."

"It's my duty as duke to marry."

Lysander swallowed his rising irritation, his fingers clenching on empty air at his sides, wishing he did not have to deal with the man. He'd had his doubts going into business with the viscount—who had a reputation for being somewhat of a gambler and a sieve with money. He'd intended to buy Treadway's shares outright, but the viscount had surprised him when he'd insisted on a partnership instead.

Against his better judgment, Lysander had agreed, thinking the viscount would accept the money eventually when he realized how much work was involved. But Treadway seemed to be steadfast. The act to expand the railway that was currently moving through the Lords would allow for a significant raising of shares, which Treadway was responsible for managing. The only remaining impediment was Bolden...and his late wife's sentimental wishes.

Lysander gritted his teeth, his mind flicking to the woman upstairs. Nève was still the key to the pretense. Once the deal was secured, they would dissolve their agreement and return to their lives. His chest burned, the tension exploding inside of him like a beast with nowhere to go.

"Finley," he called out for the butler. "Show Viscount Treadway out, please."

"But—"

Lysander didn't wait to hear the rest of the man's protests. With some desperation, he made his way toward his music room. He pushed open the doors, smelling the scent of fresh furniture polish, eyes drifting over the pristine carpets, tasteful drapery, and cozy armchairs arranged in front of the fireplace. He hadn't been in here in years. It was immaculate though the room was never used. His gaze went to the array of stringed instruments—the harp, several violins, and a cello—before falling to the gleaming pianoforte near the windows.

Air hissed out of his lungs when he strode across the room and sat on the bench. His fingers danced over the keys and then crashed down on a quick sequence of chords. The instrument was perfectly tuned as always. Finley would have seen to it. Though Lysander rarely played, all of the instruments were kept in the finest condition.

His father had always deemed music *soft*. The son of a duke could listen to musicians play, even hire them, but playing it himself was contemptible. A daughter was expected to learn the musical arts, but it wasn't the *done* thing for a son.

Yet Lysander had learned and played in secret for his mother.

His fingers ached now as they played a scale, part from disuse and part from memory. The echo of a cane crashing down on his bare knuckles made him falter on the notes. His father had caught him once, and that had been the last time he'd ever touched the instrument in the presence of the duke. Playing the scale again, he felt the ice-cold ache in his bones start to thaw before shifting into a familiar melody by Schubert, his mother's favorite composer. He was rusty, but it didn't take long to work the stiffness out.

God, it had been so long since he'd played. He could almost see the smile on her face in his mind's eye as he played Impromptu in G-flat, the dramatic notes in the middle making his chest feel two sizes too tight. She always used to say his music eased her.

It eased him, too. He'd forgotten.

He swallowed past the boulder in his throat and changed composers. Chopin, *his* preference this time, and played the introductory bars for Fantaisie-Impromptu. He let himself fall into the complexity of the piece, the pads of his fingertips dancing over the keys so quickly he didn't even have time to think about the notes that blazed from him like wildfire. His pulse slowed even as his fingers raced, the music crashing through him to loosen the knot of emotions roiling in his gut.

Exhaling, Lysander caught his breath as his fingers gentled and drifted into a poignant piece, once more Chopin from memory, Nocturne in C-sharp Minor. His favorite, but something about the melody following the beginning chords made him think about the woman upstairs. Delicate but sharp...like a steel blade sheathed in velvet. Something to be admired as well as respected. He could see her dancing to it, her lithe body extending on pointe, those slender arms held in a graceful curve.

The image of her supple form in his head was much too provocative. After the last tender notes of the ending scale, his fingers faltered and halted above the keys. The organ behind his ribs had loosened, but another had tightened with renewed pressure.

Hell, he wanted her.

Lysander leaned forward, letting his forehead rest on the pianoforte's burnished surface.

"Keep going please."

He twisted sharply around on the bench, only to find the object of his desire standing just inside the door, watching him. And listening, obviously.

"How long have you been there?" he ground out, a slew of unfamiliar emotions bursting through him, a deep sense of vulnerability being the most potent. He played for no one. Even his servants knew to make themselves scarce if and when he ever entered this room.

She's not a servant.

"Since Schubert," she replied.

"You know his music?" he rasped, though unsurprised that she would. She was a dancer after all. Music and dance went hand in hand. He almost cursed after asking the question instead of demanding that she leave, since she took it as an invitation to close the distance between them.

"Not well."

Lysander steeled himself against her mouthwatering scent as she reached him beside the bench. "Do you play, Miss Valery?"

In profile, her cheek lifted in a smile. "From time to time, though I admit I'm not nearly as accomplished as you are. You are extraordinary."

Pride swelled inside of him at her praise—an emotion he hadn't felt in ages. Certainly, he felt accomplished when he made profitable investments, but this was different. This felt profound. "It has been a long time, but thank you."

"Why?" she asked.

Lysander didn't know why he answered, but he did. "I haven't touched the piano since my mother died." He met her eyes, seeing the instant sympathy brimming in their depths. "Nearly seven years ago."

"I'm sorry for your loss." He shrugged and they fell into silence as her gaze wandered around the room, touching on the other instruments on display before returning to him. "Do you play all of those as well?"

"Some, not all. The cello is another favorite."

She wandered over to study the large red frame, a look of awe crossing her features. "Is this a Stradivari?" He gave a nod. "It's beautiful. They're so rare. You'll have to play it for me one day."

"I'll play it in exchange for a dance."

The air heated as Nève met his eyes, something like thickened honey flowing between them. Neither of them were strangers to coming to an agreement, but this kind of barter felt more intimate. *Show me yours, and I'll show you mine.* He let out a breath, about to tell her he wasn't in earnest.

"Very well," she said softly.

When she returned to the pianoforte, Lysander reached for a sheaf of sheet music on the table next to them. He moved across on the bench as he arranged the sheets on the stand and patted the seat beside him. God, he was a hundred kinds of fool.

"Sit, let's try a piece together. It's a concerto called Fantaisie in F Minor by Schubert for four hands. Do you read music?"

She gave a dubious nod, perching on the edge of the bench and squinting at the written music. "I do, but I'm passable at best."

Lysander tried not to breathe in her scent or obsess about the feel of her sleeve brushing against his. Or the heat of her thigh, separated from his by only a few layers of clothing. She swallowed nervously, that elegant throat working, and he tugged at his cravat, resisting the urge to turn and run the tip of his nose against that fragrant skin.

"Do you prefer lower or upper?" he rasped.

"I'm already on the left, so I'll play the lower. And only the first movement, please."

"Coward."

"Tyrant," she countered. "I've heard this piece, and there are four very long movements. The whole thing is twenty minutes long. I doubt I will last five."

Lysander couldn't resist teasing her. "Don't have the stamina?"

A choked gurgle burst from her. "I assure you, my musical

endurance is not in deliberation here, Your Grace, but rather it's a question of aptitude. I do not wish to be embarrassed."

"You could not embarrass yourself if you tried, Miss Valery."

"I beg to differ," she said, stretching out her fingers and hovering over the keys. "I've just heard you play, and I could never hope to master Chopin so well. You'll have to be gentle with me."

"Do you wish me to?" He turned, a hint of challenge in his tone.

Nève did not reply for a moment, but then jutted her chin, a green stare colliding with his. "Not really, no."

Lysander smirked. God, she fired him to indecent heights—that competitive spirit of hers fueled his to no end. "Ready?" he asked.

They started out slowly as she familiarized herself with the weight of the keys, stumbling a few times, but Lysander kept pace with her, never stopping. Before long, they'd entered the second movement, raced through the complicated third, and were wrapping up the fourth. Energy hummed through them in tandem, the musical connection between them messy and wild and beautiful. The last slower adagio melted into the chords, the final notes echoing in his body like a visceral pulse. Hell if it didn't feel like a climax.

Beside him, Nève's chest rose and fell, her fingers trembling. Eyes bright, she turned to him, her mouth parting in delight. "That was the best I think I've ever played. Well done, Your Grace."

He wanted to kiss her. "I stand corrected about your stamina."

"I hardly even noticed we played all four movements." Her breathless laugh rang through the room. "Honestly, why aren't you in a concert hall entertaining the aristocratic masses somewhere?"

"I am a duke."

"And?" she countered.

"Dukes do not play. We hire people to do so."

Grinning, she stuck out her tongue, and he froze in place. "So you do."

"I didn't mean you."

"Well, it's the truth. You *did* hire me. Not for music … but close enough."

That mischievous smile of hers widened, sea-glass-green eyes glittering with the remnants of her impassioned performance. Her shoulders and chest heaved with each inhale as though she were still trying to catch her breath. Lysander stared at her. Would she have that same look after orgasm—breathless and bright-eyed, and practically glowing with satisfaction?

He rose abruptly and pretended to rearrange the sheet music on the table next to them.

"Who knew you were a secret virtuoso?" she said. "What other artistic talents are you hiding beneath that fearsome ducal exterior? Do you compose sonnets in your spare time? Will you admit that you've painted the exquisite watercolor hanging on that wall?"

He looked up at the painting of a young girl holding a flower she'd pointed out. "That's actually an original watercolor from the Marchioness of Waterford."

She made a disbelieving sound, her jaw going agape. "A marchioness painted that?"

"Does that surprise you?" he asked.

"That you would have a painting from a peeress upon your walls? Yes, it does." She wrinkled her nose and shook her head with a small laugh. "And also, no, it doesn't. I've met some of the ladies of your acquaintance, and they are all rather unconventional."

"Like you."

She blinked. "I'm not a lady, Your Grace."

"Lysander."

If she rose any quicker from the bench, she'd topple over. A hand fluttered to her throat. "I couldn't possibly call you by your given name. We are not...friends."

"We've played Schubert together," he said. "And that's almost as intimate as congress, so I'd argue we are a little more than *friends*."

That lush pout fell open, and he wanted to fill it with his tongue. With his fingers. With other straining parts of him. Nève went beet red, retreating as quickly as she could until she was at the entrance. "No. No, we aren't. Thank you for the congress. Merde, I mean, duet. Oh, mon Dieu." A rapid stream of French profanity gushed from her mouth before she bit her lip. "I meant *duet*, not the other thing, you understand."

"Not congress? Are you certain? You seem quite flushed. It is a symptom of that particular affliction."

"You are insufferable, Your Grace."

Lysander didn't turn as she nearly crashed into the door on her exit, though his shoulders shook with stifled mirth. If he did, the offensive bulge in his pants would be a dead giveaway that their unusual brand of flirtation was as effective as a barehanded stroke to the groin. In fact, he'd bet his entire fortune that his little ballerina was a silken river beneath those skirts.

He closed his eyes and tried to think of the most dreadful thing possible.

Losing the Bolden property, that would do.

Chapter Eleven

Nève blinked herself awake in a blissful cloud of satin and softness. Was she dreaming? Facing the rising sun, her tiny attic room in Covent Garden was always flooded with a harsh glare at the crack of dawn. And it was always painfully loud. She cleared the sleep from her eyes and took in the deliciously darkened shadows of the room, the sweet sound of quiet, the huge bed she lay in the center of, and remembered with a start where she was.

In Mayfair.

In the Duke of Montcroix's bed.

She blushed...well, not exactly *his* bed. One of his beds. Stretching her body, she wondered if he'd ever slept on this very same mattress. His huge frame—nude, it would have to be gloriously nude—might once have been tucked into the same warm spot she now occupied. Her body went hot at the thought and then cold as reason intervened with fantasy. If Stone was in the *duchess's* quarters, he would not be sleeping, would he? He'd be doing other nonsleeping things with *someone else.*

Nève buried her head in the luxurious bedclothes and let out a groan.

Parfois, tu es vraiment bête.

She really was quite silly! Fantasizing about the lord of the manor when she was nothing but a hired hand, and would be gone in a matter of weeks, was a fool's errand. Eight weeks, to be precise. Her mind delved back to their musical interlude, and something low in her hips warmed at the memory. Dieu, his clever fingers had mesmerized her, made her imagine them running sinfully over her body and making it sing.

Congress. The audacity of him! She twisted her lips into a wry smile.

Nève shook her head with a laugh. Just when she thought she'd gotten the measure of him, the duke surprised her with a burst of sly humor and wit. That playful, teasing side of him had reminded her of the person she'd met in the alley. She'd started to think that had been a fluke, given his eternally stony demeanor, but he was still there buried underneath all of that ducal derision. She didn't think he had it in him to tease as wickedly as he had.

It was irresistibly heady.

A hard knock on the door made her sit up and clutch the bedsheets to her chest, but it was only a maid. "Good morning, miss, I'm Annie," the girl said cheerily as she gently opened the drapes and bustled over to the closet. "Lady Millicent said I can be your lady's maid if it pleases you. His lordship has left for the day, but you can break your fast in the breakfast room or on the terrace. It's a lovely morning. There was a bit of a chill in the air earlier, but it's gone now. It warmed up fast." Nève blinked at the nonstop stream of chatter, and the girl giggled with a blush. "I do love to natter on, don't I?"

"The duke's not here?"

Why did she feel disappointed that he hadn't informed her he'd be gone today? Nève gave herself a stern shake. It wasn't like he would inform his other staff about his whereabouts. He was the duke, for God's sake. He'd told her he expected her for dinner later in the evening, and that was where she would be.

"No, thank goodness," Annie said. "He left early. He was a bear this morning, frightening all the servants and sniping at poor Evans, who dropped the coffee everywhere on the carpets in a fit of fright," she said, making the sign of the cross over her breast, and Nève frowned. Was Stone truly that bad to have his servants walking on eggshells?

"Evans?"

Annie made a sighing noise and gave a dreamy smile. "The most beautiful footman you will ever see in all of Christendom."

"Oh, is he your beau?"

"Hardly." The maid pursed her lips and stopped mid-motion of setting out Nève's freshly laundered and pressed navy dress. She hadn't even noticed that the clearly competent staff had cleaned her clothing. "All the scullery maids think he's handsome, even some of the upper servants. They're all vying to get in his good graces." She giggled and covered her mouth. "That means his smalls."

"I gathered," Nève said dryly. The girl was loud and bubbly and did not have any filter on her thoughts whatsoever, but Nève liked her. At least between her and Lady Millicent, she would not be lacking for conversation or entertainment while in the duke's employ.

With Annie's assistance, Nève performed her morning ablutions and dressed before seeing herself downstairs to the breakfasting room that the girl had indicated. A mouthwatering spread was laid out and the doors to the terrace were open. Annie had been right—it was a lovely morning. Too lovely to waste cooped up indoors anyway. Not that the charming breakfast room was any hardship with its long exquisitely set table surrounded by plush chairs and a steaming sideboard covered in an array of dishes.

"Good morning, Miss Valery," the butler said from behind her.

She nearly jumped out of her skin, once more remarking how efficient the duke's staff was. Having servants bustling about and tending to her every need would take some getting used to again. She and Vivienne had done without a full staff for quite some time, but she had fond memories of those who had been in her papa's service. Their old cook used to sneak them biscuits all the time, the footmen would tell them jokes, and she and Vivi would always try futilely to get smiles out of their dour butler whose face could have been carved from granite.

Montcroix's butler was as austere, but a twinkle shone in his eyes.

Nève smiled. "And a wonderful morning to you, Finley. I'll take my breakfast outside, if that's acceptable."

"As you wish. Evans will be happy to serve you whatever you like."

She brightened at that. She was looking forward to seeing this paragon of male beauty who had the entire staff wrapped around his fingers.

"Sit over here, dear," a soft voice said, and Nève turned to see a cheery Lady Millicent. "We had the same idea to breakfast outside."

Smiling, Nève nodded. "It's a fine morning."

"Do you like the opera?" the older lady asked after she sat, while nodding at a nearby maid to pour her another steaming cup of tea. "I know dancing is a passionate diversion of yours."

Nève didn't correct her that it was much more than a diversion, but nodded. "I do, but I don't get to attend as much as I would like."

Lady Millicent tapped the newssheets she'd been perusing. "I was just reading there's a new ballet at the Alhambra for *Paquita*. Sponsored by the Earl of Lushing no less."

Nève flinched with vexation, remembering how quickly the proprietor there, Mr. Frederick Strange, had turned her away for that very production. No doubt, thanks to Lord Durand. Mr. Strange had heard her name, and his entire countenance went taut.

"My nephew loves the theater. He has always been a patron of the arts, donating money for performances. It was something my sister enjoyed as well. I suppose that's where his interest first grew—he would accompany her in their private box as a boy." Her shoulders lifted. "Until the duke discovered their outings and, well—" She broke off and sipped her tea, her mouth going flat. "It was decided that Lysander was focused on the wrong things. The duke thought she made him soft, so he made him harder."

Forgetting her irritation toward Durand, Nève's heart ached with sympathy for Stone as a boy. She'd been desperate to learn anything about him, but this knowledge felt much too intimate for comfort. She was curious, but she didn't want to care too deeply. Thinking of a young Stone being separated from his mother as a means of discipline made her chest hurt.

No, he was a heartless gargoyle. Not a lonely little boy.

There was nothing to save him from. The duke didn't need her. He didn't need anyone.

"What do you recommend for breakfast?" Nève asked. "I'm a light eater, though I am quite famished."

"Porridge and fruit? Ah, here's Evans now." Even Lady Millicent's eyes lit up.

Delighted, Nève spun around, eager to see the most beautiful footman in the history of Christendom, according to Annie anyway, and nearly fell out of her chair. The man was an honest-to-God *angel*. Like someone had plucked him from the heavens in all his perfect angelic glory and set him loose upon the world. Dark curls capped a perfectly sculpted face with brilliant blue eyes, ridiculously hewn cheekbones, and lips anyone would sell their soul for.

Ciel, no wonder all the staff was aflutter. She would be, too… if he were her type. But as pretty as she found the footman, her blood didn't heat. Her limbs didn't feel as though they were made of softened clay. Her heart didn't feel as if it were about to leap out of her chest and pledge its undying adoration.

No, only one stern, gifted, growly gargoyle of a man had that effect upon her.

And he was firmly, categorically, *emphatically* off-limits.

"Hullo, Evans," she said with an overbright grin showing all her teeth like she was some kind of performer for a tooth powder advertisement. "Some scones and fruit, please," she managed. "And coffee, if you have it."

"Of course, Miss Valery." He left to convey her wishes to the cook and promptly returned to Lady Millicent's chair.

The lady grinned fondly up at him. "And now sweet Evans

must escort me to the garden for my morning walk. It's good for my constitution, you see. Enjoy your breakfast, my dear." She stood as the gallant footman bowed, took her arm, and led her down the steps. They'd obviously done this many times before.

Laughing quietly to herself, Nève shook her head. A walk with a handsome footman would be good for anyone's constitution. Once she was served a plate of scones, butter, strawberries, and coffee, she took in the beautiful marble terrace surrounded by trellises covered in scarlet climbing roses. Stone certainly knew how to live. She sipped on a hot, fresh, nerve-shattering cup of coffee and munched on a buttered scone that melted in her mouth before she could even chew it.

Dieu, this was divine.

Nève wasn't afraid of hard work, but she had missed the comforts of being an aristocrat. The long, leisurely breakfasts and attentive servants. Hours spent playing games in the garden. Playing the pianoforte and reading in the library nook. Dancing in their private studio. It hadn't been easy to go from princess to pauper in the space of a few years, and the memory of what they'd lost felt like a gaping hole deep inside.

The taste of the scone turned a little bitter in her mouth.

Banishing the unwelcome surge of self-pity, Nève finished the rest of her breakfast, waving to a rosy-cheeked Lady Millicent, whom Evans had just escorted back inside. She was healthy, she had Vivienne, and that was all that mattered. Everything else was superficial. Money would come and go, but sisterhood would last forever. Friendship, too. Even love, one day.

"Oh, please God in heaven, tell me there's coffee. And be still my heart, you have scones!" a female voice trilled before a body plopped down in the seat opposite Nève. "I'm bloody starving."

The Marchioness of Marsden made a noise that sounded like a howling animal, and Nève realized it was the lady's stomach. She bit back a giggle and watched wide-eyed as her guest stuffed nearly an entire scone into her mouth before leaning back with a contented sigh.

"So good. I was almost about to gnaw my own arm off," she said after she was finished chewing. "I'm so hungry all the time. You wouldn't think I'd just broken my own fast an hour ago, would you? But I did. I ate a full breakfast, despite some unusual nausea that was quickly eradicated with hot sausages." She peered hopefully at the table. "You don't have any sausages, do you?"

Nève shook her head. "No, but I'm sure someone can find us some."

"No, that's fine. The scones will suffice. I don't know what is wrong with me, honestly. I woke up the other night with a hankering for blancmange."

It wasn't her place to ask, but Laila looked so utterly confused that Nève took pity on her. She'd seen this before in the corps, when out of the blue a dancer started eating more than normal or was hungrier than usual. She lowered her voice and leaned across the table. "Laila, is it possible that you could be with child?"

The marchioness's eyes went so round, she looked as if she'd seen a ghost. A gloved hand fluttered to her very flat abdomen beneath her flattering lilac dress. She blinked, sucked in a breath, and blinked again. "It's possible." Her brown cheeks flushed dark red. "Marsden and I have been rather...active lately."

"You're married. Don't apologize for being well loved."

Laila ducked her head. "When you put it like that, yes, then indeed." Her face pinched. "Don't tell the girls, will you? Vesper will be devastated she wasn't the first to know. Effie and Briar won't care, but Vesper is peculiar. It makes her feel special."

"I won't breathe a word."

A cup of fresh coffee miraculously appeared in front of her. Laila looked up agog at a smiling Evans and her eyes promptly glazed over. "Guh."

"Evans, can you bring Lady Marsden some orange juice as well as a cup of hot chocolate, and maybe some sausages, if there are any in the kitchen?"

"Of course, Miss Valery," he said.

Laila shook her head, staring unabashedly at the retreating footman. "Every time I see that man, I swear I am robbed of the power of speech, of thought, of everything conscious. Isn't he just *beautiful*?"

"Yes. Angels wept just then, when he smiled."

"To be sure." She laughed and fanned herself with her napkin. "You should see the mouthwatering fiction that Briar has written about him."

"She's written about him?" Nève asked. "What kind of writing?"

"Oh, harmless stories." Laila bit her lip and went red again. "Harmless, sultry, erotic, completely sinful stories where he's the starring hero saving the helpless damsel. They're usually unclothed."

Nève's eyes rounded. "That's... When can I read them?"

"I'll talk to Briar," Laila said, stuffing another scone into her mouth with a very indelicate moan. "But first, we need to get you outfitted for the season. Thank God your duke hasn't spared a single guinea for the expense."

"He's not my duke."

She rolled her eyes. "In all the years I've known him, Stone has never done anything like this. The man is smitten."

"He's driven, not smitten." Something inside of her chest beat its wings like a silly, captive creature that didn't know better. "You know him—he always has an end result in mind. I'm simply helping him get what he wants."

"Yes," Laila agreed. "You."

Nève shook her head and distracted the marchioness with the plate of steaming sausages that Evans had just delivered. "Mmph, God, so bloody delicious," she said, after the first bite.

"Did you know he played the piano?" she asked.

"Stone?" Laila paused, her fork midway to her mouth. "Yes. Vesper told me once that he was really talented. She heard it from Lushing."

Nève nodded slowly. "He is very good."

"Lushing said he used to play for his mother. She was a skilled violinist before she lost the use of her hands to her illness."

"How did she die?" Nève asked, curiosity bubbling. She felt strange prying into Stone's personal affairs, but the pressing need to know more about him undermined her discomfort.

"It was a wasting disease. It came upon her quickly. She was here one moment and gone the next. Stone lost the last part of himself that day."

"That's sad," Nève said. "What about the duke? His father? What kind of man was he?"

"He was...not worth our time." Laila's face tightened as she rose from her chair. She gave a small shrug with a dismissive wave. "We should probably get started with the dresses. It's going to take a while."

Nève didn't push, but she knew there was a history there. A dreadful one, if Laila's reluctance to speak about it was any indication. In any case, none of it was really her business. Squelching her curiosity, Nève rose with an agreeable smile and nodded. Whatever or whoever had made Stone the man he was wasn't her concern.

Not one bit.

Lysander was exhausted. The entire day had been tedious. After a sleepless night—his mind churning with thoughts of his father, lingering feelings of unworthiness, the fact that he missed his mother dearly, and, of course, the intriguing ballerina in the rooms just down the hall—he'd spent the entire day going over the accounts with Treadway. The finances were in bad shape. He never should have trusted the man with them in the first place, but the viscount had been insistent that he'd managed the books for years.

Huge sums of money had been allocated without saying where they'd been sent and to whom. Treadway had said they were shareholder payouts, but the numbers did not add up. He was adamant that it was a simple mistake and that he would find the error. After a day of feeling like he was bashing his head against stone, Lysander had told him to fix it and left. The discrepancies would be there tomorrow.

Hence, he was in a worse mood than when he'd left that morning.

The moment he entered Blackstone Manor, however, the roaring inside of him quieted. He must truly be wearied. Divesting himself of his outer trappings and handing his hat, coat, and gloves to Finley, he made his way to his chambers where Henry, God bless the valet, was waiting with a fully drawn hot bath.

"You deserve a raise, good man."

The valet shook his head. "You gave me one last week, Your Grace."

"Then you shall have another."

Lysander groaned as he sank into the soothing heat of the water. On evenings like this, he would eat a late meal and then work until he was too exhausted to think. The thought of that turned his stomach. Sighing, he ran the tips of his fingers on the edges of the tub and let them tap an imagined musical scale on the porcelain.

God, playing with Nève had been indescribable. She'd been better than passable. *Competent* was the term he'd have used to describe her ability, but that stubbornness he was learning was part of her disposition had driven her to be better. To attempt to match him. On the last movement, he'd barely been able to concentrate or keep up when the lower measure had dominated the melody.

Congress had been too tame a word to describe the pressure and passion of her fingers dancing across those notes—daring his to respond to the challenge. He imagined she would dance the same way, full of fight and mesmerizing beauty. He groaned, knowing it was not dancing he was thinking of right at that moment. He was tempted to let his hand drop back into the lukewarm water and take care of the aching stiffness in his groin.

Instead, he washed briskly and resorted to letting the bath cool, taking his desires with it.

"Miss Valery is waiting in the rear salon, Your Grace," Henry told him once he was shaved and dressed, all disorderly parts of him tucked away behind seventeen layers of civility, fabric and otherwise.

"Thank you, Henry."

On his way downstairs, something undefinable expanded in his chest. Nerves, if he were to hazard a guess, though Lysander didn't know what he had to be nervous about. It was just dinner for the two of them to get to know each other better. This was groundwork, nothing more. He resisted tugging at his cravat. Henry must have wound the damned thing too tight.

"Good evening, Your Grace," the butler said, and Lysander canted his head.

He stopped at the door to the salon, turning back to the butler. "I forgot to ask, Finley. How is your mother?"

The poor woman had taken a terrible fall while climbing the stairs and had been told that she would lose her foot. Lysander had sent his personal doctor to see to the woman's treatment the moment he had heard of her injury.

"Better, Your Grace," the butler said. "Your physician's remedies have helped with the pain in her leg, and he says that he thinks she will be able to walk in time with the proper care. I cannot thank you enough."

"It is nothing," he said. "Send my man of affairs any further bills that arise."

"Thank you, Your Grace."

Lysander entered the room and stood stock-still. It felt as though a runaway train had crashed straight into his chest. His pulse spiked and then dropped, the air billowing from him at the woman standing a few feet away. His companion for the evening was staring at him with an intensely curious look on her face, but Lysander could not form a coherent thought.

Even knowing that Marsden's wife had sent word about the delivery of a few of the new gowns he'd commissioned, a part of him had been half expecting the plain, sturdy gowns Nève had worn previously. Not that her beauty hadn't shone through then, but this was something else. Gowned in emerald satin shot through with gold thread, the exact hue of her eyes when lit by the sun, she captivated.

"Lost your tongue, Your Grace?" she asked, though a tremor bled through her teasing words.

He cleared his throat and swallowed. "You are stunning."

"Thank you," she said, blushing. "Laila's talent with a needle is unmatched."

"It's not the gown, Miss Valery."

Seeing that she already had a glass of sherry in hand, he stalked over to the mantel and poured himself a finger of whiskey. He couldn't understand what was wrong with him. He'd been around countless exquisitely beautiful women. What was it about *this* one that turned him into a bumbling schoolboy?

She smoothed the front of her dress, the champagne-colored gloves a perfect complement to the color of the fetching embroidery over her bodice and hem. "Thank you."

"I thought we would have dinner here tonight and get to know one another a little better."

"More congress?"

Lysander choked on his sip, nearly spraying a mouthful of expensive liquor across the carpet. She'd recovered from her embarrassment yesterday like the consummate chameleon she was. For a moment, he'd enjoyed catching a glimpse of the woman behind all the masks she wore. But now, she was in performance mode with her guise firmly in place.

A master of the role he was compensating her to play.

Lysander wondered which version was the real one, if either at all, and whether he'd ever know the true Geneviève Valery. The woman who shared the salon with him was poised and confident and ready for battle, a far cry from the stripped-down sybarite who had played Schubert with such raw enthusiasm. Who had run from him when he'd offered up his given name.

"Will Lady Millicent be joining us?" she asked, watching him.

He shook his head. "She informed Finley earlier that she is under the weather and sends her regrets."

Nève huffed out a laugh, and he lifted a questioning brow. "She didn't seem under the weather when I saw Cook sneaking up a tray of cookies and a bottle of Madeira to her room a quarter of an hour ago."

"She's supposed to be your chaperone."

"For whose benefit, Your Grace?" Her grin was full of mischief, and the sight of it pierced him like a well-tipped lance. "I did not require one the other night, and unless you insist on more displays of musical accomplishment, then I shall behave with the utmost decorum."

"I promise to keep my other ... endowments hidden."

"For the sake of a lady's tender sentiments, please do."

His lip twitched. "I thought you said you weren't a lady."

"I am whatever you wish me to be, Your Grace."

Lysander laughed, but felt a pang all the same. She *was* whatever he needed her to be, but more than ever before, he wanted her to be herself. He yearned for the sensual, honest woman from the music room. *Just like you're being honest?* The question struck him like a blow. He desired her without pretense, and yet was unwilling to lower his defenses and let her in.

The notion of *that* was nauseating.

Then what was it about her that inflamed him so? No one else treated him with such disregard for who he was. The servants scurried around him like mice that didn't want to be eaten. And in the ton, with the exception of Lushing and his rowdy set, other gentlemen and ladies of his acquaintance held their tongues, worried that their estates would be snatched up from beneath their noses, or ingratiated themselves ad nauseam, hoping to get something from him.

She's getting a bloody fortune from you.

That hadn't been through artifice, however. That had been a business arrangement, the terms of payment and product both brokered and controlled by him. Nève had nothing to prove beyond how capable she could be in the role he expected her to play. She'd acquitted herself commendably as his companion at one ball. Could she do it for an entire season?

Could *he* survive the season with her at his side?

His heart thrummed, and Lysander wasn't sure he wanted to merely survive. For the first time in his life, he wanted to do more than go through the motions, do more than fill up his hours with mindless investment concerns and mundane things that didn't matter. He wanted to *feel*. To lose himself in the music, take flight, and soar.

But leaping off a cliff had real risks. He'd done it before and been shattered. Doubt reared its head. There was safety and security in the dependable, reliable life he'd chosen for himself, even if it was routine and mundane.

He'd leave the soaring to the creatures with wings.

Chapter Twelve

Nève smiled at Evans, who served the first course of a tureen of glistening truffle cream soup, barely noticing the footman's celestial looks. No, her attention was being seduced across the table by the man who was more devil than angel.

More gargoyle than seraph.

Bold, hard, and unreservedly masculine, he was sinful, masterful, powerful, all the dratted *-fuls*. Even now, sitting on the other side of the table, it was Stone who made her body hum to life, not the flirtatious servant with his smiling eyes and full lips. Evans could be invisible for all the notice she took of him.

With effort, she focused on the next course—poached salmon in a delicate lemon butter sauce. "This is delicious."

"The chef is French," the duke said. "I thought you would enjoy the cuisine."

She faltered at his thoughtfulness. "Thank you."

"It is nothing."

It *wasn't* nothing. Just like the gowns that had been delivered earlier on the heels of the marchioness's visit. Nève warmed at the fact that he wanted to make her happy, even with a shared meal from her home. The act was thoughtful, stripping past those cold layers, to the tenderness beneath. His words reminded her of the ones she'd heard him say to Finley, the butler, on the way into the salon where she'd been waiting for his arrival. "Is Finley's mother ill?"

He blinked, then shook his head. "She had a bad fall, but she's better now."

"And you sent your personal doctor to see her? And paid all her expenses."

His face was inscrutable, but the tiny twitch of his lip caught her attention and hinted at discomfort. "Yes."

"Why?"

"Why not?" he countered, his lip flattening even more.

"Because he's your butler."

The duke reached for his wine. "He is also a person, and he's loyal. Why are you asking?"

"No reason." There was no reason other than the ember of curiosity about this remote and unapproachable duke that was now burning a hole in her breast. A purportedly heartless duke—*hadn't she called him that?*—who took care of his servants' poorly mothers, bought paintings by unconventional women, played the piano like a prodigy, bought her beautiful dresses, and hired a French chef just for her.

Who *was* this man?

Notwithstanding her base attraction to him, which only seemed to be growing, she found herself desperate to know what drove him beyond being duke and building his fortune. Who was it for? He had no heirs. He loved music, but why didn't he play more? What had he been like as a child? Had he ever played pranks or laughed—the full-belly kind of giggles that couldn't be curbed? Had he been lonely in this grand house? Who had befriended him? At least she and Vivi had had each other. Being an only child with a strict father had to have been difficult.

He's not a lost puppy, Nève!

Of course he wasn't, but she felt compassion hit her hard all the same. She took a deep breath after the dishes were cleared and the next course served. It looked and smelled like one of her favorites, poulet au vin blanc, and her mouth watered at the scent.

"You said you wanted to get to know one another," she said, fortifying herself with another sip of wine. Evans was as efficient as he was handsome and her glass was never empty, not that she was counting, though she probably should have been. "Let's say we get ten questions each with the option to pass, if either of us doesn't wish to answer. Shall I start the interrogation then? What's your favorite color?"

He shot her a look. "That's a bit juvenile, isn't it?"

"Sometimes being *juvenile* is best, Your Grace." She tasted a bite of her chicken, and her eyes nearly rolled back in her head at the burst of flavor. She took a moment to savor it before continuing. "Now stop avoiding the question and give me your answer."

"I've discovered a recent partiality to green."

Nève felt her face heat. "I would have thought blue, since you mentioned to Laila that first evening that you liked the blue gown."

"Why didn't you wear it, if you knew it was my preference?"

"I make choices for myself, no one else."

He canted his head in agreement. "As you should. Very well, what's your favorite color?"

"Black."

"I would have said red," he said. "Why black?"

"It's mysterious and endless, like a midnight sky or a bottomless lake. When I'm onstage and the lights are on me, I dance for the shadows. The darkness is...comforting when you don't want to actually be seen."

He stared at her, setting down his fork, and for a moment, Nève didn't know why she'd been so candid. "You don't wish to be seen?"

"I wish to be seen for *me*, not the role, if that makes sense."

"But you just said you are the characters you play while on the stage," he said softly, his stare earnest as though he wanted to understand...wanted to hear what she had to say.

"It's easy to lose yourself in the process of becoming others." She lifted one shoulder in a shrug and reached for her glass of wine, each sip making conversation easier. "I don't want to forget who I am."

"Who is that?"

"A sister, first." Her voice went wistful. "A friend, a dancer, a dreamer. Someday a mother, a wife. I want to matter to someone." She cleared a dry throat that felt suddenly clogged, and forced a jovial expression to her face. "Sorry, that wasn't the point of the game. Your turn. What's your middle name?"

"I much prefer hearing about you." He sighed at her pointed look. "Maxton. Yours?"

"Rose. Are you an only child?"

His answer was a short jerk of his head once dessert was served—a selection of miniature cakes and tarts. "Yes. I already know you have a sister and you mentioned that the two of you took your mother's maiden name. On the subject of names, why don't you use Geneviève? It's a beautiful name."

The sound of her true given name rolling off his tongue like he was sampling a delicacy did shocking things to her. "Only Vivienne calls me Geneviève. Nève is more of a stage name."

She selected a tiny lemon tart and popped it into her mouth, and let out an actual moan as the flavors of lemon and sugar burst on her tongue.

"Good?" Stone asked in an oddly thick voice.

"Divine."

"You mentioned that your last performance was *Giselle*?" When she nodded because she was still falling in love with the confection in her mouth, he cocked his head.

"Once." She held up one finger to indicate the sole time she'd ever danced it. It had been in the role of an understudy onstage when the principal ballerina had fallen ill.

"And which act do you prefer to dance? The first with the peasant girl or the second with the ghostly Wili?"

She swallowed, and licked her lips, unsurprised that he was familiar with the ballet. Those eyes that missed nothing tracked her movements, and his gray stare was the darkest she'd ever seen it. "That, Your Grace, is for you to discover. If I told you, it would take all the fun out of it, wouldn't it?"

"This isn't supposed to be fun. It's a job."

She lifted a brow. "We must find joy where we can take it." Nève paused to consider his question. "Very well, sometimes I prefer sweet, innocent, and sanguine Giselle in the first, but others, the Wili is the one who is free of her mortal trappings and the caprices of deceitful men."

"She does save Albrecht in the end from his fate," he said. "So she can't have abandoned all morality."

"It's a romantic ballet, Your Grace. Such selflessness is quite rare in the real world. When one is forced to adapt to difficult circumstances, innocence is the first casualty."

"You were forced to adapt?"

At the strange look—was it concern or empathy?—on his face, she clamped her lips shut, cursing the amount of wine she'd drunk. She did not need him to feel sorry for her. She was *here* and alive, with breath in her lungs and fire in her heart.

"I don't want your pity," she mumbled.

"It's not pity. I admire your fortitude." His gaze softened. "When did your parents die?"

Years. It'd been years. The last dregs of their savings had dwindled after the year of mourning. She'd been fourteen and Vivienne fifteen when they were left destitute and on their own.

"Seven years ago," she whispered.

"About the same as when my mother passed. Strange that we have that in common, isn't it?"

It was. They'd both been forced to adapt then. Blankly, Nève glanced around. When had the table been cleared? She peered over her shoulder, realizing she and the duke were now alone in the enormous dining room. She blinked. "Is that another of your questions? You have four."

"I didn't realize we were counting." A small smile hovered over his lips, his cheekbones flushed, too. Hers felt entirely too hot. How much wine had she had? Two glasses, at least, and she was not a heavy drinker.

She pursed her lips. "That's how the game works. It's a finite number of questions, Your Grace." Of course that was a lie. There had been many other questions.

"Lysander."

"I cannot," she said, her face warming more.

"You call me Stone. That's a nickname. Isn't that the same?"

It wasn't remotely the same. Stone was safe. It reminded her of what he was—a stony, hard-hearted duke. Lysander was too lyrical. It made her think there was a man with a beating heart beneath all that rock. She needed to keep her romantic illusions firmly under guard. She'd seen it too many times in the corps—women falling for men who projected who they *could* be instead of who they actually were.

She would not fall in love with a dream. She could not fall in love at all.

And never with him.

"It's not the same."

He rose and walked around the table, and she froze in place. "Join me in the small gardens for an after-dinner walk." Her eyes flew wide. When she stalled in a panic, trying to find an acceptable excuse for wanting to flee his presence and not enter a beautiful—and most likely romantically lit—garden, he held out a hand to her. "Please, Geneviève."

Oh non, non, non. She closed her eyes, hating and hoarding the memory of the sound of her name in that deep, gravelly voice, his French accent so perfect it reminded her of home. But she did not want to think of him and home in the same sentence... it led to many alarming thoughts that maybe, one day, *he* could be the safe harbor she craved. Could a man like Stone ever be home? To one woman, he would be someday.

Nève swallowed as a piercing sort of envy sank deep into her bones, scraping and burrowing deep. He would call that lady by her given name in those deep sonorous tones, entreat her for walks in the garden, stare at her with the intense silver regard that ferried a thousand intimate sentiments in one glance.

She almost shivered. Why on earth did Nève want that to be *her*? She was the fraud, the counterfeit duchess. She was nothing but a placeholder for the real thing. That hurt much more than it should, when it had no reason to. She had gone into this with her eyes wide open.

"Will you?" he asked again. "Accompany me for a short while?"

"Yes, of course," she whispered, and took his hand.

Once she was standing, his palm moved to the small of her back, and every single one of those long fingers scalded her skin through silk and whalebone as if they were gossamer. It wasn't as though other male dancers didn't have their hands all over her body onstage. Dancing with a partner meant getting very close. But their hands were not his.

Air, she suddenly needed air. A brisk walk would be *just* the thing.

They walked along the lamplit path in silence, the late air cool and fragrant from the smell of night-blooming lilies. Lysander could sense the tension emanating from Nève's body, but he couldn't pinpoint what had caused it. Was she so averse to using his given name? It wasn't that much of a stretch for an engaged couple to be so familiar.

You aren't engaged, his obliging conscience reminded him.

"This is breathtaking," she murmured, when the meandering path took them to a small landscaped pond that danced in the moonlight. "I saw this garden from my window, but it's even more marvelous in person."

"I like to come out here to think," he said. "The park at Montcroix Abbey is a hundred times the size of these, and the gardens there were my mother's pride and joy. When she was able to tend to them, that is."

Nève sighed. "How old were you when she died?"

"I was twenty-three."

He led her to one of the ornamental benches that surrounded the pond, and watched as she sat, her gaze growing pensive. Gleaming emerald skirts pooled softly around her. "And then your father remarried."

"Yes. Charlotte."

Her beautiful face screwed tight. "There's a special place in hell for a woman like her. I'm sorry you had to deal with such a betrayal from someone you trusted."

"Why are you sorry?"

She stared at him, those sea-glass eyes piercing him, as if surprised at his blunt question. "I suppose I'm sorry you were hurt."

The sentiment was moving, though unnecessary since the truth was he'd felt nothing at the time. He buried those emotions so deeply that he couldn't begin to recall what they had been. Lysander shrugged. "I wasn't hurt."

"The woman you were about to spend the rest of your life with left you for your father," she said in a disbelieving tone.

"I was there, I don't need a summary."

She blinked at his emotionless reply. "You expect me to believe you felt nothing at all when your betrothed left you for another man?"

"Believe what you want. Their choices had no effect on me."

She stared at him, frowning. "That's generous of you," she murmured finally.

"How so?"

"Because I would want to tear them apart. I still do." Her voice shook with unhidden fury on his behalf.

He gave a shrug. "That's only wasted energy, Miss Valery. Why give people like that more of myself? Any more than they deserve?"

"I don't like her, or Treadway, for that matter," she confessed. "He's a snake."

Lysander frowned. "Has he been untoward?"

"No, it was something he said that rubbed me the wrong way. That you were slow. It struck me that he didn't know you very well." She made a vexed noise and paused to collect herself. "He's the one with the railway, you said?"

"Yes."

"I don't trust him."

Lysander gave a curt shrug. "I don't care what he thinks of me, only if he will sell. I do not require guidance on how to conduct my business affairs."

"Because it's not my place?" She speared him with a hurt glance, but he stared back at her, unperturbed. It *wasn't* her place.

"No, it's not."

She wrinkled her nose. "You can be very frank."

"Yes, less misunderstandings that way."

They fell back to silence as her gaze was ensnared by the flickering surface of the water. In profile against the picturesque backdrop, like the elegant strokes of a master painter, she was even lovelier. He could watch her all night. He had the idle thought that if it had been Nève instead of Charlotte who married his father, he might not have been so indifferent. It did not sit well with him.

"By my count, we still have a few questions left each," he said.

She graced him with one of her easy smiles. "Then I believe it's my turn, sir."

"Very well," he said with a bow. "Ask away."

"What are your likes and dislikes? Besides music, do you have any hobbies? What do you enjoy doing in your spare time? What did you enjoy doing as a boy?"

"That's more than one question," he pointed out, and she hefted an elegant shoulder as if daring him to do something about it. "I like working." At her snort, he gave a reluctant laugh. He hadn't thought about hobbies in years. "When I was younger, I used to enjoy boxing with Lushing, though I haven't recently. Like music, I suppose. I used to like riding, too."

"That's a lot of past tense."

He shrugged. "I've been busy."

"Working."

Lysander nodded in affirmation. "What about you?"

She scrunched up her nose and tapped a finger to her lip as though thinking. "I don't ride. Not anymore, at least. It's too dangerous. If I took a fall off a horse, my dancing career would be over. I do enjoy a spot of cards at the tables from time to time."

Lysander peered at her. "Gambling? Truly? I can't see it."

"Because I look so innocent?" she tossed back.

"That, and it's a terrible habit." He strolled over to where she sat, and perched on the end of the curved bench. "I've seen many men and the occasional woman lose the shirts on their backs to gambling."

She shot him a snide look. "Isn't that the pot calling out the kettle? You take risks every day with your business dealings."

"That's not the same."

"You're being deliberately obtuse, Stone. You're still gambling with money. Admit that you like the rush of winning."

He warmed at the use of his nickname, despite the jab. "I do like winning, but it's not the same. We shall have to agree to disagree then." He eyed her. "So is that what this is to you? Our agreement? A game?"

"Isn't every choice in life a game? There are winners and losers at every turn."

Gray eyes met green and held, the space between them narrowing to a mere handful of inches. "I never lose, and I always get what I want."

Something fraught flashed over her face then as if she was aware of it, too, the subtle shift between them. Over the years, Lysander had made it his business to study people, to see what they didn't want other people to see, and she wanted to hide *that* more than anything.

"And what do you want, Your Grace?" A crystalline stare met his. "Land, fortune, legacy?"

"All three," he said. "And one more. You."

A slight shudder racked her slim shoulders before it was suppressed. Nève tugged her lip, drawing it into her mouth before she smiled. It was her performance smile. A competitive smile... one that beguiled and warned. One that invited someone to watch from afar but to never come too close. He didn't pay heed. He leaned in until their lips were almost touching.

"You can't have me," she whispered.

"What if I want to change the rules? What if we both want more?"

Her eyelashes dipped. "And then what, Your Grace? You make me your duchess in truth? We both know that's not what you want. You desire my body, but you have no interest in *me*. And I want the dream. I deserve the dream." She hiccuped and stood. "I'm sorry, I'm not making much sense."

His chest squeezed as he rose as well. "Nève."

She swayed on the balls of her feet, lips so close he could taste them. "Don't, Stone. I can't do this," she whispered, her warm breath fanning against his chin as they stood there, so close and yet worlds apart, before she stepped away, leaving a chasm of unsaid things between them. "I should say good night. Thank you for a lovely evening."

Then she turned on her heel and practically ran from him. Bewilderment and desire wound tight inside of him as he stood there in the moonlight, surrounded by roses. Perhaps that was for the best. She wanted the dream he could never give her.

A dream she deserved... from someone far worthier than him.

CHAPTER THIRTEEN

Nève found herself hiding behind a large oak tree, desperate for a respite from the crowds in Holland Park. It was their third garden party this week, and if she was forced to endure watching another screamingly boring game of lawn tennis or croquet, she'd pull her hair out by the roots. She'd prefer hours upon hours of grueling ballet exercises to this. Her stomach gave an obnoxious growl, but braving the refreshments tent would be an ordeal in itself.

And besides, she was hiding. Not just from people, but from the duke himself. Things had gone back to normal—meaning he did his best to embody a rock and she did her best to act as the pretty ornament—but his words from their dinner were on replay in her head.

What if we both want more?

More was a slippery slope.

More involved emotions and deep-seated, secret desires.

More was a recipe for destruction.

The duke had made no bones about the fact that he wanted *her*. At least, he wanted her physically. She'd be lying if she didn't admit that she desired him, too, but sex would only complicate things. Some girls could separate the emotional from the physical, but Nève had never been one of them, which was why she'd never taken anyone to her bed.

And she was already in over her head when it came to the duke. Stone was too intriguing by half. He was an intelligent enigma of a man with a level of complexity no one ever took the time to notice because they were too frightened or too cowed. She could lose herself in him easily, if given the chance. And she could not. He was the kind of man she would break herself upon before he would ever bend for her.

And now, Nève could not stop obsessing over what *more* actually meant. When her parents died, she'd had to think quickly and stay on her feet. Everything had been about her and Vivienne—a roof over their heads, food to eat, clothing, and basic necessities.

She'd never allowed herself to dream of the future she might have had as the daughter of a peer, and certainly, circumstances had never permitted it. But now...she *ached* for what that might look like.

A loving husband. Children. A home.

And for the life of her, Nève couldn't look at Stone without picturing those fantasies. It was foolish in the extreme, she knew. As much as he wanted to pull the wool over Bolden by pretending to be a man focused on the future and family, that was the last thing *he* wanted.

The pretense was a success, however.

After the official announcement of their engagement in the *Times*, everyone wanted to know which chit was fortuitous enough to win the unattainable Duke of Montcroix. Oh, the rumor mill abounded, and most of the commentary wasn't kind toward him, especially when jealous tongues joined the fray. While he was powerful and richer than half the ton put together—and any lady would have been in raptures at a proposal from such an influential duke—he did not possess the princely looks that would make for a swoon-worthy story.

Envy was a devil of a thing.

As expected, the tide of gossip was swift to turn against her as well. Nève wasn't a stranger to it. Gossip was used as a well-oiled blade in the corps—a slice here, a cut there—but she'd always kept herself above such conduct. So she smiled and deflected, and endured the ton's conjecture. The speculation on whether she was a fortune hunter was the closest to the truth. Said fortune would be in her grasp in a few short weeks.

Nève peeled off her clammy gloves and fanned herself with them. She peeked around the tree, her eyes falling to the duke, talking to the Earl of Bolden. At least that part of Stone's plan was going smashingly well. He seemed to be doing a fine job of convincing the earl that he was the right sort of man, now that he'd found the woman of his dreams.

She snorted. His monetary dreams.

Nève felt a twinge of guilt for the deception, but it wasn't any of her business. But that guilty feeling had grown deeper the more she and the duke stepped out together, and also because she *liked* Bolden. The love he held for his late wife was something to admire. It was what she hoped for herself one day. He sought to preserve his wife's memory and honor her wishes, which was heartwarming. She wondered at the duke, however, who was so driven by his financial interests that he couldn't understand *why* the earl felt as he did.

"What are you doing?" a voice demanded. She nearly leaped into the lower boughs of the tree as Vesper and Effie appeared on either side of her. Vesper followed Nève's gaze. "Making eyes at your duke?"

"What? No, of course not. I was in search of some privacy."

"Want a nip?" Vesper asked, shoving an engraved silver flask into her face. "It's whiskey. I stole it from Lushing's stash. I've had enough iced claret cup, tea, and punch, thank you very much."

With a chuckle at her expression, Nève took the flask and sipped, feeling the burn of the whiskey scald her throat. She fought against gagging. How people loved this stuff, she had no idea. Despite its execrable taste, she was grateful for the boost of liquid courage.

"Where's Laila and Briar?" she asked.

"Marsden took Laila home," Effie said, going red in the face and coughing from the bite of the liquor. "It was much too hot for a woman in her condition."

Laila had told her friends after confirming with her private doctor that she was indeed with child. They had all been over the moon for her.

"Briar and Lushing are at it again," Effie went on. She hooked a thumb over her shoulder. "Over there." Sure enough, the two of them were red in the face and arguing near the refreshments tent.

Vesper rolled her eyes. "Those two need to go *at it* in truth. I've tried to get them together for ages, and neither of them will accept that they are perfect for each other. They fight like cats and dogs. I bet they'd swive like it, too."

"Vesper!" Effie gasped.

Vesper shrugged. "No one can hear me."

"You don't have to be so uncouth about it."

"Why should the men have all the fun with grammar? We have tongues, too, and we know how to use them. Would you prefer I use the other word, *Effie*? The *F* one?"

"No!"

Nève had gotten accustomed to Vesper's secret bawdy talk, though it had been a shock at first for such a proper lady and the daughter of a duke. In public, she was the image of sociability and respectability, but behind closed doors, she had the mouth of a sailor and wasn't afraid to use it.

Effie handed Vesper the flask. "You're terrible, and one day, someone is going to overhear you, and what will your papa say?"

"Nothing because he'll never believe that I am any less than perfect." It wasn't an exaggeration either—Nève had learned that Vesper was generally regarded as the most perfect lady in London. Her friend tucked the flask back into a band tied above her stocking garters, and Nève marveled at the ingenuity of the hiding place. The other woman smirked and dropped her skirts. "Now come on, I fancy a spot of archery while Nève here tells us all the sordid details of what she and Stone have been up to."

"There are no sordid details to be had," Nève said. "Stone is Stone, as you well know."

Vesper's smirk widened as she waggled her brows. "*Is* he now?"

"Effie's right. You are dreadful." Nève shook her head with a laugh and swatted her with her gloves before tugging them back on. She wished she didn't have to, but heaven knew what all the other ladies in attendance would say about her then.

Have you seen *the gloveless heathen?*

Oh yes, she's the one marrying the stone effigy of a duke.

She snorted, and buttoned the gloves, even though it was so unseasonably hot that the back of her dress was beginning to fuse to her corset.

"What do we win?" Effie asked one of the servants when they arrived at the area where the archery targets were set up.

"Brooches, my lady, for five hits with twelve arrows."

They walked over to the line and took their places. Nève watched as both Vesper and Effie nocked the first of the arrows into their bows and let loose at the brightly painted targets a fair distance away. She squinted. That had to be at least thirty or forty yards. Both women nailed their marks, though Effie's was closer to the center.

Nève frowned. It looked easy enough, but she'd never done it before.

How difficult could it be?

Mimicking their side-on stances, she took the curved weapon in hand. She inspected the bow and tested its weight before nocking the arrow against the string as she'd seen the two ladies do. Then she held it up, pointing the arrow toward her target. Why did it seem much farther away than before? Closing one eye, she pulled back on the string. It was surprisingly difficult, but her arm strength was well honed from hours of ballet training. The effort was nothing compared to holding a port de bras.

She released the string and gasped at the vibration along her fingers, watching in shock as the arrow sailed wide. *Much* too wide. It was a comedic sequence of errors that followed next as the projectile toppled over a basket full of fruit that frightened a sleeping basset hound into careening toward a nearby group of people who then tumbled like tenpins. Fans and parasols flew. Punch splattered. Women shrieked and men cursed.

Nève clapped a hand to her mouth in dismay.

Amid the screeches and groans, and the furious stares turning her way, she wanted to fling the bow away and get rid of the evidence. Neither Vesper nor Effie had seen her awful shot, though they stopped to observe the commotion. Would the unfortunate victims guess it had been her arrow? It wasn't marked or tied to her in any obvious way. In truth, it could belong to any one of the dozen women standing there.

Pretend that you know what you're doing.

She grabbed another arrow and feigned confidence before nocking it and staring down her target like she'd been doing it all her life, only to falter at the dark chuckle from behind her.

"That's how you're going to play it?" a deep voice whispered into her ear.

Nève suppressed a shiver and bit her lip. She didn't have to look to know it was Stone. Her body already knew as energy hummed over the sensitive skin of her nape. The duke's distinctive scent of crisp winter and sharp pine wafted into her nostrils. "I have no idea what you're talking about," she said haughtily.

"By all means, try to get it to topple Charlotte's awful hat, if you can."

Drat, he'd seen her. "That wasn't me," she said.

"Hard to miss such an abominable shot."

Abominable? His frank assessment of the admittedly poor attempt rankled. Nève turned then and shoved the bow into his chest. "Let's see you do better then."

Stone's lip curled into a smirk as he lifted the bow, retrieved an arrow, and released it, all the while keeping her gaze. Damned if it wasn't the most seductive display Nève had ever seen in all her life—the muscles straining under his coat, the intensity of his silver stare boring through hers, the raw tension reverberating between them. Her breath hissed out when she realized she'd been holding it. There was no way he could have hit the target without even looking at it...

"You missed."

"Did I?" he returned, that storm-gray gaze still dominating hers.

They both turned. Stone's arrow was lodged dead center in the middle of her target. Unwilling to accept what she hadn't seen with her own eyes, Nève handed him another arrow. "Prove it. Do it again."

"What do I have to prove?" he asked.

"That could be someone else's arrow," she said. "Maybe even Vesper's or Effie's."

The duke's lips parted to show a hint of teeth, and she nearly fell over. Goodness, was that an actual *smile*? She was so stunned to see it that her mouth fell open. "Would you prefer I look at you again while I do it this time?" he asked.

"No, look at your target."

"I was."

She blushed, realizing just what he'd intimated. "Stop posturing, Stone, and shoot."

The chuckle that rumbled from him was earthy and rich, and the unfamiliar sound of it nearly made her keel over in shock. Nève could sense Vesper's and Effie's curious glances, though she couldn't see around the duke's large body. Suddenly, she was grateful for his size as well as the hot afternoon, knowing both concealed her very red face from her friends.

This time Stone aimed while she made sure to not be distracted by the flex of his fingers around the bow, the reach of his arm, or the erotic flick of his tongue over his bottom lip.

An amused gray gaze met hers. "Are you watching now?" he asked.

Her cheeks heated. "Waiting on you, your Grace."

The duke let the arrow fly. Sure enough, the arrow landed without a sliver of space left to spare beside the first. It would be a lie if she didn't admit that her insides were the consistency of butterscotch. Hot, melted, gooey butterscotch. It was a miracle she was even upright.

Focusing her attention back to the target, she pasted a suitably impressed look on her face. "You're very good," she told him. "This wasn't on the list of hobbies we discussed."

He shrugged. "My father insisted on the mastery of anything that involved tracking and chasing down defenseless animals. He expected precision, and I learned the easiest way to please him was to give it. Just because I do something well doesn't mean I enjoy it."

"That's good to know."

He stared at her and cocked his head. "Now come here."

"I beg your pardon."

Stone gestured with one hand. "Come here and let me teach you how to do this properly so you don't unintentionally murder anyone and ruin my plans with Bolden. The gossip will be unstoppable if I'm engaged to a murderess."

He delivered that in such a bland tone that she frowned before she realized that he was being facetious. Nève peered around him and then looked behind herself, acting as though she were searching for something.

"What are you doing?" he asked.

"Looking for the flying pigs with the forward tails because you made a joke. I mean, they have to be around here somewhere, because quelle folie, the terribly dour Duke of Montcroix might also be on the verge of cracking a real smile." She put a hand up to her brow. "Have you seen them? They're tiny and chubby with the cutest curling tails."

"You are absurd. Pigs, indeed." His lips did that quirking tilt again that made her heart flutter. "Thou dost protest too much, Miss Valery. Stop stalling and come over here."

Nothing could wipe the grin off her own face—not even Vesper's and Effie's identical astonished expressions at the Duke of Montcroix acting like a flesh-and-bone human with blood in his veins instead of ice water for once in his life. She bit back a giggle as she wondered whether they'd start looking for flying pigs as well. Goodness, his unfeeling reputation was truly ludicrous.

She was starting to believe he *could* feel. He just chose not to.

The duke leaned in when she stood in front of him, his voice low. "You're a dancer. Stance is important. You had the right of it. Turn side-on and plant your feet but leave enough flexibility in your knees to feel loose."

Nève was used to speaking of body parts—one had to be as a ballerina—but it certainly wasn't proper in mixed, aristocratic company. Not when he was a duke and everyone was pretending not to watch the couple du jour having an interlude. Nor was it decent coming from his mouth in those deep raspy tones. Or maybe it was her reaction that was indecent.

"Miss Valery, are you paying attention?"

She startled, heat singing her ears. "What, oh yes. Of course. Stance. Flexibility."

Nève glanced over her shoulder to where he stood a respectable foot away—still too close for her comfort—but she suspected that he would have to be somewhere clear on the other side of England for her not to feel his presence. He, as usual, stood impassively as though the instruction affected him not at all.

Piqued, she tossed her head. "Trust me, my limbs beneath these skirts are as loose as you need them to be."

The sharp exhale was his. Satisfaction shot through her. She hadn't meant for her voice to sound so husky, but there it was. She was trifling with the poor man in broad daylight where anyone could overhear their conversation and spread the next juicy on-dit. She could practically see Vesper's ears straining toward them.

"Shoulders back, carriage erect." The duke's voice was pure gravel now, nothing but a commanding rasp. Nève obeyed instantly. Her nipples, too, though they had nothing to do with the orders. She pinned her lips together, not daring to look down for confirmation. She could feel the bloody things! Thank heavens she was facing away from him.

"Good. Now, grip this. Left arm out." Their fingers brushed when he handed her the bow, and her body sizzled as though it housed a lightning storm.

Dieu, this couldn't be proper.

Were people watching them? Her eyes darted up and around. Of course they were. But did they *know*? Surely they could all see right through her, straight to how deliciously rattled she was by his presence. Non, non. This was a simple archery lesson, and she was overreacting. Nève sucked in a choked breath and held out the bow as he'd instructed.

"May I touch you, Miss Valery?" he asked, closer now.

She jumped. A wicked pulse began to hum low between her hips. "I beg your pardon, Your Grace?"

"May I reposition your arms?"

"Oh yes, of course," she replied.

His touch at her elbow, bending it slightly, sent fireworks careening through her. "Firm but not rigid."

Dieu, why did those innocent words sound so erotic?

Nève could only nod as he lifted an arrow and helped her situate it. A soft graze of a gloved fingertip along the underside of her arm made more sparks erupt. She could sense him inching closer, the heat from his body joining hers. "Now pull back and notch the curve of your thumb and forefinger just under the slant of your jaw. Feel the fletching against your cheek."

Nève kept her frame locked and her limbs in place without much effort, though her arm had started trembling. She made a mental note to ask the duke about a room in the residence where she could do her training. It was abnormal for her to go so long without some dancing, and it was evident in the strain on her muscles. She'd been stretching daily in her bedchamber, but it wasn't the same as performing a routine.

"Very good," the duke said, stepping away to admire his handiwork. "Chin up just a smidgen. Now when you are ready, inhale and then release the arrow on the exhale."

She did as he bid, and watched with bated breath as the slim projectile flew toward the target and sank deep. Hers wasn't dead center as his had been, but it was a respectable hit on the outer ring. She hadn't missed! Nève shrieked with victory even as the duke lifted an eyebrow at her celebration.

"Beginner's luck," he said. "Try again."

She rolled her eyes but set up another arrow, repeating all of his steps. This time, the arrow lodged even closer, in between her first shot and his.

"You are a natural," he said. "I am not surprised. There doesn't seem to be anything you can't do well. Saving dukes from cutpurses, dancing, playing the pianoforte, and now archery."

Nève blushed. "You've never seen me truly dance, Your Grace, and besides I am woefully out of practice as I haven't seen the inside of a real ballet studio in a long time." She couldn't hide the wistfulness in her voice and then gave her head a hard shake. "I can also assure you that I cannot sing worth a farthing."

"I doubt that."

Handing the bow to a waiting servant, she grinned up at the duke. "Trust me, when I sing the dogs will be howling alongside any tune of mine in a matter of moments. It's inevitable. Thank you for the lesson, Your Grace."

"You are welcome." Stone stared at her, that hard face once more inscrutable. Nève wondered if she touched her fingertip to his cheek whether it would be cold to the touch, now that all evidence of a warm flesh-and-blood man was gone. A shiver coasted over her skin—though this time, it was one of warning instead of wanting.

"You do that so well," she murmured.

"Do what?"

"Close down," she replied. "One would think you had a handle somewhere that you simply shut off like a faucet."

A muscle flexed in his jaw. "Say goodbye to your friends. I've had enough of this charade, and Bolden should be more than satisfied with our performance."

That arrow dug deep, right into the middle of her chest. She clenched her fists. Had their interlude all been for show? Nothing but a stunt to convince the earl? Tucking away her disappointment, Nève drew in a bracing breath. Everything between her and the duke was simply part of the act, nothing more.

She'd do well to remember that.

Chapter Fourteen

Lysander didn't understand why Nève was staring at him in such surprise. His request wasn't that unreasonable. She blinked. "You wish to go to Yorkshire this morning and return this very evening? Back to London?"

He nodded, wondering why she sounded so shocked. The French railway system was just as advanced as the English, and in some cases, even faster. Trains could reach speeds of over seventy-five miles per hour, and the routes that George Leeman had developed for the North Eastern Railway from London into northern England were swift and efficient.

"We'll leave from King's Cross. The journey should be less than three hours each way. We'll have luncheon there and then return. Trust me, you will be in nothing but the best of comfort." She gave him a dubious look, but nodded. "Be ready in thirty minutes."

"What shall I wear?" she asked.

He glanced at the pale green muslin dress that brought out the chartreuse in her eyes. "That will do nicely, but wear comfortable shoes."

Precisely thirty minutes later, they were ensconced in his coach and on the way to the train station. Lysander tapped his fingers nervously on his thighs and caught Nève's gaze. She smiled. "Did you pick up that bad habit from me? I tend to do that when I'm nervous."

He stopped drumming and curled his fingers into a fist against his trousers. "Coincidentally, it's an old quirk of mine as well. I haven't done it since I was a boy. One of my old tutors who knew of my love for music told me it was a good way to bring me back to the present." He exhaled, worried he'd revealed too much. The inner workings of his mind were his own business, and considering his own father had ridiculed him often for his faults, Lysander didn't advertise his shortcomings. "I'd forgotten I used to do it until I saw you do the same."

"That's smart. Did you get lost in your imagination during lessons?" She gave him a conspiratorial smile. "I did. When I was a girl, my governess said my head was always in clouds made of marshmallows and spun sugar."

"That sounds sticky." Nève burst out laughing, and he couldn't help smiling back, though it was with some discomfort, as if his own lips were rusty at it. He didn't understand why it was so easy to talk to her. She was much better with people than he was, making them feel instantly at ease in her company. "My clouds were different. My brain can get confused, and go from slow and steady to hell-bent in a handful of seconds. The drumming helped. Sometimes, a scent can be helpful, too. My mother used to smell like jasmine. If I smell it now, I can picture her so clearly."

"How wonderful," she murmured, her face turning melancholy beneath the brim of her bonnet. "I can't remember what my mama smelled like. She and Papa were so sick at the end...it erased most of the good memories."

"I'm sorry."

She nodded. "Me, too."

Lysander didn't want to talk about their parents, so he went quiet. He had no desire to answer any questions that might arise about his father. The duke was best left dead and buried. And the last thing he needed was her pity. They lapsed into silence until the coach stopped at the very crowded station.

"Where are we going, if you don't mind my asking?"

He cleared his throat. "Aldenborough. Bolden's estate."

Lysander didn't know why he'd asked her to accompany him. Perhaps the old earl's sentimentality had gotten to him. Or maybe he just didn't want to be alone. Her eyes went wide when he escorted her into the private railcar that was attached to the commercial passenger train. A luxurious saloon car with brocaded windows and ceilings in rich blues and creams greeted them.

"Well, this is fancy," she said.

"I'm not good with crowds of people and loud noises. I feel claustrophobic and it fogs my mind." When she stared at him, he shifted uncomfortably, again vexed with himself for overexplaining. He'd never done that with anyone before. They just had to accept that he was who he was. And most of the ton did because he was a duke.

"Oh," she said. "That's curious. I love people, being around them. For me, the energy is contagious, which is why I suppose I like being onstage."

"I find it crippling." He shrugged. "Though when one is a duke, a man is forgiven almost anything, even a churlish personality, a debatable lack of empathy, and an overly methodical mind."

Nève cocked her head with a wicked grin. "Debatable?"

He blinked. *Oh*, she was joking. He felt his mouth stretch in another of those unfamiliar smiles. Sparkling green eyes danced.

"No one teases you, do they?" she asked.

"Not if they want to remain employed," he said with the slightest raise of his brow, and she froze but then broke into the most beautiful smile when the corner of his lip twitched.

"Goodness, is that a *joke*, Your Grace?"

He bowed. "I am, if anything, Miss Valery, a fast learner."

Nève had seen luxury in her lifetime, but this was beyond expectation. This kind of private rail travel was exceptional. A frown pressed her brows together. While many men would have flaunted their wealth, especially *this* kind of wealth, the Duke of Montcroix did not. He seemed uncommonly neutral to all of it. He enjoyed luxury, that much was clear, but he wasn't defined by it.

The man fascinated her. He was highly intelligent and highly sensitive. She could tell in the way he asked his direct questions and gave only the most succinct and economical of answers. She'd made a joke about his debatable lack of empathy, but it was truly astonishing. Nève wouldn't call him empty of compassion…he was just remarkably spare with emotion.

She studied him surreptitiously as he read the newssheets.

Dark gold hair, groomed as always to a pristine shine. Stern, austere face with that wide mouth that didn't know what to do with itself. High cheekbones, a strong nose, and an intense gray stare that was currently hidden by a fringe of golden-brown lashes. Even in repose, he was rigid, body held upright as if it didn't dare slouch. A glass of whiskey was held carelessly in one hand.

"Why are you staring at me?" he asked, lashes lifting to pierce her with a silver gaze.

She felt her cheeks heat, but lifted her chin. "Sometimes when you're quiet, you're nice to look at."

That stare sharpened, making odd tingles erupt over her skin. "After my mother, you would be the first to think so."

She laughed and then realized he was serious. "Are you fishing for compliments, Your Grace?" The duke looked so astonished that she let out a small giggle. "I suppose that's beneath you, isn't it? You must have staff who are paid simply to bow and scrape, and exalt your ducal magnificence."

Nève was joking, of course, but his face shuttered, going distant and aloof as if she had accused him of a terrible crime. "We should be arriving soon. Do you need anything?"

"No." She shook her head, confused by his abrupt about-face. "Did I say something wrong?"

His lips pulled tight. "My father had such a decree with our servants." He paused. "And blood relatives. Esteem was not earned, it was expected, and when it was not given, the reprisal was severe. I would prefer the people who work for me to respect me as much as I respect them."

Nève did not have time to apologize when the whistle blew, announcing their arrival into York. Within minutes, they were met by a coachman and a waiting carriage. But once they were settled, she cleared her throat. "I didn't mean to cause offense."

"You did not."

But even though his face remained unreadable, she couldn't help feeling she'd hurt him somehow. To distract herself, she peered out the window at the rolling countryside, and when they came upon the drive leading up to the estate, her mouth fell open. Acres of verdant green hills and manicured gardens surrounded an enormous pond with fountains.

The castle itself, when it came into view, was architecturally stunning, with stone towers and sprawling wings, bringing to mind a fairy-tale castle in some beautiful realm. Nose pressed to the window, Nève chuckled at her whimsical thoughts.

"What was that laugh for?" the duke asked.

"It's magical!"

He frowned. "That's why you're laughing?"

She wouldn't let his passionless tone take away her joy. "How can you be so unmoved? It looks like it's straight out of a story-book. Didn't you ever dream about princesses, and knights, and dragons, and gorgeous castles?"

"Why would I?"

She huffed. "You have no imagination. What's your favorite book?"

"*Wuthering Heights.*"

Nève stared at him in surprise. She'd expected him to choose some dull treatise of philosophical claptrap to make himself sound interesting like most other gentlemen in the ton, but he hadn't. "I suppose you like Heathcliff."

"I pity him, actually," he said. "That kind of obsession is destructive. There are lessons to be learned from such a caution-ary tale. Passion like that can only corrode."

Nève had no idea why his words made her heart squeeze. It

was true; the hero had been completely consumed by vengeance, but it wasn't all heartbreak. "Perhaps, but I choose to see the hope in a story like that."

Golden brows lifted. "Hope? You live with roses in your eyes, Miss Valery."

"What's wrong with that? If one were to be consumed by sadness and doubt, what kind of life would that be? I prefer to see my glass as half-full instead of half-empty, Your Grace."

"I make sure my glass is always full," he said.

She shot him a glare. "Some of us can't always afford such luxuries."

Nève had no idea how they'd gone downhill so fast, but by the time they were strolling across the pristine, meticulously kept courtyard toward the residence, her temper was bubbling. She should have stayed in London. "Why did you bring me here? You want to prove to Bolden that you are the right buyer, but you can't even appreciate what a place like this means."

"It's an old castle."

Her mouth fell open at the way he said it, as if it were a tower of crumbling rocks. "You are blind, sir. The earl and his wife built a life here. Look at these gardens! You can see the care in almost every plant."

"That's the benefit of an excellent gardener."

Oh, she wanted to kick him! "You are missing the point," she argued. "Beautiful things grow when there is joy and love, instead of resentment and anger. That's why Heathcliff is such a tragic hero. He could not change. He could not grow. His heart was fallow."

"A fallow heart is impervious."

She scowled. "And dead. It's *dead*, Your Grace. Unable to feel anything."

As she kept pace with his ground-eating strides, she could barely appreciate the enormous velvety roses that perfumed the air.

She advanced upon him. "Stop, Stone. Smell the roses."

"I beg your pardon?" He looked taken aback, eyes wide and gazing at her like she'd lost her senses, which to her own admission, it felt like she had. "Catherine and Heathcliff were indifferent to how love changed them. Love opens your eyes to the smallest kind of beauty."

"So I must smell the roses?" he repeated slowly.

Was he laughing at her? Her scowl grew. "It's entirely figurative, Your Grace, but yes, pour l'amour de Dieu, oui."

"Alors, ça me fera grand plaisir."

The word *pleasure* on his tongue in French nearly made her knees buckle, when it was categorically the time for her knees to stay firm and upright. But it was only when he stood after carefully admiring the rose and smiled that she very nearly swooned.

"You're right," he said. "It was worth the pause."

Lysander grunted as Lushing delivered a solid whack to his gut and followed it with an uppercut to his jaw that would have knocked him to the ground if he hadn't twisted sideways at the last moment. He was distracted, which wasn't ideal in the boxing ring. But he couldn't stop his thoughts from settling on the owner of impetuous green eyes, a mouth made for kissing, and a wit bred for sparring. Bloody hell, he was in all kinds of trouble.

"Good God, man," Lushing panted. "At least pretend to put up a fight."

"I'm out of practice," he said. "I can't recall the last time I came down here."

"The day your mother died. And before that, it was the day your father threatened to disown you for going against him. And before *that*, it would have to be during our Oxford days when no girl would bed you."

Lysander scowled, lifting a hand. "It was a rhetorical question. I don't require an actual timetable."

He looked around, taking in the updated details of the boxing room. The ring had been upgraded with new mats and new ropes, the walls freshly painted. The basement room beneath the bustling tavern above wasn't as grimy and dirty as he remembered, but that underlying scent of sweat and blood was still there, ingrained in the very brick.

"So how's your fiancée?" the earl asked when they'd left the ring and settled at a table nearby for refreshment. "Looks like Vesper has taken her under her wing." He pulled a face. "Not sure how good that is."

"She's fine."

Lushing's brows shot to his hairline. "Fine? It looked like the two of you were about to burn Holland Park to ashes the other day. I felt like an interloping voyeur."

"It wasn't like that," he bit out. Though it had been. Christ, it had. Not to mention the visit to Aldenborough and the sodding roses. He'd wanted to inhale *her*.

She made all those buried feelings inside of him want to escape, when they were better off where they were. In check. In *control*.

His father had beaten that into him: *A duke never shows emotion, a duke demonstrates no weakness, a duke never bends.*

And yet, there he was...smelling goddamned roses and bending like a reed in the wind. The absurdity.

Hence the impromptu boxing session that Lushing had been only too glad to take him up on, though Lysander suspected it was for gossip rather than exercise. They'd boxed at Eton and then at university, mostly in secret, since the old duke would never have approved, and back then, it was the only physical outlet he had. Bottling his emotions because of his father had become second nature. But that was the thing about burying emotions, the human brain wasn't designed to keep all those feelings locked inside. So he'd learned to keep them *out* instead.

Until her.

And now here he was. Boxing and out of practice.

"Any news on Bolden?" Lushing asked. "Will he sell?"

"He hasn't made a final decision yet, but we are close." Lysander swiped a frustrated palm through his damp hair. It was taking too long for comfort. In truth, he wasn't sure how much more proof the man needed. He was engaged. He'd made the effort to demonstrate interest in his fiancée. In full view of the entire ton. He'd visited the damned estate and gushed about it. All the earl needed to do was sign the agreement, but for some reason, Bolden was dragging his feet. Perhaps Lysander needed to do something more drastic. Short of seducing Nève in public, he was out of ideas.

Lushing nodded at the two men who'd entered the ring they'd vacated. "Why do you want this tract of land so badly?" the earl asked. "Surely your coffers are overflowing as it is."

Lysander shrugged. "At this point, I don't want to lose."

Lushing frowned. "Bolden thinks you will raise a family there."

"Bolden will be comforting himself with the immense sum of money I'm planning to pay him," Lysander said, downing the rest of his ale and signaling for a second.

"He's not interested in the money, Stone. He wants to honor his wife's wishes."

Lysander glared at his friend. "Since when have you become so starry-eyed? Don't tell me that you fell for all that true love nonsense."

"True love is real, if either of us cads are ever lucky enough to find it."

"Did Briar tell you that?" he shot back.

Lushing's eyes narrowed, his fingers contracting on his cup. "Don't make me drag you back into that ring and pummel the snot out of you. There is nothing between Lady Briar and me, and if there were, I'd be better off girding my loins with a hundred feet of barbed wire, dousing myself in gasoline, and setting myself on fire. That woman is frightening." He scowled, and faked a shiver. "But stop deflecting. This is about you and your engagement."

"Speaking of, I need a favor. An audition for Miss Valery."

Lushing scrunched up his nose. "Have you seen her dance? Is she any good?"

"No, I haven't seen her onstage. But on that note, can you talk to your friends at the Lyceum and arrange a meeting with Falconer?"

"I can, but it's not as though she won't be recognized as the

Dour Duke's French bride. People are starting to take notice of her."

"Then arrange it in private," Lysander said.

Lushing's brows drew together, but a wicked light grew in his eyes. "A private audition, Stone? May I remind you that this isn't Mayfair, and Edmund isn't rumored to be a monk. A woman like Miss Valery won't go without attention, and if she has talent, there's no telling how that will go."

"I will be there," he ground out.

"Ha! I fucking knew it."

Lysander forced his mounting irritation down. "Knew what?"

"You like her."

"There's a difference between what your infantile mind thinks this is and ensuring she doesn't get taken advantage of. This is a betrothal agreement, not one of your romantic productions." Lysander pushed back his chair and stood, suddenly desperate to escape. "Where's my coat? I have a prior engagement."

"Is that all it is between you two?" Lushing pressed. "An agreement?"

He shrugged into his coat and jammed his hat on his head. "What else can it be? I am a duke. Marriage is a necessary construct."

"You are a harsh man, Stone. What if she wants more?"

Lysander lifted one shoulder, but he couldn't help the beat of hope that pulsed through him despite her refusal. "She doesn't. But I suppose if she does, that will be up to her."

CHAPTER FIFTEEN

The noise of heavy furniture being moved as well as loud voices directing what sounded like a horde of servants drew Nève downstairs. She had just finished replacing the ribbons on her pointe shoes, which had been left ignored for too long and were starting to fray.

Following the noise, she darted out of the way as a train of servants ferrying chairs to another part of the house came down the corridor. She spied Millicent, who was supervising all the commotion, and Nève sidled over to her. "What's going on?"

"Some kind of house cleaning," she replied with a dubious look. "Who knows what maggot my nephew has gotten in his head now. He probably did not like the look of the floorboards or the windows. It's not like this ballroom is ever used for its actual purpose."

Nève frowned. "The duke has never hosted a ball?"

"Not him. His father, yes. Lysander hated this room, especially after my sister died. She threw such lovely parties, but it's been closed up for years." Millicent's eyes brightened. "Do you suppose he's planning to host a ball? Oh, that would be delightful!"

"Perhaps," Nève murmured. He had been spending quite a bit

of time with Viscount Treadway and Lord Bolden of late, so that was a possibility. "Where *is* the duke?"

Millicent pointed. "Over there."

Following the direction of her finger, Nève stifled a gasp. Of course she hadn't recognized him because said duke was coatless, shirtsleeves rolled up and dark gold hair disheveled, carrying the end of a rolled Persian rug that had to weigh a hundred pounds over one shoulder. She blinked. Why *was* he carrying that with so many servants about? Not that she was complaining, watching the mesmerizing bunch and roll of those arm muscles as he handed over the rug to Evans.

The duke walked over to them, and Nève had to fight to take air into her lungs. "Your Grace," she greeted him, keeping her eyes fixed firmly on his face, instead of the glistening, sweaty neck that was scandalously sans cravat.

"Ladies. What do you think?"

"Are we throwing a ball?" Millicent asked.

His brow rose. "Not yet, I'm afraid, Aunt. Though ballrooms are meant for dancing and this one has been quite ignored. So I've decided to put it out of its misery and—"

"Not another study! You already have several, including my favorite salon, which you've overtaken!" Millicent blurted with a horrified look, and Nève had to hide her giggle. A pair of gray eyes met hers and slid away before he cleared his throat. "No, it's for Miss Valery." He let out a small cough. "A space for her to dance."

They both goggled at him, Nève's jaw dropping open as if she hadn't heard him correctly. "I beg your pardon?"

Millicent had an odd look on her face, one hand clapped to her breast as she stared at her nephew with glossy eyes. "Oh, you dear boy."

Those steely eyes returned to Nève's, something gentle and tender glinting in them that made her chest feel like he'd reached in and taken hold of it in his fist. "It's for you. You said you hadn't danced in some time, and, well, it's not getting any use." Cheekbones flushing a dull red, he scraped a palm over the back of his head. "It's not quite what you're accustomed to, but the men are installing a wooden ballet bar on that end."

Nève blinked in utter shock. He wasn't just clearing the ballroom for her. He was transforming it into an actual studio. "You did this for me?" she whispered.

Stiffening slightly, he let out a dismissive noise and folded his arms, those broad cheekbones of his flushing deeper. "Lushing has arranged a meeting with the manager of the Lyceum. You will need to practice, if you intend to audition."

"Stone. This is incredible." She fought the urge to scream with joy and fling her arms around him. An audition! He'd held true to his promise.

"It's nothing. It's all part of the arrangement."

There it was. That autocratic, cool answer as though it were no more than duty or part of the *agreement*, but Nève knew better. She *sensed* it. The problem was she didn't know how to feel about it. She much preferred when he was aloof and cold—that duke she could handle. This man, with his deeply thoughtful nature and unexpected kindness, she could not afford to let in. But she had a sinking feeling she was already much too late on that score.

"Thank you, Stone. This means more than I can say."

"You're welcome." His mouth opened as though he wanted to say something else, but then he closed it, and gave a clipped bow. "If you will excuse me, Aunt, Miss Valery, I have an appointment."

After he left, Nève kept a close eye on the installation of the bar, also under the watchful guidance of Finley. She needn't have worried. The specifications and height were perfect. When Millicent tottered off, Nève was left to wander the large ballroom. It was perfect for her needs, with three sets of colossal windows and lots of light. The room was undeniably grand with gold filigree work framed by ornate drapes and a massive wall of gilded mirrors on one side. She could easily imagine a splendid ball being thrown here. But given that the duke did not entertain or have any plans to entertain, she would have the enormous room to herself.

Nève watched Finley direct the last of the footmen to carry out the smaller pieces of furniture, including end tables and decorative vases. If the servants were curious, they did not speak openly, neither did they question the duke.

"Thank you, Finley," she said. "And Evans, of course."

The butler bowed, and the footman shot her a mischievous grin over his shoulder. It was a good thing she was quite immune to that smile because the way to her heart obviously wasn't a pretty face... clearly, a balance bar in a ballroom was all it took to make her swoon.

Why had Stone done this?

At times, he was so impossible to read. After their last outing to Aldenborough, he'd kept his distance, and Nève wasn't quite sure how to react, so she'd followed his lead. Stone hadn't accepted any other social invitations in the past week, and she'd hardly seen hide or hair of him. Then again, he'd been busy in here.

Doing this for *her*.

Nève closed the doors and spun in the center of the room. Though what looked like Stone's pianoforte had been moved into the far corner—the sight of which made her blush—and unless he played for her, she would have to imagine the music, but that was no hardship. Most of the pieces she danced to were in her head anyway.

Inhaling deeply, she performed a few simple stretches, pliés, and floor exercises to acclimate her stiff limbs until her body felt warm and liquid. Thankfully, she'd chosen a light morning dress today, and she reached underneath to untie and remove the smaller walking crinoline. There, that was better. She tucked the sides of the excess fabric into the ties of her garters so that the length would not tangle in her legs. It was indecent how the muslin clung to her limbs, but no one was here to bear witness.

Removing her shoes, Nève tied her slippers and rose en pointe. Her toes ached, but in the best way. At least they weren't blistered and bleeding. Not yet, anyway. A ballerina's toes were sometimes the stuff of nightmares.

With another inhale, Nève began one of the later movements for *La Sylphide*, channeling the lyrical soft motions of one of her favorite ballerinas, Marie Taglioni, the Comtesse de Voisins, who had perfected the role some thirty years ago. Her father had created the ballet just for her. Nève smiled, feeling her body fall gracefully into the familiar arrangement of the sylph dancing in the forest, her feet twisting and pirouetting to the melody of imaginary violins in a complicated sequence of fouettés en tournant. The whipped turns made her breathless.

The comtesse had also composed *Le Papillon*, the role for which Nève had been the understudy in Paris before Lord Durand had chased her away. Imagining the light sounds of the musical score in her head, she began the solo movement for the butterfly, the short little hopping, chassés, and complex battements, snatching the breath from her. Soon, energy flooded her limbs and she spun and leaped, letting the dance fill her body until the end position on bended knee.

Slow clapping filled the room, and Nève stood so quickly she almost tumbled. Her skin tingled with belated awareness as her gaze fell on the duke, who stood in a corner near a door at the far end of the room. "Oh, Your Grace, I didn't realize you'd come back," she blurted. "I thought you had an appointment."

"I do, soon."

"Oh."

Her gaze swept him, only just noticing in the time he'd been gone, he'd changed. He was back to the put-together, immaculate duke she knew, from the tip of his well-groomed hair to his polished Hessians. A part of her mourned the loss of the rumpled look from earlier when he'd carried the rug...the version of him with the beating heart, against whom she had little defense.

"You are spectacular," he said in a low rumbling voice, eyes lit with admiration.

A flush of pleasure filled her. "I am not at my best."

He pushed off the wall and stalked closer, that unreadable gaze of his fastening to her heated face. The ballroom was huge, and yet Nève felt crowded by his presence. Ballet always made her feel full and on edge, but this feeling was different. It flooded her body from the tips of her sore toes to the hair on her head. The duke's eyes fell to her tucked skirts, darkening at the sight of her exposed legs, and Nève hurriedly tugged the fabric from their holds. The soft muslin brushing against the sensitive bare skin of her upper thighs made her catch her breath. She bit her lip, and a sound like a growl ripped from the duke's chest.

Dieu...

He prowled closer yet, and her breath stuttered in her lungs as she smoothed the flimsy skirts, wishing she hadn't removed the dratted crinoline.

"It's improper, I know," she began, her voice hoarse. "But I thought I'd be alone."

"Don't apologize," he told her.

Fists clenched at his sides, he stopped a few feet away. Thank heavens. Nève let out the breath she'd been holding.

A smoldering stare met hers. "Which ballet was that last one?"

"*Le Papillon*," she replied, her tongue thick and uncooperative in her mouth. "Taglioni's. It premiered at the Paris Opera a handful of years ago. I was the understudy for Farfalla, the butterfly."

"You should have been its star."

Heat suffused her. "Thank you, but there are many others much better than me, Your Grace. More so now that I have not been dancing every day." She paused. "In truth, I had forgotten what it felt like to dance just for the sake of dancing. For the sheer pleasure of it."

His eyes dilated at the last, focusing on her lips. "How so?"

She lifted her shoulder. "I danced to feed my sister and myself, to keep us warm with a roof over our heads and not on the streets or begging for charity. When you need to do something to survive, it can lose its spark."

"And you lost yours," he guessed.

A grateful smile curved her lips. "Thanks to your generosity, I'm discovering it again. The inner passion I had as a girl." She let out an embarrassed laugh.

"You are welcome."

Nève blushed and swallowed. "You've given me a reprieve from the exhausting life of Geneviève Valery, an intermission between acts that I didn't know I needed."

She didn't know why she was confessing all of this, but she wanted him to know just how much the small thoughtfulness meant to her.

"Why were you ousted again?" His brows drew together. "If I recall, you mentioned when we first met that it was something to do with a rotting, rodent-souled roué?"

Nève blinked. Her memory of their meeting led her back to the steps in the square when she'd been fuming at her lack of luck and cursing a blue streak at the man who had brought her to that point. "I was not myself then, Your Grace. I was…angry."

He arched a brow. "That temper of yours is part of the reason you dance so passionately. Your emotions rule your every step."

"The theater director says I should focus on technique."

"Technique can be taught," he replied. "True passion for the dance cannot."

She lifted her shoulder in a shrug. and they fell into silence before he took one step forward. It was nothing, a few inches, and yet she felt the space between them shrink. "Who was he?"

"Who was who?"

"The roué?"

Nève exhaled. "What does it matter?"

"It matters to me."

The shadow of a bruise colored the bottom right side of his jaw, and she frowned, closing the distance between them before she could stop herself or realize what she was doing. Her fingers lifted to the discolored skin, visible now that the fine layer of scruff had been removed by his valet. "What happened here?"

"Nothing." His answer was a low rasp that did things to her. Heated things.

"It doesn't look like nothing."

His tongue peeked out between his lips. "Lushing got in a lucky blow, that's all."

"You were brawling?" she asked, eyes going wide. She could not imagine the stoic duke resorting to fisticuffs.

"Boxing."

She nodded. "Ah, yes, one of the precious few hobbies you mentioned."

Nève blushed, realizing her fingertips were still touching him. Her hand fell away.

"Will you refuse to tell me his name?" Stone demanded in a harsh whisper.

With a sharp inhale, Nève shook her head to clear it and stepped away. Oui, she needed to put some distance between them before she did something unapologetically foolish. Focus on Durand. The thought of that rat-faced, selfish bastard never failed to invoke fury. "You don't know him. A French marquis."

"His name," he asked, a muscle coming to life in that hard jaw.

"Why are you so insistent?"

He scowled. "Why are you evading the question?"

"I don't need you to fight my battles for me, Your Grace," she said. "And in any case, Durand is in the past."

"Durand," he repeated.

Blast it. Nève actually quaked at the deadly look in his eyes. "He's nothing, Stone. The man is a worm and not worth the trouble. Trust me."

But her words had no effect on him whatsoever because without another sound, the duke turned and quit the room. She shook her head, wondering what had set him off this time. It wasn't as if he were going to sail to France and pummel the man into a pulp.

Though Nève had to admit . . . the idea was distinctly gratifying.

CHAPTER SIXTEEN

Christ. Catching Nève mid-dance had damn near unmanned him.

He'd never seen anything more exquisite than the vision of her in that room, moving like liquid flame across the polished floor. The skill of that lithe, supple body as it had whipped around and around and around, her toes kicking out in brisk beats, had rendered him speechless. But it was the look of pure, unhindered joy on her face that had made his heart crash against the stone walls of its tomb.

Even now hours later as he lay in bed, she consumed his thoughts. Cursing his lack of sleep and restless state, Lysander shot out of bed nude and stalked to the window, the gardens shadowy and dark under cover of a moonless night. He scrubbed his hand over his chin and ground his jaw. He needed to put his fantasies to rest and go back to bed.

He had an early meeting with Treadway the next morning about the railway company's books. Something wasn't adding up, and Lysander had to get to the bottom of it before any unethical practices came back to kick him in the arse. Which meant getting some sleep instead of dreaming about the beautiful ballerina down the hall.

Lysander stared back at the mess of bedclothes, indicative of his chaotic state. His hand drifted down his abdomen, catching the tip of his swollen cock, and he hissed at the excruciating fullness. Hell, he should just deal with it and go to sleep. Instead, he reached for a discarded pair of trousers, dragged them on, and left his bedchamber.

Silent footsteps and several turns took him to Nève's closed door. There was no sound coming from within. He let out a grunt. Why would there be? It was the goddamned middle of the night, and he was the only fool awake, pining for something he could not have.

You are pitiable, Lysander Blackstone.

Swallowing his self-despair, he turned again, headed downstairs, and was wandering aimlessly through the kitchens when he crashed into a stool that made an unholy clatter. At this rate, he'd awaken the entire household. When he heard footsteps on the servants' staircase, he let out a low curse as a light flickered on.

"Your Grace?" a sleepy-eyed Finley asked, clothed in a sleeping cap and robe. "May I get you something?"

He shook his head. "No, go back to bed. I'm working late and will be in my study."

"Very well, Your Grace."

The butler nodded and left, taking his lamp with him. The staff was used to his eccentric work habits at night. But Lysander didn't head to his study. He walked to the music room instead. Since the pianoforte had been moved to Nève's makeshift ballroom, his fingers grazed over the cello. As she had guessed, this one had been made by Antonio Stradivari, and he'd paid a fortune for it. In his current mood, he did not want to handle it. Lysander selected a second, newer instrument made by John Betts, who had designed it based on the Stradivari model.

Pulling out a chair, he sat and arranged the cello between his open knees, placing the neck of it against his chest, before reaching for the bow. The pads of his left hand hovered over the fingerboard and pressed down as he drew the bow lightly over the strings. The low, rich sound filled the space. It had been so long since he'd played, and yet, the music came back with an ease that surprised him.

Closing his eyes, he started with Bach's little-known cello suites, which he knew by heart. The familiar scales eased him before he descended into another melody of his own arrangement, the composition mournful and hopeful all at once. His fingers held a vibrato and then sped up along the strings before slowing to something more poignant. All he could see in his mind's eyes was Nève dancing, her slender body graceful and elegant. Fluid arms, sinuous torso, and those endlessly long legs...

Bloody hell, did he *mean* to torture himself? He came to an abrupt halt.

"Don't stop." She stood like the ballerina nymph she was, clad in a gossamer white wrapper, her dark hair tied into a loose knot.

"What are you doing out of bed?" he asked, his voice sounding hoarse, like it hadn't been used in decades. He swallowed past the sudden lump in his throat.

"I heard a crash before, and when I investigated, I saw you come in here," she said. "It's my turn. You watched me dance today, so it's only fair that I get to watch you."

"Go back to bed, Geneviève, or if not, shut the door behind you."

With a visible shudder, she sucked her lower lip into her

mouth, and desire shot through him. He put the cello to the side and watched her eyes hood at the sight of his scandalously shirtless state. For a second, he did not know if she would stay or leave, but after a few fraught heartbeats, she closed the door.

He kept himself firmly in the chair—any decisions about where they went from here would be hers to make. She was the conductor of this concerto.

"You are spectacular." His own words echoed back to him.

Lysander canted his head as she traced the periphery of the room. "Thank you."

He waited with bated breath and a drumming heart until he felt her creep up behind him, but still he didn't move. A gust of air hissed out from between his lips as he felt her fingertips dancing over his shoulders. Or maybe he had imagined the ephemeral sensation because he wanted her to touch him so badly.

But he hadn't imagined it. Not when her hands drifted through his hair and she murmured, "So soft."

"What are you doing, Nève?" he rasped.

"No," she whispered. "Call me Geneviève."

"*Geneviève*." It was part groan, part plea. "You don't have to do this."

"No, I don't."

Her fingers dug into the bunched muscles at his nape, and he held himself painfully still. While it was frustrating not to see her—not to be able to read her expressive face for a hint of what she was thinking—she was leading this dance. She would face him when she was ready. "Then what is it you want?"

"What I want is simple," she replied quietly. "Call it an amendment to our original agreement if you will."

The original agreement was bound by payment. Lysander wanted this to have no ties to the first. He shook his head. "Let us make a new one."

"Terms?"

He groaned as her fingers kneaded lower. "Just two. Only consent and...pleasure."

Her breath feathered the hot skin at his ear. "Then I agree, Your Grace."

Blood simmering, Lysander wanted to scoop her in his arms, but he forced himself to remain in place, letting her set the pace. She released his shoulders and moved to stand beside him. At long last, he could see her beautiful face and those glimmering sea-glass eyes that held so much emotion.

"This is madness," she whispered. "But I fear I'll burst if..." She trailed off.

"If what?" he asked.

"If I don't touch you." Her teeth sank into her lip. "If you don't touch me."

A chuckle broke from him. "I know exactly what you mean."

After a few protracted moments, she lowered herself to sit in his lap, a gasp leaving her lips at the feel of him against her hip. Surprise lit her eyes, but not embarrassment. She was not a prude, his tempestuous ballerina. No, she wouldn't be. He admired that about her...her natural confidence and her complete ease in her skin. "I have a confession to make first."

"Then tell me."

Nève blushed, the pink blooming along the velvet curve of her cheek. "I have never done this before."

"Propositioned a man?" he asked with a grin.

An answering smile tugged at her lips. "I love when you smile," she whispered. "It makes me feel like I've won something of immense value."

"Why?"

"Because you don't do it often." She let out a breath and met his eyes. "And no, that's not what I meant. I mean lie with a man. I've never done it before."

Lysander blinked. "You're a virgin."

"Don't sound so shocked, Stone." Her laugh trickled through him. "I know some dancers have a fast reputation, but not all of us take lovers, despite the temptation or ample opportunity. And it just so happens I didn't want to be with anyone in such an intimate way. At least until now."

With that, she leaned in and kissed him, her tongue flicking lightly across the seam of his lips. Lysander jolted into action, his mouth dancing with hers in teasing sips and velvet nudges. The shallow kiss was hot, explosive, even as he kept his hands where they were. He didn't need them, not yet. Hell, she was so fucking sweet—she tasted like passion, sugar, and sin. Her tongue teased his, daring it to chase hers back into her mouth. He nibbled at her lips, drinking her in and wanting more.

"Wait." He broke away.

Her eyes glittered and her mouth was wet. "Yes, Your Grace?"

"Why now?" He drew in a breath. "Are you doing this out of obligation?"

She laughed. "To you?"

Lysander gave a short nod. He was not unwitting enough to ignore that he held the power in their relationship. Nève shook her head, her palms going to his chest like twin brands scorching his skin. They slid over his muscles, and his breath caught in his lungs. Devil take it, he was going to explode just from her touching him.

"Answer me, please," he bit out.

"No. This is my choice. I want you." A fingernail scraped around his nipple, making him shudder. "But now, Your Grace, we need to make sure that *you* know what you're getting into."

"What do you mean?" he growled as those torturous fingers trailed lower, skipping over the ridged rise of his abdomen. His cock leaped, and a satisfied smile curled her full lips.

God, she might be inexperienced, but there was nothing innocent in that sultry, knowing expression. It was the look of a woman who knew her own power.

Soft lips brushed his brow. "I have a temper and like to do things my own way."

"I am ruthless and have no heart," he countered.

Her mouth slicked over his. "I'm willful and stubborn."

"I'm callous and cold."

She reared back, lust-bright eyes searching his. "I burn hot."

"Then burn us both."

Lysander growled, took her hips in his hands, ran his palms up her spine, and dragged her to him. Her breasts crushed against his chest as his tongue plundered her mouth. She kissed him back just as fiercely, all lips and teeth and voracious hunger. Nève kissed as she danced, with passion and purpose.

His hands hovered at the ribbons to her wrapper. "May I?"

"Yes," she whispered. "Yes to all of it."

With a groan, he tugged at the ties, letting the wrapper slide from her creamy shoulders. The night rail underneath left little to the imagination, the lace bodice hugging the top of her bosom making him salivate. He couldn't wait to get his mouth on her soft pliant skin. But first, he had other plans.

Gathering the fabric of her night rail in one hand, he tugged her hem high, exposing her trim ankles and svelte calves. He wanted to trail his tongue over every inch of her. He would soon. Lysander lifted her easily and turned her so that her spine was pressed to his chest. He closed his knees and swung each of her legs over his. The position was deeply erotic. What would follow would be, too.

"What are you doing?" she mumbled.

He bit her neck between her shoulder and nape, not enough to break her delicate skin, but enough for her to still. He soothed the sting with his tongue until she moaned. "Playing you."

"Oh," she whispered on a throaty sigh.

"Arms up," he commanded, and the feel of her graceful back arching against him nearly ended this before it began. He breathed her in, and his fingers wandered down the front of her, easing her bodice down and fondling wanton handfuls of each breast in his palms. He rolled the taut, tender peaks of her nipples between his thumbs and forefingers. Her whimper of pleasure was music to his ears.

"Don't stop," she whispered when his hand stilled on her flat, linen-covered stomach. He wanted nothing more than her bare skin, but patience was required. And care. He wanted this to be good for her. "Please, Stone."

"Lysander."

She pushed up into his hand, obstinate to the last. "*Stone*."

He tweaked her left nipple as his right hand stalled just above her mound. "Call me Lysander, or this stops."

He felt her laughter echo through him, even as she leaned back, arching voluptuously, chin tilted sideways to offer him her lips. "Kiss me, Lysander."

He savored the three syllables of his name for the smallest moment before lowering his head to oblige her command. Biting her bottom lip as his hands delved beneath the hem of her night rail, he inched his feet apart. Nève gasped as her knees mimicked the path of his, her long legs opening like doors to the greatest of treasures. Lysander groaned, relishing her sharp inhalation when his fingers found her bare, exposed sex.

Fuck, she was drenched.

"Is this all for me?" he rasped in her ear.

She wriggled her arse against his cock and then moaned as the friction of his fingers pressed into her. "As much as all that is for me."

He ground his hips upward. "It is. But later."

He strummed his playful fingers into her cleft. Now was only for her.

Nève's entire body vibrated as Stone—*Lysander*—played her like a skilled maestro. She felt as though her body was at the mercy of every single scrape, pluck, and swirl of his fingers.

A thick finger pressed into her, and she bit back her moan. Dieu, the way he touched her, stroking along her soaked center, was maddening. A soft stroke here, a pinch there. Something that felt like a vibrato on a spot that made her want to scream.

His tongue tormented her ear, teeth scraping against the sensitive lobe, and she lifted her jaw for another drugging kiss. This time, she bit him, making those storm-cloud eyes darken with lust. His left hand slid up her throat, holding her to him as their kiss grew more fervent. She wanted him to let go of that exacting control for once in his life.

She wanted him to *let go*.

Hungrily, Lysander kissed her, devouring her lips as her body wound tighter and tighter, one finger and then two spreading her. Impaling her. She tugged wildly at the ends of his hair, daring him to strum her harder. To *work* her harder. Her virtuoso didn't disappoint. Nève gave herself over to him and to the sensations building in her body until his thumb pressed into the bud at the top of her sex. The crescendo lifted her and took her under, her cries of pleasure consumed by his mouth.

"Beautiful," he murmured against her lips, when her body finally quieted.

Nève slumped against him in a boneless heap, her limbs askew and her heart pounding like she'd just done fifty fouettés en tournant without stopping. She felt giddy and weightless, and thoroughly satisfied. Lysander drew his knees together and turned her so that she was cradled into his chest.

She smiled up at him, an idle finger trailing over the hard line of his jaw. "That was enlightening," she murmured. "I suppose I now have an intimate understanding of why you're such a talented musician. Parts of me are still humming."

Her tone made him chuckle, the rumbling sound vibrating through her own body. Heavens, how she cherished the rare sound of his laughter. Effortlessly, he stood, scooping her up, and she looped her arms around his neck, pressing her lips to the wild pulse at the base of his throat. "We're not done here yet, Your Grace," she whispered against his skin.

"We're not?"

She bit him. "I seem to recall an order for us both to burn, and yet, I'm the only one in flames." She tugged his face down to hers and kissed him hard, sighing with pleasure as the taste of him filled her. "I want to see you undone."

"Should we find a proper bedchamber?" His voice emerged as a raw growl.

Nève shook her head. "I like this room. It suits us. We're on even footing in here. You're not a duke. I'm not a woman on the wrong side of the ton. We're a musician and a dancer. No more, no less. United simply in our passion for music and art."

The duke stared at her as if she'd said something profound, and Nève frowned. She hadn't, but perhaps at the core of it was that he also wished to escape the weight of who he was.

"You're right," he rasped. "It does suit rather well."

She gave a startled squeak as he deposited her on a chaise longue at the far end of the room. Nève swallowed hard. She'd felt his size, and now she wanted to see him.

Her eyes locked with his and then drifted down to his rumpled clothing. "Those need to come off, Your Grace."

"What about your clothes?"

"You had your turn. It's mine now. Strip."

There was outrage sparking there—a warning that she might

be crossing the line of ducal propriety—but there was fire, too. And lust. So much lust it took her breath away. Lysander Blackstone, the fearsome Duke of Montcroix, wasn't used to being ordered about. Her eyes narrowed at the deepening flush over his cheekbones...and he might *like* it!

She was delighting in her newfound power when, with one flick, his trousers dropped to the floor, and suddenly, she couldn't articulate a single word. His wicked smirk was worth her incoherent mumble, because by every star in the night sky, he had to be the most exquisitely formed man she'd ever seen. Nève couldn't stop staring. Strong and honed, his legs were thick and dusted in blond hair. Her eyes fastened to the equally thick organ between them, and her throat went dry. "Ciel, you're perfect."

The duke came down on one knee between her legs and took her mouth with his. Her night rail went flying, tugged off her body by expert hands until she lay as naked as him.

"Your body is the perfect one."

"I'm as flat as a crêpe."

His fingers found one of her small breasts, kneading it. "I happen to love crêpes."

She could only gasp as his finger plucked her nipple like a string on a harp. Who was she to complain? Nève filled her own palms with him, roaming over his muscled back, skipping down the indent of his spine, and finally cupping the firm globes of his buttocks. Dieu but the man was hard all over. She giggled thinking of the words she'd said to Vesper: *Stone is Stone.* Well, now, she could, in fact, confirm that that was categorically true.

He. Was. Rock. Hard.

Everywhere.

She'd felt the prod of him earlier, when he was lodged beneath her bottom, but now, aligned with her slick, bare core as he was, she was aware of every single solid inch. Inches that were soon to be buried inside of her...somehow. Her bubble of laughter took on a hysterical pitch.

"What's so funny?" he asked, pressing hot, wet kisses down her neck.

"Nothing," she said.

He tweaked her nose. "Tell me."

"The ballerinas in the corps love their bawdy talk, but I'm certain that the men they've been with have to be half your size." She wriggled her hips, making them both gasp when the crown of him notched intimately against her. "I was thinking that you're going to need a mallet to get that in there."

He laughed, and the sound made her smile and scowl at the same time. "I've seen what your body can do, and trust me, it can take me," he said.

"Doubtful, but you're the one with the experience here."

Lysander took her nipple into his mouth, making warmth descend straight through to her sex, and ran the fingers of his right hand down her ribs. The sensation—both erotic and ticklish—made her body arch up into him. When his hand reached the outer part of her thigh, he hitched up her leg, bent at the knee, and then walked his fingers across the back of her calf, extending her leg.

"So flexible," he murmured.

"Perks of being a dancer," she said with a delicious shiver at the hedonistic stretch.

His lips found her ankle, and Nève gasped as the new position made him press up against her in an explicitly carnal way. She'd never felt so exposed, so decadently open. She loved it. And from the look on his face, so did he.

"My ability to perform a front split proves nothing, Your Grace," Nève said, squeezing the globe of his arse and nipping at his jaw. She bent her knee and hooked it around his shoulder, making him groan as his huge body anchored hers to the chaise.

"Then we shall have to get right to it, I suppose," he said, voice thick with desire. Gray, almost black, eyes met hers. "Are you certain?"

Nève could see the strain on his face, in the corded power of his neck, the passion etched in every line of his features. His lips, usually so stern, were fuller and wetter, bruised from her attentions. Deep color filled those prominent cheekbones. Dieu, he was beautiful. She wanted him deconstructed and unstrung. She wanted him lost to everything. Lost to her.

She wanted to see the stony Duke of Montcroix shatter.

"Yes," she said, and rolled her hips. "Now, Lysander."

He did not wait, angling his hips so that the rounded crown inched into her body. Head thrown back at the sensual invasion, Nève bit her bottom lip, fingers grasping his shoulders, nails biting into his skin. Her body was more than prepared to receive him, but the unfamiliar stretch still ached. Her other leg came up to hook around the base of his thighs as he breached her tight passage. She let out an inaudible curse in French.

"Are you in pain?" he asked, halting abruptly, his voice raw.

"Don't you dare stop, Lysander, or I will cheerfully murder you."

At the mumbled threat, he laughed and nudged her nose with his. "Where on earth did you come from, Geneviève?"

Gracious, she loved when he said her full name. "You found me in Covent Garden."

"I think you found me." He grinned down at her—a full no-holds-barred grin that lit his eyes and showed his teeth, including one charmingly turned incisor.

One golden eyebrow quirked. "What?"

"You're so beautiful, Lysander," she whispered.

"I think all of this pleasurable sensation might have you confused, my lady. I am not and will never be a handsome man."

"You are to me," she said. "You've always been." The soft admission slid out of her, and for a moment, Nève worried that she might have spoiled the moment by being too maudlin, but he did not seem to notice. Though it was quite hard *not* to be emotional, when a man was about to enter her body for the first time. Then again, that had been her choice, not his. She forced levity into her next words to get her back to level ground. "Come now, Your Grace, there's good virtue to be taken."

"I'd prefer it to be given," he replied in a tender voice that made it clear he *had* noticed.

She kissed him. "It's yours."

Lysander pressed forward, the impossibly thick girth of him filling her to the brim. When he was fully seated, they both groaned, and when he started to move, Nève could hardly think. Her mind and body were overwhelmed with him. She felt the pleasure coiling and growing inside her body, the start of the unending fouettés snatching her breath.

"I want you to come again," he said, rocking into her.

Nearly there already, Nève reached her fingers down between their bodies and circled the part of her that ached. It didn't take much. When her sex began to tighten around him, he growled with deep satisfaction. A few more strokes, and bliss swallowed her whole. Her knees had shifted to bracket the sides of his hips, and Nève held on for dear life as his body drove into hers. He wasn't gentle and she didn't care.

In this moment, she belonged to Lysander Blackstone.

And in the next, when he came undone, roaring his release to the heavens—his strikingly beautiful face overtaken by raw, unguarded pleasure—he was hers, too.

Chapter Seventeen

It was impossible to do any work without thinking of her every time his thoughts wandered, which was much too often. Lysander sighed, slumped back into his chair, and closed his eyes. Visions of intertwined limbs and writhing bodies, and the memory of how sublime it had felt to slide into Nève's warmth, burst behind his eyelids, making him crave her even more. He felt his trousers pull tight, and he shifted irritably in his seat. This was hardly the time for arousal, though where Nève was concerned, his body seemed to have its own mind.

Focus!

Lysander cursed under his breath. He had an appointment with Treadway to square away the railway's finances, but the slippery bastard was late. With so many eyes on him, Lysander had to make sure the ledgers were clean, especially since there had been some new rumblings in Parliament. The bill he'd recently championed through the Lords was meant to govern investments in rail and shipping companies, protecting investors against dishonest trading, bribery, and illicit commissions. Treadway and Clareville Railway had come up as a potentially suspicious enterprise during discussions, taking Lysander by surprise.

Just when he was about to summon his carriage and go looking for the man himself, a whistling Treadway strolled into his study as though he didn't have a care in the world, and plopped his lanky frame into an armchair. "Got any coffee, old chap?"

"I'm sorry, Your Grace," Finley said. "The gentleman did not give me a chance to announce him."

"The proper address is Your Grace, Treadway," Lysander ground out, irritated that the man thought it fit to walk into his home without being announced, but it wasn't Finley's fault. He dismissed the butler with a nod, and turned back to Treadway. "This isn't a hotel, and you're late. You were supposed to be here two hours ago."

"You're in a mood, *Your Grace*." The corner of Treadway's lip lifted into a mocking grin. "You don't see me demanding for you to address me as the Right Honorable Viscount Treadway, do you?"

Lysander pinched the bridge of his nose between his thumb and forefinger and squeezed hard. "My time is valuable. Did you bring the documents?"

Treadway picked his teeth with the corner of a nail. "Working on it."

"The meeting with Bolden is next week," he said in clipped tones. "Once we have the property in hand, I will start the demolition. The finances, including the investor shares, for the railway must be in order. I need to see the share distributions and associated funds."

"Don't worry your tedious little brain, Your Grace," Treadway said, making Lysander clench his jaw with rage. He remembered that Nève had picked up on the viscount's unflattering opinion of him once before. He hadn't thought it mattered then, but it did now.

"My tedious brain is losing its patience, Treadway."

"You'll get them. Why do you need them so badly, anyway? It's just the usual columns of shares and stock prices that you've already looked through. The company is solvent and the investors will get the dividends promised."

Lysander narrowed his eyes. "Which is what?"

"A hefty return on their investment." Treadway patted his gaudy waistcoat, and Lysander took in the obviously new kit. The viscount was a wealthy man, having inherited some thirty thousand pounds from his late father, but he was notoriously careless with money.

"The latest accounts, Treadway, by tomorrow," he said.

"I need at least two days."

Lysander gritted his teeth. "Tomorrow."

Ignoring the threat, the viscount gave a placating nod. "So how's your ladybird?" he asked. "Looks like you and the French chit are getting cozy."

Lysander swallowed his disgust. Had the man always been this unctuous? Or was he only noticing it since talking with Nève, and her mention of dancers being treated like commodities? About how *she* was treated by men like Durand? It rankled because men like Durand and Treadway were much too common, assuming everything was their due. He shook his head to clear it. Now was not the time to get riled up on Nève's behalf, though the recollection of Durand harassing her tied his already strained humors into knots.

"Have you sampled her yet?" Treadway was saying. "Can't hurt to get some practice in before you fill her with heirs."

Lysander's simmering ire boiled over. "Get out."

The viscount's eyes went wide, but he practically tumbled out of his seat in his haste to stand. "I was jesting."

"Jest elsewhere. Leave."

After Treadway departed, apologizing and mumbling inaudibly, Lysander released the breath he'd been holding. The tension in his limbs and clenched fists remained, however. He did not subscribe to the patriarchal notion that a woman was the weaker sex whose only value was her womb. That a woman was less intelligent, less capable, or less competent.

Geneviève Valery was proof of that.

She and her sister had fallen into poverty through no fault of their own, and she had found a way out of it. A way that society might have frowned upon, but one in which she'd used a talent at her disposal, stayed out of the workhouse, didn't beg for charity, and kept her integrity. Most men would not have been so industrious, so determined.

Or so brave.

He'd seen Nève on her way to breakfast before he left this morning, and she'd graced him with an unguarded smile that had eased his mind. He'd worried that what they'd done last night would change things between them, but it hadn't. And why should it, he reminded himself. They'd both agreed to the terms.

A knock on the door had him frowning, wondering if Treadway had returned, but it was only his aunt. "Thought you might like a spot of tea."

"Just the thing," he said, hoping it might help. "You know me so well."

She set the steaming teacup in an open spot on the desk, her eyes roving over the plans and documents he'd been poring over. "You're still going ahead with this railway?"

"I am," he said, and then noticed her frown. "Is something the matter?"

A smile curved her lips. "Did you know that the Countess of Bolden and I used to be friends?" She pointed to the area marking the Earl of Bolden's property on one of the maps. "She loved that place, and you're planning to tear it down."

"It's a building, Aunt," he said. "And the countess is deceased."

Something like pity flashed over her face before she patted his arm. "Not everything can be placed in tiny little black-and-white boxes, you know. It might be a building to you, but to my friend, it was everything. Not just a house, but a home. A legacy. A life well spent."

"This deal will be my legacy," he said, with no little irritation.

"There are more important things in life, Lysander. Perhaps one day, you might wish to build a home yourself for a family. Find companionship. What about Miss Valery?"

He scowled. "What about her?"

"That was a nice thing you did for her with the ballroom."

He frowned. "She needed the space to practice. It was pragmatic, not nice. Don't read anything into it, Aunt."

"It was thoughtful," she insisted. "And it made her happy."

Lysander blinked. Yes, it made her so happy that she'd offered her virginity to him in return. Another transaction, of sorts, though thinking about it in those terms was discomfiting. As was the familiar sensation of dread that was beginning to seep into his belly—that feeling of impending disaster.

"She makes you happy, too," his aunt continued.

Nerves spiking, he flinched. Happiness was a trap. One he'd learned when his mother died, taking all the joy from his world and leaving him with the brute who should have died instead. The very same father who had delighted in killing anything that had brought them joy while she'd been alive. Trips to the theater? Forbidden. Glazed cakes for dessert? Gone. His favorite horse? Sold. His mother's gorgeous heirloom pianoforte? Burned. The duke had been merciless, and as a boy, Lysander had learned to show no pleasure in anything. To bury his emotions until it had become second nature. As a man, those protective habits were part of his very marrow.

Why then were his insides churning at his aunt's words? Could she sense something within him that he himself had not? He was used to fumbling at discerning other people's emotions, but he'd always been in control of his own. Yet he couldn't deny that these past weeks with Nève had felt different. *He'd* felt different.

He hadn't felt so *alive* in years. And it was terrifying.

Nève hummed happily to herself as she took a turn in the duke's small gardens with Vesper and Laila at her side. It was a beautiful day and she didn't want to spend all of it indoors, even if she was in love with her new dancing space.

Her friends had begged to watch her practice, and Nève hadn't had the heart to refuse. The ladies' enthusiasm had been contagious, and by the time she'd performed a piece from one of her favorite small ballets called *La Naïade et le Pêcheur—The Nymph and the Fisherman*—they had been in tears. In truth, Nève hadn't danced so well in a long time.

Her body felt new, every plié a discovery, every jeté a delight.

Nève wrapped her arms about her middle, feeling a delicious twinge echoing from her core. The ache between her legs had long since mellowed, but heat filled her cheeks at the recollection. Dieu, the duke had mastered her body. Kissed it. Touched it. *Owned* it. And she'd loved every single minute of it. Nève ran a hand down her flat stomach as she stopped to smell a yellow rose in full bloom. They had not taken any precautions, but there was little chance of conception. Her courses had never been regular.

"Do you miss dancing onstage?" Vesper asked Nève, pulling her from her thoughts. "I can imagine you in the glamour of the stage lights. So fabulous!"

She opened her mouth to say yes, but then paused. To her surprise, Nève didn't. Ballet and the stage used to be synonymous, but now they weren't. Long ago, dance used to be her passion, her *everything*. But as dance turned into something she *had* to do to live, somewhere along the way, passion had turned to drudgery. It was a shocking epiphany.

She shook her head slowly. "No, not really. Being a ballerina isn't as glamorous as it seems. My feet are thanking me for the reprieve. Blisters, missing toenails, and open wounds? Non, merci. Honestly, I would much rather dance for the pleasure of it. Vivienne would love to teach children one day and have a school of her own. It's a dream, of course."

"Not you?" Laila asked.

"No," Nève laughed. "Unlike me, she would make a marvelous teacher. I don't have the patience for it, but I do have a good head for figures and could help with the management of day-to-day duties."

"I think it sounds like a wonderful idea," Vesper said. "Have you heard from your sister? Is she well?"

"She wrote to me last week. Now that she can put weight on her toes again, she's in a much happier place. She misses me and can't wait for me to return." Nève exhaled, thinking of the audition Lysander had arranged for her and how her future might change if she impressed Mr. Falconer. It was everything she'd hoped for, and yet now the chance to audition felt like a hollow victory.

"Could she come here?" Vesper suggested with a bright grin. "You're one of us now, officially part of the Hellfire Kitties club. She could be, too."

Laila snorted. "That is categorically the worst name I've ever heard."

"What's wrong with Hellfire Kitties?" Vesper said, making claws with one hand and letting out a pretend hiss that made Nève grin.

"It's dreadful."

Nève couldn't help bursting into laughter at the two of them. "Maybe she can," she replied noncommittally.

It was odd. Normally, whenever she thought of what had befallen her sister, Nève couldn't control the rush of rage. This time, however, she felt hopeful. That Vivienne's dream of opening a school might soon be a reality when Nève secured the balance of her money from Lysander.

It was a harsh reminder. Playing house, entertaining friends, and getting intimately involved with Lysander was a recipe for heartbreak. Hers, not his. Nève blinked, coldness seeping through her veins.

She stumbled, and Vesper was quick to steady her. "Are you well?"

"Oh yes," she replied. "I must have tripped over a root or rock."
Or cold, hard facts.

"I have to say, Nève, you are having a wonderful effect on Stone," Laila said, making Nève's heart skip a beat. "Apparently the whole household is in a tizzy that he's been using the music room, which he hasn't done in years."

Her throat went tight. "Is that so?"

"It was something he did often with his mother," she said. "Marsden told me years ago that when they were at Eton, Stone had a hard time expressing his emotions, especially with a father like his. The duchess encouraged music as a form of communication. When he plays, it's…" She trailed off, a sad expression on her face.

"Transcendent," Nève finished softly, then paused to draw in a fragrant breath of the roses that grew along the path.

She stopped to smell another, her fingers caressing the soft petals, and flinched when a thorn stabbed her thumb. Staring at the tiny bead of blood, she let out a breath. Beauty, like ballet, had sharp, jagged edges. They both came with a cost, but some things were worth it.

Even *him*.

She felt no regret for offering him the gift of her body. Lysander, as ruthless as he was with others, had cared only for her consent, and her comfort. She could not have asked for a better lover, and in truth, it would be hard to let him go when the time came. But let him go she must.

Just as she would say goodbye to these ladies.

Her situation was only temporary, after all.

Everyone knew to avoid Lysander when he was in a foul mood. His patient butler, the footmen, the expensive French chef, the wide-eyed maids, they all scurried out of his way like ants evading a boot.

Not even a visit to the boxing ring and pounding Lushing to a pulp had been enough to put him to rights, nor had the copious amount of whiskey he'd bought his friend afterward to make up for it. His head was a mess, and he knew exactly what had caused it. Or *who*.

Hell, he never should have let her in.

All his posturing earlier about getting rid of weakness had been bullshit because letting her in meant that everything he'd carefully pigeonholed over the entirety of his life wanted *out*. A round of boxing could hardly hold up against a lifetime of repressed desire. She wasn't his weakness. She was his ruin.

With Charlotte, he'd been satisfied that his life was in line with what his father expected. She'd been a suitable choice of bride with a suitable face, a suitable dowry, and a suitable pedigree for marriage to a duke. Clearly, his father had agreed. Lysander had told Nève that he'd felt nothing when Charlotte cuckolded him. That was a lie. He'd felt powerless.

He'd been emasculated by his own father.

And he'd vowed never to feel that way ever again. And he'd kept that vow, using the strength his father had once deemed a weakness—his methodical, logical mind—to acquire business after business, amassing riches that were unmatched among his peers. And with riches came power.

Power could not disappoint. It could not cheat or steal. It laughed in the face of setbacks and reveled in the wake of victory.

Power did not care about trivial things like emotion. Power was impervious. Power was control.

Lysander scowled. Then why did he feel so goddamned *defenseless*?

He knew why.

He stalked through the house like a wild wolf on a rampage. "Where is she?" he demanded of a wary Finley.

The butler quailed, then formed a mutinous look. "I'm not certain, Your Grace."

His eyes narrowed. Was the butler protecting her from him?

"Do not take that tone with poor Finley, Lysander," a feminine voice said from the top of the stairs. "Even though he's used to it by now." To his vexation, the voice didn't belong to the woman he was seeking. He turned his cold gaze to his aunt, who met it with a cool one of her own. "Perhaps you should calm yourself before doing anything rash, Nephew."

"What is it you expect me to do? I am a duke, not a ruffian. I simply wish to know where my future duchess is." He glared over his shoulder, looking for Finley, but the butler had vanished along with everyone else.

"You've been drinking," she said, descending the staircase with a discerning stare to his flushed face and bruised knuckles. "And brawling."

"Does that surprise you?"

She paused. "You've never been a man who solves problems with his body instead of his brain. What has gotten under your skin so?"

Lysander's chuckle was guttural and humorless. "You have to

ask?" Understanding lit her gray eyes and then amusement. He bristled. "What about any of this is funny, Aunt?"

"I much prefer for you to discover it on your own, dear boy." She gave his arm a fond pat and then turned toward the foyer. "The one you seek is in the library." Millicent took two steps before halting. "If I may offer one piece of advice, Lyssie-lad, tread carefully." His wretched aunt actually cackled. "She bites back."

Lysander blinked as a wicked voice reminded him that she truly did. He had the teeth marks on his shoulder to prove it. *No, no. Focus.* He was here to reaffirm the terms, to restate their positions. To take back the control he'd so stupidly ceded. Correction…that his *body* had ceded when it had been overtaken by lust. His brain had been robbed of reason. Of its good sense. And he needed to restore order within himself.

Striding down the corridor to the library, he found her standing next to one of the floor-to-ceiling bookshelves, her fingers drifting over the spines of the books. Her beauty—all sinuous lines and sylphlike grace gilded by the fading sunlight from the enormous stained glass window—took his breath, and for a moment, he forgot what he'd come to say.

Order. Power. Boundaries.

Lysander cleared his throat. "I need to speak with you."

Nève whirled, happiness in her eyes dulling by the heartbeat as she took in his grim expression and registered his hard tone. He hesitated. The wild roar in his chest had quieted, but suddenly, he felt unsure.

Her reply was as cool as he deserved. "Then speak, Your Grace."

"What happened last night cannot happen again," he said quickly, glancing around to make sure they were alone.

He saw something he couldn't name flash in her eyes, but it was gone so quickly he wondered if he'd imagined it. "I agree." Her voice was steady and her expression placid.

Prepared for a feminine outburst or some such, Lysander opened his mouth and closed it. Nève propped one palm on a slender hip, drawing his eye to that slight curve and remembering how his lips had traced it. Desire heated his veins before her words sank in like a dousing of icy water. "You do? Why?"

"I said I agree," she said. "Once was more than enough."

"That's it?" he asked, searching her face, for what, he wasn't sure.

"I'm confused, Your Grace. Isn't that what you wanted? What you came here to speak with me about?" At a loss, he stared at her. Why was *he* questioning his own command, while she was the epitome of composure? Irritated at himself, Lysander's lips tightened. Nève frowned but didn't back down. "And don't look at me like that either. I'm not one of your servants you can order about."

Oh, he relished the fire falling from her lips. Though it struck him that he shouldn't be so affected by her show of emotion.

"But you are," he replied, prowling forward. "You work for me."

She laughed but there was no joy in it. "That may be so, but you don't scare me, Lysander Maxton Blackstone. I'm not one of the easily frightened people you bark at because you have a deficit of compassion and need to compensate to feel big."

He smirked. "But I have nothing to compensate for, Miss Valery. I *am* big."

The blush erupting on her face was its own reward, even though he should not take any pleasure in it. "Your ego is truly astounding, Your Grace. There's no honor in blowing one's own trumpet."

"I shall be sure to judge you fairly when you do it then."

Curse his deuced tongue! The whiskey and her nearness were combining to bedevil him. He'd come there to set things straight between them, but by God, he couldn't resist the desire to provoke her, to see that temper and passion twine in her eyes. Almost as good as seeing it bloom when he was inside her.

No, no, no.

Her cheeks were crimson, but she tossed her head. "You just said what happened between us cannot happen again. Forgetting already? Tsk, tsk. I suppose I did warn you about falling into your dotage, Your Grace."

"Last night, did it *feel* like I was in my dotage, Geneviève?" His reply was silky.

A puff of air escaped her lips. "Self-praise is no praise at all."

He lifted a brow, his traitorous blood on fire, and cursed Lushing's Scottish whisky between breaths. "But good things should be praised."

This was a disaster and not going at all as planned.

"Do you wish me to stroke your ego so badly, Your Grace?" she asked, watching him struggle with the stranglehold of his own desire and idiocy. Her gaze dropped to the crowded front of his trousers displaying an erection that didn't even have the decency or loyalty to hide. "Or is it something else you wish to be stroked?"

Yes, please. Rather than let his overeager cock turn him into the sorriest kind of fool, Lysander feigned disinterest. "The ball is ever in your court, Miss Valery."

"Is it? Because you seemed to have served up a match-winning point." She laughed softly to herself and nodded. "You want to know why I am in agreement?" She did not wait for his answer. "It is because you and I will end," she said. "I will leave and we will each go back to our own lives, free from entanglements and expectations. You will charm the earl and have your land, and I will earn my five thousand pounds. You'll go your way and I shall go mine."

Her words should have appeased him, but instead, Lysander felt only a dull sense of emptiness. He breathed through suddenly tight lungs, wondering if he'd just made the worst mistake of his life.

He cleared his too-tight throat and gave her a small close-mouthed smile. "Excellent. I'm glad we are in agreement."

She didn't smile back, her face unreadable. "If there's nothing else, Your Grace?"

"No, that's all."

When she eased past him, he let her go, despite the indescribable urge to pull her into his arms and beg her forgiveness for being the stupidest man in the history of the world. But he kept his mouth shut and his arms glued to his sides.

A shallow cut now would save him a deeper one later.

Chapter Eighteen

Nève stood in a corner of the ballroom, fidgeting as she watched the Duke of Montcroix from afar. He hadn't spoken to her since their confrontation in the library, and she was both saddened and relieved. Gracious, the wild, unhinged look in the duke's eyes in the library had nearly knocked the bluster from her. Goading a man like Lysander Blackstone was simply asking for trouble. Then again, she'd never been the kind of woman to shy away from it.

A woman had to have a backbone to survive as a dancer. Ballet was a cutthroat business—eat or be eaten, strike or be struck. As a result, Nève usually met trouble head-on... even when it might be the sensible thing to pause and think. Confronting the duke in his obviously awful frame of mind had been like flying a red rag in front of a snorting bull, but she hadn't been about to let him run roughshod over her.

He was right, however. They both needed space.

Was it foolish that a part of her had wanted him to reject her levelheaded words? To push her up against the bookcases, lift her skirts, and have his wicked way with her instead?

Oh, la vache!

She fanned her suddenly hot cheeks, wishing she could step outside for some air.

"Goodness, this is a crush." Laila made her way over, furiously fanning herself as well, followed by Vesper, Effie, and Briar.

Vesper snorted. "How Lady Saunders felt everyone she invited could fit in this sweltering ballroom is anyone's guess."

"It is hot," Nève agreed.

Effie peered over at her. "Do you need to borrow my fan, Nève? Your face is like a ripe tomato."

"I have one." She lifted it with a flourish, not bothering to explain that her face was red because of the very maddening Duke of Montcroix and not the stifling warmth of the ballroom.

Briar let out a groan and tugged at her bodice from behind her fan. "This is awful. Shall we play a round of cards? I wager it's much cooler in the game room."

"Isn't that for the men?" Effie asked.

Briar rolled her eyes. "This isn't the eighteen twenties, Effie darling. Women are allowed to gamble, too."

Effie swatted at Briar playfully, but her pale face seemed even more ashen than usual. "No, I know that. I just meant...Lord Huntington might be in there, I think."

"Who is Lord Huntington?" Nève asked.

Vesper scowled. "No one at all. An annoying fop who thinks he's God's gift to women. He's been positively cruel to poor Effie simply because she refused to kiss his sanctimonious rear end during her first season."

Nève took her friend's arm in a show of solidarity. "Good for you, Effie."

"Come on," Briar said. "He won't dare cut her with all of us there, especially the Marchioness of Marsden and the future Duchess of Montcroix."

Nève died a little inside at the sound of the title, but squashed it down.

She followed Briar and Vesper into the game room, which was much less crowded than the ballroom and what felt like a million degrees cooler. They found an empty felt-covered table and sat. "Shall I deal then?" Briar asked. "Vingt-et-un? You know it, Nève?"

Nève lifted a brow. Know it? She grinned and cracked her knuckles, earning her a few chuckles from the other ladies. "What are we betting?" she asked. "I haven't brought much money with me."

"Oh, we don't play for money. We play for secrets." Nève blinked as Briar continued. "Winner gets the right to ask one secret of her choice. Loser must answer truthfully."

Nève shrugged. How bad could it be?

Obviously, *not* as easy as she expected ... because these women were old hats at this game and Nève lost the very first hand. Vesper shot her a thoroughly wicked look. "Inquiring minds want to know ... is Stone a generous lover?"

"Vesper!" Laila huffed, her eyes darting to a hot-cheeked Nève. Nève gaped. "Guh ..."

"Is *guh* good?" Briar teased.

"This is not proper," Nève stammered. "We ... I ... haven't ..."

Vesper laughed. "We're not proper amongst ourselves, silly, and the secrets have to mean something, otherwise it's just another game."

"Some questions are confidential though," Laila said. "And she's new to us, which means she gets a pass on that one."

"Then I pass." Nève shot Laila a grateful look even as Vesper looked put out.

What happened between her and the duke was private, and Nève wanted to keep it that way. The game went on, and Briar took the next round and held Laila in her sights.

"Do you prefer to be on the bottom or the top?" Briar asked with a wicked gleam in her eye.

Effie let out a high-pitched giggle, and Laila went beet red. "Top," she squeaked.

The scandalous thoughts that bombarded Nève's head were enough to put a saint to shame. She didn't even want to think of the duke's enormous frame spread out like a masculine feast beneath her. Once was enough, her mind screamed, but her body did not listen. It was as though her every wicked thought were suddenly transparent on her skin.

A chortling Vesper waggled her brows and pointed at her. "Guess that answers my earlier question then."

Nève laughed and shook her head. "One of these days, Vesper, you will fall head over heels for someone and it will be the end of you. Then we shall torment you with these dreadfully crude questions."

"That day will be when hell freezes over, dear friend. I am destined to be the queen of the spinsters."

"I think love finds us when we least expect it," Nève said without thinking.

All four women goggled at her, but Laila was the first to speak. "Do you?"

Nève laughed, shrugging off the sudden air of expectancy.

"Alors, I am French and I am a seller of dreams, especially onstage. What do you expect? Love is my game."

Play resumed, and she sighed with defeat as Laila took the next win. "Nève," she said, and Nève blanched.

"Go on then, out with it," she said with resignation.

"When is your birthday?"

"In two weeks," she replied, relieved that Laila had gifted her with an easy question. "The sixth."

"Brilliant!" Vesper squealed. "Does Stone know?"

"Does Stone know what?" a voice as smooth as dark velvet interjected from behind her, and Nève let out a gasp.

She bit the inside of her cheek hard. "Nothing of concern, Your Grace."

"Her birthday is in a fortnight on the sixth," the ladies volunteered helpfully, and she glared at them, but their delight only grew. The rotten meddlers.

The duke had said he'd wanted distance between them, and distance he would get.

Lysander crossed the hall of the foyer, his footsteps tapping impatiently against the pristine marble. Everything had been arranged down to the last detail, and it had taken some finesse to get all the pieces in place. He resisted raking a palm through his neatly combed hair. Henry would have his hide if he so much as mussed a single strand.

His palms were clammy and his stomach felt disordered. This had been the *right* thing to do; no need to read anything more into it.

You don't celebrate the birthdays of your other employees like this.

Scowling, Lysander tugged at his collar. Nève wasn't *just* an employee. She was more than that—her role as his fiancée, false though it was, deserved attention. Now that Lady Vesper and Lady Marsden knew about Nève's birthday, they would never let him live it down if he ignored the occasion. It was bad form, and he couldn't have it getting back to the Earl of Bolden that he did not celebrate the birthday of his betrothed in grand fashion.

A noise drew his attention as the source of his inner chaos stood at the top of the staircase. His breath shunted in his lungs at the vision in deep carmine silk standing above him like a queen about to address her subjects. Spine locked, chin high, and descending with liquid grace, she moved like an ethereal creature spun from dreams and moonlight.

A sylph in all her mesmerizing glory.

"Thank you for the gown, Your Grace," she said, breaking the spell that had held him mute. "It's lovely."

Fashioned with a delicate lace overlay and elegant seed pearl beadwork sewn into the bodice and hem, it was a gorgeous gown, but it was the lady wearing it who made it unforgettable. The rich red silk made her skin seem luminous and her green eyes glow like backlit emeralds.

"Thank Lady Marsden," he replied in a hoarse voice.

Nève didn't look surprised, though her eyes warmed. "I knew it had to be one of hers. She's extraordinary."

You're extraordinary.

She reached the bottom of the staircase, and Lysander could not move. He had something to do, something to give her, but couldn't for the life of him remember what.

"Your Grace?" Her soft voice washed over him.

Blinking, he pulled out the diamond-and-garnet necklace burning a hole in his coat pocket. The rose-cut gems surrounded by clusters of diamonds shone like fire and ice in his fingers as he held them out. "There's one thing missing. May I?"

She gasped, eyes going wide. "No, I couldn't possibly..."

"It's a gift. I want you to have it." When Lysander fastened the necklace around her creamy throat, his fingers lingered. He couldn't stop himself from savoring the velvet feel of her skin while he affixed the clasp. As he'd hoped, it suited her. "There. Beautiful."

Her lips parted as she stared at him, a gloved hand going up to touch the dangling gemstones, and for a moment, he wanted to lay himself bare. Give way to all the impossible feelings crowding up inside of him, but they stuck uselessly in his throat.

"Why are the two of you just standing there mooning at each other?" Millicent shrieked, hustling down the staircase in a froth of rose-colored satin. "We're going to be late. Come along now!"

Lysander cleared his throat as his aunt speared them with a look that was both doting and ferocious. He nodded. "After you, Aunt."

"You didn't have to do this, you know," Nève said when they were all ensconced in the carriage. "My birthday is nothing special."

"I wanted to." The confession slipped out of him, but he found that he did not regret it, especially when her cheeks flushed with pleasure.

"You both look lovely tonight," he said as the carriage pulled away into the street.

"Thank you, Nephew." Millicent let out an approving noise as she peered over at Nève. "Oh my. My sister's necklace looks lovely on you."

Nève startled, fingers going to it again as her eyes met his. "This was your mother's?" He nodded. She looked like she wanted to protest, but at his look, she firmed her lips and placed her hand back in her lap. "Where are we going?" she asked instead.

"Patience, Miss Valery."

"Do you *know* me? I'm not a very patient person at the best of times." She huffed and poked Millicent. "Do you know where we're going?"

"It's a surprise."

Nève pouted, but the ride passed quickly. When they arrived at their destination—the Lyceum—her jaw gaped as her eyes caught on the posters plastered outside of the theater.

ROYAL LYCEUM THEATRE

His Grace, THE DUKE OF MONTCROIX has the honor to announce
that he will host

A GRAND BALLET

presenting *Le Papillon*

PERFORMANCE BY: Farfalla, Emma Livry; Prince Djalma, Louis Mérante; Hamza, Louise Marquet; Patimate, M. Berthier; Mohamed, M. Dauty; Zaidee, Mlle. Stoikoff; Ismail Bey, Emir, M. Lenfant; Leila, Mlle. Lamy; The Diamond Fairy, Mlle. Simon; The Pearl Fairy, Mlle. Mauperin; The Flower Fairy, Mlle. Troisvallets; The Harvest Fairy, Mlle. Scholosser.

"What is this?" Nève whispered, staring at him. "How did you do this?"

At absurd, astronomical expense, he'd bought out the Paris show for a few consecutive nights and brought her former colleagues here for this evening's very special performance; as he watched her now, it was worth every cent.

"Bon anniversaire, Geneviève," he said.

She swallowed hard. "You've fetched the entire company here?"

He nodded. "Yes."

"I don't know what to say."

"Say nothing." He lifted her knuckles and grazed a kiss over the back of her gloves. "Just enjoy the evening."

Her eyes glittered with unshed tears as he escorted her through the nearly empty foyer. His aunt had been right—they were later than expected—and most of the audience had already taken their seats.

Once they were settled in their private box, Nève looked around, her eyes wide with awe. "This is indescribably beautiful."

Lysander had the same thought, but not about their surroundings—he could watch *her* for every minute of every day.

"Have you never been to the theater?" Millicent asked.

Nève smiled. "Not very often on this side of the stage. At least, not since I was a child when I went with my parents and sister." Her shoulders lifted. "And never in a ducal box. This is rather special. Thank you," she said to him, her eyelashes fluttering down.

"You're welcome."

The lights dimmed, the curtain raised, and the performance

of *Le Papillon* began. It took all of Lysander's composure to keep his eyes on the stage instead of on the woman seated beside him. The story was similar to other romantic ballets—a beautiful young woman transformed into a butterfly by a wicked fairy and rescued by her true love only after many harrowing twists.

Nève's fingers counted the beats and tapped against her knee, lifting with each jeté. Her face was a mirror of passion, reflecting everything that happened onstage, and when intermission came, she was practically vibrating with emotion.

"Dieu, they are fantastic! I forgot how incredible Emma and Louis are."

Lysander smiled and nodded to Millicent that it was time. "Your turn," he said to Nève.

Her expression was comical. "My turn what?"

"I've made arrangements for you to dance the pas de deux in the next scene." When he saw the look of horror on her face, he patted her arm. "You told me you were Mademoiselle Livry's understudy, so you're already acquainted with Monsieur Mérante, are you not?" He smiled when she gave a bemused nod. "Go with Millicent. Have no fear, you will be in disguise."

"The dancers will know," she whispered.

"Both Mademoiselle Livry and Monsieur Mérante have been sworn to secrecy. Trust me, no one will say a word." He paused. "Unless of course you do not wish to."

"I would love to."

With a dubious look on her face, she followed his clucking aunt. He chuckled as he heard Nève admonishing his aunt about keeping secrets. It wasn't long before the second act began, and he waited eagerly for the scene in which Nève would replace Emma on the stage.

Lysander's breath caught as Nève appeared, dressed in filmy white tulle, a glittering butterfly mask concealing her identity.

From the moment she rose en pointe, she was all he could see.

All he could *feel*.

Her effortless grace, the movements of her arms, the extension of her legs, the blissful expression on her face had him utterly enchanted. Each time she looked out from behind the mask into the audience, their eyes connected.

Though she couldn't see him, it was a jolt in his spine—a visceral understanding that she was dancing for *him*. He could feel it keenly. This butterfly was his.

Only his.

CHAPTER NINETEEN

"Nève, you were marvelous!" the principal dancer, Emma, squealed in a whisper as they crossed paths in the shadows of the wings.

"Shh! No one can know it's me." Nève hugged her friend hard. "I've missed you. How's Vivienne? Have you seen her?"

Emma's eyes warmed as she pranced back to the stage. "She's well! I saw her last week. Walking and itching to dance."

Relief filled her at the news.

"Nève, you wretch!" someone shrieked, and she turned to see Vesper. Of course the hoyden would be in on it. The woman could not keep her nose out of anything exciting. They embraced and rushed behind Millicent to the private dressing room she'd used earlier.

"You were bloody breathtaking," Vesper said, grinning. "I can't believe Montcroix actually pulled this off. Who would have thought he had a romantic bone in his body?"

No one, not even her.

Nève had a thousand questions of her own but was in a state of shock as she changed out of the dancing costume and back into her gown. She untied the slippers from her feet and handed them to Millicent, who packed them away carefully into a box.

On impulse she kissed the older woman on the cheek. "Thank you, Millicent."

"Don't thank me," she said fondly. "I only followed instructions. Bring you here, help you dress, bring you back. He planned it all."

It was inconceivable the lengths Lysander had gone to for *her*. Nève couldn't fathom it. No one had ever done anything like this. Ever. It was almost a dream. When she was finished dressing, she hugged Vesper again, if only to convince herself that she *wasn't* dreaming.

"One more thing, dear," Millicent said, and fastened the necklace to Nève's neck. Breathless, Nève touched her fingers to it. She didn't even want to imagine how much it was worth or think about the fact that it had been his *mother's*. Why on earth would Lysander let *her* wear a priceless family heirloom?

"That's pretty," Vesper said with a grin. "That from your fairy godfather, too?"

Nève blushed, her entire body going indescribably warm. "It's on loan."

"Bloody hell, what is *that* look?" Vesper said, and then her eyes rounded at Nève's soft expression. "If you've fallen in love and didn't tell the Hellfire Kitties, there'll be the devil to pay."

"I'm not in love with him."

Something protested in the vicinity of her heart. *Was she?*

When they returned to their seats, Nève nearly tripped over her own toes as the man himself appeared at the curtained entrance to the box, stern and forbidding. Her pulse skipped its usual beat, but something was different now. She'd poured her heart out on that stage, telling the duke in dance what she could never say in words. Because he'd made himself clear in the library, and she'd agreed. And she always kept her vows.

Lysander's expression softened, and he gestured for them to sit. When Nève took her place beside him, Lysander leaned over, his voice low and only for her. "You were utterly spectacular down there, the most exquisite ballerina to grace any stage."

His quiet praise filled her with pleasure. "Thank you."

The ballet had already resumed, but Nève could hardly focus on the rest of it. Even with his aunt there, she was acutely conscious of the man sitting next to her. He was so stony and unapproachable on the outside, yet a man who was truly empty of compassion would have never gone through so much effort and expense…not for *her*. Then why did he? It was an extravagance and indulgence that she did not deserve.

At the end of the performance, the curtain fell and the entire theater broke out in applause as the dancers took their bows. Nève stood, her mind whirling as she followed the duke and his aunt out of the box to the reception hall where champagne was being handed out to the delighted patrons. Suddenly, she was swamped by four familiar faces as her friends converged upon her. From their expressions, she gathered that they were all in on her secret adventure.

"You were gorgeous," Laila whispered.

"Splendid, just splendid," Briar said, clapping her on the shoulder.

Effie had tears in her eyes. "It was so beautiful!"

Nève smiled, her heart almost bursting with pride. "Thank you."

"Goodness, I'm parched," Vesper said. "Shall we find some refreshment?"

Briar gave an enthusiastic nod, making her dark curls bounce. "You, garçon, over here!"

Nève suppressed a giggle at Briar's sharp whistle as they swarmed the poor server and his tray of drinks. Once more, a bittersweet chord resonated in her chest at the thought of leaving them behind. She would miss them terribly. She would miss *him*, too.

Of their own volition, her eyes met a pair of intense gray ones across the room. The Duke of Montcroix seemed to be deep in conversation with Lord Bolden, but his attention did not stray from her.

"He'll ruin you," a venomous voice said from behind her.

Nève turned, unsurprised by the sight of the Duchess of Montcroix, her pretty face twisted with spite, even as she smiled. "Your Grace, how perfectly charming to see you again. I see that barb in your mouth is still steeped in poison."

"Curious tongues are wagging," she drawled loudly. "Why would a man go through all the hoops of ferrying the entire cast of a ballet across the channel for one single performance? Why would he go through such expense? For a special prize perhaps?"

"You will have to ask him," Nève replied coolly.

The duchess made no effort to lower her voice. "Unless of course the prize is already tarnished."

Nève's temper boiled over, but she kept her voice to a hushed whisper. "Insult me again, Your Grace, and you will regret it."

Instead of taking the warning to heart, the duchess sneered.

"Oh, good Lord, you truly are a marvelous actress, aren't you?" Nève's heart dropped to the floor. Did she know? Truth glittered in the lady's malice-filled eyes. This time she did lower her voice. "I followed you after intermission and saw your little caper. You really were quite good onstage. What more are you hiding, I wonder?"

Nève went cold. "What do you want?"

"For you to go back from whence you came," the duchess replied. The way she said it implied that where Nève hailed from was lower than the gutter. "Leave and never return."

Nève clenched her jaw, unwilling to bend to a bully, even though the woman could jeopardize Lysander's scheme to the ton if, in fact, she did know something. "Perhaps you should take up acting yourself, Your Grace. You seem to have quite the gift for it. Though I am sure if the duke got wind of your unfounded accusations, he would have something to say."

"I saw you," she said through her teeth.

"Saw what?" a deep baritone interjected as Lysander appeared at her side with the Earl of Lushing and the theater manager of the Lyceum in tow.

"Nothing, chéri," Nève said sweetly. "Your very kind stepmother was just saying how much she enjoyed the ballet, and that she was interested in contributing a sizable donation to the Lyceum. Isn't that wonderful?"

The manager's eyes widened at the prospect. "Oh yes, of course! That is incredibly generous, Your Grace. We are always in dire need of funds. So, so generous!"

Nève didn't dare look at Lysander, but she felt him nod, surprising her. "The dowager is a great patron of the arts."

"Dowager?" Charlotte shrieked with a horrified look.

"Out with the old, in with the new as they say." Lushing let out a bark of laughter and canted his head. "Don't worry, Your Graceless, I'm sure Montcroix will have a dower house readied with your name on it. With any luck, said dower house will be a tower surrounded by a moat. Dower tower! Good God, my cleverness astounds me sometimes."

Nève pressed a hand to her lips to keep from grinning at the earl.

Snapping with rage, Charlotte's eyes bored into hers. "This isn't over."

She stalked away before Nève could reply.

The manager of the Lyceum, whom she recognized as Mr. Falconer, leaned toward her, his voice low and earnest. "Brilliant audition, Miss Valery," he said. "You have a place in my company, if you want it. I apologize that I let gossip stand in the way when you first came to my theater."

Overwhelmed, she could only stare at him. *Audition?* Had the duke confided who she was? He must have. "Thank you. And you're forgiven, we all make mistakes."

Truth be told, Nève didn't know how to feel. It was the only thing she'd ever wanted since coming to London, and her heart felt curiously hollow. Lysander peered down at her with a slight frown. "Is everything well?"

"He offered me a job."

"Of course he did. You're outstanding."

A nearby footman took their empty glasses, and Nève pushed her chaotic thoughts to the side. She would consider the offer later and make a decision when she was more clearheaded.

"What was that about with Charlotte?" Lysander murmured, while Lushing and the theater manager were engaged in conversation.

"She followed me during intermission," Nève said. "I'm sorry but I think she saw me get changed for the role of Farfalla. She can ruin things for you with Bolden."

"Don't worry about Bolden," Lysander said. "The deal was inked this morning. I am now in possession of two hundred hectares of prime Yorkshire estate."

"That's wonderful news. Congratulations!" She peered up at him. "You must be happy. Aldenborough is beautiful."

He nodded. "I am satisfied."

At times, it was shocking how apathetic he was. This news should have delighted him, and yet he showed such little excitement over something that had to be momentous. Nève knew now that his stoicism wasn't a mask, it was just his natural response to most situations.

Except music and making love…

Heat filled her cheeks, and she gave a small cough.

"I'm glad," she murmured, a strange sadness filling her breast and making it hard to breathe. Would he terminate their agreement, now that he'd achieved what he wanted? It was the most practical thing, and she knew that the duke was nothing if not pragmatic.

He took a hold of her hand and she froze, her green eyes rising to meet his beautiful gray ones. So much swirled in them… those silvery depths that were usually so unreadable stormed with indecision and hope and something that looked too much like affection. Or maybe that was a construct of her needy and suddenly desolate heart.

"You are more than welcome to stay until Lady Vesper's birthday party in a few weeks. I know you were looking forward to it and she was, too. It's no hardship." He trailed off, looking uncharacteristically helpless as though he had much more to say. "Nève, this is hardly the place, but I—"

But whatever Lysander had been about to share was rudely interrupted by the arrival of a very loud and very foxed Viscount Treadway, swaying as he held four glasses of spilling champagne in his grip. One was unceremoniously thrust into her face. "Drink up, Miss Valery! Nève, can I call you Nève? Very well, Nève, we have reason to celebrate! A toast to my dear friend here, lovely Nève, whose future husband has pulled off the coup of the century by convincing that cranky old codger to sell!"

Lysander frowned, his lip curling with distaste. "You may address her as Miss Valery. And you are drunk, sir. Compose yourself."

"You should be drunk, too! We're going to be filthy fucking rich!"

Nève sidestepped the man as he teetered toward her, his eyes fastening to her bosom before he licked his lips. She felt a frisson of disgust, but before she could say anything, he turned around and wandered away.

"So he's happy about your prospective railway, I take it?" she said.

The duke frowned, staring after the man. "He should not be celebrating. I'm still waiting for the full accounting of his company's shares. I refuse to invest in an unethical company, and for whatever reason, he is stalling on providing me with the updated figures."

"Talk to the employees," she said.

His stare pinned hers. "What did you say?"

"If you don't have the documentation, talk to the people who work for the company. They'll tell you soon enough if they're happy with the terms of their employment, and I wager a few of them will know local investors. Then you can ask about the returns they've gotten, or not. Besides, if the business is corrupt, the finances won't be recorded in the books. They will have been scrubbed."

"You are brilliant," he said, eyes full of respect.

She blushed. "I've been catching up on some of the developments in the papers. You would be surprised at how many hardworking and honest men have been cheated by railroad investment schemes. As horrid as it is, it's quite common. I read about the bill you helped push through the Lords to protect ordinary investors." She shot him an appreciative smile of her own. "That was admirable of you."

"It was needed. Dishonesty and bribery are rampant."

"Do you think the viscount is hiding something?"

"I don't know," he said. "But I intend to find out."

Nève exhaled, summoning her courage to ask what it was that he'd been about to say before, when her friends approached. The group was closely followed by some of the ballerinas who were still in costume, as was the custom following the performance. Besides Emma and Louis, most of them wouldn't have known that she had danced briefly with them tonight, but it was wonderful to see them all the same.

The smile froze on her face when a man walking behind the dancers came into view. What the hell was Lord Durand doing here?

She waited until he was nearly upon her, and watched as his eyes widened in surprise, falling from the top of her head to her gown to the tips of her toes. "Nève Valery, it *is* you! What a charming surprise to see you here," he drawled, the sound of his voice making the hairs on her nape rise.

"The surprise is mine, I assure you." Nève pinned him with a glare.

His grin was feline. "I thought I was mistaken earlier, but here you are."

Before she could scream that he stay a far step away from her, Lysander moved forward, his stance aggressive and his new position placing her slightly behind him as though he meant to protect her. She inched forward to put them on equal footing, keeping her glare focused on the marquis. "Who are you?" the duke demanded.

"The Marquis of Durand." He eyed Lysander with a circumspect look, that oily grin still firmly in place. "Who are *you*? Her new protector?"

"I am her *fiancé*." The duke's voice sounded like ice cracking. "The Duke of Montcroix."

"Haven't you done well for yourself," the marquis said to her, a sneer curling his lips.

Nève felt Lysander stiffen at her side, the menace rippling from him in waves, and she placed a gentle hand on his sleeve. "He's not worth it, Your Grace."

Durand laughed, the sound mocking and cruel. "You dare insult me. *You?*"

"You will listen to the lady, sir."

"Lady? Is that what she told you?" Durand asked, his gaze going comically wide.

Nève felt more eyes and ears perk their way—some of the people here could scent blood in the water like sharks on the hunt. They might be dressed in gowns and jewels galore, but beneath all the trappings of civility, they were vicious. She didn't have a title to protect her, or a fortune to her name. She had only her integrity and her dignity, and both would be trampled without much provocation.

She lifted her chin with quiet pride. "My father was a viscount, Lord Durand."

"And my mother is the queen of England."

"I speak the truth. My father was Viscount Reeves."

The whispers grew. Or was that her imagination? Other dancers were making the rounds, so conversation would rise and fall. She couldn't be sure whether people were paying attention to them or not. Nève glanced to her friends, who were keeping an eye on the interaction and simultaneously trying to herd people away.

"Sure you are," Durand crooned in a way that made Nève sick. "Shall I now address my little bird as the Honorable Nève Reeves?"

"I'd prefer you not to address me at all." Though her voice shook with nerves, Nève was proud of herself for standing up to the man who had caused both her and her sister such misery.

Durand opened his mouth to retort, but the Duke of Mont-croix forestalled him with a lifted palm. He didn't raise his voice, but the threat in his words was made worse by his hushed, fore-boding delivery. "Enough of this. If you ever approach my fiancée, her sister, or any of these women without their explicit consent, I will ruin you, Durand."

The marquis was stupid enough to reply. "Who do you think you are?"

"I'm not a man who coerces helpless women and then hurts them when they refuse to comply." When the marquis paled at the accusation but scoffed in disdain, the duke watched him like a hawk watched prey. "I assure you I mean every word. I will have you living like a pauper in the streets of Montmartre begging for your supper within the year. Now get the hell out of my sight!"

No one in Nève's adult life had ever stood up for her before. She was always the one fighting the battles and dealing with the fall-out. Being defended so superbly shouldn't have made her as calf eyed and weak-kneed as it did, but if her friends weren't there, finding an alcove and dragging Lysander into it would have been her first priority.

"That was rather exciting, wasn't it?" she blurted, her voice breathy.

The duke stared down at her, his gaze so intense that Nève barely noticed when her friends slipped away, Vesper squeezing her arm with a knowing grin. Wait, what *did* Vesper know? It wasn't like her every emotion was transparent and written all over her . . . that she was falling head over heels for this man. She swallowed down the excessive moisture in her mouth. Oh, bon Dieu, *was* it?

She wet her lips. "It seems we are both facing our demons tonight, Your Grace. What is the universe trying to tell us, do you think?"

"That trouble is thy name."

Nève gaped at him, seeing the gleam in his eye. "Did you just make a *joke*?"

"It happens on occasion."

"And by that, you mean hardly ever."

Her eyes ran up his chest to his snowy-white cravat to meet his, stormy and dark as though he could sense the chaotic churn of her thoughts. Admiration, gratitude, and desire surrounded her heart in tight-meshed bands. The physical pull was familiar, but the newly nascent feelings woven into it had her on precarious ground. It felt as though her skin were going to split apart from the pressure of them.

She swallowed hard. "I know you said everything between us is business, but what you did tonight for me was…" Her throat went tight. No words jumping to mind could translate the sheer enormity of what she was feeling. To her mortification, her eyes burned with unshed tears. "It meant more than you could ever know."

"Good," he said softly.

Nève reached for his hand, her fingers brushing over his gloved knuckles. His palm curled over hers, dwarfing it, as he held tight. For once, she didn't want him to let go. "Dance has always been precious to me, but I confirmed something tonight. Something I said to Vesper. I thought I might be wrong, but it was more than clear." A tremulous smile grew. "Your gift gave me the chance to recognize something so important. One that became crystal clear when the manager offered me a place in his company."

"What?" he asked huskily.

"That the stage is a prop...I don't need to dance for other people." She let out a slow breath, feeling the truth and power of her words. "Up there, for the first time in as long as I can remember, I wasn't dancing for the sake of an audience or a wage. I chose *me*, and it felt wonderful."

His head cocked in surprise. "You don't wish to take Falconer's offer at the Lyceum?"

"No, I don't think so. Ballet is part of me." She tapped her heart with her free hand. "It will always be here, but the stage isn't what I need. It became a cage."

Something moved over his face—understanding, perhaps—and he nodded. "When something you love becomes something you resent because of circumstance."

She shouldn't have been surprised that he understood. It was what music was to him, after all—equal parts salvation and snare. Compassion filled her. His ability to feel through music was so tied up in loss, no wonder it hurt him to play.

"Yes, exactly," she whispered.

"I suppose the trick is to find what made you love it in the first place. Not always easy, but I'm glad you have." He squeezed her palm. "I feel the same about music, recently."

They stood there in a moment of complete accord, underlying emotion and unexpected connection heightening everything else. The press of their fingers. The wild beating of her heart. The need gathering like a hurricane in the pit of her stomach. The look in his eyes.

"Lysander." His name emerged on a sigh of pure want.

Flecks of silver burned in his irises, the haughty, sullen curve of his lips a seductive trap set only for her. He licked them, and her pulse tripled in her veins. They were in a roomful of people, and she could not have cared less. It was only them. Always ever them.

"Stop looking at me like that," she whispered.

"Like what?"

Uncaring of their public position, her voice was breathless with want. "Like you want to break all your rules."

His voice was soft. "And would you stop me if I did?"

Bravely or stupidly—she had yet to decide which—she pushed up onto her toes, her lips as close to his ear as she dared without scandalizing the patrons milling around them. "No, I wish to break them all."

CHAPTER TWENTY

"Geneviève." He breathed her name through his lips, eyes glittering with a primal, untamed desire that matched hers.

He did not throw her over his shoulder, but the firm, assertive grip on her fingers had almost the same effect. She wanted those big hands all over her, moving her pliant, needy body to his every whim. Heat bloomed along her nerve endings, and her breasts tingled in her bodice as he drew her from the hall. Nève burned as the gazes of her friends followed their departure, but she couldn't bring herself to care. Vesper would undoubtedly be in a froth of *I-told-you-so* delight.

The duke didn't speak as they hurried through a dark corridor, and Nève was operating on sound alone when she heard a door click open and snick shut. "Where are we?"

In response, her mouth was blanketed by a hot, furious, and demanding set of male lips. Grasping her hips, Lysander walked her backward until the rear of her thighs hit a hard surface. A table or a desk, if she had to guess. The loss of vision only seemed to heighten every other sense; the crisp masculine scent of him, the enormous feel of him, the sound of the growls tearing from his chest, his taste...Oh, Dieu, his *taste*. Like sin and darkness.

Like the devil she craved.

"Lysander," she begged, rolling her hips into his, her body aching to be filled. She clutched at his coat, desperate to feel him, and feel him she did. His pelvis ground into hers, the friction between them making her gasp. She hissed with frustration at the layers of clothing and crinoline between them. She wanted them gone! His hot mouth nipped at her chin and slid down her throat before climbing back up to her ear. Teeth grazed her lobe and bit down.

"God, I could eat you alive," he said, his breath feathering over her sensitive skin. "Gorge myself on the banquet of your body."

He nibbled down her jaw to her parted lips. His huge frame caged her in, looming over her and bending her backward. Nève's supple spine curved obediently, and his gratified groan filled her with pleasure. His tongue speared into her mouth as his fingers tugged on her chin, forcing her to open wide to his greedy demands. Nève gave in with a smothered gasp as his mouth dominated hers until she was in a whimpering, needy state.

"I wanted you the moment I saw you on the staircase," he said hoarsely. "And I burned when you danced on that stage."

"I liked knowing you were watching me," she said, tangling her fingers in his soft hair.

Warm palms slid over her swollen breasts, yanking down her bodice, until cool air kissed her already painfully peaked nipples. The duke lifted her onto the flat surface of the desk before his mouth closed over one taut bud and sucked. Nève arched with a cry as raw pleasure streaked from her breasts to her shivering, damp core. Switching to her other breast, his tongue flicked against the pebbled skin.

Lysander wasted no time in reaching below her skirts to untie her crinoline and the tapes of her drawers and sliding both from her body. "One taste," she thought she heard him mutter.

The weight of him disappeared, and Nève fought to see in the darkness. A broad, wet swipe against her throbbing sex had her shuddering and falling back against the desk. Surely that wasn't what she thought it was… A second sinuous stroke, followed by the heady sound of his groan, had her fists winding and clenching in her skirts and a cry breaking from her lips.

Oh, Dieu above… his mouth was on her. *There.*

And it was shockingly glorious.

He sucked like he had on her nipple, and Nève nearly saw stars. His tongue flicked against her sensitive flesh with maddening strokes, the pleasure curling and building inside of her like a wave. His fingers danced up her inner thigh, and when she felt one of them breach her inner walls, her entire body seized. The wave crested and broke, pleasure barreling through her as Lysander's relentless tongue continued its sensual assault. One cataclysm crashed into another, and her vision went white. With a final soft lick, the duke stood and she was glad for the darkness, heat filling her cheeks at what he'd done. He touched her as if he adored her, as if each taste were a cherished gift.

She'd loved every second of it.

Nève felt his hands at her waist, drawing her upward on wobbly feet. His lips found hers, and she tasted herself on him, making her cheeks scorch even more.

"I can feel you blushing," he whispered huskily.

She hissed out a breath. "That was… indecent."

"There's no shame in pleasure, Geneviève." Heavens, the erotic way he said her name was almost enough to send her careening anew over the edge. Nève rubbed against him—he was still so hard—and moaned when her lower half brushed his. Her well-sated but greedy sex wanted more.

She drew a finger over his wet bottom lip. "May I try that? With you?"

His growl was almost inhuman. "Yes, but not now. Right now, I need to be inside you."

Oh, God, Nève wanted that, too. She wanted to savor every second. In this moment, in this dark room, she belonged to him, body, heart, and soul, even if he didn't know it. Even if she could never *confess* it. She was his; he was hers. No more barriers or boundaries between them. Just passion flowing through them like the sweetest of music. Like a final encore.

"Where did you go just then?" he whispered. "You went so still."

Nève blinked, feeling her eyes sting, and grateful for the cover of darkness. She slid her arms up around his nape and found his lips, kissing him. It wasn't a tender kiss. It was raw and devastating and soul destroying, but she wanted to be destroyed. She wanted to crash over him with all the love she had to give. Her palm drifted to his right pectoral, heartbreakingly gentle, in direct opposition to the violence of their kiss. "I'm here, Lysander. I'm right here."

"I need you so badly," he whispered against her mouth.

"I'm yours."

The rustle of clothing was her only warning before he turned her around and she felt a gust of air against her skin, and then he was there, the hard heat of him a brand. A gentle palm slid against her back, guiding her down until her face was pressed against the cool wooden surface, while his legs kicked hers apart. She felt exposed and vulnerable, but she trusted him. The girls in the corps had spoken of this position, but in bed, never over a desk.

In a *public* theater. It was deeply erotic.

Soft fingers danced along her ribs before cupping her hip and pulling upward so that her spine was arched. Even in the darkness, she could imagine how wickedly carnal she would appear— half-clothed with skirts draped over her buttocks, legs parted wide, her lower half on salacious display, and a huge god of a man behind her, hard and ready.

Her breath stuttered in her lungs as the tip of him breached her entrance, and with one stroke, they both groaned as he seated himself to the hilt. Nève could feel her body stretching to accommodate his size, but it was nowhere near as uncomfortable as it had been the first time. She felt deliciously full.

"Christ, you're a vise." With a wicked grin, she squeezed her walls around him, making him choke out a gasp. "What was *that*?"

"Pliés are a great way to strengthen the pelvic muscles," she said. "And a dancer's control over her body is impeccable."

"Don't," he bit out just as she did it again. "Fuck!"

Lysander drew back and shoved forward, his hips slamming into hers as his movements grew increasingly more erratic.

"You're diabolical, woman," he said. "But two can play at this game."

With that silky threat, he braced a palm against her ribs and pulled her up so that her back was flush against his chest. He was still firmly lodged within, but the new position made him touch a place inside her that had her brain turning to mush. And now his hands were free to torment her breasts before arrowing down to the screaming bundle of nerves at the apex of her sex. The flick of those clever fingers had her moaning even as his body punished hers from behind in the most carnal of ways.

"Too much," she moaned. "I'm ... Lysander!"

He kissed her nape. "Soar, my butterfly."

Those words set her free, and Nève did as she was told, releasing beautifully as she clenched and crashed around him, feeling him join her as his body seized and spent inside her.

Lysander's mind was lost in a haze of mind-numbing gratification.

He was dimly aware of Nève's slender body beneath his, but what was left of his brain was functioning enough to have most of his weight positioned on his elbows. He didn't want to crush her, after all. They were still joined, though his body was softening. He'd taken her like an animal, though she hadn't complained.

"I changed my mind," she murmured. "This was heaps more thrilling than being onstage in front of all those people. This definitely wins."

"Better than ballet?"

She laughed. "No, but perhaps a very close second."

Smirking with satisfaction, Lysander pushed upright, straightening and reaching for a handkerchief from his breast pocket. "Stay," he told her when she made to rise as well.

"What are you doing?" she squeaked, when he passed the cloth gently over her body.

"Housekeeping," he quipped.

Her husky chuckle was music to his ears. "Another joke? Goodness, Your Grace, we'll have you performing comedy on this very stage before you know it."

Grinning foolishly in the darkness, Lysander cleaned himself before tucking his half-stiff cock back into his trousers. The throaty sound of her laughter was enough to have him raring to go again, but bringing her in here had been a risk as it was. He helped her locate her crushed crinoline and get it back in place under her skirts, though the intoxicating scent of her had nearly made him repeat Act 1 of their erotic interlude.

Later, he promised himself.

"I can't see a thing," she said. "My hair is probably a mess."

He frowned. "Stay put. There's a light in here somewhere."

The gas sconces sizzled as light flooded the room.

Lysander's gaze found Nève where she stood, and he nearly stumbled over his own feet. Fuck if she wasn't the most beautiful woman he'd ever beheld. Wild, damp tendrils of hair framed her luminous face. Her cheeks were flushed, her lips swollen and red. Her green eyes glowed in a post-release haze. She looked gorgeously satisfied, and all he wanted to do was have her again.

Her palms flew up. "What is it? It's my hair, isn't it? I must look a fright."

"You are the most exquisite thing I've ever seen."

"Oh." Her hands fluttered in midair, her blush deepening.

"But yes, your hair is an absolute ghastly fright."

Her smile was like the sun coming out on a stormy day, and Lysander basked in the blinding warmth of it. "Ha! Three jokes in a row. It appears that a bracing round of carnal activity is good for your poor, sickly, brooding constitution, Your Grace."

"I'm inclined to agree. Are you volunteering to nurse me back to health?" He grinned back at her, and her eyes glittered with delight.

"Do you know you have a dimple?" She poked at her left cheek. "Just there."

Lysander blinked. "Do I?"

She nodded, walking toward him, reaching up to brush a lock of hair off his brow. "Only when you forget to keep it prisoner, of course."

His heart squeezed. The pad of her fingertip traced down his cheekbone to where the shallow indentation would be before she angled her palm to cup his jaw. Capturing her wrist, he stared down at her. Everything he was feeling bubbled up into his throat, choking him with nerves. More than anything, he wanted to beg her to stay, but that other coldly rational part of him veered toward his casing of stone and security. It had *never* failed him.

"What are you thinking?" she asked.

He cleared his throat. "That we should probably be getting back before our absence is noticed."

"I think that ship has long sailed, Your Grace," she said dryly. "The best course of action at this point is to slip out an exit, find a carriage, and make a quick escape. At least, that's how the gentlemen did it back in Paris."

Something venomous filled him. "You have experience with that?"

She shot him a look. "Yes, and I sewed my virtue back together just for you."

"That's not what I meant," he said.

Nève eyed him. "Then what did you mean?"

Raking a hand through his mussed hair, he blew air through his teeth. He was confused and not thinking straight. "Nothing. You're right. Let me find Millicent and make sure she has a way home, then I will meet you outside. Or would you rather go inside and I find the coach?"

Eyes going wide, she shook her head. "Not looking like this, I can't. They'll see right through me. Point me in the proper direction and I'll meet you at the carriage."

Lysander walked her to one of the other exits and watched as she made her way toward his ducal coach, before closing the door and heading back to the main hall. Taking a breath to compose himself, he reentered the foyer de la danse. It hadn't been that long since they'd left, no more than twenty minutes, but their joint absence would not have gone unremarked.

He ignored Lushing, who shot him a grin and a wink, and moved to where his aunt stood in conversation with a few people, including Marsden's wife and Lady Vesper.

"Aunt," he said. "I'm taking Miss Valery home as she isn't feeling well. I can send the coach back for you later, if you prefer."

"Oh, what is the matter?" Millicent asked with a frown.

"It's nothing serious, I assure you."

Lushing strode over and clapped his hand on Lysander's back. "I couldn't help overhearing what you were saying about the lovely Miss Valery. I might have some experience with this malady. Is the lady short of breath? Fluttering pulse? Locking muscles? Loss of consciousness?" Lysander's glare promised pain, but the bastard just grinned. "I could go on, if it's helpful."

"Nothing you do is ever helpful," he growled.

Lushing smirked. "But I beg to differ." He gave a thoughtful nod. "There are also convulsions, occasional screaming, and pleas to God. It can get quite severe."

Lysander scowled at the rake. "She has none of those symptoms, don't worry. Stop blowing hot air." He turned to the rest of the group. "Ignore him. Please enjoy the rest of the party. Nève would want you to."

"Lady Millicent can ride with us," Lady Marsden offered, hiding her grin behind her fan. "We have plenty of room in our carriage."

"Thank you. Then I bid you good evening."

He nearly stopped and punched Lushing in the mouth when the man called out "Watch her closely. Those symptoms have a tendency to escalate."

Lysander lengthened his stride instead. When he got outside the coachman was already waiting in front of the building. Nève was ensconced inside, and he climbed in to settle in the seat opposite her. She pinned her lips in between her teeth and then met his gaze shyly.

"I want to thank you for a wonderful birthday," she said. "Every part of it was incredible."

Lysander couldn't help smirking. "Every part?"

The minx rolled her eyes, though her cheeks lit a delicious pink in the gaslight of the carriage. "Is that all you men think about?"

"We think about other things, too," he said, crossing one ankle over his knee. "Like eating and sleeping."

"You only think about working, remember?"

Lysander canted his head. "I *used* to only think about working.

You've gotten under my skin of late and I seem to have developed a few terrible habits."

"All work and no play makes Jack a dull boy," she said.

His mouth quirked. "Tell that to Jack when he's in the poorhouse singing for his supper and jumping over candlesticks to escape the authorities."

"I think you of all people can afford a few indulgent habits, Your Grace."

Smiling at her wry expression, Lysander leaned back against the squabs, his long fingers drumming across the top of the bench. He studied her, the thought of what his life would be like once she was gone crossing his mind. Would it return to the colorless, laughter-less version it had been before? Would the loss of her presence leave a hollow carved out inside him? His throat felt like he swallowed a mouthful of sawdust.

"What will you do when you return to Paris?"

"Open a school with Vivienne. That's been her dream for years."

He nodded. "Not yours?"

"I always thought ballet was everything, but…dreams change," she said softly and then ducked her head as if she'd said something she hadn't wanted to say. "I don't think I will ever stop dancing. Ballet is too much a part of my blood, but I've had enough of the limelight. And men like Durand."

"He's a snake."

She shrugged. "Then by default the same can be said of many of the other gentlemen who sponsor ballet dancers."

"Doesn't make it right."

"No, it doesn't. What you said earlier though in the foyer, about consent, makes all the difference. A woman should be able to choose what she does with her own body. Many of those ballerinas have limited options—a sponsor means opportunity. Vivienne and I were lucky we didn't have to rely on a man's charity. Between us, we had our savings and we lived frugally, until her injury at least."

"Is that why you agreed to our arrangement? You needed money?"

She nodded, her mouth twisting with an edge of bitterness. "The transaction is a double-edged sword. It makes it both scandalous and safe. Scandalous because it's money for my company. Safe because the expectations are set."

"I've never considered that."

"Your wealth and position give you power, but my ability to choose gives me mine." She gave him a soft smile. "Tonight meant something special because of that same choice. The chance to dance in that particular ballet was closure in itself, considering it was my final real performance." Nève exhaled. "How did you manage to do it?"

"Lushing is on good terms with the director of the Salle Le Peletier. He's a pain in the arse most days, but even I will admit that the man has connections everywhere." He shrugged. "I simply made them an offer they could not refuse."

"Sounds familiar."

It wasn't accusatory or cruel, simply a statement of fact, but a knot still formed in his throat. "It's not the same. You have to know that all this ... it was for you."

Dark lashes fluttered down to hide her expression, and he

almost raised his hand to tilt her chin up so that he could see every single secret buried in those green eyes. So that he could cherish this moment. Seeing her like this, so beautifully strong and powerful, it shook him to the core. He wanted nothing more than to see her this happy. *Always.*

His mouth opened and closed...the fervor of the words tumbling through his head expressing what he could no longer deny. *I love how you make me feel. I like having your presence near. I love the warmth of your laughter in the coldness of my life. I don't want to spend another day without you.*

He desperately wanted to keep her. To beg her to keep him. To amend their agreement.

To persuade her to stay.

Because without her, he was helplessly, hopelessly lost.

"Stay." The word was a grated whisper, barely audible. A plea from the depths of him that had escaped his stranglehold on his emotions.

She glanced up at him, brows pleated. "What did you say?"

Lysander exhaled. She hadn't heard him, and perhaps that was a blessing in disguise. Vivienne needed her. She had a life in Paris. He had a railway to build. A project to complete. Their paths were always meant to diverge.

Their eyes met and held for a suspended moment. *Don't leave*, he wanted to shout. His bloody eyes pricked, even as his fingers keyed a frantic rhythm into his thigh. He could show her his heart with music, but there weren't any instruments near, bar his own unskilled voice.

He fought the mental habit that twisted up his tongue. "I know that you have to go back to Paris." Choosing his words carefully, he took in a measured breath. "But I was wrong when I said I wanted things to remain businesslike between us. I wish we had met under different circumstances, but I want you to know I don't regret a second of this. Of you. I could never regret you, Geneviève."

"I don't regret anything either," she said softly. The poignant look in that glossy gaze flayed him to the bone.

Because after Vesper's birthday party, she knew it would be goodbye, too.

CHAPTER TWENTY-ONE

"Stop thinking about her," Lysander growled to himself. "She's done her part. Now it's time to do yours, and get this railway finished."

He was sick of the fucking railway.

After Nève's brilliant suggestion, Lysander had sent his man of business north to interview the employees for Treadway's Clareville Railway, and the report had come back a day ago. It was worse than he'd suspected, given the viscount's reticence to provide the final accounting. Stories of drastically reduced dividends, misappropriated funds, delaying payments for monies owed, and new shares being offered at artificially inflated prices were the worst red flags.

"What are you muttering about over there?" Lushing asked from where he sat on the sofa, with his third glass of whiskey in hand. "You said thirty minutes. We've been here over an hour. I thought the sale with Bolden was resolved."

"I'm waiting on fucking Treadway."

Lushing squinted. "The foxed fool from the ballet?"

He nodded. "The figures from his report don't line up. Are you any good with numbers?"

Lushing made a face. "I copied your arithmetic homework at Eton, remember?"

"Fair enough."

Lysander couldn't decide whether Treadway was being willfully deceitful or was simply unaware of the solvency and practices of his company. He was all too familiar with indolent aristocrats who cared only about maintaining their extravagant lifestyles, even if it meant cheating others, and if that was the case here, then his instincts about Treadway would have been dreadfully off.

He couldn't recall the last time he'd made such a mistake.

A dark-haired, green-eyed, svelte ballerina came to mind, but he shoved the thought away as quickly as it had come. She was the best decision he'd ever made. Not telling her how he felt, however, was a mistake, but that was neither here nor there. His only regret was that he should have been more concerned with the viscount's obvious attempts to evade him, instead of the silken feel of Nève's lips or the sound of her laughter or the way she looked when she was dancing. Or the fragrant scent of her that pervaded every breath in his lungs.

A dark chuckle broke free from Lushing. "From that besotted look on your face, you're thinking about your ballerina instead of ledgers."

"She's not my ballerina. And I am hardly besotted."

Lushing wrinkled his nose and poured himself another glass. "She's your fiancée, no?"

Lysander scrubbed his palm through his hair, wanting to get some of the weight off his chest, and who better to confide in than his best mate, one who was well on his way to being foxed and might not remember anyway?

"What if I told you we weren't engaged? That it was all a ruse? That she's a dancer I met in Covent Garden and paid her to play a role for the sake of this deal?"

"If that were true, I'd say you were the coldest bastard in London." His friend blinked. "Is it?"

"Yes. I hired her."

"Fuck, Stone. That's ruthless, even for you."

He let out a long breath, struggling with the words. "That's not all. I...care about her."

"So marry her. What's the problem? Any woman in England would salivate to be a duchess, even yours I'd wager."

"She's not like that." He slumped into his chair. "It's complicated."

Grinding his jaw, Lysander dug his fingers into his palms. He felt deeply and disproportionately out of control. Not only was this deal not proceeding as it should, his arrangement with Nève would be ending soon. His instincts felt off. His priorities were skewed. He was more preoccupied with losing a woman than he was with losing a business contract worth hundreds of thousands of pounds.

He was so close to success...and yet, his deepest desires had changed.

He had changed.

He didn't care about the railway. Or Bolden's property. Or any of it. For the first time in his adult life, he felt uncertain of his course.

"Gracious, you look positively ferocious," a laughing voice said from the doorway. "I didn't realize Lord Lushing was here as well. Shall I come back later?"

Nève. Even the sound of her voice was an unexpected balm. Lysander glanced up, noting how lovely she looked in a lavender morning dress. Then again, she could wear a sack and make it look good.

"Miss Valery!" Lushing hollered. "The lady of the hour!" Lysander sent him a horrified glance, hoping he would keep those loose lips buttoned, but the earl ignored him. "We were just talking about you."

She smiled. "Were you? Good things, I hope."

"Yes, Stone was—"

"What is it, Nève?" Lysander asked quickly, cutting him off from inserting his inebriated foot into his mouth. "Do you require something?"

A pair of amused green eyes met his. "I wanted to see if you were free for luncheon with me."

"I'm afraid I will be poor company," he said, though the offer was tempting. "My humor is a bit frayed at the moment from attempting to reconcile these numbers. And Lushing is of absolutely no help besides drinking all my good liquor."

"It's excellent liquor," the earl agreed. "And meant to be drunken." He paused. "Drunked. Drunking. Something like that."

Lysander rolled his eyes, and Nève hid her giggle behind her hand.

"May I have a look?" she asked, walking toward him. "My papa always said I had a good head for figures as a girl. I used to remind him of the people who never paid him back the money they borrowed or the interest. Perhaps a fresh perspective is what you need."

He blew out a breath of relief. "These are the ledgers for the Clareville Railway, and these are the sums my man of business was able to uncover from local investors as you so cleverly proposed."

Shy pleasure lit her eyes before she leaned over the desk. It was an innocent position, but the sensual thoughts running through his head were far from it. But he liked the easy feel of this, too, and the warm familiarity of her slim form beside his, as though she belonged there. If Lushing weren't in the room, he'd pull her into his lap and bury his face in her hair. Hold her for hours until the world fell away.

"I see what you mean," she said, pointing at a column of numbers. "There are discrepancies in terms of income and payouts in almost every instance. The figures are tiny enough to escape notice."

"So an error?" he asked, leaning down to inspect the ledger.

She shook her head. "It would not seem so. The numbers appear to be inflated by the same amount each time, but I am not an expert."

"No, you're right. I missed it before, but I see it now."

When she stared up at him, he saw something flare in her eyes at their nearness, but she focused her attention back on the columns. Her lips moved as though she was redoing the calculations in her head, and then she nodded. "They don't match up."

"Your Grace," Finley announced. "Viscount Treadway is here."

Lysander straightened. At least the cad had the decency to wait to be announced this time. "Send him in, please."

The man waltzed in without a worry in the world. "Heard you were looking for me?" he said. "Oh, hullo, Miss Valery. And Lord Lushing, too. I didn't see you sprawled over there."

"Viscount Treadway," Nève said with a nod while the earl gave a half-hearted wave.

His grin was ingratiating. "So formal. Call me Bart."

Lysander headed that one off quickly, stepping in between them and blocking Treadway's view of her. He knew he should ask her to leave, but he didn't. "The numbers don't add up, Tread-way. Can you explain that?"

The viscount's smile vanished. "As far as I know they're accurate."

"They are wrong. I've triple-checked them myself."

"That's impossible, you must be mistaken," Treadway insisted, and Lysander frowned. If he was acting, he was doing a fine job of it, but numbers did not lie. Mathematics was an exact and exhaustive science.

"He's not mistaken," Nève interjected. "I've checked them as well."

The viscount's gaze narrowed on her like the stare of a snake awoken from sleep, and Lysander's senses prickled. For a moment, the man's easygoing demeanor slipped. If Lysander had blinked, he would have missed it, but the sly, furious look was a signal that the viscount wasn't some incompetent, oblivious dandy. Was it all a charade?

"Leave the menfolk's work to the men, love," he drawled.

To Lysander's surprise, Nève laughed. "Women can also perform simple addition, *Bart*. Sex isn't a condition for basic aptitude." She walked to the door, a smile on those full lips. "But I'll leave you to your menfolk affairs."

Sharp green eyes met his, and dear God, he wanted to kiss her. When she was gone, he met the probing gaze of the viscount. It was filled with scornful amusement. "Do you make a habit of letting your women do your work for you, Your Grace?"

"I don't *let* her do anything."

Lushing stood, weaving unsteadily on his feet. "Should I go?"

"No, stay," Lysander said. Without him, a murder might be committed, and he needed a witness.

Treadway scowled. "Where did you say you met her again?"

"I didn't."

"*When* did you meet her then?"

Lysander's voice was pure stone. "None of your business. I want you to explain these numbers to me or our deal is off."

He saw a glimmer of that deception again as the viscount's mask fell away, displaying a flicker of pure unmitigated rage. "I told you. The finances are solid. You would trust that woman's opinion over what I'm telling you?"

"I would trust my own, and I can add very well, Treadway."

The viscount stood and paced, agitation evident in every step. "How do you know she wasn't planted by someone? To come here and stoke trouble? The numbers were fine several months ago. Things haven't changed between then and now."

"You're not selling inflated shares?" Lysander asked.

Treadway halted, tension blasting from him. "Where did you get that information? Was it from *her*?"

"Not directly no."

"Indirectly then," Treadway snarled. "Can't you see that she's a spy? Someone must have put her in your path just so she could discredit me and ruin the progress of our railway. Someone from the North Eastern Railway. They want the land for themselves! I told you they've been sniffing around."

"She's not with North Eastern," Lysander said.

The viscount's face was almost purple with rage. "Damn it, Montcroix, listen to me! I'm telling you she looks familiar. I'm certain I saw her with George Leeman—"

"For fuck's sake, stop grasping at straws, you cretin," Lushing muttered. "She's not a spy, she's a ballerina he found in Covent Garden."

Dead silence ensued. Lysander wanted to throttle his fool of a friend with his bare hands, but the cat was out of the bag now.

The viscount gaped at him in shock. "But she's your fiancée." Lysander said nothing, kicking himself internally for confiding in Lushing, who didn't even realize what he'd inadvertently done with his poor choice of words. Treadway's eyes grew wide as delayed understanding filled them. "Found? You sly dog. You faked the engagement to win over Bolden."

"Our deal is off," Lysander said with a tired exhale. "I can't do business with a man whose employees are inadequately paid and terribly overworked. Or someone who manipulates revenue and expenditure to keep himself in lavish style. You lied and committed fraud."

Lysander was well aware of the hypocrisy, considering he'd fashioned a ruse to win over Bolden, but it wasn't the same as cheating honest and hardworking investors of their money. Still, a ripple of unease slid down his spine.

"Now see here," Treadway sputtered. "Montcroix, this is an outrage!"

"Get out." Lysander folded his arms. "Evans, please see Viscount Treadway to the door. Thank you."

"Montcroix!" the viscount screamed as Evans did as he was

bid, the large footman taking the viscount in a firm grip. "You'll regret this!"

The truth was Lysander already did. Sweeping the papers violently from his desk, he let out several choice oaths. Months of work, now lost. A fortune, gone.

He glared at his friend. "Give me one good reason I shouldn't pummel you right now. What the fuck were you thinking telling him that about Nève?"

Lushing stared at him, wide-eyed. "It was a secret?"

"Well, it's not now, is it?" he ground out.

"Hell, mate. I'm sorry. He was just going on and on that she was some dreadful spy and that's the last thing she is!"

Lysander clenched his fists. Lushing had intended to defend her honor, but still . . .

Fuck, he needed to focus on something else. Something *good*. Without another word to Lushing, he stalked from the study to where Finley stood in the foyer. "Where is Miss Valery?"

"She's taking luncheon on the terrace, Your Grace," the butler said.

"Thank you. Summon the earl's carriage please and make sure he gets home."

"Yes, Your Grace."

It was amazing what the sight of her did to his frazzled, muddled senses. Upon seeing that head of dark hair, poring over the newssheets while she munched on a piece of roasted chicken, the agitation brewing inside of him eased. Not completely, but enough for him to not want to break something with his bare hands. Preferably Treadway.

Dismissing the hovering servants with a curt wave, he approached.

"May I join you?" he asked. She smiled and pushed the chair to her left out with a stockinged toe. His lip curled. "No shoes? How scandalous."

"I have them," she said blushing. "They are just under the table. I admit my feet are still quite sore from the performance the other night. Dancing in new ballet slippers that haven't been broken in is a terrible idea." She glanced over his shoulder. "Where's Lord Lushing? Will he be joining us?"

"Not in his condition, no." Lysander sat and gestured toward her. "Let me see."

"Let you see what?" she asked, a faint blush cresting her cheekbones as she stared at his extended hand in adorable confusion.

"Your foot," he said slowly, opening his palm.

Those green eyes of hers went wide. "The servants, Your Grace."

Lysander almost chuckled at the aghast look on her face as she craned her neck to see if any of them had overheard. "Don't worry, I've dismissed everyone." His tone went husky. "Do I need to remind you about other places I've touched with my tongue? A foot—a covered foot at that—is nothing."

"Your Grace!" she hissed, but desire crept into her eyes.

"And besides, this is my house." He flexed his wrist and put steel into his voice. "Foot, now, Geneviève."

Her slender throat worked at the command, but a fire burned in that feral green gaze. Slowly, so as to convey that she did not have to obey but was choosing to do so, she lifted a slender leg and placed it in his waiting palm. She flicked her tongue across her lip with the tiniest of gasps as he cupped her heel. Her skin was warm beneath the white silk stockings, and very carefully, he placed her foot in his lap.

"Now the other."

"Lysander," she protested softly, but he wasn't having it. He *needed* to touch her. Staring at her, he waited in silence until she sighed and raised the other foot to rest beside the first. Glancing down, he could see hints of swelling beneath the fabric on her tender skin, and with the utmost care, he began to rub her feet. "Ohhh." Her moan of bliss made him grin. "That's heavenly."

"I am a man of many talents," he said.

"Clearly."

"Does it hurt?" he asked after working both feet from toe to heel, and then frowned at what looked like mottled shapes on her arches beneath the thin silk hose. "These bruises were from the one evening?"

"This isn't so bad. Ballet can be worse than pugilism." He stilled, and then lifted a finger to summon someone. Nève ducked her head and went crimson when he murmured something to Finley, whose gaze remained firmly averted in the other direction. "I thought you said you dismissed the staff!" she hissed when they were alone again.

"Finley is very discreet, and you gave me an idea."

"Which was?" She went quiet again, when the butler returned to deliver a small pot before leaving. "What is that?"

He uncapped the pot. "A salve I use on my knuckles after boxing. It helps with muscular pain." He stroked over her silk-clad ankles, voice a rasp. "May I remove your stockings?"

Blushing furiously, she nodded after a protracted beat, her

breath hitching when his hands slid under her petticoats to the ties at the top of her knee. They both went still when his fingertips met warm flesh. *So soft.* Lysander blinked. He hadn't quite thought this through...how she would feel. How very much he wanted all of her completely bare.

His blood thundered in his veins at the warm texture of her skin as he painstakingly unrolled each stocking until the curves of her lower calves were visible. He wanted to press his lips to the creamy lengths, breathe in the scent of her, and lift those skirts higher to trace those tantalizing dips and hollows all the way up her slender, muscled thighs.

"I'm sorry my feet are hideous," she said in a breathless rush and shoved the fabric down to her ankles, with a nervous look toward the door.

Smiling at her modesty, he rubbed the salve into the ball of her left foot and massaged in small circles that made her groan and her eyes flutter closed. "I love touching you."

Her lids snapped open and narrowed with reproach. "Lysander. You're making this much harder than it has to be."

"I don't understand," he said, genuinely perplexed. "It's the nice thing to do."

She stalled him with soft fingers and then placed her feet into her slippers one by one. "It is, but things aren't always so simple. When you touch me, I want more. And we both know that more is a slippery slope with us." She stood and bent to kiss his cheek, the imprint of her lips scalding. "We shouldn't tempt fate any more than we already have."

He wanted to throw fate into the fucking void, but he nodded, respecting her wishes. Lysander cleared his throat. "I understand.

Since we have more free time, I did want to ask if there was anything you would like to do while you're here?"

Her green eyes lit up. "I wouldn't mind going for a ride."

Lysander's gut clenched with need. He'd offer to be the mount if he didn't think it would be the most vulgar suggestion in the world, but that was how bloody desperate he was. "Tomorrow. I'll make the arrangements."

CHAPTER TWENTY-TWO

With some trepidation, Nève eyed the riding habit in the mirror. The ensemble, another of Laila's, was beautiful—a rich hunter green with cloth-covered buttons down the front and a smart cream collar—but perhaps she'd bitten off more than she could chew. She hadn't ridden in years, not since she was a girl.

She tugged at the excess fabric draped on one side, and the ingenious front split in the skirts that allowed her to wear a pair of fitted breeches beneath. At least she wouldn't be bare-arsed if she took a tumble. Nève let out a breath and released the skirts before her helpful lady's maid deftly pinned the smart matching hat to her head.

"Thank you, Annie," she said.

"You look lovely, miss," the maid said. "That color brings out your eyes a treat." She shot her a shy grin. "The duke will love it."

The duke wouldn't be looking at her riding habit if she fell off her bloody horse and embarrassed herself. Nève shook her head with a wry laugh. She made her way downstairs and outside to the courtyard, toward the mews where Lysander was waiting with a groom busy saddling a massive glossy brown stallion and a smaller gray horse. She took a cautious step toward the pair, her nerves getting the better of her as the gray pranced prettily.

"Come meet Belle," the duke said. "She's my most docile mare."

"She doesn't look very docile." Nève narrowed her eyes at the beautiful creature. Why did she suddenly get the feeling the horse was doing the same and sizing her up? Best to not show that she was afraid. Animals had a secret sense about these things.

She'd ridden before; she could do it again.

It's like doing a pirouette—you never really forget.

With the groom's help, she clambered up the mounting block into the saddle, settling herself with both legs on one side, her upper leg tucked into the slipper stirrup. The duke mounted his horse with much more effortless grace than she had.

"Take this, miss," the groom said, handing her a crop.

Nève shook her head. "I don't like those. I wouldn't want to hurt her."

He gave her a lopsided smile. "It's not meant to harm her. It's to guide her, you see. Because of the sidesaddle, there's no stirrup over here. A gentle touch is all you need."

"Oh."

She took the crop gingerly, angling it down the mare's right side. The horse didn't seem bothered by the presence or the slight graze of it, so that was reassuring. Her seat felt comfortable at first, but once the horse began to move, the gait made her feel like she was going to topple off. But she was a dancer and she knew her body. After anchoring her weight toward the right hip bone and keeping her posture upright, she felt a bit more confident.

"Lead her once more in a circle, Lorrie," the duke said to the groom.

"Yes, Your Grace."

He eyed her after they'd completed the turn about the court-yard. "How do you feel?"

"Good." The groom released the lead, and Nève frowned. "Stop right there. You're not continuing to guide the horse?"

Lysander chuckled. "Belle will follow Samson. You can do this."

"I still feel that Lorrie should come," she said stubbornly. "What if I fall?"

"You don't trust me to catch you, butterfly?" His voice was even, but the pulse it elicited between her legs was wicked in the extreme.

She swallowed. "I do."

"Good."

Gingerly, Nève held her balance as they walked through the yard, and relaxed after a few moments when she realized that Belle wasn't going to throw her off the first chance she got or take off running the minute she saw open road. In fact, the mare trot-ted quite docilely beside Samson.

After a few minutes, Nève forgot about her nerves and let her-self enjoy the ride.

"You're a natural," Lysander told her.

"Thank you," she said. "Once you have the beat, it's a matter of keeping your body in tune with it."

They rode in silence for a while until they were inside the park. It was a smidgen before the fashionable hour, so it wasn't yet crowded. Nève couldn't help noticing how well the duke carried himself in the saddle. His coat strained across the muscles of his back and shoulders, and she knew the strength and feel of both intimately. *Without* clothing. Nève's fingers tightened on the reins as a rush of warmth filled her. Dieu, if she didn't stop ogling the man, she was going to slide off the dratted horse.

"How did things go with Treadway?" she asked in an attempt at distraction.

"I ended it."

She'd pulled back on the reins so sharply that Belle came to an abrupt halt. "*What?*"

Lysander steered his mount around so that they were face-to-face. "His company was corrupt. He lied and cheated his employees and his investors. He wasn't the man I thought he was."

She frowned. "But what about Bolden's property? Can you find another railway company to partner with to continue your plans?"

"I suppose."

Her frown deepened. "You *suppose?*" She looked around and pretended to peer into the nearby glade. Then twisted her torso to the other side and did the same. Then she raised her hand to her brow and gazed into the distance.

"What are you doing? Looking for flying pigs again?"

"Looking for the single-minded, work-driven, hard-arsed Duke of Montcroix. I heard he was missing, but I did not believe it."

That stern mouth curved, a hint of a dimple making her gulp. "You think he has a hard arse?"

Oh, hell. She really was going to slip off the blasted horse. "You are playing with my words, Your Grace."

Lysander inched Samson closer so that their knees were nearly touching. "I've heard that the duke's been missing for weeks, ever since he got lost in Covent Garden, as a matter of fact."

"Has he?" she whispered.

"A ballerina butterfly rescued him and stole him away to her realm. Showed him that there could be light and happiness in his life. That he might not have to be alone if he was willing to change."

No, she wasn't going to fall off, she was going to bloody swoon. Everything inside of her felt tight—her lungs, her throat, her heart. "And did he? Change?"

He didn't answer, only stared at her. Nève was mesmerized by the look in his eyes. She'd never seen them so full of light, like a pool of molten mercury shot through with silver shards. It felt as though everything was hinging on this moment—like the full breath a dancer took before leaping into the arms of her partner and trusting him not to drop her during a lift. Nève inhaled, waiting.

A shrill voice cut between them breaking the magical moment. "Your Grace, I must have a word."

No, Nève wanted to scream as Lysander steered his horse a step away to greet the incoming riders. Lysander's stepmother... and Lord Durand. Her stomach went cold at the first glimpse of the woman's face and her calculating expression. Durand, that slimy bastard, had to have told her who Nève was. She should have known he would not have left quietly, not after being embarrassed by the duke in front of the entire company.

"What do you want?" Lysander said, his voice retaining none of his earlier heat.

"For you to get rid of this diversion of yours." Her eyes glittered. "I insist on you not sullying the family name."

Nève bristled, ready to fight her own battles, but Lysander beat her to it.

"She's not a diversion." His mouth flattened. "May I remind you who is duke here, Charlotte."

"Lord Durand told me who she is," she went on, and Nève couldn't help seeing that they were attracting attention. Two barouches and a curricle had slowed. "A French ballerina who has been passed around by every gent—"

The poise drained from Nève like water through a net.

Lysander growled. "Finish that statement, I dare you. I will see you to Northumberland for the rest of your days."

The lady blanched and sealed her lips.

His icy glare found Durand. "I told you what would happen, and here you are, causing damage to a young woman who has done nothing but reject your unwelcome advances." The duke's smile was a slash of viciousness. "Enjoy the poorhouse, my *lord*."

Durand paled to the color of parchment before yanking on his horse's reins and cantering away.

"Lysander, I only wanted to—" Charlotte began, but the duke cut her off. Nève had never seen such a look of utter violence on his face.

"I did not care that you cuckolded me in front of the entire ton. I did not care when you left me to marry my father. But I very much care now that you show me respect."

"But she's…"

"She's what?"

Charlotte sent her a look of such contempt that Nève felt it in her bones. "Durand's leavings."

Lysander started to laugh, and Nève looked up at him in surprise. "And you were my father's, and yet you expect me to have you."

But it wasn't what he'd said to Charlotte, it was what he *hadn't* said. Why hadn't he defended her? She wasn't Durand's anything. Nève knew by now that the duke only responded to things he felt required explanations—it was the way his strange mind worked—but the fact that he didn't even care to address the slight done to her *hurt*.

Durand's *leavings*. He knew that wasn't true. He believed her when she said she'd refused Durand. Hadn't he?

Nève didn't think, she bolted. Thankfully, Belle cooperated and allowed her to keep her dignity intact. She ignored the duke's sharp shout, ignored the stares of the other riders, ignored everyone on the road. All she could think about was getting back to the mews. But she must have made a wrong turn somewhere or cantered past the turn because within minutes she was…lost.

Nève let out a sigh and dismounted. She needed to stretch her cramped legs. But once that was done, she would simply have to rescue herself as she'd always done. Luckily it was broad daylight and there were many people on the paths. Directing the horse around, her way was suddenly blocked by a man in a flashy curricle led by a pair of matching horses.

He was well dressed so she did not panic when he descended. Until she saw his face.

"Viscount Treadway. What are you doing here?"

He grinned and she did not like it. The veneer he wore was wavering.

"The question is Miss Valery, what are *you* doing here?"

She waved an arm, frowning as he raked her body with a lascivious gaze. "What everyone else is doing, sir. Taking the air on horseback."

"Taking the air, are you?" He licked his lips in a manner that made her flesh crawl. "Shouldn't you be under the duke, fulfilling your duties and taking *him* on your *back* instead? After all, isn't that what he hired you for?"

Nève blinked, shock blanketing her at his crass statements. But it was the last one that gutted her. How did he know about their arrangement? "I don't know what you're talking about."

"Don't you?" He closed the distance between them, trailing a finger down her arm. "Montcroix and I spoke of you just yesterday."

Her heart plummeted. How could she have been so wrong about Lysander? "Step back, sir."

He didn't heed the warning, that loathsome finger trailing back up to her shoulder. "How much would you cost, I reckon?"

"I am not for sale, sir."

He sneered. "Surely you're not that good that Montcroix wants you all to himself?"

Nève dropped Belle's reins. "No, you're just that contemptible."

His nostrils flared in disgruntled ire. "Is that a word they teach dancers in the corps while your arse is in the air?"

"I was born a lady, you sorry excuse for a man. Now leave me alone."

"Or what? You'll scream? No one will believe you. I'll just say you're my wife and you need a firm hand. Not right upstairs, you see." That oily smile appeared again, and this time, Nève felt the first inkling of fear. He could do just as he'd said and most people would turn a blind eye. Wives were property, and a man—especially one with a title—could do as he wanted. It was the reason her new friend Briar was such a fierce advocate for women's rights. But Briar wasn't here. Neither was the duke. No one was.

She had only herself and her wits.

"So, how much for a night?"

Ignoring the blare of alarm in her head, Nève stepped into his space. "I told you. I. Am. *Not*. For. Hire."

His fingers tightened cruelly. "You stupid, vain har—"

But he didn't get another word in as Nève swallowed the pain from the bite of his grip, wrenched the split in her skirts apart, and swung her knee up as hard as she could. But he must have sensed the attack because he sidestepped to his right at the last moment so her knee glanced off his left thigh. Treadway's mask fell, and all she could see on his face was pure, unholy wrath. Out of the corner of her eye she saw his hand tighten into a fist and lift.

Non. She might be a woman, but she wasn't helpless.

With all the force she could muster, she brought the crop up between his legs, the hard leather connecting with a snapping sound that made her wince. Before pain clouded it, Treadway's expression was almost comical. He toppled over, screaming and clutching his ballocks as he writhed on the ground.

"Espèce de lâche!" She spat on the mewling coward. See how he liked being threatened and manhandled! Then she used his body as a mounting block to clamber back on her horse, leaving him a keening mess in the dirt.

"Nève!"

Determined to find her way, she was heading back the way she'd come, and recognized the duke racing toward her on

Samson just as she heard him call out her name. She pulled Belle to a gentle stop, shoving back the feelings of relief and, worse, happiness at the sight of him and focused on the fact that he'd told Treadway about their agreement.

"Treadway approached me," she said when he halted, his face searching hers.

He stared. "What?"

"Treadway," she repeated calmly. "He's over there around the bend. I won't apologize for his state. I fear I might have drawn blood, but he deserved it." She let out a breath and with it the agony gnawing at her nerves. "He sought to procure my services."

She watched Lysander carefully, and when the guilt bled across his expression for a scant second, Nève felt nothing... nothing but a numbing coldness slivering through her veins. "You told him."

"No, I did not," he said. "I told Lushing, and he told Treadway."

Her eyes went wide with horror. "I'm the subject of parlor room discussion?" A guttural laugh ripped from her. "The things he said, the things he *expected* from me as if you had declared me a courtesan peddling her wares in the hallowed streets of Mayfair!" She lowered her voice to a mimicry of his. "'When I'm done here, old boy, you should give her a go. She's worth every penny, trust me, but only when I've finished.'"

"Stop this," he said.

"Why?" Tears stung her eyes. "A duke's *leavings* are better than a marquis's, aren't they?"

"I've never called you that."

"But Charlotte did, and you said nothing. A rose by any other name... I am what I am. A light-skirt for hire."

His lips flattened. "Enough of this. You're being vulgar."

"*I'm* being vulgar?" She bared her teeth. "I haven't even *begun* to be vulgar, Your Grace. I mean truly, I should put a higher value on myself, shouldn't I?" She stared at him. "It's important to recognize your worth. Isn't that what you said? Excellent advice. I shall be sure to use it in future negotiations."

The duke stared at her, mouth slack and face unreadable. She could see the wheels in his head turning as he sorted through all the information, but this wasn't that hard. Admitting he was wrong wasn't difficult. Comforting her shouldn't be either. When he didn't say anything at all, she thinned her lips. Her insides felt so hollow, so empty, as though her heart had been excavated from her chest. She felt tired, drained, and *used*.

But she was better than this.

"We're done here," she said.

"May I remind you that we have a binding agreement, Miss Valery," he said in such a curt voice, it nearly stunned her. She swallowed. She shouldn't have expected anything less from him, this duke with the stone heart. Oui, he saw things in stark black and white, but this was beyond ridiculous. He truly was a heartless monster if he couldn't see what was wrong here.

"As if I could forget." Exhaling, Nève grasped the reins, head high and taking a page from his book of cold detachment. "In two weeks, when I complete my part of the bargain, I will leave for good, and that will be the end of that." She didn't look at him as she nudged Belle to canter forward. "Service complete. La fin."

The end.

Never mind that her heart was fracturing. Never mind that tears blurred her vision. Never mind that she'd taken the leap and crashed for it. Letting herself care for a man who did not actually possess a heart, despite all her own reservations, had been her own fault, no one else's. Her choices, and all their consequences, were her own. Like fractured bones, her heart would mend.

Eventually.

CHAPTER TWENTY-THREE

What had he done wrong? Staring into his drink, Lysander blinked, replaying the scene in his head. It wasn't *his* fault that Lushing had blurted the truth to Treadway. He'd explained that to her, and she'd gone down a path he'd found hard to follow, one that included that bastard Durand. Why did Nève care about what *he* thought about Durand? The man was a bottom-feeder who had no bearing on the two of them at all. The way the whole situation had escalated had left him in a state of frozen shock.

We're done here.

The words had gutted him, and all he'd managed to do was make things worse when he'd balked and burst out that they weren't done because they had an agreement. In that instant, it was all he'd heard, that she was done with him. Lysander knew his reply had been wrong, even if it was the truth.

Lysander exhaled. How had he fucked up so monumentally?

Because you don't know how to function, you dolt.

You ruin everyone you touch.

Lysander narrowed his eyes as the liquor in the half-empty bottle he held in his hand gave its harsh rebuttals. Or perhaps that was his conscience speaking and not, in fact, a whiskey bottle.

Because whiskey bottles could not talk. Being drunk solved nothing, of course, but at least it numbed him enough from having to feel anything at all. He *hated* feeling. He hated feeling irritable, miserable, and so fucking guilty.

God, he hated that he'd hurt her.

That Treadway had hurt her...because of him. Indirectly, yes, but he, *Lysander*, had still caused it. It was his fault.

After he'd collected the viscount in Hyde Park, gratified as he'd been to see the piece of shit still moaning about his whipped cock and balls, he'd carted the cretin back to his residence and dumped him on his doorstep. But before Lysander had taken his leave, he leaned into the man. "You're lucky she dealt with you so kindly. If I ever find out you touched her, you'll be gelded for life, I promise you."

He'd wanted to beat the bastard into a pulp, but getting himself home to Blackstone Manor—home to Nève—took precedence. The viscount would be held accountable and charged for his crimes. For now, he needed to talk with Nève, apologize, make her understand—*beg* her to understand—that he'd never intended to hurt her. But when he arrived, Finley informed him that the lady was indisposed.

The next day he was told that she'd gone out with her friends. He'd given strict orders to be instructed when she got back, but either she'd slipped in unnoticed or Finley and Evans had decided to mutiny. Lysander had strongly suspected it was the latter. They were both fond of her. His entire staff adored her.

Everyone had fallen in love with her.

Everyone.

The knot in his throat thickened. Lysander hadn't seen her in days, and the week was quickly slipping through his fingers. Five days left with her. Four days left. And now three.

Soon it would be one and she would be gone.

You're soft, boy. His father's laugh echoed in his head. *Stupid and spineless.* Lysander tipped up the bottle, trying to block out the duke's unwelcome voice, but the man was as unrelenting as a specter as he'd been in life. *Have I taught you nothing? You're a dunce. Pathetic. Losing your head over a woman. Now look at you, brought to heel like a dog. Goddamned useless.*

"Fuck you," Lysander muttered. He flung the bottle into the empty hearth, watching as the glass shattered and the liquid sloshed over the stones. He wasn't useless or weak. Letting Nève in hadn't been weakness.

A knock on the door made him look up from where he was slumped in the armchair. "Go away!" he roared.

Whoever it was did not listen, damn them to purgatory, and rattled the door instead. Without warning, the locked door splintered open on its hinges. A large man emerged from the wreckage. *Evans.*

"Pack your bags and get out," Lysander growled.

"No, Evans, go back to your duties," Millicent said crisply, following on the footman's heels. "Thank you for your assistance."

Lysander scowled as the footman left. His scowl deepened further at the disappointed look on his aunt's face. Millicent sniffed before wrinkling her nose. "You smell dreadful." Her expression turned stern. "Enough of this, Nephew."

"I wish to be alone, Aunt," he said.

"You've had enough time alone doing God knows what in

here." Millicent cocked her head, her mouth a flat line. "What happened between you and Miss Valery?"

He swallowed, the sound of her name like a stab to the gut. His tongue felt thick in his mouth, but she lifted her brows, waiting in cool silence. "Leave me to myself. I only cause harm where none is warranted." He poked himself in the chest. "What's in here may as well not exist, because what's up here"—he jabbed at his temple—"doesn't fucking understand. And innocent people get hurt in the process."

His aunt didn't bat an eyelash at the profanity. "Nève has a generous spirit. Have you explained or apologized?"

He should have been surprised that his aunt had guessed the center of his turmoil, but he was not. "She refuses to see me."

"Perhaps for good reason."

He let out a half laugh, half cry. "Don't you think I know that? It was my fault, all of it."

Millicent stared at him as though she were trying to peer inside his soul, and he frowned. "Do you care for the girl?"

What he felt for Nève was more than care...he *loved* her. But all he could hear was his father's voice in the back of his head, berating him for his flaws and telling him he could never be any good for anyone. "I can't love her the way she deserves. I'll always say the wrong thing, or not say what she needs to hear. I'm too dense. Too broken."

"You are not dense or broken," she bit out, making him gape at her. "I never want to hear those words come out of your mouth ever again, Lysander Blackstone!"

He dropped his head into his hands, unable to process all of the emotions flooding it. Shame, desire, guilt, sorrow, fear. If this was the cost of love, he didn't know if he could pay it. Everything around him felt as though it were spinning off its axis.

"It's not foolish, you know," his aunt said gently, reading him. "To let someone in."

"It makes you weak."

She cupped his chin. "No, dear boy, that's the last thing it does."

"He always said that."

Lysander didn't have to explain who he meant. His aunt's face darkened with anger. "Your father was a horse's arse."

A huff of laughter escaped him. "Have you ever been in love, Aunt?"

Millicent's face softened. "So it's love, then?"

"All I know is that it feels like nothing inside of me works without her."

With a compassionate look, she patted his arm. "Then don't let her go. If she cares for you in return, and I believe she does, the words you find will be the right ones."

On impulse he hugged her. She looked taken aback, but she returned the embrace. "Thank you, Aunt."

"Of course, Lyssie-lad," she told him gently. She shook her head and wrinkled her nose again. "In the meantime, summon Henry to get you a bath and then a meal."

She'd been right. After he had a long bath and a meal, his head felt clearer, and now, he had a plan. He blinked. A very public plan, but it was better than letting her go without a fight.

He would have to grovel. Lysander didn't care.

He would crawl if he had to.

Nève stared at her friends in nervous silence. She'd just dropped the bomb that her engagement with the Duke of Montcroix was off and she was going to be returning to France, and they were all gaping at her with near-identical expressions of shock. She gulped. She'd owed it to them to give them the truth—or at least as much of it as she could bear. They now knew she'd been hired by Lysander to play a role, but telling them that her engagement was equally false felt disingenuous given how much of her heart she'd given the duke during their time together.

Laila's eyes were sad. "What, *no*!"

"You're leaving?" Effie shook her head in denial. "You can't leave. You can't just end an engagement."

"Engagements end all the time," Nève said. "We simply don't suit."

"You *do* suit," Vesper argued. "I've never seen anyone suit so well. You're perfect for each other, and I happen to know quite a bit about matchmaking."

"I agree with her," Briar put in. "And I never agree with her."

Nève didn't have the heart to tell them it had all been a lie from the very start. A practical means to a profitable end. The arrangement had never been meant to last. "I wish it had worked out, but I will be all right, truly. My sister is in Paris, and well, my life is there. You'll all write me, won't you?"

"Nève, this feels wrong." Effie, who was usually the quietest and meekest of the four, looked crushed. "You have to stay."

Dieu, she would *not* cry, but the tears pricked all the same. "I can't. Vivienne is injured and needs me."

No one could argue with that.

"We shall write, visit, show up on your doorstep so many times you will be sick of us, and you'll wish you had never met us," Laila promised.

"I could never wish that."

Vesper lifted a teacup in a morose toast. "You will always be part of the Hellfire Kitties."

Briar snorted and burst into giggles. "Capital name!"

"That is not our name," Laila protested, while Effie dissolved into snorts, too. "It is the worst moniker ever invented. I refuse to allow it."

"Shall we vote, ladies?" Vesper suggested. "Allow Nève to be part of our official naming?"

They all cheered, and Effie lifted her cup. "The Taming of the Dukes Club?"

"Dukes are overrated," Briar said, "and besides, Laila is a marchioness. How about Tea and Strumpets? Like crumpets, except flirtier and dirtier."

Vesper chortled. "Not bad. Nève, any suggestions?"

The tears threatened, especially when they all looked at her so expectantly. Her chest felt tight. "I always thought the four of you carried yourselves like true queens. Queens Club?"

There was dead silence and then a chorus of exhilarated screams ensued. Vesper grinned and whispered, "Queens Club, also known as Hellfire Kitties."

"I forbid it," Laila said and then giggled. "I mean it, Vesper. Don't you dare!"

As they burst into a fresh wave of laughter, Nève had never felt so loved and accepted as she did in that moment. Not for the first time, she found herself wishing circumstances had been different.

Nève smiled sadly. She had never imagined she would find one bosom friend during her time in London, much less four of them.

"See you at my birthday bash tomorrow?" Vesper said, leaning over.

Her stomach roiled with nerves at the thought of the ball. While she and Lysander hadn't discussed the particulars, a tasteful, amicable parting had been the plan all along. Vesper's party would be the perfect time for Nève to officially end her engagement. Nève had no idea whether Lady Charlotte had spread what she knew, but if the duchess had, the gossip would not be in Nève's favor. Worse yet, if Treadway had spilled their secret, the scandal would be enormous. At least she wouldn't be alone. Her friends would be with her. And then she would be gone.

"Wouldn't miss it."

Vesper gave her a mock glare. "You better not, because you know I'll find you."

Nève laughed. She didn't doubt the threat for one second.

Following the tea party, the rest of the afternoon passed quickly, and she holed herself up in her bedchamber for the evening. The last thing she wanted to do was cross paths with Lysander. After Vesper's party, she could put everything in London behind her where it belonged and move on.

Passing yet another sleepless night—her dreams didn't care about her resolutions during the day and were filled to the brim with the duke—Nève spent most of the day in the library. Thankfully, Finley had imparted that His Grace was out. With the help of Henry, his valet, Evans and Finley as well as Annie, she'd successfully managed to avoid Lysander for four days. But as happy as she'd been about not running into him, a part of her mourned not seeing him either.

She missed *him*.

Millicent also made herself scarce, which Nève appreciated. She didn't think she could keep her wits together in the kindly older woman's presence. It was hard enough not to cry at the smallest thing.

Even now in the bath, getting ready for the evening, she felt her eyes burning. This would be her last ball. Her last party in London. She was sure *he* would be there. Or maybe he wouldn't. Maybe she would never see him again.

Annie bustled into the bathing chamber, startling her. "Miss, you're going to be more than fashionably late to Lady Vesper's party if you don't hurry."

"Must I?" Nève hated that her words sounded like a pathetic whine as she stepped from the bath and wrapped herself in a length of toweling.

"Yes." The declaration came from Millicent, who marched in behind the maid. "You must. She is your friend, and it will mean the world to her that you're there."

Throat tight, she glanced up at Millicent. "Is His Grace planning to go?"

"He's in chambers." The lady shook her head. "Some emergency session in Parliament about that crooked viscount."

"He won't attend tonight?" Nève asked.

Millicent shrugged. "I don't know." Her eyes narrowed on Nève. "Are you asking because you wish for him to go or you wish to continue to avoid him? Or is it both?"

"Am I that obvious?"

"It's obvious that you are not yourself and haven't been for days," Millicent said. "If it's any consolation, I've never seen my nephew in such a bellicose state either. I have no idea what happened between you, but the two of you need to talk and come to some agreement."

Nève winced at her unknowing choice of words. "I'm still recovering from the last one," she muttered.

"What was that, dear?"

"Nothing," she said with a sigh. "You're right, of course. Perhaps later after the ball."

Despite her reluctance, with Annie's expert help, Nève managed to get ready quickly. Her gown of choice tonight was simple. She did not want to be noticed, but inasmuch as it was one of Laila's designs, it was still beautiful. Lines of pale buttery gold silk fell in a waterfall of panels to the floor, the bodice and each flounce edged in delicate blond lace and embroidered butterflies.

The symbolism of the butterfly made her heart ache.

But it was time to let go.

Nève gave herself a critical look in the mirror. Annie had styled her curls in a flattering side-swept coiffure tucked into place with a delicate rope of pearls and a single yellow rose that had been plucked from the garden. A pair of pristine white gloves, and gold heeled slippers embossed with roses and a butterfly appliqué that had been designed for the gown, completed the ensemble. It wasn't as extravagant as some of the ball gowns she'd seen, but it was elegant and understated. Laila was truly a godsend.

"You look beautiful, miss."

"Thank you, Annie. You've outdone yourself."

The maid held herself around the middle and twirled about the room. "Have a dance for me, will you, miss?"

Nève sent a fond smile. "I will be sure to do so."

She descended the staircase, half expecting to see Lysander waiting for her. Disappointment welled when the only person in the foyer was Millicent, though Nève squashed it down when the older lady clapped her hands and wiped at her eyes. "You are so lovely, Nève dear."

"Thank you. So are you."

Millicent was dressed in a dark blue ball gown trimmed with black bows in an interesting zigzag pattern around the hemline. Nève wondered if it was one of Laila's fashions. In the coach, she listened with half an ear to Millicent's chatter, but was lost in her own thoughts.

"Millicent," she said softly as the coach rumbled through the streets. "I want to tell you something. The engagement is off. I wanted to be honest with you because you deserve that. It was a false arrangement all along." She did not mention the exchange of funds, but she did not have to. *Arrangement* did the job quite well enough.

The woman's face fell, but it seemed to be from resignation rather than surprise. "I suspected there was something, but aristocratic marriages are made on settlements all the time. I had hoped whatever had brought you two together would turn into something more."

"It was simply not meant to be," Nève said, reaching for the woman's hand. "I'm returning to Paris, but I want you to know how much it has meant to get to know you these past weeks."

"For me as well," Millicent said, the shine of tears in her eyes. "You've been such a delight to have around, and apart from these last few days, I've never seen my nephew so happy. I think he'd forgotten how to laugh until you." She put a trembling hand to her throat as though overwhelmed with emotion. They relapsed into silence, but when the carriage came to a stop, Millicent put her hand over Nève's and squeezed. "Don't give up hope just yet."

Nève blinked at the odd sentiment, but the coach door opened, and then they were walking up the marble staircase to be announced by Vesper's very efficient butler.

"Lady Millicent Templeton and Miss Geneviève Valery."

Upon entering the ballroom, Nève waited for the sense of awareness to prickle under her skin that the Duke of Montcroix was somewhere near, but it never appeared. She rubbed her arms and swallowed the enormous lump in her throat.

He hadn't come.

Chapter Twenty-Four

From the outside balcony, Lysander watched the woman of his dreams walk through the ballroom like a queen and greet Vesper and her friends with a smile that lit her eyes. She *gleamed*, his gorgeous butterfly, outshining every other woman in the room.

Dance after dance, she laughed and spun, charming them all.

It was his penance, he decided, for the unfathomable hurt he'd caused her. To watch her in the arms of others, while he stood here in the shadows. Lurking like the villain of the story instead of the hero. He *wasn't* hiding, he just needed to calm himself, pick the right time, the right moment to approach her and hope that she would give him a chance, one he wasn't sure he deserved.

"I thought I saw you loitering out here," a familiar voice said.

He groaned. "Lushing, go away. I am not in the mood."

"Why are you peering through the windows like a pauper begging for crumbs?" He gave a loud gasp. "Are you planning to win her back? I've heard that your engagement is off."

He stared at his friend in disbelief. "What did you just say?"

"Miss Valery has said your engagement is off." Lushing let out a breath with a frown. "Everyone is shocked, except Charlotte, who is in raptures."

Lysander's head was spinning with an explosive cocktail of

emotions. Who cared about Charlotte? Nève had told people the engagement was off? It felt like someone had gutted him with a ragged knife, and for an agonizing second, he couldn't take in a single draft of air. Christ, was this what dying felt like? A slow collapse of every organ in his body, starting with his heart?

"It's not off," he wheezed.

Lushing's brows rose. "Are you certain? I heard her say it with my own ears."

"I love her," he burst out.

"Does *she* know that?"

"That's why I'm here. To beg her to take me back, if she'll have me." He stared at his friend in mute desperation. "God, you have to help me."

Lushing puffed his chest. "Well, I'm not God, but yes, as your best and only friend in the world, I shall offer you my sword and my shield."

Lysander stared at him and rolled his eyes. "Never mind."

With a protesting Lushing on his heels, Lysander walked into the ballroom, his eyes searching for one person...the one who had snatched his heart right out from under him, before he even knew it had been lost. Their eyes met, and he did not attempt to hide his regret and sorrow, and even when he saw that spine snap straight and her own gaze shutter, he did not lose hope. None of this was about him.

It was about *her*. He'd come here to make things right.

Lysander strode through the crowd, with eyes for no one else but Nève, and frowned with frustration when a woman blocked his way just before he reached her. "Move, Charlotte."

"Don't be a fool, Lysander."

He glared, tempted to push her aside. "The name is Montcroix."

"It's over between you," she said with malicious relish.

"It's not." *Not yet.*

Her eyes glittered with spite at the unhidden hope in his voice. "Your father would turn in his grave to see you prostrate yourself thus, at the feet of a common dancer no less. Where's your pride?"

The sudden hush in the ballroom told him that people were listening. His skin itched, sweat beading under his collar, as the usual sense of disorientation rose within him. He forced his brain to calm and tapped his fingers against his thigh, Schubert the first rhythm to come to mind. And then he imagined the scent of lemon and vanilla. Everything inside of him went blissfully quiet.

"Pride is irrelevant when it comes to her," he said. "It means nothing."

Charlotte's laughter was harsh, though her eyes went a bit wild. "Oh, this is rich. How the lofty have tumbled!"

He stepped around Charlotte and faced the woman he'd come here to win. "May I speak with you in private, Miss Valery?"

Eyes glittering with unshed tears, she opened her mouth, but any reply was drowned out by Charlotte. "Why don't you tell everyone who she is? A ruse to convince poor Lord Bolden of your good intentions. Treadway told me everything. This is all a show for that parcel of land you so coveted."

Lysander froze as the chatter in the ballroom erupted. But none of that mattered. The only important thing was Nève. Even if everything fell apart, he had nothing left to lose by baring his soul to her.

"What is this?" Lord Bolden said, shoving through the throng. "You tricked me?"

Fuck, he had not expected Bolden to be here. Lysander fought off the cloying pressure on his senses from everyone in the room, the loudness of the crowd, and turned to see the earl's disappointed face. "At first, yes. That was my plan. But, I swear to you, Lord Bolden, everything changed. I've changed. That's why I am here, to tell this woman how I feel."

Bolden's stare slipped to Nève. "Is that true?"

Nève bit her lip and nodded at the earl. "I'd hoped it might be," she said softly, and Lysander felt his heart swell with encouragement.

A loud laugh ensued at that, and this time, Treadway was the man to take the stage. Despite hobbling as if it pained him to walk, he had a spiteful look on his face. This was a production in thespian fashion, but he supposed that trial by fire was his fate. Nève was worth every second of it.

His mother smelled like jasmine.

Nève smelled like lemon and vanilla.

Schubert's last four-hands movement came together in a blistering, beautiful crescendo.

Lysander's eyes lifted to meet the man he'd so unceremoniously deposited at his home after the debacle in the park, knowing that revenge was the viscount's goal. "Treadway."

"You are a master of the long game, Your Grace," he spat. "If your fervent avowals are so true, then why are the plans going ahead for demolition?"

Nève's stare snapped to his, as did Bolden's. Her voice was whisper quiet, even as his stomach sank. "You're demolishing Aldenborough?"

"The railway has to be built," he explained patiently. "That doesn't change what I feel for you."

Her eyes flashed with pity, and it was with a sharp sting that he realized the pity was for him. "But it does, and if you can't see that, then you haven't changed at all. You're still the same man you always were."

"It's a thing, Nève." For the life of him, he couldn't reconcile the two. The matter was one of pure logic, finances, and pragmatism. The most efficient way forward for laying the new tracks, even without Treadway's corrupt company, was still through Aldenborough. Sentimentality had no part in his business decisions. "I'll buy you another castle."

Her laugh was a hollow sound as she shook her head. "You can't buy everything, Your Grace, and it's not just a disposable thing. The sooner you realize that, the sooner you will understand why this could never work. Why *we* could never work."

"Wait, please, Nève."

But with one look to Lady Vesper, she was ushered from the ballroom in the arms of her friends, and he was left standing there...alone and utterly helpless to regain the only thing that had ever mattered.

Her.

CHAPTER TWENTY-FIVE

The money had been deposited on the apartment for a ballet studio that Vivienne had found in a lovely little neighborhood with a view of the Seine in the Marais. It had been two months since Nève returned to France, and in that time, their lives had changed. The apartment above the studio was also well suited to their needs, with three bedrooms and more space than either of them could have dreamed of. Come autumn, Vivienne's dance school would be full of eager new students. Even if Nève was miserable, she had never seen her sister look so happy.

Thanks to the Duke of Montcroix's funds.

Money she'd *earned*.

Nève rubbed at her chest, easing away the pang there. The pain after leaving had lessened as each day passed, but still whenever she thought of Lysander, she was still gripped by an inconsolable grief. A defining sense of loss.

Despite what had happened between them, she felt as though she'd left a piece of her soul across the English Channel, one she'd never get back. Two days had become two weeks and then two months...and soon, two months would be two years. She only had to put one foot in front of the other and go through the motions that everything was fine…that her heart wasn't irreparably shattered.

It was easy to pretend for others.

Not so easy to lie to herself.

How could she miss someone who had hurt her so badly? When she thought of how he'd come to Vesper's party, his heart on his sleeve, the hope rising inside had almost given her wings. But then when news of the demolition and his plans to go forward had come to light, she hadn't known what to feel. Nève knew his mind worked in much narrower ways, but it'd been a slap in the face. He *was* Heathcliff from *Wuthering Heights*. Stuck in old patterns. Though, sometimes, in between all the hurt and anger, it was compassion she felt for him.

"Isn't it perfect, Geneviève?" Vivienne squealed for the dozenth time.

She ignored the pang that her full name brought with it and nodded. "It is."

"Tiens, I cannot believe we've done it, thanks to you, anyway!"

Nève had told Vivienne the truth when she returned to Paris in a flood of tears, leaving nothing out. She'd needed to purge so that she could heal, and her sister's outlook had been enlightening: love was a game meant to be played, just as life was meant to be lived. One either won or lost, but loss was what made the winning worth something. Nève had protested that she wasn't sure it'd been love, but Vivienne's expression had been priceless.

"You think with your head and your heart. I *know* you—and you wouldn't have given your affection so easily, if it hadn't been worth the risk."

Vivienne had always been able to see right through her.

Though she'd sacrificed her heart, all hadn't been lost, however. Some of the money had gone to the school that would support her and her sister. The rest went into savings and a fund for starving or destitute dancers. In the end, Lysander had given her six thousand pounds...the extra was a dividend, his solicitor had written.

She'd kept the gowns as agreed. Some could be sold, others she would save. The diamond-and-garnet necklace he'd given her on her birthday, however, she'd left in her bedchamber. Nève hadn't been able to bring herself to keep it. A necklace like that—a family heirloom—was meant for the future Duchess of Montcroix.

Squinting in the sunlight, Vivienne sauntered toward her after locking up, and arm in arm, they walked toward the Seine and the Île de la Cité, where the beautifully Gothic Cathédrale Notre-Dame de Paris and Nève's favorite place stood. "Oh, I forgot, a postcard came for you."

Nève's heart leaped, but when she took the correspondence, she saw that it was from Laila. She'd received letters from all four of her Queens Club friends, but she'd written only once to inform them of her change of address and progression on the studio. Writing them without thinking of Lysander had been too much to bear. She hoped it would get easier.

"What does it say?"

Nève frowned, and flipped the cardstock around. "Nothing."

"That's strange," Vivienne said in an odd tone of voice that made Nève look up and freeze. She blinked, and blinked again.

A few feet away on the edge of the stone Pont Neuf, a group of well-dressed people stood—faces Nève recognized—and then they screamed in unison, "Surprise!"

A more rounded Laila, Lord Marsden, a beaming Vesper, Effie, Briar, and Lushing. She found herself combing their number for another...but of course, Lysander wasn't there. Nève bit her lip and buried her foolish disappointment. Why would he be?

He was probably neck-deep in railway construction. In one of Laila's letters, she'd mentioned that Treadway had been convicted and forced to pay back money he'd skimmed from his poor investors, but Nève had read in the newssheets that the Duke of Montcroix had entered into a staggering deal with the North Eastern Railway. She didn't begrudge him his success.

"What on earth are you all doing here?" she said as she found herself engulfed by her friends. She laughed in confusion. "I mean it's wonderful to see you, but what is the occasion? We already celebrated my birthday."

"We come bearing gifts," Vesper screamed. "Er, I mean gift. Singular."

Nève laughed. She'd missed her friend. "Whatever for?"

"They're here because of me." The delicious baritone slid through her like the softest silk.

Heart beating a frantic cadence, Nève turned in slow motion... and there he was, a bouquet of yellow roses in hand. Her throat went dry at the sight of his painfully beautiful face, all sharp angles and hollows, the sinful curve of those stern lips. She left his eyes for last...and fell into them.

She couldn't speak. Couldn't move. Couldn't breathe.

He approached with tentative steps.

"I understand now," he said simply. "Aldenborough wasn't just a place."

Oh dear God. "You're here."

He nodded and glanced up to where Lushing and the rest of her friends stood. "I've come to understand a few other things, too. One, Lady Laila has a powerful right palm, two, Lady Vesper knows words that would make a sailor blush, three, Lady Evangeline's animals leave surprise droppings everywhere, and four, Lady Briar knows people I wouldn't want to cross paths with." He drew in a breath. "I was wrong about so much, and I've been the most horrible excuse for a man."

"A complete nick-ninny!" Vesper's voice chimed in.

"Maggot-pated," Briar shouted.

Lushing, not to be outdone, roared, "A puny little lobcock!"

Nève pinned her lips at Lysander's solemn expression, though he made no effort to defend himself from their unflattering descriptions. He leaned in with a whisper. "I'm not puny."

She couldn't help it...she laughed.

The look of wondrous delight on his face shot straight to her heart. Oh, Dieu, she did not know how much more of this she could take, but she had to be honest. "You hurt me."

He nodded solemnly. "I know and I am so sorry."

"You didn't defend me with Charlotte," she whispered. "I shouldn't have had to hope for you to do that. And your plans for Aldenborough. I thought you saw what it meant...to me. To us."

"I'm sorry I didn't say what I should have to Charlotte. I never wanted you to feel that you were anything less than wonderful. You're the sun to my shadows, Geneviève." Voice breaking, the duke swallowed hard, eyes hiding nothing from her, leaving himself bare. "What you said about me at the ball was right. I was blinded by my own convictions, by the way I've always done things. It's not an excuse, but I know I'm not my father. I'm not whom he groomed me to be. Not anymore. You showed me that I could let myself be *happy*. That I was safe with you. And I want you to be safe with me."

The knot in her throat expanded. "Lysander."

"I love you, Geneviève." Nève almost sobbed when he dropped to his knees in the middle of the filthy street. "I want to be the man who deserves *you*. I want to earn every smile, every kiss, every touch you deign to give. I want the chance to prove I can be worthy of you. I'm not asking for forever, but if you could find it in your heart to give me another chance, I promise to earn that forever."

"What took you so long?" she asked, her own voice shaky.

He looked pained. "I wasn't sure if you would forgive me when I couldn't even forgive myself."

"What if I want forever now?" she whispered, feathering a hand through his soft hair.

Those beautiful gray eyes lit with so much hope it made her soul clench. "Then forever you shall have. Forgive me, love?"

"I do. I love you, Lysander." She grinned and wound a lock of dark gold hair around her finger. "Now get up off the ground and kiss me properly. A duke never kneels."

The look in his eyes as he stared up at her nearly set her on fire. "This one does, especially when he hopes the woman of his dreams will put him out of his misery and save him."

"I think we'll need a new agreement," she said breathlessly.

He rose, sliding his hands to her waist. "My answer is yes to all the terms, as long as yours is yes."

"No negotiation?"

Her duke shook his head. "I surrender wholly to my lady's mercy, though I must warn you that surrender is not submission."

Oh, Dieu, her knees went weak at the sultry promise in his tone.

With a wicked grin that made his dimple appear for a full second, he took her lips with his. Dimly, Nève heard the screams and hoots of her friends, but she didn't care. She didn't care about the people or their audience, or the fact that a duke was kissing her in public in the middle of Paris.

She cared only about him.

Many pleasurable hours later, Lysander lay back with a gratified sigh on the tiny cot that was masquerading as a bed. An exhausted, sated Nève lay cocooned in his arms. It was a miracle that both of them even fit on her bed, but it wasn't as though they'd made use of it. No, their frantic coupling, following an evening full of food, friends, and laughter, had occurred on nearly every available surface in her spacious new rooms. After two full months apart, they hadn't been able to get enough of each other.

He ran a finger down her nose. "What are you thinking?"

"I was wondering if you are truly sure this is what you want."

Lysander let out an exasperated noise. "Yes, my love. I want you."

Green eyes peered up at him. "I have a temper."

"People call me Stone because I'm emotionless," he countered.

"I think whiskey tastes like dirt."

"Heathen." He inhaled her hair and gave a mock growl. "I

can be stuck in my own head and find reading people nearly impossible."

"I have hideous toes," she said.

"I love your toes." He reached down her leg and brought her ankle up, marveling at her suppleness before kissing said toes.

"You're the most attractive man I've ever met." She turned in his arms to face him, her fingers wandering down his chest.

"That's not a flaw."

She kissed him. "You started it, and I'm done with faults. I only want to celebrate wonderful things," she murmured, that teasing palm sliding down to his abdomen. He felt his well-used cock stir again as her knuckles traced each indent along his tense muscles. Christ, he'd never be able to get enough of her. They'd fucked hard and fast the first time, and then made love slowly for hours, and yet, he couldn't contain his arousal when she touched him like this...when she looked at him like he was her whole world. His love smiled up at him before she grazed right over his crown. "You're clever, loyal, strong, passionate, wise, and all mine."

"Yours," he whispered on a sharp inhale, unable to articulate anything else while she was stroking him like that. He'd tell her how wonderful she was later...and every day until forever came.

" 'Whatever our souls are made of, his and mine are the same,' " she whispered.

"What's that?"

"You don't recognize your favorite book? For shame, Your Grace, it's *Wuthering Heights*." Her hand dipped lower again, grasping him. "We're the same, you and I."

He bit out a chuckle that turned into a groan as she applied gentle pressure. "I can't think when you do that."

"Lysander Blackstone at a loss? I like that very much."

She started to move her palm over his thickening cock, making him swell even more, and he stalled her with his own hand. "What are you doing?"

"I have plans," she told him.

Lifting up ever so gracefully, she shifted to the end of the narrow bed and kissed her way down the path her fingers had taken. By the time she reached the destination in nibbles and bites, his cock was so hard it hurt. She held him in her fist, running her thumb over the crown of him and gathering the bead of moisture. Holding his gaze, she lifted it to her lips.

He groaned. "Geneviève."

"Salty," she pronounced. "Like moules frites, a bit briny and a bit earthy." She cocked her head. "What do I taste like?"

"Une tarte aux pêches, hot out of the oven."

If possible, his cock swelled more at the memory of her on his tongue. He sucked in a breath as she caressed him from root to tip. "I've never done this before, but the dancers in the corps all talked about it. I admit, I'm curious."

When Nève bent to take the tip of him into her mouth, Lysander's eyes nearly rolled back into his head. She was going to be the death of him. She took her time to discover what made him tense and groan her name. What she lacked in experience, she made up for in enthusiasm, and it wasn't long before Lysander felt the pressure coiling at the base of his spine. He reached down and heaved her up onto his chest, watching as she aligned her hips over his and brought him home. They both gasped when she was fully seated.

Posting her hips, she let out a puff of laughter, and Lysander lifted a brow at her wicked expression. "Dare I even ask what is going through that head of yours now?"

"Riding lessons," she said, rising and easing back down. "I find I much prefer being astride, however."

"You are an excellent student," he agreed.

"Shall we move from a trot to a canter, then?" She didn't wait for him to reply, increasing her speed with a rocking motion that made her moan. Her head fell back, her beautiful face alive with passion and exertion. God, she was so fucking beautiful. Lysander almost forgot the sensations in his own body, so caught up as he was in hers. Her elbows dug into his chest, and her movements grew more erratic as she chased the culmination of her own pleasure.

"Lysander, oh…" The release hurtled through her, kicking off his own, and for a moment, they both hung suspended in bliss. Her brilliant green gaze met his. "Je t'aime."

As she crashed in a tangle of limbs over him, he ran his palm down her damp spine, holding her to him as his pounding heart slowed. "I love you, too, my butterfly."

Hours later, she rose and stretched her body in a sinuous motion that reminded him of a feline. He propped himself to his elbow and watched while she did a slow arabesque. "I love to watch you dance."

She peered at him over her shoulder. "Naked?"

"Especially," he said, waggling his eyebrows.

Kneeling on the floor, she winked at him and reached for a pair of ballet slippers from a box. "I saved these." He recognized them as the ones from the ballet in London that she'd danced months ago. Entranced, he stared as she wound them up her bare calves, and then stood, rising en pointe in the middle of the room with her arms held gracefully above her head, all lithe lines and sensuous curves that he'd kissed for hours.

"You're stunning."

She fell into an elegant curtsy. "Why thank you, Your Grace."

He canted his head. Smiling, she did a sequence of jumps, crossing her pointed toes one over the other, and then performed a glissade that ended in a pirouette. When her hips swayed and she folded in half en pointe, winking at him from between her legs, Lysander nearly swallowed his tongue. "Come here, my love. Let me feel that you're real."

She lifted and pushed a pointed toe into the middle of his chest. "I'm real."

"And mine."

"Yes."

He yanked and she fell on top of him with a breathless laugh. Perched lengthways over his body, she propped her chin on his chest, and peered at him through a warm, contented gaze.

"Not to ruin the mood, but when do you plan to go back?" she asked. "As much as I want to keep you in my bed forever, I know you have duties."

"I would not mind that, but since Vivienne's given her blessing, I hope to convince you to return to London with me." He drew in a slow breath, his heart racing again, but this time for a very different reason. One that made him feel suddenly shy. "I happen to have a very desirable piece of property called Aldenborough with a beautiful home just waiting for the right owners."

Her eyes shot up, light hitting the green with so much love that he blinked. "I thought it was gone."

"No. I want to keep it and perhaps one day..." He trailed off, feeling strangely vulnerable. "Fill it with children."

Nève frowned in confusion. "You wish to open a school at Aldenborough?" As soon as she said it, she caught his wry expression, rolled her eyes, and laughed at herself. "Oh, you mean your children..."

"*Our* children, if you want them."

Her expressive face fell, and Lysander frowned. Her voice was hesitant when she spoke. "I do, but I don't know if I can. My courses have never been regular because of ballet."

He stared at her and gathered her into his arms. "My love for you is not conditional on whether you can give me children, Geneviève," he said softly, tucking a strand of hair behind her ear and tracing his fingertip over her jaw. "You're mine, perfect as you are, in every way."

She swallowed and shook her head. "But you're a duke. You'll need heirs."

"I need *you*, and we will cross that bridge together, if and when we come to it." He kissed the rest of any protest from her lips. "No more discussion. Now, about marriage, however..."

Her smile was tremulous. "Are we negotiating, Your Grace?"

"Always."

Clearing her expression of amusement, she feigned a serious face. "Very well then, Your Grace. Assuming you propose—"

"So proposed."

She poked him with a finger in his side. "That does *not* count as a proposal. You will do it with the aplomb befitting a duke and the ladylike, demure daughter of a viscount."

"Where is this demure lady you speak of?" He pretended to look around and earned a sharper poke for his efforts.

"Arse."

Lysander winked, and filled his palms with hers. "Indeed, and what a nice one it is, too."

"Be serious," she admonished.

He assumed a suitably grave expression. "I'm always serious about all parts of your delectable body."

"If...and when the time comes, after our wedding, I am willing to try for a baby. I mean I want us to try."

His grin was wolfish. "You don't have to convince me. I'm looking forward to all the *trying*. Trying inside, trying outside, trying all day long. I am your humble, enthusiastic, and dedicated servant."

"You're far from humble and you're insatiable."

"Only for you, my love."

With a happy smile, she rested her cheek on his chest, drumming her fingers in time with his heartbeat. After some time, Lysander had almost thought she'd fallen asleep before he heard her soft voice. "I don't know if I thanked you for coming here to find me."

"I had to," he said. "I have it on impeccable authority that a body can't survive without its heart, and you've had mine in your keeping since the day we met." He met her melting green eyes that were filled with so much love he could hardly imagine it was all for him. "Where you go, I go."

"Is that a promise?"

Lysander smiled, feeling it overtake his face and not bothering to curb his joy. He wanted her to see it...to see him. "Pour toujours."

Forever with her would never be long enough.

Epilogue

Sixteen Months Later

"Hurry up, lazybones!" the Duchess of Montcroix bellowed in a voice that would make any Covent Garden market fishwife proud. "Allons-y! Let's go. We're going to be late."

Her husband grabbed her around the waist, making her shriek as he nearly dislodged Annie's painstakingly elegant coiffure. "Who's getting married again?"

"Vesper's third cousin, twice removed. And considering it's our own former footman, we have to be in attendance."

Lysander glowered. "Evans is lucky I let him go with a generous allowance."

Nève shook her head at his look. It had been such a scandal—the lady who had fallen for the devastatingly handsome footman—but it was only afterward that Nève had learned that Vesper had orchestrated the whole thing from behind the scenes and practically shoved the two young lovers together at every turn. Pleased as punch with her efforts, she'd declared that love didn't care about social classes and that the two were meant to be together.

Never mind that Evans was a footman, and the girl was a lady.

While Nève was the last one to make judgments on such things, she did wonder at how quickly everything had happened—barely within months of their meeting, and now Evans was going to be a father. When Nève had asked the footman if he was excited about the baby, he'd looked mildly perplexed as if he hadn't quite thought it through. He'd thought it through enough to get his bride-to-be up the pole, however.

That had nearly set Lysander off, considering it had happened under his own roof.

It had only been at her urging that he'd relented and not given the boy the thrashing he insisted he deserved. Nève had argued that mistakes happened, and sometimes, all one really needed was a second chance. The duke had glowered at her and then promptly dismissed the man with a sizable settlement, at least enough for him and his new bride to be comfortable for a few years. Sadly, the lady in question had been disowned, but with Vesper on their side, their future wasn't too bleak.

"You're too soft on him," Lysander grumbled.

"Be nice," Nève told him. "No matter how it happened, they're with child, and they need all the help they can get. He's not a duke with endless coffers at his disposal. And besides, Evans was always perfectly sweet to me."

"The pretty ones always get away with everything."

She reached up to stroke his face. "You're beautiful to me."

"Speaking of children..." Her husband's hand curved lovingly around her middle, cupping her barely there infant bump. "How are you feeling, my love? How's my tiny caterpillar in there?"

She shot him a dry look. "Are you calling my baby a bug?"

"It's a baby butterfly, love. And stop evading the question."

Nève bit her lip. "It's not so bad today."

After the fourth month, her nausea had reduced significantly, but she still had frequent bouts of queasiness. The pregnancy had been a shock to say the least. Nève had teased Lysander about being extra virile, but at the duke's personal physician's guidance as well as Vivienne's advice via many letters, she'd changed her diet, eating more, and eventually, her courses had returned, though they'd remained erratic. Despite the low odds, they'd been hopefully optimistic.

Vivienne had explained from her own research that the suppression of menstruation had to do with Nève's excessive hours of dancing and her low levels of body fat. But once she made a few changes, her body had become healthier. Healthy enough to astonishingly conceive. The pregnancy, thus far, had not been easy. Each day felt like a battle, but she'd go to war for this child with her stalwart duke right at her side.

"Are you certain you wish to go?" Lysander asked, watching her expression like a hawk. "We could stay here and I could rub your feet and make you feel better."

"You have no idea how tempting that sounds."

He stared at her. "When this is over, I'm taking you back to Aldenborough."

Lysander had given the estate to Nève as a wedding present, and she and Lysander had busied themselves with returning it to its former glory. While it wasn't as enormous as his ancestral seat, it meant something special to both of them.

Married life with Lysander had been everything she'd hoped for and more. It was passionate and all-consuming, and yet they each had the necessary space to be themselves. While he was learning to look past his own views and take how she saw things into account, their relationship still took patience and love. The singular, stringent way his brain worked made him the brilliant man he was, and she would not change him for anything. Though she often felt like kicking him for being much too punctilious at times, kissing usually won out. It was an excellent strategy for redirection, as she'd discovered.

"Greydon is back from his travels," Lysander murmured, folding the newssheets he'd been reading earlier. "His father died a couple of years ago."

"Who?"

"Aspen Drake, the Duke of Greydon, an old friend. His estate adjoins Lushing's father's."

She frowned. "How have I never heard of this old friend? And how have the girls not mentioned him either?"

"No one thought he'd ever return." Lysander shrugged. "Should make things interesting either way for however long he decides to stay this time. The reason your friends haven't spoken of him is that he and Vesper have history."

Nève perked up, ignoring the swell of nausea. "History?"

"Friends for years and then"—he made a gesture with his palms—"something happened. No one actually knows. There was a huge scandal about his father being committed."

"Curious." She *was* curious, but then a wave of dizziness hit her. She blanched and wasn't quick enough to hide it from her eagle-eyed protector.

"We are staying home and you are resting," he said in a tone that brooked no argument. Usually it was a tone that heated her blood and had her tearing his clothes off, but now she was only grateful. "Evans will understand. Don't worry, I will send a messenger with our regrets."

In truth, Nève was grateful to stay at home. Within a quarter of an hour, they were settled together in the library, her feet in his lap and her head on a mountain of pillows. She let out a groan when he massaged her bare feet. "I hate feeling like an invalid."

"You are not. You're hard at work making another tiny human. Don't be so harsh with yourself. I'm very partial to you and this versatile, creative body, you know." He lifted her ankle to kiss it. "Every single gorgeous inch of it."

Something that wasn't nausea fluttered in her belly. "How partial?"

Heat turned his eyes to silver as her husband's big hand slid up her knee. "Shall I distract you, my love?" he asked with a sideways kick of the hard curve of his mouth that never failed to drive her to folly.

"Do your worst, Your Grace," she said.

His hand crept higher, making her breath hitch. "I prefer to think of it as my best, Your Grace. That's what my duchess deserves, after all."

She sat up and impulsively kissed his lips. "I love you so much."

"Never as much as I love you."

Nève stared at the man she adored, who adored her in return, and felt so full. Her stone gargoyle had turned out to have the biggest heart of them all.

ACKNOWLEDGMENTS

This book would not exist without many wonderful people. To my hands-down brilliant editor, Amy Pierpont, a tremendous thank-you for giving *Always Be My Duchess* such a wonderful home at Forever, as well as for your smart, spot-on revision notes, all the emoticons and hilarious comment bubbles, the brainstorming and passionate chats, and your excellent grasp of these characters, my story, and where I needed to go. Thank you for getting me there with so much enthusiasm, humor, wisdom, and care.

To my spectacular agent, Thao Le, this book is dedicated to you, not only because you are literally the Jedi of agents and one with the Force but because I legit wouldn't be here without you and all your efforts. Thank you for being such an awesome advocate and a wise adviser through thick and thin. I'm so grateful to have you in my corner.

To Sam Brody, thank you for all your emails, for keeping me honest with turnaround times, answering all my pesky questions, and wrestling the Godzilla of documents into submission. You're a wizard of all the things! It's been a joy to work with you.

A tremendous thanks to the entire production, editing, art direction, cover design, sales, and publicity teams at Forever for all your efforts behind the scenes, including the fabulous Dana Cuadrado and the wonderful Jodi Rosoff, who so kindly included me in publishing events long before this book came out. So much goes into the making of a book, and I'm so grateful for everything you all do. Rock on, Team Forever!

A huge shout-out full of adoration goes to the very talented women in my writer and reader groups who keep me sane on this wild publishing roller coaster, inspire me, read my first drafts, invite me to events, and send me absurd TikToks. I have so much love for you. Your friendship means the world to me. To all the readers, reviewers, booksellers, librarians, educators, extended family, and friends who support me and spread the word about my books, a tremendous thank-you for all you do! I appreciate you more than you know.

Last but not least, to my family: Cameron, the love of my life, and our three amazing children, Connor, Noah, and Olivia, my heart would be empty without you. Thanks for all the assists, including getting me coffee, tea, and snacks when I'm on deadline...and reminding me to shower. I know, I know...we'll have that vacation soon, I promise!

READING GROUP GUIDE

A Letter from the Author

Dear Reader,

Thank you so much for picking up *Always Be My Duchess* and joining Lysander and Nève on their unconventional, impulsive, heartwarming, and definitely steamy adventure while they figured out what trust, hope, and falling in love meant for each of them. I hope you cheered for them as hard as I did on their way to a hard-won happily ever after!

This was such an incredible story to write. Not only did I get to write about some of my favorite things—grumpy heroes, dauntless heroines, ballet, and France, with a nod to my favorite '90s rom-com films—but this was my first book about a neurodivergent hero. At first I didn't set out to write Lysander this way, but while I was writing this book, I was heavily entrenched in therapy for my own neurodivergent teenage son that I found myself writing so much of his characteristics into my hero—smart with a slow processing speed, binary thinking, methodical, fixed on routine, anxious, direct, and no time for anything beyond what he sees as the milestones for success. However, his capacity for love is deep and infinite, and once given, his loyalty is unshakable. As such, Lysander and his HEA will always hold a special place in my heart.

As far as ballet, I attended a ballet school for nine years with the Caribbean School of Dancing, advancing through the international Royal Academy of Dance program, though I was by no means prima ballerina material. I loved it, however, and even performed multiple productions onstage at the Queen's Hall performing arts center in Trinidad when I was a girl.

It was very interesting researching ballet during the nineteenth century, especially since dance and music were so romanticized in art. Behind the scenes, however, conditions were less than palatable, and dance was viewed as a disreputable profession. In Paris, girls entered the ballet at a young age, working toward positions in the corps de ballet. They were often poor, isolated, and vulnerable to exploitation and harassment. The wealthy, powerful patrons of the Paris Opera—called abbonés—were little more than predators, allowed into the foyer de la danse for an enormous subscription fee, who often made propositions to the dancers to become their mistresses. According to my research, in some cases, mothers even advocated for their daughters to make these arrangements because of the stability, money, and protection they offered. These rich patrons had huge control over who received roles and who did not. In my story, my heroine fends off the advances of one such man and pays the price for it when she's fired from the production and barred from every reputable theater in Paris and London. But she is determined not to be a casualty of adversity, despite the odds stacked against her.

Nève was inspired by a few nineteenth-century ballerinas, including Carlotta Grisi and Marie Taglioni. Grisi started dance at age seven, earned roles onstage from the age of ten, and was on tour by fourteen. Her first performance in *Giselle* led to instant fame. In 1858, Taglioni had her first major role at sixteen in *La*

Sylphide at the Paris Opera. After Taglioni retired, she taught social dance to high society ladies and children in London. She was also known for choreographing one ballet, *Le Papillon*, in 1860. Emma Livry, who is mentioned in my story as a friend of the heroine, danced the principal role in this ballet, however she died tragically onstage when her ballet costume caught fire from the gaslights in 1863. The ballet troupe that the hero hires for Nève's birthday was the actual cast of *Le Papillon* performing onstage in France during that period!

My heroine was such an interesting character to write. Given the power dynamics and the transactional nature of the plot (money for companionship), she had to be strong in her convictions and have a deep sense of self and female agency. As a dancer who has faced many challenges in her life, she knows what her limits are...and what she's willing to do to meet, cross, or change them. Like many women, we've faced hard choices in our lives, but all we can do is use the information we have at hand and make the best decision for ourselves. My heroine also needed to be someone who could not only challenge and wholly accept those idiosyncratic parts of the hero but stay true to herself in the process.

One last note on the epilogue: While Nève and Lysander are able to conceive despite Nève's complications with amenorrhea, I am intimately aware that this is not the outcome for everyone who struggles with infertility. Like Nève, I, too, struggled with amenorrhea (indirectly related to dance) and was told that I would not be able to have children. And yet, despite two of my three pregnancies being high risk and one with infertility complications, I am beyond thankful that I was able to overcome the odds. My heart goes out to each and every one of you who have traveled this journey.

Hope you enjoyed reading Nève and Lysander's story as much as I enjoyed writing it! Thanks for reading!

xo,
Amalie

DISCUSSION QUESTIONS

1) Despite feminism being an anachronistic concept, it was not anachronistic behavior, especially for women in historical times who wanted to break free of traditional roles or expected rules of conduct. Nève's actions would have been considered vulgar by her aristocratic peers, given that she has gone from a viscount's daughter to working as a ballet dancer in an effort to provide food and shelter for herself and her sister. If you were in Nève's shoes, would you have chosen to follow or flaunt the rules of society?

2) There was a distinct lack of support toward any kind of female agency during the Victorian time period, especially by men when it came to women and women's rights. What did you most appreciate in the heroine's approach to fighting against male power dynamics in the ballet world: a) not giving in to the indecent proposal made to her, or b) doing what she had to do in order to keep dancing? Do you think there were any other choices she could have or should have made? What might you do differently in a similar circumstance?

3) In a time when modesty was renowned and women's bodies were fully covered, ballerinas wore skimpy clothes, were

sexualized and fetishized, especially when viewed through the male gaze. Despite how much ballet was revered in art, many had pejorative opinions about it as an occupation, and actresses/ballerinas were considered to be women of loose morals. Do you think this has changed from the eighteenth century to contemporary times? Or do you think such stereotypes still exist, and women in this occupation still face criticism and bias? Why is that?

4) Lysander is a neurodivergent hero. In that era, there would have been no diagnosis of such a condition, and even if he had been seen by a doctor, one of the most common treatments of any behavioral malady was laudanum. As such, he has taught himself how to be successful and driven within the parameters of his disorder as well as on the heels of abuse from his father for being dim-witted and slow. How did your opinion of the hero change as you read the book and you embraced him through the heroine's eyes, especially when it came to his mental and behavioral challenges? Did it change your opinion of either of them as well? Did either or both of them experience personal growth via their interactions with each other?

5) The story is set in the Victorian era with ties to specific economic and social structures in both railway development and ballet. Real figures, like Emma Livry, the ballerina, or George Leeman, head of the North Eastern Railway in England, were interwoven with fictional characters to bring a level of authenticity and breadth to the story. Do you feel these historical figures enhanced the story or would you prefer all your characters

to be fictional and/or leaning toward historical fantasy (creative liberty taken with events and characterization for the period)?

6) One of the biggest considerations in writing historical romance is writing for an audience that is reading through a modern lens. The patriarchal structure, archaic social customs, as well as the lack of rights for women make it a challenge to write feminist concepts that modern-day readers will connect with without sanitizing some of the ills of history. Is it difficult to keep our own contemporary thinking from influencing the reading of a historical fiction story? Are there some themes that remain the same going back to the nineteenth century? Which symbols and/or themes in the Victorian context do you feel still resonate today?

7) In Regency and Victorian times, the aristocracy was very privi-leged, influential, and elite. Access to those circles was highly guarded by both station and fortune. Lysander hides Nève's true identity to pass her off as a member of the gentry with connections to the peerage. Did you take away a greater under-standing of what a couple like the heroine and hero might have faced during this time and place in history, from peers and friends, especially coming from such a disparate social and class gap? What kind of challenges and gossip might they have faced, individually and together?

8) One of the works quoted and passionately discussed in the novel between the hero and the heroine was *Wuthering Heights* by Emily Brontë. Do you think there is a correlation between

Heathcliff and Lysander, and do you see any parallels between them? In terms of personal desire, obsession, social classes and conflict, and the means a man might use in pursuit of what he wants, do you see similar themes at play? How so, and what was done differently in *Always Be My Duchess*? What other themes do you see?

9) Simone de Beauvoir was a French writer from the early twentieth century, nearly half a century from when *Always Be My Duchess* was set. One of her quotes on la condition féminine was, "No one is more arrogant toward women, more aggressive or scornful, than the man who is anxious about his virility." In the Victorian era and particularly the world of the demimonde, misogyny was common, and the heroine faces two kinds of men—those as described in de Beauvoir's quote and those whose "virility" isn't defined by sexism. How has Lysander's attitude toward women, and the heroine in particular, defied this kind of typecasting for the era? What did you appreciate best about him?

ABOUT THE AUTHOR

Amalie Howard is a *USA Today* and *Publishers Weekly* bestselling novelist of "smart, sexy, deliciously feminist romance." *The Beast of Beswick* was number five on *Oprah Daily*'s "Top 24 Best Historical Romance Novels to Read" list, and *Rules for Heiresses* was an Apple Best Books selection. She is also the author of several critically acclaimed, award-winning young adult novels. An AAPI, Caribbean-born writer, she has been interviewed and written articles on multicultural fiction that have appeared in *Entertainment Weekly*, *Ravishly* magazine, and Diversity in YA. When she's not writing, she can usually be found reading, being the president of her one-woman Harley-Davidson motorcycle club #WriteOrDie, or power napping. She currently lives in Colorado with her husband and three children.